Nothing Serious

Nothing Serious

EMMA MEDRANO

MICHAEL  JOSEPH

PENGUIN MICHAEL JOSEPH

UK | USA | Canada | Ireland | Australia
India | New Zealand | South Africa

Penguin Michael Joseph is part of the Penguin Random House group of companies
whose addresses can be found at global.penguinrandomhouse.com

First published 2024
001

Copyright © Emma Medrano, 2024

The moral right of the author has been asserted

Set in 12/14.75pt Bembo Book MT Pro
Typeset by Jouve (UK), Milton Keynes
Printed and bound in Great Britain by Clays Ltd, Elcograf S.p.A.

The authorized representative in the EEA is Penguin Random House Ireland,
Morrison Chambers, 32 Nassau Street, Dublin D02 YH68

A CIP catalogue record for this book is available from the British Library

HARDBACK ISBN: 978–0–241–59969–3
TRADE PAPERBACK ISBN: 978–0–241–59971–6

www.greenpenguin.co.uk

To everyone out there feeling lonely.
I promise you're not doing it alone.

This novel portrays sensitive issues like body dysmorphia, eating disorders, domestic violence, PTSD and allusions to sexual abuse. Check in with yourself and take care of your mental health while reading. A list of resources and places where you can get support is available at the end of this book.

'We are all so afraid, we are all so alone.'

Ford Maddox Ford

Nicki

I unbuckle my seatbelt. This is my last chance to change my mind. I get out of the car, my hand shaking as I grab my handbag.

I stare up at the front door. It's too late to turn back, isn't it? My feet take me up the path to the door. I press the doorbell, and it starts to hit me. I'm standing at the door of a man I've never met and whose existence I was unaware of until a few hours ago. He might kill me. I am an idiot.

I wait. I'm a few minutes late; I'm not desperate. The door opens. There's a moment when I don't know his name, and then I remember: Adam. Adam is wearing a t-shirt and jeans, white on denim. His skin glistens in the yellow sheen of the ceiling light. He must have just left the shower.

'Hey,' he says. 'Come on in.'

'Thanks.'

I step inside. I don't like the smell of his cologne and he's used way too much. The hallway is tight and there's not enough room for me to escape feeling his every breath on my face.

He's looking me up and down as if he's inspecting a product he has purchased. My profile picture's a few years old; my face is more lined now, my body thicker and softer. His lips are pursed and he might be disappointed. Well, I'm disappointed too.

I don't want to be in this cramped hallway with half a dozen pairs of trainers overflowing the rack. I don't want him to touch me, but he does. Slipping his fingers between mine and putting his nose to my hair. His presence feels disruptive, but I invite it, reaching for his belt buckle, opening my mouth to allow his tongue in.

'Come here,' he says.

His fingers slide from my grip and he takes a step back. I greedily inhale the unpolluted air. He opens the door on his right and waits, smiling, as I bend down to take off my shoes. He should ask me something mundane now, like if I found the place okay, or if I want something to drink. I wish he would. My throat is dry. The silence is unsettling, as if we're strangers waiting at the same bus stop.

I follow him into the bedroom. It smells like a teenage boy and there's a dirty plate on the desk. The bed is in disarray, the duvet halfway on the floor.

I open my mouth to ask for a drink, and he kisses me, both hands on my neck. He tastes like mouthwash. The kiss is too urgent, too hungry; his pace is impossible to match, his teeth bang against mine. I return it anyway.

He's already tugging on my sweater, and I raise my arms and allow him to remove it. I suppose this is what was to be expected. This is why I shaved and put on lotion and drove across town with deodorant and a spare pair of underwear in my handbag.

There's a growing bulge in his jeans. He massages my breasts over my bra, clumsily fondling them like he's checking for tumours, his breathing fast and excited.

I'm so thirsty, and I want to say no. But it's too late, it's too awkward. It's time to go through the motions.

Afterwards, he still doesn't offer me a drink. He basks in the afterglow with his arms outstretched and leaves me to bend down over his bathroom sink and lap up the tap water. I wash my face, trying to erase every molecule of him from my skin, and he's snoring by the time I return for my clothes.

I sob in the car. I promise myself I won't do it again. The sex was sub-par; I didn't like the way he moaned, the taste of him disgusted me.

What did I expect?

I'm disgusting. I'm unclean. I'm changing my panties in my car, spraying deodorant on my pits and fixing my hair in the rear-view mirror. I angle it to the side so I don't have to look at my face.

I dry the tears from my cheeks and drive home in silence.

When I get home, I close and lock the door behind me as quietly as I can and tiptoe into the bathroom. I put all the clothes I was wearing straight in the laundry basket, shoving my underwear deep into the pile. Then I shower for a long time, until the scalding water and furious rubbing of the loofah have turned my skin red and I smell of vanilla and macadamia again. Not of his cologne or his sweat.

My hair wrapped in the towel, I sit on the toilet lid, shaking. Watching my hands and waiting for them to still. I take deep breaths. When I'm steady enough to reach for the propranolol, I take two pills instead of one.

My face isn't red any more. My eyes are no longer wet and puffy. Slowly, the trembles subside.

I go into the bedroom and slip under the duvet, trying not to breathe too loudly. He shifts, his face contorted at the disturbance, turning away from me.

'Nicki?'

'Yeah,' I whisper. 'It's me.'

2

Amber

When Mr Miller started, we all fancied him. For approximately five minutes. Until he opened his mouth.

He was standing behind the desk with his hair tousled and tie crooked on the first day of the year, really rocking the confused and dishevelled professor look. His skin tanned and his smile blindingly white. There was the promise of a muscular chest and some tight abs under the wrinkled shirt.

And then it turned out that Mr Miller didn't go through puberty. He straightened his back and started saying, 'Hey, hey,' with the voice of a dog's squeaky toy, high and weak.

'Oh my fucking god,' said Marnie.

'Is he doing a funny voice?' said Kim.

Mr Miller didn't switch back to a voice more appropriate for a man of six feet and thirty years. He went on to introduce himself and teach the entire class as if someone had just kicked him in the nuts.

English hasn't been the same since. Mr Miller's voice doesn't command respect, so he gets none, and I think he's used to it. We don't work during his classes, and we don't shut up when he tells us to. We're supposed to be quietly reading *King Lear* right now. I'm texting Dan; my book isn't even open.

Marnie, chewing on a piece of gum, leans towards Kim and asks, 'Do you think he's ever got laid?'

'Nah,' says Kim. 'His balls haven't even dropped yet.'

'If he kept his mouth closed,' I say, seated right behind them. It's a little loud; I just want them to hear me.

'Imagine him talking dirty.' Marnie snickers. 'Gross.' She doesn't turn around.

Mr Miller is sitting oblivious at his desk. We're barely audible in the collective murmuring of the room. There was a time when he tried to keep the class in order, squeaking out for us to keep it down and stop talking and pay attention. That time is long gone. At this point, I only have a vague idea of what he's taught this year.

'Oh my god,' Kim says. 'Imagine swiping right on him and showing up to the date to *that*.'

Marnie bends over snorting. 'Ew! This is why I'd never use Tinder.'

'There should be a warning label on his profile,' I say.

'Guys.' Kim puts a hand on my desk. 'We should make him a Tinder profile.'

Marnie freezes, her finger curled around a thick strand of hair. 'Kim, you're a genius.'

'I'm serious,' she says. 'We should seriously make an account using his picture and see how many girls he gets.'

I volunteer my phone, sticking it between them before they have a chance to use one of theirs. If we use my phone, I can't be excluded. I download the app while Kim scans his Facebook profile for pictures.

'Any shirtless ones?' Marnie whispers.

I look up at Mr Miller. Hard to imagine him shirtless, with that awkward little smile like he's trying to gather the courage to get the classroom quiet. He looks like he could have a sixpack, but he *feels* like he absolutely can't have a sixpack.

'Sadly not,' says Kim.

'Aw,' says Marnie.

A piece of gum lands on her desk and some boys start laughing behind us.

5

'Oh my god, Kevin!' she shouts. 'That's disgusting.'

Mr Miller gets brave. 'Kim,' he says, 'please keep your voice down.'

She gives him the finger with a side of nail extension. Any other teacher would get pissed about that, but he just looks a little sad. His smile quivers. He says nothing.

'It's done.' I open the app and both of them turn their chairs toward me. 'It wants a phone number.'

'We can just use yours, can't we?' Marnie places her chin on Kim's shoulder.

'Yeah,' I say, because I'm trying to be cool, and if you're cool you don't care about random people finding your number online and calling you. 'Why not?'

She smiles at me, her lips shiny with lip gloss. 'What name do we want to use?'

'Kevin,' says Kim.

'Gross,' I say, typing it in.

'Everyone,' Mr Miller says. 'Can we please stick to our quiet reading?'

His eyes move across the classroom and for a moment we make eye contact. It makes me feel weird, like he knows what we're doing.

Marnie sighs. She picks up her phone and sends us a message in the group chat: *Make him queer.*

What age range? I text back, and Kim replies, *18 to 100. He's not picky.*

We stick to the group chat after that. They look at my phone and text me the answers I should give to all the questions. Kim sends us her favourite pictures from Mr Miller's Facebook albums. He's not a big selfie guy and most of it comes from tags on other people's posts. But we get a few good ones; a bathroom-mirror selfie where he has stubble, one where he's at the top of Arthur's Seat, a final picture someone else has taken of him in the wilderness with hiking boots and shorts that show off his strong hairy legs. They laugh, hands over their mouths. I'm a little scared by how often they look at him, comparing him to the Mr Miller in the pictures and giggling. I don't say anything because I know it isn't very cool to be worried about detention. Mr Miller doesn't realize. He sits at his desk, his eyes blank, like he's in a different world. I guess that's why he doesn't notice us.

It's too easy. Soon we're swiping right on every girl with hair extensions and fake tans and every topless guy with abs that the Tinder gods send our way, quietly laughing our asses off. Unaware of it all, Mr Miller rubs his forehead at his desk and checks the time on his wristwatch.

When Melissa joins us in the cafeteria, Kim and Marnie are swiping on my phone as I chew on a carrot stick. Melissa's in advanced English because she wants to do journalism; she's never had the pleasure of sitting through one of Mr Miller's classes. I get excited to see her. I think she'll like what we did earlier, I think she'll find it funny.

'What's this, then?' she asks, sliding in next to me with her tray filled to the brim. She's the special breed of skinny girl that can eat a mountain without gaining a pound.

Sometimes I hate being seen with my friends in public. I'm so much bigger than all of them.

'Just a little something we did in English.' Kim passes her the phone. Marnie's grinning.

'Oh my god, is that Mr Miller?'

'It sure is! He has, like, three matches already.'

Melissa looks through the pictures on his profile. 'Damn, he's fit.'

'Hey, no cheating on my brother,' says Marnie.

Melissa sticks her tongue out at her. She and Brandon aren't officially dating, but they've hooked up enough times for it to count. Especially considering how obsessed Melissa's been with him for over a year. I've known her since reception, since we were practically toddlers. She's had a lot of crushes and I've been with her through all of them, but none have been as big as her thing for Brandon. He came into our lives along with Marnie, Kim and Dan when we entered sixth form. Up until then, it was just Melissa and me.

'This your phone?' she asks, nodding at me.

'Yeah.'

She passes it back to me.

'We weren't done with that!' exclaims Kim.

'What do you want to do?' I ask.

'Text one of them, obviously. Send a flirty message.'

'Oh baby,' says Marnie, stretching her fingers in preparation for the challenge, 'I'm the queen of flirting.'

Melissa's looking over my shoulder, her pale cheeks flushing pink. A hoot of laughter erupts behind us. She nudges my arm.

'Look who's over there.'

I turn my head in the same direction as hers. A few tables over, facing our backs, are Brandon and Dan with some of their other friends. Neither of them is looking in our direction right now. Brandon's busy shoving an entire sausage down his throat and Dan's one of the guys cheering him on. Melissa shakes her head, smiling.

'They're so fucking gay,' she says.

'Uh, yeah,' says Kim. 'As gay as they are homophobic.'

'Uh-huh,' I say. 'They're adorable.'

Marnie is leaning across the table with her fingers on my

phone screen and her stomach pressed against the edge of the table.

'This one,' she says. 'Give me the phone back, Amber.'

I don't give her the phone, but I allow it to be pulled from my hand. Her nails, long like Kim's, tap against my screen as she types.

'Hey cutie,' she reads aloud. 'That shirt is becoming on you. If I were on you, I'd be coming too.'

Kim's water goes everywhere when she breaks into hysterical laughter, splashing my phone in the process.

'Hey!' I say. 'Be careful with my fucking phone.'

Melissa is laughing too, snorting through her nose like she always does. I snatch my phone back and wipe it with my sleeves. I glance over my shoulder and make eye contact with Dan. He pulls out his phone and my heart flutters.

'Sorry,' Kim says. 'It was just too good.'

Marnie shrugs. 'I can't help it.'

'I guess this is why you don't get laid,' says Melissa, poking the fork through her chips.

'Excuse me?' Marnie tilts her head. 'I promise we'll get a response.'

I'm not listening any more. A notification appears at the top of my screen, a text from Dan.

Hey sexy

Those jeans make your ass look good

I turn to look at him. He gives me a quick wink and a big grin. I hide my red cheeks with my hand, shaking my head at him. He shrugs and I sigh.

Worth a shot, he texts.

Keep trying, I reply.

3

Nicki

I pop a Plan-B like a Tic Tac in the car. I shove the carton in my pocket before I get out. Seagulls are circling the skies, screeching. The wind nearly blows me off my feet.

I let myself inside the little semi-detached with the untended front garden, my face full of hair. There's a pile of envelopes and leaflets rustling under my feet and I sigh. I'm always the one to take care of it.

'Hello, Edith!' I lean down to pick up the mail. 'It's Nicki.'

'Oh, come on in, dear.'

I enter the living room, where Edith is sitting on the sofa with the telly on, playing one of those daytime soaps that have been airing since she was young. Edith is a small woman. Her curly hair is short and grey, and her smile is wide with oversized dentures. She's a nice respite in my day. She's the only one of the old folks who hasn't called me a Paki. Of course, that's because she can't see me well enough to tell what my skin colour is, but you take what you can get.

I plop myself down on the couch next to her. 'I have some mail for you.'

'You do?'

She smiles at me with her nearly blind eyes as I sort through what she's received. I end up with two envelopes and three leaflets.

'Do you want your leaflets or letters first?' I ask.

'The letters, please.'

I read out her bank statement to her, and then her electricity bill. I say I'll help her pay it in a couple of days' time; it's not urgent. She blinks at me, the smile unyielding.

'And then?' she says.

'Then we have a couple of leaflets. One from Gennaro's—'

'No more letters?'

Edith's smile never fades, it's constant. But in this moment, it doesn't seem to reach further than her mouth.

'No.' I put a hand on her shoulder to ease the disappointment. 'Are you waiting for something?'

She shakes her head and some of her usual spark returns. 'Oh, no, it doesn't matter. Do read out what the leaflets are selling.'

I tell her about this week's deals at Lidl and the new garage a few streets down. She doesn't stop me even though she's not the one who does the grocery shopping, and, for obvious reasons, she doesn't own a car. There are a couple of leaflets she wants to keep. I put them in the glass bowl on her coffee table, which is always overflowing with them until I throw the older ones in the bin.

'There we go,' I say. 'You have me for another hour. Do you want to have dinner or shower first?'

'I'd like to eat,' she says. 'Does the kitchen need cleaning?'

'I'll give it a good scrub. You wait here and I'll get it all sorted.'

'Thank you, dear.'

I smile at her. No one else ever thanks me. They live under the assumption that since this is what I'm paid for, my salary is thanks enough. I hope Edith knows how appreciated it is.

I leave her on the flowery couch in the room with the bright yellow wallpaper. This house is eternally stuck in the sixties, though I suppose it's unfair to criticize the interior design of a blind woman.

In the kitchen, I discard the Plan-B carton in her bin, pushing it under some tissues so none of the other carers will see it. The worktops are covered in crumbs. Alice was probably here earlier. Alice is one of the worst when it comes to cleaning.

'What are we in the mood for?' I ask as I open the fridge.

'What do I have?'

I should have checked before I asked. There isn't much apart from a block of cheese, some milk, and a mouldy collection of expired vegetables. I'll need to do the grocery run again.

'How about a cheese toastie?'

'Sounds lovely,' says Edith.

She has a photograph on her fridge of a young family: a man, a woman and a toddler. They're standing on a lawn, the mother holding the child and the father beaming at the camera. I've never asked who they are.

I step aside and start preparing her dinner.

Tom is already home when I get there. He's at the kitchen table on his laptop when I come in and hang my handbag over a chair.

'Hello there,' he says. He's sunburnt and his glasses are dusty again.

'Hi. What are you doing?'

'Nothing much.'

Well, I know what that means. I place my arms around his neck and have a peek. He's looking at a two-bedroom bungalow on Zoopla. It's in Hove. It has a fireplace. I can almost feel the longing emanating from his chest, mixed with the nausea at the price.

'This place looks good,' I say.

He hums. 'Yeah, we'll just need to work forty more years to afford it.'

I don't know why he tortures himself like this, always looking up properties for sale, when he's well aware that we won't be able to buy unless we win the lottery. We don't even buy lottery tickets.

'Are you hungry yet?' he asks, forcing his voice to a cheerier state.

I check my wristwatch. It's barely six.

'I can eat soon. I'll just hop in the shower and change out of my uniform.'

He closes the laptop and stands up. 'Chicken?'

'Sure, why not?'

He smiles and puts his arms around me. Up until now, it was hard to tell, but he's in a good mood today. I relax into his embrace and he kisses me on the forehead as we sway back and forth.

'How was work?' he asks.

'It was all right. Mr Anderson's broke his hip, is all. He doesn't quite enjoy needing help to shower.'

Tom snickers into my ear. 'You know, sometimes I think I should be jealous of you touching another naked man.'

I can feel it again, the smell of Adam's cologne, his dick in the same hand that I'm now pushing onto Tom's chest.

I shake my head and giggle. 'Don't be silly.'

'So I shouldn't be?'

I feel sick, struggling to maintain a smile. He can't be allowed to sense the rivers of guilt and shame that run within me.

'He's as old as the BBC,' I say.

I kiss him, desperate to smooth the wrinkles of suspicion around his eyes. If it would make a difference, I would apologize a million times over.

'Well, at least you're getting paid for it,' he says.

I run a hand through his hair and change the subject. 'How was your day?'

He shrugs. 'Ah, same old. Moved a couple that couldn't be arsed to pack their own boxes and thought we'd be able to get it done in two hours. A three-bed house and all.'

I try to press my face into his shoulder, but he takes a step back. He grips my arms and holds me outside kissing distance, forcing me to eye contact.

'Hey,' he says. 'You sure you're all right?'

I force a smile that strains my cheeks. 'Yeah, course I am.'

He observes me carefully, a strand of hair hanging over his right eye. I nearly stop breathing. I nearly tell him everything. My phone is burning a hole in my pocket.

'You seem a bit distracted,' he says. 'Have been, for a couple of weeks.'

I shake my head. 'Nah, I'm fine. Just a bit tired.'

He raises both brows, eyeing me with scepticism.

'Tom, I'm all right.' I take his hands off me. 'I am.'

'Promise. Tell me there's nothing going on.'

I plant a kiss on his cheek. 'Nothing. I promise.'

In the bathroom, I turn on the shower and sit down on the toilet lid. I get the propranolol and take the phone from my pocket. And as I swallow the pills, my heartbeat slowly settling, I start swiping.

4

Amber

Flat on my back on Melissa's bed, I'm staring at the posters on her ceiling. She's always hung them there instead of on the walls. This is how she likes it, she says, where she can look at them when she's lying in bed.

I've watched the posters on her ceiling change over the years, from My Little Pony to High School Musical to Fall Out Boy, to whatever they portray now. I don't know who these K-pop stars are, all skinny with dyed hair. It's too late to ask; I don't want to out myself as ignorant.

A lot of things changed when we started sixth form. Mostly Melissa. She dyed her hair pink and became obsessed with getting a bellybutton piercing; it got infected twice and she still wants to get it redone a third time. She's still my best friend, but I don't think I'm hers any more.

Marnie is painting Melissa's nails a glittery purple. 'You need a manicure,' she says.

I'm bored, but Kim has my phone. She's on Tinder again, making fun of people's descriptions and showing us the most awkward pictures.

'Oh my god.' She's shaking her head and smiling. 'They're all so desperate.'

'That's why they're on Tinder,' I say.

'Are you judging us?' Marnie looks up from Melissa's fingers, rolling her eyes at me. 'Just because you're in a loving long-term relationship. Sigh.'

'Of course you can't have a loving long-term relationship.'

Kim doesn't raise her eyes from the phone. 'Everyone knows bisexuals aren't capable of monogamy.'

Pride rises in my chest. Melissa's never managed to get a commitment from Brandon, and Kim and Marnie are eternally single, but Dan's been my boyfriend for two months. Not bad for the fattest friend. We spent almost a year being acquaintances because of the others; he's Brandon's best friend. I had no idea he liked me until the first time he texted me and he asked if I wanted to go to the pier. I thought other people were coming too, but it turned out to be a date.

'Match!' Kim exclaims.

We crowd to the phone screen like it's a Victoria's Secret sale. Our match isn't pretty. Her teeth are big and her skin has been blurred too much, the tell-tale sign of acne.

'Horse Mouth,' Melissa says under her breath, and Marnie snorts. Melissa looks so happy; I wish she'd look that happy when I'm the one laughing at her jokes.

'Give me,' Marnie says, and takes my phone.

She types away.

'Do you want to go to Nando's?' asks Melissa, inspecting the seven fingernails that have been painted.

'I don't know,' says Kim.

'Nah,' I say, trying to come up with an excuse. 'Mum wants me home by nine.'

Marnie passes the phone to Melissa and she chuckles. I snatch it from her hand.

'The poor girl,' says Melissa.

Marnie's sent another message. *I just lost my teddy bear :(can I sleep with you instead?*

A collective groan goes through the room.

'Just wait and see,' Kim says with a smirk.

'I mean, she is typing,' I say, staring at the little dots.

We wait with barely suppressed giggles. I look at her profile. Horse Mouth's name is Jessica. She's twenty-six. She likes rollerskating, but I don't read more than that. I'm already bored.

Haha, if you play your cards right ;)

'Oh, baby, we're in,' says Kim. 'Mr Miller's about to get some.'

'Wait, are we actually texting her back?' I ask.

Kim looks at me like I just asked what shape the Earth is. 'Well, duh, what else is the point of this?'

'So are we setting up a date or something?'

I feel stupid. It isn't helped by Marnie's eye roll. I guess I'd thought all we were doing was getting someone's interest and then ghosting them.

'No!' Kim laughs. 'Come on, Tinder isn't for *dating*.'

I want to tell them that I'm not a child, I know what Tinder is for. I spoke before thinking. Now I grit my teeth, angry at the humiliation.

'Yeah, I know,' I sneer. 'I meant a hook-up, obviously.'

Marnie claps her hands. 'Get some.'

Melissa laughs and inches closer to me. She puts her chin on my knee, and for a second it's like we've gone two years back in time. It's just me and her, and as far as I'm aware, Kim and Marnie don't exist.

Marnie bursts my bubble. 'Come on, text her.'

What you up to?

Melissa squeals with joy.

'Poor Horse Mouth,' Kim says under her breath.

A few minutes go by.

'Nando's?' Melissa says again, and no one replies.

I check if I have any texts from Dan. I don't. A notification dings.

Horse Mouth: *Not much, wbu?*

I look to the others for guidance.

'Say same,' says Marnie. 'Tell her you're bored.'

Melissa nods encouragingly. I do as I'm told.

Two texts arrive in quick succession:

Haha me too

Up to anything tonight?

'Bitch is thirsty!' Kim says.

Marnie makes a victory gesture. 'Horse Mouth wants some of that sexy just-got-kicked-in-the-balls voice.'

'What next?' Melissa says. 'I mean, she obviously wants to meet up.'

'Get her to a club,' Kim says.

'Let's tell her to meet us at PRYZM,' Melissa says.

'Ew, not PRYZM,' Marnie says. 'That's where old people go.'

'We're supposed to be an old person, dumbass.' Kim rolls her eyes.

I put together a message asking if Horse Mouth wants to go to a club tonight.

'It's Thursday, though,' I say. 'She probably has work tomorrow.'

'Who cares about work if you can smash?' Marnie sings, her finger moving up and down with the pitch. She wants to be a singer, but she's not very good.

Horse Mouth still replies quickly. I feel bad for how desperate she is. I bet we could send Mr Miller to meet her and she'd clasp her hand over his mouth and climb him anyway.

Yeah sure, I've never been

Trying to play it cool, as if she's not already soaking wet.

'Ooh, baby, we're in,' Kim says.

'Mr Miller's in,' I correct her.

'I bet we're getting him more action than he's had in his whole life.'

Melissa asks, 'What do we do now? Just let her show up at the club and be disappointed?'

Marnie shrugs and then falls onto her back beside me. 'I dunno. Amber, just set up the meeting and all. I bet you'll get some real funny messages.'

'That's so *mean*,' Melissa says, smiling. It's strange, because I don't think the Melissa I knew before last year would have enjoyed this. She used to be so *nice*.

Kim pushes herself up to her feet. 'Do you guys still want to go to Nando's?'

'Yes!' Melissa and Marnie shout.

I have to fight the urge to join them. I keep my eyes trained on the phone screen, trying to pretend that I don't care.

'Amber.' Marnie looks at me. 'You'll send us the screen-shots, yeah?'

I nod.

'I'll text the guys and ask if they want to join,' Melissa says.

Marnie groans. 'Please don't! I don't want to hang out with my brother, that's disgusting.'

'I disagree,' says Melissa. Marnie shoves her in the side so she almost topples over, then she turns back to me. 'You sure you don't want to come even if Dan's there?'

I roll my eyes. 'We can be apart for five minutes, you know.'

'Just asking!'

A notification on my phone registers at the bottom of my vision. It's Horse Mouth. She's asking if I want to see her in a red or green dress. I reply that I want some pictures before I decide, winky face.

Horse Mouth sends me two pictures of herself, wearing a green mini dress with spaghetti straps, and a strapless red one with a slit. Her breasts can barely be contained by these slutty creations. I don't like Mr Miller, but he doesn't deserve this. I'm glad he doesn't have to deal with her.

Oh my, the red one

'Let's go,' says Marnie. 'We can walk, right? I can't be arsed to get on a cramped bus.'

I sit on the edge of the bed and wait for them to get ready. Melissa goes to pee, Marnie brushes her hair, and Kim applies more mascara to her already thick and spidery lashes. They're giggling in front of the mirror, talking in voices low enough to make me feel like I'm being deliberately left out.

We leave when Melissa comes back, and the cold air outside hits me like a wall. I pull my jacket tighter around me as Marnie lights a cigarette. We continue down to the street and Melissa stays by my side, the usual bounce in her step.

'You sure you don't want to come?' she asks again.

'Positive.'

'Please?'

'No.'

'You gonna tell me why?'

'I already did.'

She rolls her eyes. 'Whatever. You taking the bus then?'

'Yeah.'

She runs up to the others and puts her hands on Kim's back, jumping up and down like she's threatening to piggyback her. The bus stop is in the other direction. When they turn right, I pause for a moment, and look at their backs and the smoke rising from Marnie's cigarette.

'Bye!' I call out.

'See you tomorrow!' Melissa shouts without turning her head.

Kim raises a hand as acknowledgement.

I put my head against the window of the bus. My bones vibrate with its shifts and shakes. It's already dark outside; it's the season of red leaves and the occasional frosty morning.

There's a text from Dan asking if I'm also coming to Nando's. I say no, and he doesn't ask why. Horse Mouth is asking me if we're meeting outside PRYZM, and I stop replying. Her meeting with Kevin is two hours away; way too early to plan, Horse Mouth.

I could tell her not to show, but I'm desperate to make up for my embarrassing shortcomings in the art of Tinder catfishing. They asked for this. They want this. Marnie told me to get the screenshots. A part of my brain is whispering that if I don't get them, I'll be exposed as boring and childish. If I give them the screenshots, they'll think I'm fun and cool.

Brighton goes by outside the window, grey and wet from the last rainfall; colourful houses and long, empty beaches. I'm already checking Instagram to see if they're at Nando's yet, refreshing every two seconds for pictures from the night I'm not part of. There's a grumble in my stomach.

Horse Mouth texts: *Kevin?*

All her messages are marked as seen, but it's only been five minutes since I last replied. Five minutes doesn't warrant a double-text, Horse Mouth, is what I want to write back. Instead I hold my silence, my temple slamming against the window with every turn.

Nothing new on my feed yet.

Mum isn't home. I catch a whiff of her perfume, but it must only be because she recently left. Her keys aren't in the bowl on the chest in the entrance hall. From experience, I know it isn't likely she'll be back in the next few hours. The best part of having divorced parents is the alone time. I settle on the couch in the lounge and turn on the telly. Still nothing on Instagram.

I put my feet on the coffee table and my neck over the backrest. I spend the next two hours switching between different channels, trying to find something worth watching, and getting distracted by my phone.

I forget about Horse Mouth until she starts texting me again.

Be there in ten

I stare at the screen; I don't open the app. This is the last chance I have to save her night, and I don't take it. Getting these screenshots is my only way of inserting myself into their night at Nando's, to stop them from forgetting about me because I'm on the other side of town. I wait for the messages to trickle in at an increasing frequency over the next half-hour, and I imagine her standing in the club in her red dress with her hair so full of product it would catch on fire within three feet of a flame.

I'm here
You on your way?
We said 10 right?
You here?
I'm at the bar
Are you coming or not?
?????

Maybe I shouldn't be so harsh on her. Loneliness will make you do crazy things, and Tinder is full of lonely people. I take the screenshots and send them to the group chat. Melissa sees them first, but she doesn't reply. I wish she'd say something.

I want her to think that I can be just as funny as Kim and Marnie, that I know how to catfish. By now her hands will be sticky with chicken and their table full of empty plates and dirty napkins, unless they're already hanging out in the car park, watching the boys on their skateboards. Melissa laughing her phony just-for-Brandon laugh.

I remain staring at the screen, hoping that she'll respond.

It takes Horse Mouth way too long to send that final text: *Fuck you.*

That's when I unmatch with her.

5

Nicki

The worst part of a hook-up is the awkwardness of the aftermath. There's no way to leave that isn't a bit weird. There's nothing to talk about with this stranger I don't even like. I'm lying naked next to a man whose genitals have been in my mouth and I have no idea what he does for a living.

The sheets are covered in sweat. I'm careful not to move and end up in the wet spot. Adam's bed isn't a wide one. I can't adjust myself without accidentally brushing against his hot, sticky skin, and I've had more than enough of that.

His chest rises and falls as he catches his breath. He smiles at the ceiling and gives a short laugh. I shrink into myself, making my body as small as possible so I don't have to touch him. So that in case there's a god out there, maybe he won't see me naked in this bed with a stranger's semen between my legs.

'You've got some stamina,' Adam says. 'I can barely keep up.'

I know. That's why he kept moving me on top, letting me do the work. Too lazy to even move his hips.

He turns to me. 'You're stronger than you look, you know.'

'I guess,' I say. 'Do a lot of lifting at work.'

'Oh, yeah? What'd you do?'

I bite my lip. I don't want to tell him anything about myself. It feels like a slippery slope to admitting that I have a life at home with Tom.

'It's not that interesting,' I say.

'Come on, tell me.' He pushes himself onto his elbow. 'What line of work gives you biceps like these?'

He grabs my upper arm just a bit too hard. If he let go fast enough, I would be fine. But he lingers there, his grip tight over my slick skin.

I manage to let out a weak, solitary, 'No,' and suddenly I'm somewhere else, and it's no longer his hand. The world spins and my eyes roll back into my head. Both my arms are held hard and tight behind my back. I'm not in a bed, I'm kneeling on hard linoleum floor. My mouth is being forced open with fingers strong like pliers and my cheeks are wet with tears.

'No,' I whisper, shaking my head.

'What's wrong?'

Adam's back. His voice is low and distant but I cling to it, I hold on hard enough that I manage to brush his hand off me. I can still feel my arm muscles pulled taut, the thumb stroking my lower lip. I say no again, but I don't know if my lips deliver the message.

'What's going on?'

I don't recognize the voice this time. I gasp for air. Gripping the sheet, I manage to pull myself up. In a blur of faces and hands unzipping a pair of jeans and my own tears, I see Adam sit up, naked and confused. I force my nails into the palms of my hands and inhale. I hold on to the pain for as long as I can, like an anchor dragging against a bare ocean floor. All I know is that I need to get out of here before it gets worse.

'Was it me?' he asks as I'm pulling on my jeans.

I can't reply. I'm too busy holding on to reality. The vision of the unzipping jeans returns again and again, the zipper slowly being pulled down.

'Did I do something?'

I think I shake my head. Then I'm fully dressed, almost losing my balance as I shove my feet into my shoes. I stumble out of the room. I'm not aware of what Adam is doing. If he says anything else, I can't hear him. Suddenly a cool wind hits my face and I don't know where I am.

I spin around on the driveway and try to locate myself. I don't recognize my surroundings and I can't see my car. I'm crying. My knees are being forced onto the floor and my arms are twisted painfully behind my back.

No.

I catch sight of Adam's door, and suddenly I remember where I am.

I walk down the street until I find my parked car, my arms wrapped around myself as I shiver in the cold. I fumble in all my pockets for the keys until I find them in the last pocket I check. The car beeps and I throw myself inside.

Safely in the car, I press the lock for the doors. I used to fear these episodes so much that I would try anything to stop them. Wallace taught me that it's no use. There's no way to fight it, he told me, so just let it play out, and then it'll be over. I often think about him when this happens.

There's nothing to do now except surrender myself to the unzipping jeans and the pain in my arms. It's time to live through it again. I lean back and let it happen.

I come to in my seat. The neck-rest is hard against the back of my head. I blink. I turn my head. On the pavement across the street, a lady is walking a Golden Retriever. My head throbs and my eyelids are heavy.

I shake myself back into consciousness and start looking for my phone. I'm on the brink of panicking when I feel it with my hand, lying on the passenger seat. At some point I must have put it there.

I check the time. Two a.m. I can't be sure, but I think I left Adam's well before midnight. I have no memories of the time I just lost. I have only the vaguest idea that it started happening in Adam's bed and I had to scramble to leave. Bits and pieces replay in my head, of the confused look on his face and his mouth moving without me hearing any of the words.

My phone is full of messages. There's two from Adam: *Are you okay?* And *Did I do something?* There are more from Tom.

Where are you?

Missed call.

When will you be home?

Missed call.

Pick up the phone

Three missed calls.

Come home now

And that's it. Fear starts to build up inside me. I clasp a hand to my aching forehead and close my eyes for a minute. I'm so tired.

I'm sorry, I'll be back soon, I write.

He reads it immediately. He doesn't reply. I gulp.

I go through my usual routine; change my panties and put the old ones at the bottom of my handbag, spray deodorant on my pits, brush through my hair in the rear-view mirror. I use baby wipes to clean my nether regions of all traces of Adam. I look like a mess, my hair tangled and my eyes red and swollen.

I focus on taking deep breaths. There are still tears escaping the corners of my eyes and I carefully dry them off with my fingers, trying to force them to stop.

I open up Adam's texts again, my fingers hovering above

the screen. In the end, there's nothing to say. I can't explain to him what happened here tonight, what happened all those years ago. Let him wonder. My head hurts too much to formulate an apology. I don't need to see him again.

I drive home. It takes longer than it should. I'm too tired, my eyes sliding shut and my reflexes slow, to dare go at a pace that doesn't warrant honking and overtaking. Time and again I look over at the phone on the passenger seat, hoping to find it lighting up with a reply from Tom, and every time I'm disappointed.

A lump grows in my chest.

I pull into the parking spot nearest our building. And I wait. For what must be at least ten minutes, I can't bring myself to exit the car and go home. There's nothing I want more than to fall into bed and let myself drift off, and yet I'm tethered to the car seat, my hands shaking.

I carry my pills in my handbag for moments like this: when the anxiety gets overwhelming and I find myself gasping for air. I take one and it burns my throat as I swallow it dry. It's going to take some time to kick in, but finally I force myself to open the door and get out. What will happen is inevitable. I've nowhere else to go.

The cold air bites at my skin like tiny midges. I leave the handbag in the car; I'll pretend I forgot it. I can't let him find the dirty panties or used baby wipes.

Inside the building, I take the stairs up three floors. Checking if the lift is functioning is a waste of time I can't afford. It usually isn't.

Despite the late hour, the living room is fully lit. Tom is sitting on the couch with a can in his hand. His post-work beer is traditional, but he got off hours ago. I can't see any other cans. I can't determine how many more he's had.

'Hey,' I say.

'Hello.' He doesn't look away from the telly.

I hang my key on the hanger and open the bedroom door. I'm hungry, but I'd have to walk past him to get to the kitchen.

At the creak of the door, he speaks up. 'Are you not going to say goodnight?'

I open my mouth, my mind racing for a response.

'I was just going to take my shoes off.'

'Well, you should be going to bed. It's half two.'

I hear the sound of the telly turning off. I close my eyes.

'I'm sorry I'm so late. Kate was plastered, and it took ages convincing her to go home. I didn't want to leave her to herself.'

'Why not?'

I don't dare look over, but I hear him get up. He's coming towards me.

'I just wanted to be a good friend,' I find myself whispering. He probably doesn't hear me.

'Why didn't you call and let me know?'

'My phone died. I had to charge it at hers before I left.'

'Show it to me.'

'What?'

He's standing next to me now, holding out his hand. I keep my eyes glued to the floor.

'Show me the phone.'

I quietly pull it from the back pocket of my jeans and place it in his open hand. He's taken off his glasses; that's a bad sign. He lights the screen up. I hold my breath. If Adam's texted me again, I'm dead.

'It's only at eight per cent, Nicki. Why wouldn't you leave it to charge longer?'

I force a small, futile smile. 'Because as soon as it turned back on, I could see all your texts. You told me to come back, silly.'

'Don't call me that.'

Something inside me sinks deep and heavy like a rock. There's a point of no return that I can always sense, and this is it. He moves in close, his breathing strained.

'Do you think it's silly for me to worry about you when you're not home on time?' he spits. 'Because I don't think it's fucking silly to worry that you're dead in a ditch somewhere.'

I maintain my harsh eye contact with the dust on the carpet.

'You know that's what happens to women like you,' he says. 'I'm not making this shit up. You know it's true. Do you know why prostitutes get killed so often? Because blokes can tell just how worthless they are. They can smell their used-up cunts from miles away and they know they're doing society a favour if they off them.' He leans down until he's level with me. 'And that's just how it is with you. There's something you've radiated since you were eleven years old. There's something about you that pulls these bastards in and you know it.'

I do. Whatever I exude, he's right that it's there. Since the first time the boys at school groped me, I've known it. Whatever I do, it keeps happening. Wallace taught me that, too. I take a shaky breath.

'Are you listening to me?' His voice is louder now, harder.

'Yes.' Mine is barely audible. 'There's something wrong with me.'

He laughs. Sometimes it's a comfort, a sign that his mood is good and all is right. Sometimes it's a warning, low and scornful.

'Yeah,' he says, 'so what would you be doing without

me? You'd be raped on the fucking daily, like the useless slut you are.'

I nod. I deserve this.

'So you'd better treat me with some gratitude,' he wheezes. 'You'd better appreciate just how good you have it and treat me a shit-ton better than you do right now.'

My voice breaking, lips trembling, I say, 'I'm sorry.'

My phone hits the ground with a thud and a crack.

6

Amber

I've been running for fifty-four minutes. I've never been this sweaty. When I step off the treadmill, my legs feel weak and jiggly. My knees almost cave and I lean against the handrails, catching my breath. The world is unsteady and I'm dizzy. But the monitor says I've burned three hundred calories.

I check my phone. There's finally a response from Melissa.

Omg I'm so sorry, I completely forgot

Ten minutes ago. Well over an hour after we were supposed to meet outside the gym. I waited in the changing room for ages before I gave up.

No worries, I reply. *Just finished, wanna hang after I shower? I'll come to yours.*

I should be mad that she stood me up, but I want to see her. Just her. I want us to sit in front of *The Great British Bake Off* and shout out instructions even though neither of us bakes. But she always wants to talk about Brandon and I can't watch *Bake Off* any more, not with all those cakes and pastries. All I want is some time with the old Melissa.

I wipe down the handrails and stretch, blasting music in my earphones.

When I leave for the changing room, Melissa's texted me back.

Not tonight, soz, Brandon wanted to hang out

I sigh. Of course, always Brandon. Any plan will be cancelled if Brandon decides he has time for her.

That's okay, dw

★

I shower at home; I always shower at home. I get out of the bathroom and I'm still starving.

I cave and go downstairs to the kitchen. There isn't much in the fridge that doesn't require cooking. I hear Mum's heels tapping into the room and I slam the fridge closed.

'Hello, honey,' she says. 'What're you doing?'

She's wearing a thicker coat of make-up than usual and her hair is curled.

'Nothing. Just checking what's for dinner.'

'You'll have to figure it out yourself tonight if you need to eat, but do make sure it's something healthy. I'm going on a date.'

'Oh, okay.'

This explains the low-cut dress and carefully blow-dried curls. She takes a glass from the cupboard, her bracelets clinking on her wrist, and fills it with wine.

'Who is he?' I ask.

'Just someone from online. Divorced, sporty. He's an accountant.'

She drinks, careful not to let her lips touch the glass and ruin the lipstick. My mum is pretty. It's a weird thing to say about your mother, but I can't help but be aware of it. I know men like her. She blossomed after the divorce, losing weight and getting injections; she used to look like one of the regular mums, but now she's like someone from reality TV. Unfortunately, she didn't bless me with her genes. Or the money for breast implants.

'I hope you have fun,' I say.

'Thank you.' She cocks her head to the side and smiles at me. 'Did you go to the gym today, Amber?'

'Yeah, I just got back.'

'Well, that's good.' I can sense her eyes drifting up and down my body. The smile isn't real. 'How'd you get on?'

'I ran for fifty-four minutes. It was tough.'

'Oh wow.' She smiles. 'That's good. Well done.'

I shrug. 'I guess.'

She puts her empty glass on the worktop and pats me on the shoulder.

'Have a good night, honey. Love you.'

'Love you too.'

She exits the room in a cloud of perfume and hairspray. I put her glass in the dishwasher and drink some water to keep myself from eating.

I go back upstairs and look out of the window from my room. My mum is by the gate, wrapped in a thick coat. I flop down on my bed. My legs still ache. I scroll through the contacts on my phone, looking for someone to talk to. I click on Melissa. She's read my last message but hasn't replied.

I decide to leave her alone. I don't want to look desperate. There's Marnie and Kim, supposedly. But we don't talk about things like this. I don't tell them about my life. I don't think we've ever texted each other outside of the group chat. They're Melissa's friends, not mine. I can't tell them about how fat and sad and alone I am. They don't want to hear that. I know exactly the face Marnie would make and the uninterested stare I would get from Kim.

I call Dan. After Melissa, he's the next best thing. He picks up fast.

'Hey, Am. What's up?'

'Nothing, just wanted to talk to you.'

There's a pause. 'Do you want me to come over?'

I consider it. 'Maybe not.'

'Ah, I get it.'

What am I supposed to say after that?

'Listen, Amber, I'm playing *GTA* right now . . .'

'Okay. Do you want to hang up?'

'I can call you back later, though.'

I close my eyes and sigh. He won't call me back.

'When do I see you again?' I ask.

'Tomorrow at school, I guess.'

'You know that's not what I mean.'

He chuckles. 'You trying to get me alone?'

I smile. 'Maybe.'

'Let's say Wednesday, yeah? We can hang at mine.'

'Sounds good.'

'Great, so . . .'

'Yeah, off you go. Back to your game.'

'Thanks. See you.'

Beep. And I want to call him back and say that on second thought, he can come over now. That my mum isn't home. That I'll do whatever he wants as long as he keeps me company.

I get up and look myself in the mirror. I carefully inspect every blemish on my face and squeeze the folds of fat on my body. If I change my position, maybe I'll look thinner. I don't. I suck in my stomach. There's no point trying to fool myself.

I get back on my bed and back on my phone. There's a single notification and it's from Tinder. When I open the app, I tell myself I just want to see who this match is.

It's a guy this time. His pictures show a lot of abs and the band of his Calvin Klein boxers. It seems more Grindr than Tinder. I wonder if Mr Miller is actually gay. His voice does sound like he is.

There's nothing better to do, so I return to swiping. I swipe right on everyone, just wanting to see which of all these people would be willing to sleep with the guy that teaches me about syntax.

After a few minutes, I have a new match with one of the

people I went past without paying attention to the profile. She only has one picture. For some reason, she's fully clothed in it. She's leaning against what looks like the pier railing, water behind her, looking to the side, her dark hair flowing over her face. From what little I can see of it, she's decent-looking for someone over thirty. Her eyes are closed against the wind, her smile bright. Her skin is dark; she might be Indian.

What intrigues me is how little she seems like someone who would be on Tinder. Ab-guys and Horse Mouths are to be expected, not this. Her bio is surprisingly predictable, though. Two simple words: *Nothing serious*.

'You're a genius,' Marnie said to Kim when she suggested getting Mr Miller a Tinder.

Melissa liked it too. She found it hilarious, giggling turning into deep belly laughs. And that was just texting, that was just leaving Horse Mouth alone in a club on a Thursday night.

I have a lightbulb moment. What if I get this woman to actually fall for Kevin? The screenshots from Horse Mouth went ignored, so I need to give them more. *That* will be hilarious. That will make them all crowd to my phone, praising my cat-fishing skills, laughing at all the conversations between 'Kevin' and his girlfriend. And Melissa, in particular, will love it.

I never thought I'd say this, but I wish I had one of Marnie's awful pickup lines.

I write: *Hello gorgeous*.

And I think that I'll break her heart if that's what it takes for Melissa to see in me whatever it is that Kim and Marnie have seduced her with. I press send.

The message is read.

A few seconds pass. Then a couple more. And I wait.

And then:

Nicki is typing

7

Nicki

The skin around my left eye is dark and sore. My eyelid is swollen, the eye bloodshot. I hate the way I look right now. There was a time, back when I was young, when I would have tried to cover it with make-up.

I don't wear make-up any more. It would warrant too many questions, now, to appear one day with foundation so thick it's like a second layer of skin. Under it, always, the inescapable colour of purple-toned grey that you can never fully cover.

So at work, I act as if I have nothing to hide. When Charles asks, as I'm pleading desperately with him to take off his underwear so I can get him in the shower in the ten minutes we have left, I tell him I walked into a doorway. He asks if it was because I was looking at my phone and I tell him that I was texting my mother and not paying attention.

When Ursula exclaims, 'Oh, darling, you look dreadful!' I tell her I rolled onto the nightstand in my sleep. She doesn't believe me, her eyes narrowing into suspicious slits under her too-long fringe. She asks if it's my husband, and I tell her I'm not married. She asks if it's my father, and I tell her I don't live with my family. Even as she puts one pill after another on her tongue and swallows them, she tells me how she knows this is the custom with Muslims, but she doesn't agree with it.

Every visit leaves me tired, catching my breath in my car before I drive on, dragging my feet up every set of stairs. But the day is busy, and I don't have time to rest. The longest break

I get is when I spend twenty minutes in the car eating a Greggs sandwich for lunch, washing it down with a can of Coke, the crumbs getting onto every inch of my car's interior.

Edith is my last visit. I've looked forward to it all day, but I still feel uneasy when I arrive. She's my last visit, and I don't want to go home.

'Is that you, Nicki?' she asks as I enter her living room.

She's bent over the TV stand, holding on to it for support.

'It is indeed,' I say. 'What're you doing? Let me help you.'

'I'm looking for the button to switch channels. I've lost my remote.'

I grab her around the waist and help her stand up straight. It doesn't take much to support her small frame. I'm so happy she won't mention my black eye, that her vision doesn't allow for identifying such things even as she looks me straight in the face.

'Here, I'll take you back to the couch and try to find it.'

And I do. She's barely landed on the cushion before I spot the remote on the floor next to her coffee table, unmissable against the blue carpet.

'Wouldn't you know, here it is.'

'Oh, thank you dear, you're a doll.'

She sounds tired, groaning slightly as she adjusts onto the couch. She might be in pain, but Edith's not one of the complainers. I doubt I'd notice a broken bone with her unless she was lying on the floor. She holds out her hand to me and I place the remote there, she grips it tight and runs her fingers over the buttons to identify which are which.

'Would you like any help with that?' I ask.

'No, thank you.'

She begins switching through the channels, waiting a mere

second before she moves on to the next one. No, I truly don't want to go home. I love it here; the lack of expectations, the thank you that comes after every task I perform, the comfortable ambience of the telly always playing through the walls from the lounge. When I'm here, everything is predictable. As soon as my shift ends, I don't know what will happen.

'I'll get you sorted for the night, yeah?' I say.

Edith nods, her eyes trained on the telly. I close the blinds over the windows. She has a lovely view over the barren fields leading to the sea, the tall, yellow grass moving with the wind. I would like to ask her if she remembers this view, if she can summon the lights of the pier in her mind's eye when she opens the window, feels the breeze on her face, hears the seagulls and smells the distant seaweed. What a terrible thing to remind her of.

'Would you like a cup of tea?' I say as I move toward the kitchen, even though I know the answer.

'Yes please.'

When it comes to her evening routine, Edith's a creature of habit. I put the kettle on, take out the lavender tea she has before bedtime and pick out a cup. While I wait for the water to boil, I close the curtains in the kitchen and wipe down the worktops that whoever prepared her dinner has left dirty. Alice. I take my time, not bothered if I finish late. It's some extra time to breathe.

The news is playing in the lounge, and then Edith calls for me. 'Have I got any mail?'

'I don't know, Edith. Did you get any this morning?'

'No one gave it to me.'

'Then I can't say. They don't deliver this late. Who was here earlier?'

'Alice.'

I roll my eyes. 'Well, I can't do anything except ask her tomorrow. She'll be off already.'

'Okay. Thank you.'

Her voice is soft, defeated. I return with her tea and check the bowl on her coffee table. There's a little tourist leaflet about the Lake District that I don't recognize, and that's all. The others probably throw out all the ads.

'Are you waiting for something?' I ask.

She takes the cup of tea and brings it to her lips, blowing gently on the surface. 'Oh, I was only asking. Could you check my voicemail, then?'

I smile, a hand on her shoulder. 'When would you have missed a call, eh? Did you go out today?'

'Perhaps when I was in the shower. Sometimes I don't hear the phone, you know.'

The only time I've heard her phone ringing, it was a telemarketer that she chatted about flowers with for ten minutes until the poor sod hung up. Nonetheless, I dutifully force myself upon her ancient voicemail, a black box with buttons that's connected to her telephone. It takes me a minute to figure the dusty thing out, and then the mechanical voice proclaims no missed calls.

Edith says nothing, holding her cup with both hands.

In the bedroom, I take out her nightgown and place it on the bed. I close yet another set of blinds and make sure everything seems clean and in order. I wash her dishes, and then I stand leaning against the worktop and listen to the telly in the next room. The dread is growing within me. The dread of what awaits me at home.

'How about I get your meds now then?' I say eventually.

'Whenever you say so, my dear.'

I take deep breaths. I want to linger in this house longer.

The medication is all that's left, and then there's nothing standing between me and the end of my shift. I bring myself to open the cabinet and prepare the pills.

Tom isn't home. He's left the bedroom light on but his shoes aren't in the hall. I stand inside the front door for a minute, disappointment coursing through my veins. I thought this might be the case.

He's not here, but I want to be held. Everything needs to be made right again. We both need to be forgiven and I need to know he still loves me.

I call him inside the front door, still wearing my shoes. He answers, his voice tentative.

'Where are you?' I ask.

'I'm at Dave's, just having a pint.'

'Are you going to be back tonight?'

There's a moment of hesitation.

'No,' he says. 'No, I don't think so. I think I need a bit of time.'

'Tom.' I almost laugh.

I'm ready to forgive and move on. I've said I'm sorry. What more can I do?

He sighs. 'I don't know what came over me. I wish I could tell you how sorry I am.'

'It's all right. I should have told you where I was, and I should have come home earlier.'

A pause. 'I don't like myself very much when I'm angry.' I've never seen him cry, but sometimes I hear his voice break, just a little, and it twists my heart. 'I just can't control it. I snapped. And I can't bear to see what I did to you.'

I catch sight of my reflection in the mirror on the wall. The mirror is long, and it makes me look so very small. I stare at the ugly, dark spot around my eye, the angry redness around my iris. No wonder he can't be around me with this reminder.

'I'm okay,' I say. 'Really. All couples fight, Tom.'

A sharp intake of breath on the other end of the phone.

'Nicki, I swear it won't happen again. I can't get it out of my head, the sound of you . . . of you . . . Fuck me. I'm an arse.'

'No, you're not,' I say. 'If you were, you wouldn't care what you've done, you wouldn't be wanting to get better.'

'Why are you waiting for me to get better?'

'Don't you talk about my boyfriend that way.'

I'm scared I'll start crying, my chest is full of sobs.

'Your boyfriend's not worth anything.'

I want to say fuck you, you don't get to decide that.

Instead I whisper, 'Will you come home tonight? Let's talk.'

'Not tonight. I need to think. We should both . . . we should both start thinking about if we're good for each other.'

I tremble. I feel heavy. All the blood goes from my head so suddenly I almost fall.

'Of course you're good for me.' I can barely speak, the words come out weak and broken. 'You're the only thing keeping me together.'

I listen to his breathing. I try to keep myself from falling apart, but all I want to do is lie on the floor and cry until he comes home.

'You said it won't happen again,' I whisper. 'And I believe you.'

Silence. And then, 'I don't know if you should.'

'I love you!'

It's almost a cry; a desperate, defiant scream. He'll say

I deserve better, but I know it isn't true. There is nothing better. There is no one else I want. No one will know me as completely as he does and love me despite myself.

'I don't want to hurt you,' he says.

'I'm telling you it's okay!' I'm yelling now. 'I should have been back sooner!'

I don't want to yell at him, I want to comfort him. It isn't his fault I keep doing these things to him. Deep down, I don't think he even truly knows why I evoke such reactions from him. Sometimes I want to put my phone in his hands and show him the app, show him what I write to all these other men, tell him what I do with them. Then he'll know just how much I deserve his anger.

'Please,' I whisper. 'Please,' louder.

His breath is heavy. There are voices in the background now, and I can't hear what they're saying.

'Give me a minute,' he says, not to me, but to them, his voice muffled and his tone different. It's his voice for the boys.

'Tom?' I say. 'Don't leave me.'

'Nicki. Do you think I want to?'

I have no words. No, I know. But I'm difficult to live with.

'I'll probably stay here tonight,' he says. 'I'll . . . I'll see you when I see you.'

There are tears on my cheeks. I have so many things I want to say, so many ways I want to scream at him to stay with me, to come back, to love me, to not let me go. I'm drifting. I don't have time to say any of them before he's hung up, and I'm holding the phone in my hand, staring at his name on my cracked screen.

I call him back. He doesn't pick up. I wait until I reach the voicemail and I call again. I want to tear my own hair out.

The voicemail a second time. I scream. The world around

me is so distant and unclear and there's no telling what's real. I need something to hold on to or I'll lose sight of land.

I cry on the floor of the lounge, banging my head against the wall until it aches. My hands are shaking and my throat hurts, my eyes burn. I wish there were a single person in the world whose hand I could reach for right now.

Trembling, gasping, crying, I reach for my phone. I open Tinder. Everything is blurred through the tears. I can't message Adam. He's seen too much of the things I don't want anyone to know. I search my memory for who else is an option.

Jared, who was sweet, up until the moment I told him to stop and he grabbed me by the hair and kept going. I never went back. I never responded to all the texts he left me in the days afterwards.

Bob was nice until the end. He cooked for me. But he was getting clingy and cuddly.

So many other names I don't remember, so many men I'll never see again.

It's not Bob that I want, just someone.

So I'm on Tinder again. My standards are low. If he smiles, I swipe right. If he wants me, that's good enough.

And suddenly I have a new match. Kevin, white and thirty-six. He's wearing ugly cargo shorts, but there's something kind in his eyes. His bio is embarrassingly cliché.

I love long walks in nature and the kind of wine I can't afford

I want marriage and kids in the long run, but for now, I'm willing to start with a movie and see where things go

He's too good for me, so I won't message first. A man with eyes like that is someone I would snap in half, just like Bob. When they post shirtless pictures showing off their hip bones, when all they're looking for is sex, that's when I'm the right person. That's what I'm good for, nothing serious. Men like

Kevin are the kind that want to look into my eyes during the act and tell me afterwards that they want to see me again.

But when they message me first, I can't refuse them. I need someone to keep me afloat, even if I'll take him down with me.

And Kevin messages me first.

8

Amber

Hi handsome

And suddenly I'm out of things to say. I know how to flirt as Amber; I can do the blushing and the hair twirling. Dan isn't funny, but I can laugh at everything he says. I don't know how to flirt as a man with a mortgage.

Tinder is a buffet for women. She probably has two other matches messaging her right now, and Kevin needs to stand out. I don't know how to make her want him. I'm a chubby seventeen-year-old, not a sexy mountain climber with a full-time job.

What would Mr Miller say? The green circle stares at me. I scramble to my desk and rummage through the pile of homework and assignments that's built up over the term. There's one for English in there, a list of writing prompts that we were allowed to choose between.

Which historical figure would you like to meet?

Which historical figure would you like to bring to the present?

I wrote 500 words on MLK and how much he'd love the lack of racism today. That's not what I want to do to Nicki if I'm going to have any chance of pulling this off. The third question has potential, though.

If you could be anyone throughout history, who would you choose?

Now that's interesting. That makes Kevin fuckable.

So I write: *If you could be anyone else in the world, who would you choose?*

And I wait.

I don't expect her to give me an interesting answer. I think she'll probably name some random celebrity; give me a reason to roll my eyes and have some fun at her expense with the others when I show them this conversation.

I would be my mother, Nicki writes. *So I could be kinder to her than she is to herself.*

There's something raw and tender about these words. If she reveals her deep, dark secrets to Kevin, just imagine how impressed the others will be.

I don't really know what to do. I figure I should approach with caution, slowly slither my way in like a snake.

Well, that makes my answer a lot more boring, I write.

She replies in seconds. *What is it?*

Was going to say Leonardo DiCaprio

Why?

The models he shags

Good point. I can't say I blame them

Oh yeah?

He's gorgeous

I groan. It's the kind of thing my mum would say. He's way too old.

I don't disagree, I say.

Wouldn't you?

Absolutely

Me too

And before I can reply, *But to be fair, you don't need to be DiCaprio to get with me.*

I don't know if she means it in a general sense or Kevin in particular, but judging by the context, I think she's hitting on Kevin. Hard.

Oh yeah? Who do you need to be?

You, for example

I grin like an idiot at my success. It feels like there's no way I can mess this up now.

You flatter me, Nicki, don't let it go to my head

No, I want it to go somewhere else

I laugh out loud. I'd love to see the look on her face if she were ever told that she spoke like this to a teenage girl.

Do tell, I write.

I think you know what I mean

Just want to make sure

I try my hardest to summon the language and texting manners of someone who grew up in an era without mobile phones.

Nicki: *It's the one that's growing right now*

Kevin: *A bold assumption*

Nicki: *Am I wrong though?*

Kevin: *Didn't say you were*

Nicki: *Is it maybe even throbbing already?*

It's strange, going along with her flirtations. By her profile, she's thirty-four years old, and because this is Tinder, she's probably even older than that. I have to appear a lot more sexually experienced than I am.

Now why would I tell you that and spoil the surprise?

You're right, I'd like to find out myself

I barely have time to blink before it all becomes much more graphic.

I want to taste your precum

I want to lick you up and down until you're screaming

I'll go so slow you'll beg me to do more

I'm blinking at the screen, my mouth open. What am I supposed to say to that? Just a minute ago I had her in the palm of my hand, and now she intimidates me. It feels like she could eat me whole. My crotch feels uncomfortable, something nervous stirring in my stomach. I remind myself who I'm talking to.

I type and delete. Her circle goes red, then green again. She's waiting. If these screenshots are going to be seen by my friends, I have to act like the person they need to believe I am.

Kevin: *And what else?*

Nicki: *I'll let you fuck me, as deep and hard as you want*

Kevin: *You like that, huh?*

Nicki: *I love it*

Things feel really strange and difficult and confusing, and I don't know how to keep going. I don't want to talk about sex any more. I try to think of something else to say, another topic to bring up.

Kevin: *Maybe I should take you out to dinner first*

Nicki: *There's no need*

Kevin: *Why not?*

Nicki: *Says so in my bio*

Kevin: *A girl like you's got options, why don't you want anything more than a fuck?*

Nicki: *Can't a girl get horny?*

I say nothing, giving her time. In person, this would be an awkward silence. Over text, I feel like a police interrogator aiming the spotlight at her face.

A girl can take care of herself, I write.

What's the fun in that?

Her responses are coming quickly now, short and concise. Snappy and defensive. I can feel her trying to pull away from me as I'm reeling her in.

Before I get into bed with someone, I just like knowing why she's there

Look, I just want a bit of fun. I didn't come here to get judged

I ain't judging

Then accept the offer or leave it

My throat is dry. I'm losing my grip and I can't think of an excuse. Kevin should be jumping at the chance to get inside her pants. But Kevin doesn't exist.

I'm not that kind of person, I say. *I don't want to fuck someone I've only known a couple hours.*

A couple hours is all I've got

I put the phone on my bed and drag my hands through my hair. I hate accepting defeat, but it might just be time.

Then this isn't happening tonight, sorry

And she leaves Kevin on read.

I never double-text, but Kevin isn't me.

I'd like to keep talking, though, see if anything comes of it in the future

The minutes go by and she doesn't come back. I feel deflated and disappointed. I look at her profile picture, carefully studying the expression on her face for something previously unnoticed.

I'm disappointed, and yet. Nicki likes Kevin. She thinks he's funny. She was practically clamouring to unzip his trousers. I bet I can go further.

9

Nicki

I wake up in a stranger's bed; his name is Marcus. I glance over at him. He has terrible teeth. He's my age, but he's already losing hair and attempting very badly to cover it up with a terrible backcomb. In the light seeping through the barely closed curtains, I can see that his hair is muzzled and frizzed from sleep. He sleeps facing me, his mouth open. I catch his breath in whiffs of wheezy snores; it wasn't bad last night, but now it smells like something died in his mouth.

What day is it? Tuesday. I have therapy today.

I'm not here. I'm watching this sleeping man through a screen. I try to concentrate on feeling the weight of the duvet on my body, the softness of the sheets against my bare skin, but when I lift my hand and look at it, it feels like someone else's. It obeys my instructions, but it doesn't belong to me. This body is like something I'm controlling in a video game. I thought this feeling was completely normal until I started seeing Wallace. He told me it's called disassociation. He said he'd try to help me come out of it. His attempts never really worked.

There's a soft, quiet yelp from the bedroom door and I freeze. Something scratches on the door, and I remember the cat that Marcus introduced me to yesterday while I sat on his couch waiting for him to serve me a glass of water. The cat that I had to insist he locked out when we moved to his bedroom. He wanted to let the damn thing inside because it was meowing so desperately, and he said his flatmate would get upset. Oh god, I slept with a man who has a flatmate.

Other memories from the previous night return to me in damaged fragments. Did we use protection? Did I enjoy myself? I can't remember the last time I enjoyed it. I can't piece together the answers from the brief, unconnected images I have.

I focus on the cat's scratching to bring me back to the world. It's like my ears are stuffed with cotton wool. I sit up slowly. My phone's on the nightstand and the time is 6.05. In the distance, an ambulance siren grows fainter. I stare at the piss-yellow curtains and listen to Marcus's snores. The scratching at the door interspersed with soft meowing.

This isn't my life. I look down and my legs seem to be so far away. This isn't me.

I get dressed without waking Marcus. Once or twice he turns slightly and I freeze, holding my breath, but he is still again. As soon as I open the door the cat yells and shoots inside. It's a white, hairy thing that looks like it ran face-first into a wall.

I drive home and shower. My tears are mixed with the shower water and the shampoo. It's become something of a ritual. I like the way the water washes everything away, the way it muffles the sounds of my sobs.

Tom still isn't home.

My therapist takes one look at me and exclaims, 'Goodness, Nicki, what happened to your face?'

She moves in closer to inspect me. I want her further away.

'A bit of an accident. Banged my head against the extractor fan.'

Leela giggles, a hesitant smile growing. 'Well, I do like to say that cooking is an extreme sport.'

I hum in response. She finally backs off and returns to her swivel chair, dragging herself out from behind the desk with an awkward waddle. Her room doesn't look like the therapists' offices you see on telly. It's clinical and impossible to distinguish from a GP's, the walls a harrowing light green and the desk housing an assortment of document holders, pen cups and a laptop. My chair is plastic and uncomfortable, it has a wobbly front leg.

'How are you today?' asks Leela.

Her hands are clasped on her lap and she looks at me like a parent looks at their child, her eyes shining with an abundance of understanding and acceptance. Every trivial problem I mention is met with a frown or a gasp or a sound of dissent. I compare her to my memories of Wallace. He was smiley too, but he laughed a lot, he joked around. He never looked quite so serious or so concerned. Took everything in stride, acted like fixing me would be the easiest thing in the world.

'Not too bad,' I say. 'Had a bit of a row with Tom a few days ago, but I'm fine.'

Not heartbroken, not distressed, not floating through the day like a film I'm watching. I'm fine.

'And what was the row about?'

She looks too concerned, her brows furrowed, her lips pursed. Nothing is too small and insignificant with her.

'I was out later than I'd said I'd be,' I say. 'My phone died and I couldn't let him know, and he was worried. That's all.'

I don't know if it's my imagination, or if her eyes truly drift over to the bruise around my eye. It aches.

'Do you think it was warranted of him to be upset with you?'

I twitch. 'I didn't say he was upset with me.'

'If it led to a row, I'm sure he must've been upset, mustn't he?'

I inhale deeply. Leela watches me, and I'm sure she's more observant than she seems, with her askew glasses and colourful skirts and disorganized desk.

'Yes,' I say. 'It was warranted. I should've let him know.'

She nods. I sense disapproval.

'Has the argument been resolved?' she asks.

My bottom lip wobbles. I can't allow myself to cry in front of this woman.

'No. He spent the night away and still hasn't come home.'

She cocks her head to the side like an inquisitive puppy. 'And how do you feel about that?'

So many things. And so little. This isn't real. I'm not here. I shrug.

'Does it make you worried?'

'A bit, I suppose.'

'Are you worried he won't come back?'

Terrified, I want to say. Please tell me it will be okay. I won't believe you but I want you to try.

'Yes,' I whisper. 'I love him, and I don't . . .' I breathe in, keep the tears at bay. 'I don't know how to be alone.'

It's quiet and tentative. It's a first attempt at sharing something real with her, as she keeps reminding me that I must. I regret it as soon as the words leave my mouth.

Leela smiles compassionately. 'I understand that. It's been a long time, hasn't it?'

I nod. 'Six years.'

'A person's not a stable ground to build a life on.'

Too late for that.

'I know,' I say, snappy.

If I knew she wouldn't judge me, if I knew she wouldn't tell me I should leave, I might tell her everything. But she doesn't know what Tom and I have been through, she doesn't understand what we are to each other. This isn't something anyone would understand.

I look away.

'How do you cope with these worried feelings?'

Marcus's hairy chest. The cat screaming outside the door. Crying in the shower. I shake my head to get rid of the images.

'I don't know.'

'I mean, what did you do that night, when he didn't come home? Did you do your breathing exercises, did you journal, did you treat yourself to something nice and relaxing?'

I'm on my knees, his hand in my hair. He tastes disgusting. Make it stop.

'I guess you could say that.'

'I'm only asking because I know you have a hard time coping with arguments and feelings of abandonment,' says Leela. 'Trust me, Nicki, it's more than normal to find these emotions difficult. Especially when you come from a background of childhood abuse.'

'I'm not a statistic.'

She is silent for a moment. There's a question in her eyes. I'd like to squirm, but it would feel silly.

'Do you have anyone to confide in?' she asks.

The question confuses me. That's what she's here for, scribbling in her notepad and pushing her glasses further up her nose. It's like a cashier in a supermarket asking if you have anyone to show you where the apples are.

'Of course I do,' I say. 'I have Tom.'

'Yes, of course you do,' she agrees, smiling, nodding, as if

I didn't fully grasp the question. 'But not right now. So who do you have to talk to about the things you can't tell him?'

It feels like she knows, like she can smell Marcus on me through the shower gel and deodorant. I swallow. I simultaneously want to divert my eyes and act as natural as possible to avoid suspicion. And I say nothing.

Because that's the answer. I don't have anyone. I used to have Kate, and I shared things with her I never thought would see the light of day. But Kate isn't here any more.

'I don't need to talk to anyone,' I say. 'What's the point in dragging other people through my shit?'

'We all need someone, Nicki. That's just the way humans are.'

I feel myself closing up like a clam, holding tightly on to my pearl of emotions. She's wrong. If she knew the whole truth about me, she'd know just how much. It is lucky I have no one to confide in. It's a good thing that no one knows me fully.

'Correct me if I'm wrong,' says Leela, putting her hand to her chin, 'but I feel as if there's a wall between us.'

There's a wall between me and everyone, I want to tell her. If I reached out for you, I'd touch glass. Isn't it obvious? I've seen her every other week for half a year now and I never tell her anything.

'I don't know,' I say. 'Maybe.'

'I know you've had trauma related to therapy in the past,' and I flinch at these words, straining not to scream, 'but it's important, if we're to get anywhere, that you let me in.'

I stare at her. Yes, I want to say, you know what happened. I used to think therapy could help me, I used to believe that whatever was broken inside me could be fixed. Instead it fucked me over even more. I opened up to Wallace. I never told Leela that I came to my first session with her because of

56

Tom. He'd told me I needed to get better, I needed to get help; he couldn't cope with the nightly nightmares and screaming, didn't know what to do during all the flashbacks. So I'm not letting her in, because the last time I did that, it didn't work out. Letting her in wasn't part of the deal.

'Yeah,' I say. 'Maybe so.'

She raises her hand and knocks on an invisible door. 'Knock knock.'

'Who's there?' I say.

'Change.'

I choke back a laugh. She sounds like a self-help book sometimes.

'Are you willing to try that for me?' she asks, a smile of encouragement. 'Are you willing to try opening the door just a crack?'

I grip the side of the chair. No, I don't want to.

'Sure,' I say.

She leans back. 'So tell me. How are you doing?'

I open my mouth and close it again. Part of me wants to go for it, crash and burn as it might. Another part of me is terrified. Both parts are aware of the futility of trying.

'I'm not sure I'm here,' I say.

He's back. When I put my key in the door, I realize it's unlocked. I'm as light as a feather, my head swimming, stepping inside.

He comes out from the living room, his face set, and I love him. I love him when he squints at what he's reading because he doesn't agree with it. I love him when he tries to cook for me and something is always burnt. I love him when he strokes my cheek and looks as in love with me as I can ever imagine anyone being.

I love him so much my breath catches and I almost burst into tears.

'Hello,' he says. 'I didn't think you had work today.'

I swallow hard, attempting to gather myself together. 'I didn't,' I croak. 'I had therapy.'

'Oh?' An eyebrow rises. 'How did it go?'

I close my eyes. It's tiring to think of. I can't imagine trying to explain to him how difficult it is. He's delusional enough to believe that if I get the proper help, one day I'll be okay.

'It was all right.'

We are silent. He looks away.

'God, Nicki.' His voice is pained. 'Your eye.'

My hand goes to it instinctively. My cheekbone burns at the contact. I don't wince. I don't let him see.

'It's okay,' I say. 'It's not as bad as it looks.'

'Hurting you is the worst thing I've ever done,' he says, quietly, eyes squeezed shut. 'I don't understand how I can hurt the thing I love the most.'

And despite myself, I smile. Even as my eyes burn and lip quivers, I smile.

'I forgive you.'

'I don't deserve it.'

I take a step towards him, reaching for him.

'Yes, you do,' I say. 'You deserve more than you know.'

I should have known he would come back to me. Waves disappear, but they always come back to shore. The water pulls away, but it returns. Tom always comes back. He crashes into me. We cling to each other with desperation, hurting each other with our need. I grip him as tightly as he holds on to me, convulsing silently.

'I think I need help,' he whispers. 'I get so angry and I lose control. I don't want to hurt you, I never want to hurt you, but I can't stop it.' He sounds distraught and his mouth wobbles.

I stroke his hair and I nod. 'It's okay. We'll be okay.'

'I don't know how to leave you.'

'Then don't.'

I kiss him. He kisses me back, harder. Violently, urgently, we bang our teeth together and rip each other's lips open. My fingers tangle in his hair and I'm pressed so tightly against him that I can barely breathe.

Before long, he's pulled me into the bedroom and out of my clothes. He pauses over me, naked on the bed, and looks at me. I'm scared, for a second, that my body will reveal to him who I gave it out to last night. He puts his hand on my cheek.

'You are so beautiful,' he says.

I could cry, because no one else has ever called me beautiful. The first time he did, so many years ago, I did cry. I cried as he confusedly held me, asking what was wrong. Trying to choke out how I couldn't believe that this was real.

'I love you,' I say.

And I'm here again. I exist. His tongue on my skin, my skin again, my legs wrapping around him at my command, and they're my legs again. I'm here. And I belong here.

10

Amber

We wait outside the classroom for Mr Miller. The other girls are talking about something that happened on a show they're all watching, a show I haven't seen a single episode of, names I don't recognize.

'Guys, do you want to see something fun?' I say.

'Shoot,' Melissa says.

Marnie shrugs, her expression unenthused. Kim reluctantly abandons her phone as I pull up my own. I show them Kevin's conversation with Nicki. Melissa's expression changes in the smallest way, her lip twitching and her eyes narrowing with concentration. She's the one who slowly scrolls down the chat as they all read.

'That's juicy,' Kim says.

'Wow.' Marnie takes another long drag of her cigarette. 'This bitch is nutty, isn't she?'

'It's kinda sad, isn't it?' I say. 'I mean, she's pretty pathetic, to be honest.'

Melissa still hasn't said anything. I used to be able to read her every thought on her face; I can't decode it any more.

'Only thing that's sad is how fast it ended,' Marnie says.

And finally Melissa gives me a sign. It's a small smile and a nod.

'Nah,' I say. 'I bet she'll come running back with her tail between her legs.'

'Now that would be fun,' Kim says.

Melissa's phone buzzes and she gets it out of her pocket.

Marnie groans at this, and I know why. I don't think Melissa ever had her phone on vibrate before she met Brandon. As she looks at the screen, a smile grows across her face.

'Look what Brandon sent me!'

It's a cute little hamster video on Instagram. He didn't even include a message, but I won't point this out to her.

The moment is over so soon. No one's looking at my screen any more. I'm left holding the remnants of Kevin and Nicki, everything I was so proud to show them. I still think they'll return to me soon, once they're done talking about boys.

'Jesus, what happened to your phone screen?' Kim asks.

Melissa chuckles. 'Dropped it.'

'Why wouldn't you get it fixed?' Marnie says.

Marnie's a little clueless. Her dad's a pilot; they've got a pool in the backyard and a cleaner that comes round twice a week while her mum does yoga in the home sauna. Melissa, mean-while, lives in a two-bed flat, where her younger sisters share a room and their mum sleeps on the couch when she isn't at work at the nursing home. Just a few months ago, Melissa cried to me about how she doesn't know how she'll afford going to uni.

She looks at her screen, typing out a response to Brandon. She purses her lips together tight, doesn't answer the question. I can't make out what she's typing from this angle, not without looking suspicious.

'You know he's never going to date you,' Marnie says, nonchalantly.

'You don't know that,' Melissa says.

'Yeah, I do. He's my brother.'

Melissa rolls her eyes.

'Whatever,' Marnie says. 'I'm just saying what we're all thinking.'

Which is true. If Brandon wanted anything except sex, he

would've told her by now. She's a little bit sad sometimes, Melissa. I'd like to pick her up and shake her to make her figure shit out.

Mr Miller appears, a pile of papers under his arm. He walks quickly, his face towards the ground, like he's late. He isn't.

'Good morning, girls,' he says as he passes by, like he already knows we won't respond.

'I guess I better go,' Melissa says. 'Class is about to start.'

'Are you seriously going to be mad at me about this?' Marnie says loudly.

Melissa shrugs.

'Marnie, leave it,' Kim says. 'Who gives a shit?'

Melissa gives me a look. I can't tell what it means. Then the look is gone, and she's heading away without saying goodbye. Without the conversation returning to Nicki and Kevin.

'She's so sensitive,' Marnie complains.

'I mean, what did you expect?' Kim says. 'He's like, the only thing she cares about. You know she gets pissy about it.'

And when they walk through the classroom doors after Mr Miller, it hits me. They don't care about the Tinder stuff. It's tame. It doesn't hold their attention. I haven't done enough. But I remember the smile on Melissa's face, the little nod. I remember the seconds they were all quiet and fully focused on my phone screen. They do like it. I just need to do more.

I shove my phone in my pocket and go after them.

After class, I wait by the gates as the students well through them. My hands stuck deep in my pockets, I watch the crowds grow thinner and disperse. Dan is late.

On the other side of the gate, there's a group of skinny blonde girls chewing gum and chatting. I watch them, catching a word every few seconds. One of them is wearing a crop top, revealing a pale, flat stomach. I'm mesmerized by the sight of it, hard and straight like a plank, as if she has no use of inner organs. I bet I could put both my hands around her thin waist, my fingers touching.

I put my arms around my own stomach and try to fade into the wall.

Dan finally comes scampering down the drive.

'Hi,' he says. 'You all right?'

'Yeah, fine. Why?'

He shrugs. 'Looked a bit thoughtful.'

'Well, I have thoughts, twat.'

He laughs and I smile at him. I run a hand through his curly hair, get my fingers tangled in the locks.

'I've got my bike,' he says. 'You don't mind, do you?'

I shake my head, and he gives me a lift on the back of his bike, where I bump along with my thighs chafing against the sides of the rear rack. I hold on to him tightly, burrowing my face into his neck, my nose tickled by his hair. It's not often I get to touch him like this. He's not a cuddler.

He likes to go fast, releasing the brakes to let us shoot down the hills, and I like the wind in my hair and the drop in my stomach. I feel light, floating. I weigh nothing.

It's romantic, in a way, that I trust him this much. I trust him to slink between cars and past pedestrians; I trust him to slam on the brakes with all his strength when we reach a red light; I trust him to take every turn, even as we're almost sideways, and it feels like strands of my hair could almost be touching the asphalt. I smile, closing my eyes, squeezing his chest so tight he takes one hand off the handlebar to tap me on the wrist because he needs to breathe.

I love him, I think, as I watch him put the bike in the shed in the communal garden behind his house. This is what it's like to love someone. My heart fluttering, stomach light, cheeks hot. When he turns back to me, I kiss him on the lips. It's awkward, his tongue pressing against mine, his lips a different rhythm. I pull away.

'I love you,' I say. I've said it before, but never this seriously. With my voice just flat and honest.

He smiles awkwardly, his mouth opening to speak but no words coming out.

'It's okay,' I say. 'You don't have to say it.'

I turn away to escape the embarrassment, the hard, heavy cloud of weirdness in the air between us. There's a tremble in my lip and I force myself not to cry over something this small. It's silly.

I don't need him to tell me he loves me. But I want him to tell me he likes me. I want him to say how much fun he has hanging out with me and how happy I make him, touching my arm while he does, then interlacing our fingers and putting his face to my cheek. He wouldn't do such a thing. He wriggles his hand out of mine at every attempt I make. When I put my head on his shoulder, he always moves away.

'Are you hungry yet?' he asks, walking past me toward the building.

'No,' I say. 'Thanks.'

The house has two stories, and his family has the top one. He walks up the stairs with hurried steps. I can tell he's trying to escape me and the cloud of weird that I brought with me.

He unlocks the front door and goes straight to the kitchen and takes out a bag of string cheese from the fridge.

'Do you want a Ribena?' he asks.

I hesitate. There's a lot of sugar in Ribena, but I don't want to make a fuss in front of Dan. A few sips should be fine. I can skip dinner.

'Thank you,' I say. I lean against the worktop and he hands me a bottle.

The place is very quiet. I'm nervous now.

'We're home alone,' he says, like he's just read my mind.

I'm watching his mouth as he bites off a piece of cheese.

'Oh yeah?' I say.

He nods. My breathing is strained, the Ribena bottle quivering in my hand. Something unspoken hangs in the air between us, lives in his eyes. Why am I scared?

'Want to go to my room?'

I hum in response and we go to his room. The cables of his Xbox lie strewn across the floor from the telly to the bed, the curtains are closed. He's got a chair which is overflowing with dirty laundry, and he doesn't clear it for me. He sits cross-legged on the bed, expecting me to follow, and I do. I drink my Ribena and he finishes the cheese. There are children in the gardens below now, laughing and squealing.

'Do you want to watch some stuff?' he asks.

'Sure.'

He gets his phone out and we scroll through TikTok. His feed doesn't look anything like mine, and I'm not very interested. He snorts instead of laughing. I'm barely watching. I'm too aware of our close proximity, the falling and rising of his chest, the smell of Axe mixed with a hint of sweat because he took his shoes off.

He moves closer. I sit still.

'Amber,' he says.

I look to him, and he leans over and kisses me. Again, it's awkward. Teeth and tongue everywhere. I don't like the fact that I must taste like Ribena. I'm still holding the bottle in one hand, and I don't know what to do with it now.

We make out for a few minutes, his phone lying on the bed,

the videos still playing in the background, the Ribena still in my hand. He puts his hand on my thigh and I struggle to breathe, then keep going. My mouth is dry, my lips dripping with a mix of both of our saliva. His hand reaches under my shirt, stroking my belly. I allow it. And then he touches my boob, clasping it a bit too firmly, squeezing hard enough that it's painful.

'Dan.'

'What?'

'Please stop.'

His hand lingers for a moment and then retracts.

'What's wrong?' He cocks his head to the side, watching me intently.

My lip quivers. 'You know I don't want to do that.'

'I wasn't doing anything. It was just a bit of touching.'

I look down. He puts a hand to my cheek.

'Amber, I wouldn't do anything you don't want me to.'

'I'm sorry,' I whisper.

'What are you sorry for?'

'This. Being so childish, not being able to give you what you want.'

And I want him to tell me that it's bullshit, it's only me he wants, whatever he can have of me. And I want him to tell me that it's okay and he loves me anyway. He shrugs. He says, 'It is what it is.'

I forced my way in here today, and I've been nothing but a disappointment.

'I'm just not ready,' I say.

'I get that,' he says, picking up the phone again, returning seamlessly to the video. 'It's fine. Really.'

But it doesn't feel fine. I clasp the Ribena in my hand, try to unhunch my shoulders, try to watch the TikToks again. I glance at him from the corner of my eye. He snorts again, amused. I try to smile. There's no reason I shouldn't be happy with such a loving, patient, understanding boyfriend. But I don't feel happy; I feel ashamed.

I pull my hood up, the wind whipping my face and the tears stinging my eyes. Like a child I tread home with my panties dry and my innocence intact.

It's embarrassing to be a virgin at age seventeen, terrified of the idea of being touched. I'm the girl who wears one-piece swimsuits instead of bikinis. I'm the girl who changes in the toilets before PE, quickly covering my rolls and folds before I show myself to anyone. Not the girl he wants.

I kick a small rock as I walk, angry at myself. Dan is too kind to me, saying it's fine. I know what he wants, but I don't know why. It's like he doesn't see just how disappointed he'll be when he gets to see all of me, how awkward it will be when he finds me too heavy to have on top.

I pull my phone out, ready to call Melissa. I used to do this all the time when I felt upset. Now I hesitate, my finger hovering above her number. Melissa wouldn't understand. She's been having sex for two years like a normal person. Worse, the fact that I haven't slept with Dan yet would inevitably reach Kim and Marnie, not out of malice, but simply because of how gossip-worthy it is. Kim and Marnie talk about blow-jobs and orgasms; Marnie has a vibrator. She showed it to us, once, during a sleepover when we'd had too much to drink while watching a terrible horror movie.

I'm a child compared to them.

There's one way I can reclaim my dignity. There's one way I can appear to be the person I should be. There's one person I've managed to fool into thinking I'm someone I'm not. I open Tinder and message Nicki. A simple *Hi stranger, what's up?*

I put my headphones in and continue the rest of the walk with the music at the highest volume I can stand. Nicki's replied when I come home and check my phone inside the front door.

I'm sorry

I know you want to hook up, but I don't. I can't do that any more

A wave of relief goes through me. This is perfect. I won't have to fend off her advances in the future. All I need to do is convince her to become interested in anything about me except what's under the waistline.

That's so funny, because I can't hook up with you at all

I was visiting relatives in Brighton when we matched, but I live in Australia

I'm just messaging you because I like meeting people and you're cool to talk to

She leaves me on read for a few minutes. I wait patiently, biting my nails in fear that she won't reply at all. I look around my room and there is nothing else to do. I can hear my mum downstairs, laughing, which means she has someone over. The accountant, maybe. It means I can't switch aimlessly between channels on the telly, hoping to find something or someone I can laugh at.

You're kidding me

I open the app again too fast. I say, fuck, under my breath but it's too late to go back. She's online and knows I've read it.

I'm not, I'm literally in Perth right now

Why are you in Australia?

Why not?

You're not pulling my leg are you?

I spend a few minutes googling for pictures of Australian backyards, dismissing anything too high quality, until I'm deep enough down the hole that I find one that looks like it was taken through a window.

Nicki: *Wow, you grew all those yourself?*
Kevin: *I have magical fingers*
Nicki: *Too bad you're on the other side of the world*
I laugh out loud.
Answer the question, she says.
Wanted to be able to look out of the window and see the sun instead of grey skies and rain
The quintessential British experience
I haven't thought about Dan for a few minutes now. Nicki's made no attempts to virtually take Kevin's clothes off, and she's still texting him back.
You haven't deleted your profile, Kevin says.
Did I say I would? she replies.
You said we won't be hooking up
Well, we obviously won't now
Would you mind if I keep messaging you anyway?
For a while, nothing. I start to get flustered, worried that I went too far. Then she's typing again and I exhale.
I'm not looking for anything serious, she says.
I know that from her profile. And of course it won't be, because I'm not Kevin. I'm a girl in my final year of school doing this because I'm bored and too pathetic to impress people any other way. This is nothing serious at all.
Don't worry, Kevin texts back. *There's no risk of that.*
I'm scared she'll say no and there's nothing I can do about it. It shouldn't matter if I fail; she's one of many. But I'm not only trying to prove something to the others, but also to myself. I want to know I can pull off this act. I want to know that I can convince a person that I'm someone I'm not.
She says, *Okay then.*
And I smile.

II

Nicki

I am tired but content. I am rolled up next to Tom in bed. He's splayed out over the duvet that he stole from me in the night and left me freezing and grasping for. There's a single ray of sunshine getting in through the crack between the curtain and the wall, lighting a straight line across his chest.

I get up, careful not to disturb him, and wrap myself in my robe.

The kitchen tiles are cold and refreshing. I decide to make breakfast. It's past seven and Tom starts work at nine. He doesn't call in sick when I ask him to; he doesn't like lying to his boss because they're friends. I can hear the seagulls outside. They're louder in the mornings before the sounds of neighbours drown them out.

I heat up beans and fry some eggs and sausages. I set the table for us, take out the bottle of orange juice from the fridge. By the time his alarm goes off, I've turned on the coffee maker and the kettle. I've picked out his favourite mug, the Star Wars one, and when he leaves the bathroom, stumbling into the kitchen in his boxers, his chin shadowed by stubble, pushing his glasses up the bridge of his nose, I have the tea and coffee ready.

He looks at the set table, the plates full of eggs, sausages and beans.

'I love you, woman,' he says.

He kisses me and I smile into his mouth, a mug in each hand held out behind his back.

'I love you too,' I say.

We sit down to eat. He's a fast eater, throwing half a sausage into his mouth and washing it down with some orange juice.

'This is so good,' he says, fork pointed at the sausage.

I smile. 'It's Tesco's.'

'I don't care. You did something to them.'

We eat, chatting about work, brushing past my last therapy appointment. There's a furrow of his brow as I skirt the subject, but he doesn't press it. We laugh together, clinking our glasses and saying cheers.

I can't stop smiling. His presence in the room is like a light switch that illuminates something I couldn't previously see. My eyes are full of sleep, my head heavy, but I'm happy.

I stay at the table after he's finished, put his plate in the sink, and gone to get dressed. I listen to the shower and the opening and closing of the wardrobe doors, the cursing as he's putting on his shoes and can't find the shoehorn.

He comes back in fully dressed and shaven. He kisses me on the cheek, his chin smooth and smelling of aftershave.

'Have a great day,' he says.

'You too.'

His hand lingers on my hair and then he leaves, the door slamming shut behind his heavy footsteps, the key jingling in the lock. I remain in place, the smile carefully maintained. But it's difficult, now, to make it reach my eyes. One of my hands is wrapped around the mug in which my tea is turning cold. Most of my food remains uneaten; half a sausage, an egg with a bite in the side, the liquid from the beans slowly spreading across the plate.

This isn't me. Wearing a robe in the kitchen of a flat that has my name on the lease. A table full of coffee, tea and orange juice. It wasn't me, cooking for the man I love, stirring the beans while the sausages were sizzling in the pan and the water in the kettle came to a boil. It wasn't me, laughing without inhibition, leaning over the table to kiss Tom's face.

It's not the kind of person I am. I don't deserve these things. I feel wrong and out of place. I feel like an intruder in my own home. My tea's too cold to drink.

There's something inside me tugging and pulling for the men I don't know in houses I'll never see again, pulling my hair, slapping me, spitting in my face. That's where I belong. My dad used to tell me that, and I used to think he was full of shit.

I look down at my plate; I don't have an appetite. I get up and put my leftovers in the bin. There are dishes in the sink that need washing, but I'm tired. Where's the contentedness now? I look for it in my heart, pushing my feet into the ground to remind myself that I'm here I'm here I'm here.

It's gone. All that's left is this feeling that I'm in the wrong place.

I have too many hours to kill before work. It's in moments like these it hits me just how empty my life is. I could do with a hobby or a friend. When I came home from Adam's, I told Tom I'd been with Kate. I haven't seen Kate in five years. As far as I know, she could be dead or on the other side of the world. Kate was the one I could turn to from year three onwards. A whole lifetime, and now nothing.

So I turn to Tinder, not because I want to, but because that's what I always do. There doesn't seem to be any alternative, until I glimpse the conversation icon in the corner. Then I remember he exists. He's like something out of a fever dream sometimes, a vague outline of a person whose facial features I can't make out. But he's there.

I message Kevin: *Brighton to Australia.*

I sit down on the couch. I feel a bit ridiculous. It's exposing, it's humiliating, to be the one to message first. To admit I have a need for him, that I have thought about him in his absence.

I glance at the picture of me and Tom framed on the wall. It's from Naples, the only holiday we've gone on together. That one time he agreed that we should treat ourselves. In November, when the prices are lower and tourism non-existent, he's smiling with red cheeks and my beanie's slipped down to my eyebrows. It was a beautiful week, full of pasta and long nights on walks through the city and long mornings between the sheets in our hotel room.

I'd like to go somewhere else with him. The money's there, I think, but he's saving it for a house now. The home he's always dreamed of.

When I look back on my screen, Kevin has replied.

Australia here, over

I write, *How's the weather?*

Raining burning koalas

And venomous spiders?

No, those are coming up through the toilet

The photograph is still in the corner of my vision and I want to turn it against the wall so that he won't see. It doesn't make sense, after everything I've done, to feel so guilty about this.

Kevin: *How's the day treating you?*

Nicki: *I'm good, got a couple hours to myself before work*

Kevin: *What's work?*

Nicki: *It's what you do to get money*

Kevin: *Haha, so funny, now answer the question*

I take a breath. I want to think of something glamorous, I want to be someone different. *I'm a secretary for a law firm*

So you're a phone-answerer?

Basically, what about you?

He's logged out and takes a minute to get back to me. I take the chance to move from the lounge to the bedroom, where I stare at the bed we share together and instead go to the kitchen, where we had a beautiful meal just this morning. I decide on the bathroom and sit on the toilet lid with my toes on the fuzzy bathmat.

Kevin: *I own an e-commerce company*

What do you sell? I ask.

Art prints

And then, *Yes, that boring.*

He might be making this up, but I don't care. I'm pretending too. Aren't I always? It's refreshing to meet someone else who mistook life for a costume party and turned up in disguise.

Not as boring as answering the phone

Depends on who's calling, no?

You hitting on me, Australia?

We agreed that wasn't happening, didn't we?

I feel disappointed that he didn't say yes. And I'm surprised. If phone sex and naked pictures aren't what he's after, then what?

Nicki: *Are you going to let that stop you from trying?*

Kevin: *Depends on how you answer my next question*

Nicki: *Which is what?*

Kevin: *What's with the No More Hooking Up?*

I flinch. This is unexpected, unwanted. It takes me some time to figure out how to respond. The truth obviously isn't an option.

I don't know what it adds to my life, I write, slowly, weighing the words with my eyes before I press send.

That's fair, he says.

I realize that I can stop texting him right now, and it

wouldn't make a difference. I don't have to say goodbye. Nothing would be missed. I can block him and time will move on just like in the days before I swiped right. Work tonight, Tom asleep when I get back, then he'll wake me up in the morning with slamming doors and running water. I can leave this conversation.

Why don't I?

Are you still there?

Yes, I write. *Sorry, just thinking.*

About what?

I'd quite like to go travelling, I say.

12

Amber

The accountant has been promoted to boyfriend. His name is Stuart. Mum said he's sporty, but he doesn't look it; he's balding and his stomach is round. He greets us at the table, nervous, shaking my hand like it's a business meeting.

'Hello, Amber,' he says. 'I'm Stuart. It's nice to finally meet you.'

'You too,' I say.

Mum wraps her arms around him and kisses him on the cheek, leaving a light imprint of lipstick when she pulls away. I go to sit down and Stuart hurriedly pulls out my chair for me.

'Oh, thank you,' I say, not sure what the situation requires. It's a first.

It's weird when he tries to push it back to the table when I'm seated. It catches against the floorboards and he wobbles it back and forth, loudly scraping the floor. Mum sits beside me, and Stuart on the other side. I find it awkward sitting between them, the chair opposite me empty.

'I hope you'll like the place,' Stuart asks, his eyes roving between us, his smile fake. 'The steak is delicious.'

'I'm sure it's lovely,' Mum says, eyeing the place. 'Amber, won't you take your jacket off?'

'I'm cold,' I say, because even with the jacket this restaurant is chilly.

'Not a problem,' Stuart says. 'Keep it on, no worries.'

I grab a menu and start scanning it. There are no calorie

amounts and I'm getting flustered, forcing myself to look from the pasta section to the salads, where there's nothing that I want. Instead I keep drifting back to the good stuff. A cheese-burger; I imagine it juicy and filling, grease running down my wrists. I haven't had a burger in ages, and I can feel myself sali-vate at the thought of it. God, they have mozzarella sticks as a starter. I clench my fists into balls.

Mum watches me as she opens her own menu, her eyes a careful warning. I wonder if she's seen me lick my lips and swallow hard. My stomach hurts.

'Would we like to start with any appetizers, ladies?' Stu-art asks.

'I'd like to have a go at the shrimp, if you don't mind. Let's split it.'

'And for you, Amber?'

I stare at the starter section and think about the mozza-rella sticks, but now my throat is dry and I take a minute to speak.

'She's all right,' Mum says. She smiles at me. 'She's not got a big appetite, though you might be fooled into thinking otherwise.' She gives me a friendly shove with her hand.

Stuart laughs. I felt bad for him for a minute; I pitied him because he's dating my mother, but he erased all my compas-sion with that laugh.

The waitress appears, red-haired and tall, an apron wrapped tightly around her waist.

'Are you ready to order any drinks?'

'Yes,' Mum says, 'we'll just have a bottle of water for the table, please. Stuart?'

'Could I have a pint of Guinness?'

'Of course. Anything else?'

'We can order our food now, can't we?' My mum looks to

Stuart, who nods in agreement like an obedient dog who's just happy to be included.

'I haven't decided yet,' I say.

'Oh, that's all right, they have Caesar salad, Amber.' She smiles at the waitress. 'That's her favourite.'

The waitress scribbles it onto her little pad. My cheeks burn with embarrassment. Stuart says nothing.

'I'll have the shrimp for a starter, and the carbonara,' my mum continues.

'And I'd like the chicken, but could I have it with chips instead of rice?'

'Of course. Is that all?'

She looks to me and I divert my eyes back to the menu. It's full of things that sound much more appetizing than a Caesar salad. Tonight, I'll be staring at my secret stash. My fingers will itch to open it and devour everything in there. It's going to be hard.

My stash is in one of the storage boxes of my Ikea Kallax. I collect food there. I never mean to; I know Mum's right. But every time I go to the shop, I end up loading things into the trolley that aren't meant to be there. The cravings are easier to control when the bag of cookies isn't sitting right in front of me. When it's right there and Mum's debit card is in my pocket, my hand develops a mind of its own. It takes what it wants.

Afterwards, I throw away the receipts. Mum doesn't check her bank balance; I know, because Dad used to complain about it, back when we still talked more than twice a year. She never sees me lug a bag full of sweets up the stairs, sneaking like a burglar.

'Yes, thank you,' Stuart says. 'That's all for now.' He turns to me. 'The Caesar salad here is lovely, by the way. I've tried it before.'

The waitress leaves and it's weirdly quiet. Mum twists her gold bracelet around her wrist, glimmering when it catches the light from the chandelier, and Stuart checks his watch. I whip my phone from my pocket and open Instagram under the table.

'So, Amber.' Stuart clears his throat awkwardly, encouraged by my mother's half-smile. 'What year are you in again?'

'Thirteen.'

'Oh, yes, Gemma told me. That's an exciting time! Are you applying to university then?'

There's a surge in my stomach at the reminder. UCAS closes in less than a month, and I've been desperately trying not to think about it.

'Yeah, pretty much,' I say.

'What are you going to be doing?'

It feels like an interrogation, my breathing becoming strained.

'I don't know.'

His smile cracks wider. 'If you're thinking of something artsy, you don't need to be worried about telling me. I won't judge.' He puts his hands up. 'In fact, I would quite have liked to do music myself, but it wasn't really an option.'

'Okay,' I say.

'You're lucky to be doing it now, you know. There are so many more interesting fields that didn't exist back when I was younger.' He shakes his head.

'I guess,' I say.

Mum looks at me. 'Amber, you're not being very conversational right now.'

I know she isn't angry at me. She's embarrassed.

'It's all right,' Stuart says. 'I was grilling you about something you didn't want to tell me, wasn't I? If you ask me, it's insanity to ask people as young as yourself to choose a course for the rest of their life – how can you ever be expected to make that decision already?'

The waitress returns with our drinks, handing out glasses left and right with a big customer-service smile that twitches in the atmosphere at our table. I want to leave just as badly as she does. As soon as she's gone, I look back at my phone.

Mum's pouring our drinks. I can feel Stuart's hesitant gaze on me, his mouth opening to speak and then closing, quickly, as if he's realized that his thoughts aren't worthy of being spoken. I scroll down Instagram.

'When I was her age,' Mum says, 'I knew just what I wanted to be.'

Stuart beams at her like she's perfect in his eyes. A pang of sympathy hits me and I wish it away.

'Oh, yes? A determined young woman, were you?'

'Were? Still am, excuse me!'

She chuckles and he laughs, reaching his hand for hers across the table. He rubs her wrist with his thumb and I roll my eyes.

'Amber Cox,' my mum says, her voice rising. 'Don't you roll your eyes at me!'

Her voice is fake and full of laughter. It's a performance, her offended facial expression carefully crafted. Stuart clucks at her, smiling.

'And please put your phone down,' she says. 'We're having a nice meal together, aren't we?'

I hesitate. There's a picture on my feed, uploaded ten minutes ago on Kim's account, of her, Marnie, and Melissa in front of a full-body mirror. My breathing is suddenly shallow, my lungs small.

'Amber!'

'Yeah,' I say. 'Sorry.'

I shove the phone back in my pocket and it's heavy there, I feel it through the denim no matter how I adjust myself. My fingers itch to reach back for it. I'm sure the picture isn't from today, it can't be, but I'm also not sure, because I think that was the top Melissa was wearing in school today.

'What's on there that's more interesting than us?' Mum says, her lash extensions clipping.

'Ah, Gemma,' Stuart says. 'What isn't more interesting than two old fools like us?'

She cackles, but she won't have liked that. She doesn't like being referred to as old. Ever since she turned forty, she treats it like a curse word.

I get up. 'I need to use the bathroom.'

'Be back before the food comes so Stuart doesn't eat yours!'

Their laughter ringing in my ears, I make my way through the restaurant. I'm trying to walk normally, pretending not to be rushing towards the toilets like I have diarrhoea, but I find my feet quickening with every step. I'm struggling to breathe. The sudden movement of getting up from my chair made me a bit dizzy. The world is unstable.

As soon as the door swings shut behind me, I get my phone back out. Today, at school, Melissa had a small braid in her hair that swung in and out of visibility between the strands. This is definitely the outfit she wore today, but I can't remember with Kim and Marnie, so I zoom in on Melissa until I spot the little braid. I commented on it because she rarely does anything except let her hair hang wild and loose. She shrugged and said she's trying something new. But when Kim said it looked pretty, she giggled and said, 'Really? Thank you!'

I can hear the blood pulsing through my head. This picture's from today, posted twelve minutes ago. The background is Marnie's bed with her sheepskin rug thrown across the pink duvet.

They never told me they were hanging out tonight. I never told them I was busy.

The caption says *love these bitches*, with a yellow heart at the end because that's the one Kim uses, and no capitalization because she always writes like this on Insta.

I check that all the cubicle doors are open so no one else is in here, and then I support myself against the marble sink and aim my face at the ceiling. I squeeze my eyes shut and breathe carefully, deeply, trying not to cry. It would ruin my delicate mascara and leave lines in my foundation. My throat feels shaky with tears.

Maybe it was spontaneous and unplanned, I tell myself. Maybe I've missed messages from one of them asking me to join. It's useless. I know I haven't. I've been deliberately excluded, and not only that, it's been publicly declared. Just the three of them, like they're a whole crew, and not even a mention or a tag, not a comment that says *Wish Amber was here with us!* Just a whole lot of likes and people saying they're gorgeous. And they are. Without me, they are.

I convulse with silent sobs, resolutely forbidding my eyes from shedding tears. But my brain keeps whispering that they must've done this before. And it keeps telling me that I've always known this.

Something shifted when we started sixth form. We'd never worn make-up or done our hair for school before, but Melissa showed up one day with sparkly eyelids and her hair ironed aggressively straight. The clothes she wore were different. The things she wanted to do were different: go shopping, go to Starbucks, party, buy a fake ID.

It wasn't her fault. It was Marnie and Kim. They turned her into one of them, but I've always known they never wanted me. She was the one they started talking to in the cafeteria, complimenting her boots. She'd had a fight with her mother about those boots; they cost more than a week's worth of groceries for all of them.

love these bitches

It doesn't matter that I started doing my make-up too. It doesn't matter that I got a boyfriend first. They don't like me, and they never will, because I'm fat. But not only fat. There's something else, something intangible, separating me from them. Melissa used to have it too. Maybe she still does. Maybe she's better at hiding it.

Does it matter? Melissa's like them now. She doesn't like me either.

I remember once in year eight when I got my period in class. It was unexpected, it's always been so irregular. I cried in the girls' toilets as I stuffed my underwear with toilet paper and tried to wipe everything off my skirt. I'd left my jacket placed over the stain on my chair, and I was shaking when I walked back to the classroom with a bunch of paper in my hands, terrified of having to wipe my chair down without anyone seeing. But when I came back, there was nothing on my chair. Melissa smiled at me and squeezed my hand when I sat down, confused and overwhelmed. She told me later that she'd intentionally knocked over her water bottle so it fell onto my desk and she could wipe everything down discreetly.

I get my phone again. The caption feels so aimed at me. The whole post feels like it was meant for only me to see, so that I would finally get the message. Leave us alone, Amber. We don't want you here.

I like the picture. I comment, *Omg, you're all stunning!* Thirst emoji.

I wipe the remnants of tears from the corners of my eyes and inspect my make-up. It's fine. My eyes look a bit red, but I don't think anyone will notice.

My screen lights up with a notification. Kim has replied to my comment: *Aw babe, but u!*

Yeah, the stash is going to look tempting tonight.

13

Nicki

I'm wearing blue plastic covers over my shoes. I understand why. The floors are wooden and white, they feel rustic, and there's a large, fluffy rug in the lounge. It's raining outside, pouring, and the inside of the plastic is wet and brown by now. My hair is as wet as if I've showered.

We're not the only ones here; there's an older couple, retired, there's a family of two parents and two kids and a large bump that will soon be a fifth member.

Tom is standing in front of the large glass sliding doors in the kitchen. The garden is small, fenced in by tall wooden walls. It must look lovely during nicer circumstances, but now the grass is muddy instead of green, and everything is grey and wet. He smiles back at me as I approach, puts an arm around my waist.

Leaning my head against his, I know he must be imagining that this is ours. He must be pretending that he can't hear the older couple mumble among themselves or the estate agent showing the younger family around the kitchen, bragging about the white goods.

'What do you think?' he asks.

It doesn't matter what I think, because we can't buy this place anyway. He knows this. He likes to pretend. We have done this before. He has periods when we'll go to several viewings a month, and then it will be another year before he speaks of it again.

Maybe if we take out a high-interest mortgage. Maybe if

we move to a different city, give up the dream of Hove. Maybe if we get a two-bed house and rent out one of the bedrooms.

'It's lovely,' I say.

It's white, it's plain. Everything is bare. It looks newly built, it lacks character. It's the white bread of homes. I grew up with colours and carpets and tapestries and a dozen ornaments on every flat surface.

I say, 'I just wonder how much the bills would be.'

He hums absently and I wonder if he's elected not to hear me. There's a smile on his face. I wish I could give this to him. I wish I could give him everything he wants.

'I love it,' he says. 'It's beautiful, isn't it? You'd love the closet space.'

'Yes,' I say, because there's no harm indulging his fantasy. But there's a lump in my throat that I can't swallow.

The toddler runs roaring through the room with a stuffed dinosaur in his hand.

'I'd like to have a look at the bedroom,' I say.

'I'll join you in a bit,' says Tom. 'I have a couple of questions for the agent.'

I slip from his arm and leave the room. It doesn't matter what he asks the agent, we won't be buying this house. The agent's jovial laughter follows me into the hallway. I open a door and find the master bedroom. It's large, a grey carpet across the floor, a built-in closet spanning the entire wall opposite the bed. I drag my hand along the dresser, feeling the wood. I can hear the feet of the little kids along the hallway outside. It makes me feel out of place.

This is a house for people like that family. It's squeaky clean and pretty, like them. Three happy little children and two happy adults. This is a house for children to run wild with dinosaur toys. Not a house for me to swipe through Tinder in the bathroom. Not a house for our fights.

I leave the bedroom. In the lounge, the older couple are putting their raincoats back on and Tom is speaking to the agent. I touch him on the shoulder and say I'll wait outside in the car, then smile politely at the agent.

'Should I take your details so I can give you a call and discuss mortgage options tomorrow?' I hear her ask.

'Yes,' Tom says. 'That would be great.'

I tear the blue plastic off my shoes and go outside. I let the rain take me. It's cold. It drums hard against my shoulders and my head and it gets inside my coat, running down my skin. The older couple are getting in their car, the man holding an umbrella over his wife. *I'm not like these people*, I think. Why am I here?

When we get home, I take off all my wet clothes and sit on the couch in my damp underwear, covering myself with a blanket, shivering. Tom has a rule that we don't turn the heating on until November. I spend all of September and October wrapped in multiple layers, counting down the days.

Tom plops down next to me in his bathrobe. He shakes his head and the water from his hair goes everywhere, splattering the couch and me and the wall. I hold up a hand and laugh.

'Stop it!' Half-heartedly.

'What, can you get any wetter than you already are?' he says.

He sinks back onto the couch. I twist and wring my own hair out, letting the water pool on the carpet.

'You didn't like it very much, did you?' he asks.

I smile an apology. 'It's not really my style.'

He shrugs. 'Well, not like it matters anyway. We can't afford to buy.'

'Yet,' I add, like he always does.

'When's the last time you looked in the savings account, Nicki?' Tom is getting agitated, exasperation seeping into his voice. 'We're not buying for forty years. And then we'll be retired, so we won't be buying anyway.'

I inch closer to him, carefully. Withdrawing and approaching can both cause him to direct his frustration at me now, so I do what I feel inclined to. I put a hand on his shoulder.

'You don't know what life will look like in ten years,' I say.

He doesn't push me away, but he doesn't acknowledge my attempts. He slaps a hand to his forehead and rubs at the skin.

'You know what the worst part is? Yesterday I moved a couple into a million-pound house in Hove. A million pounds. They have three bedrooms between the pair of them, in case they get bored of the one, I guess.'

It's not often his hope deserts him this fully. Tom sees silver linings where there are none. It concerns me to see him like this. It's always the beginning of a downward spiral.

'Tom,' I say. 'Do you mind if I ask you something?'

'What?'

'Have you tried getting help yet?'

He groans. 'What are you talking about?'

'After the last time we had a fight, you said . . .'

I let the sentence drift off into nothing. I move away, as discreetly as I can, creating a safer distance.

'Well, how are they going to help me?' he says, his voice louder. 'You want me to see a therapist like you do?'

'I didn't say I wanted you to,' I try. '*You* said—'

'Give me a break,' he says. 'I don't need the kind of help you're thinking of. My problem's that the system is rigged against me and I can work ten hours a day making next to nothing and I'll never be able to own a fucking home. No therapist can do anything about that.'

He stands up, he shoots from the couch like he has to get away from it. I want to curl myself into a protective ball like an armadillo.

'I'm so tired of this bullshit!' he yells.

There's shouting, so much shouting. It's my dad. My dad is angry at me and I don't know why.

'Tom,' I whisper. 'Tom, I'm going back.'

But it's not Tom, it's Dad. He's bent down in front of me, his hands on his thighs, staring at me.

'What did you do?' he says.

I can hear Mum in the background screaming at him, pleading for him to stop. I move my hands around, trying to feel something. A couch. I grip the cushion tightly, digging my nails into it.

'Jesus fucking Christ.' It's Tom. He's standing in the middle of the room looking at me.

'Please help me.' I force the words out, fight hard to make a sound.

Dad grips my ponytail hard, yanking my head back. His breath is hot against my face, sour, smells garlicky.

'What did you do?'

'Don't hit me,' I say. 'Please don't hit me.'

'Please, Nicki,' Tom says. 'Not right now. I can't deal with this right now.'

All I manage in response is a whimper. I can barely see him. He's so small and so distant and I reach for him, but he's too far away. He fades in my vision. He's replaced by my dad.

'No, no, no,' I say.

It's not real. Is it? It feels more so than Tom right now.

I'm sobbing, still reaching for him, hoping if I just get to feel him, I'll know that he's here.

He looks so angry. He's gesticulating, his mouth moving quickly. My mum is screaming.

'I'm going to Dave's.'

No, I think, and he's gone. Well and truly gone.

I scream for him and he doesn't come back. I'm alone with Dad. Mum is banging on the door. Why is he angry?

14

Amber

It's hard to look at them.

English is the first class of the day, and there they sit, their desks pulled closer together than they're normally placed. I slide into my usual spot and say hi. It comes out weakly, pathetically, smiling is difficult.

'Morning,' Kim says.

Marnie only gives me a look, a single twitch in her lip, and returns to chewing her gum. I take out my books and the pencil case, acting like it matters to me where they're placed on the desk and I'm so absorbed in organizing them that I can't speak.

I should go and sit somewhere else. Kim shifts uncomfortably and they're silent now, their chatter died down as soon as I appeared. Maybe it was me they were talking about. Yes, I should sit somewhere else, but that's even more embarrassing.

They start talking about how Marnie's parents don't want her to move to London, even though it's the best for the arts, even though they can afford the rent.

'They have to let you if you get into ACM! That's so impressive. And you've definitely got what it takes.'

Oh yes, the Academy of Contemporary Music, Marnie's dream. She doesn't have what it takes. Her voice is okay in the way that it gets her compliments at karaoke, and all her friends are amazed at her videos on YouTube, but it's nothing compared to the tens of thousands of others trying to achieve what she wants.

'Yeah, honestly,' I say. 'You're amazing.'

She flicks her hair over her shoulder. 'Oh, stop it.'

Mr Miller looks haggard. It's a far throw from his usual dreamy looks, with the perfect skin and bright eyes. His skin isn't clear today. There are bags under his eyes and some stubble on his face. Suddenly his appearance matches his voice. He's staring at the windows with dead eyes while he waits for the class to arrive and settle.

I start scribbling in my notebook. Last night, I started making a list about Kevin. I have to turn him into a person if he's going to be convincing. I don't know much about him yet. Looking at Mr Miller makes it easier. He's palpable. I wonder what his family looks like, where he grew up, what he likes to do in his free time.

Goes to the gym (obviously)

Siblings?

I cross out the question mark and decide that he has two, a sister and a brother, both of them still living in Brighton. They're not close. That means I don't have to talk very much about them.

Mother is retired

Father is dead (?)

Favourite colour: green

Favourite food: Thai

'All right, everyone,' Mr Miller says, rising from the chair. 'Let's all settle down a bit.'

Kim is balancing on the back legs of her chair and rolling her eyes. Marnie briefly looks up at him from her phone.

He clears his throat. 'Okay then, who did the reading?'

I don't know what the reading was. I'm not sure anyone does. No one says a word. Mr Miller's face is tired and drained. He sighs.

'Okay, please open up your books and do the reading I assigned you last week. I'll put the page numbers on the blackboard.'

He starts writing on the blackboard and people start chattering among themselves. I almost feel bad for him.

Likes cats, not dogs

Newly single after a long-term relationship

Marnie glances over at me. 'What are you doing? Are you actually doing schoolwork?'

'Ew,' I say. 'I'm just making a to-do list.'

'That's so organized of you,' she says, and I can tell that being organized is a bad thing in this context. It's uncool, not spontaneous enough, not carefree enough.

'It's nothing,' I say. 'I'm just busy. It's not like I care.'

She moves back, her hands up in a defensive gesture, like I'm being overreactive. 'Hey, I don't give a shit.'

Because of course she doesn't. That's what this is about. Marnie's cool enough not to care, and I care way too much. I care that I'm too fat. I care that Melissa and I aren't the same any more. I care that Kim and Marnie don't like me.

And I care that Nicki buys the lie I'm selling her. I look down at the notebook and feel stupid. I shouldn't be putting this much effort into it. It's nothing serious. I tear the page out and crumple it up.

That night Dan texts me. *Amber*, he says, *are we ever going to have sex?*

I freeze, my finger in the middle of a scroll, when the notification comes. It must have been on his mind since last time, just like it's been on mine. We haven't even spoken since then.

Of course, I say. *I've told you, haven't I?*

Yeah, you said we'll do it, but like, that was ages ago

It was two months ago

And I still can't even touch your boobs, and that's fine, I'm not trying to put you on the spot. It just doesn't seem like you want to

I do want to

I type it out and I'm scared to send it. It feels like it will commit me to something.

But I do want to. I'm not a fucking Catholic. I get horny, I masturbate, I've watched porn and I don't want to be a virgin when I go to university. I don't want to keep being the one pretending to understand what the others are talking about, laughing along as if I have stories of my own.

Sometimes I think I should do it just to get it over with. There's no need to enjoy it. At least I'll have done it. But then I think about the way rolls form on my stomach when I bend, and I think about my thighs rubbing together, and I think about how it will all look to him when he sees it for the first time.

We don't have to, he writes. *You can just tell me if you don't want to.*

He's so good to me. There must be something wrong with me. Despite the way I look, there's a guy here that really wants to fuck me. And for some reason the idea of it gives me heart palpitations and acute asthma.

I want to, I say, *I'm just not ready, okay?*

He doesn't reply.

15

Nicki: *I haven't heard from you in a few days*

Kevin: *Sorry, been busy*

Nicki: *That's all right, I'm not a priority*

Kevin: *Of course you are*

Nicki: *Why? You've only spoken to me twice*

Kevin: *More like 3 times*

Nicki: *Wow, we're getting serious*

Kevin: *I'm just saying I like you*
Sorry I was gone a few days

Nicki: *It's okay*
What have you been doing?

Kevin: *Had to make a last-minute business trip to Auckland*

Nicki: *Your life is very difficult*

Kevin: *I know, right?*
How are you, you okay?

Nicki: *I'm doing good, nothing much going on*

Kevin: *Do you ever feel like someone expects something of you
that you can never give them?*

Nicki: *Like what?*

Kevin: *Like something that should be simple
And you really want to give it to them, because you should,
and there's no reason not to
Except you just can't do it*

Nicki: *Yeah, I know that feeling. Like they think you're
someone you're not*

Kevin: *I don't suppose I'm lucky enough that you've found a*
   solution?
Nicki: *I wish*
   What is this about?
Kevin: *There's a woman I've been seeing*
   Not seriously enough to delete Tinder, obviously
   But she wants something more, and I just don't think I can do
   that yet
Nicki: *Have you told her that?*
Kevin: *Pretty much*
   She says it's okay and she's willing to wait, but I know she's lying
   I know what she wants, and it doesn't feel right to ask her to
   wait for it, and for what?
   Me? I'm not really worth waiting for
Nicki: *Do you know what I think you should do?*
Kevin: *Please*
Nicki: *Tell her about me. I think that should send her running*

16

Nicki

Leela's wearing purple eyeshadow. 'So,' she says, smiling widely. 'How are you today?'

I nod. 'Good.'

'How are things with Tom? I remember you had an argument last week.'

'That's all right now.' And my eye is no longer sore and red, you have to look carefully for any trace of the bruising.

Leela does her head-tilt. 'That's all right? Does that mean there's something else now?'

I'm overwhelmed with anger. She reads too much into what I say. She pries. There's always a sense that she believes I can't solve my own issues, and she's wrong about that. Whatever she thinks about me and Tom, she's wrong about that too.

I take a deep breath, forcing myself to remember that this is her job. This is what I'm here for.

'No, we're fine,' I say. 'Things are great.'

I think about how we made love that night, fingers laced, looking into each other's eyes. I think about the morning I made him breakfast and we had such a wonderful time and I should do that again, and I can, I might as well do it again tomorrow. I don't let myself think about the fight after the viewing. I can't think about how he left me by myself. He had every right to. He's not obligated to take care of me.

'Well, I'm glad to hear,' Leela says.

There was a delay, though. She waited a moment, regarding what I'd said, disbelieving me.

'Would you like to tell me about how the argument was resolved?' she asks.

'I apologized,' I say.

'Did he?'

'Of course.'

Annoyance seeps back into my crevices; I don't like being observed. I don't like being evaluated.

'Did you come to understand each other?' Leela asks.

I nod, biting my tongue. She waits for me to speak. I listen to the clock ticking on the wall.

'Nicki,' she says. 'I want you to be as honest as possible with me. Is there anything that would help you feel more comfortable speaking to me?'

Stop being a therapist, I think.

'No,' I say. 'It's fine. I feel fine.'

She looks at me under her fringe, eyes searching. 'Are you sure?'

Her expression unnerves me. It's such an obvious attempt at projecting a certain message: I see you. You are safe. You are heard. But I don't feel safe. This room reminds me of too much. Of Wallace. The first time I walked in there and he shook my hand and smiled and offered me a chair. God, I was hopeful. I was stupidly hopeful.

'Yes,' I say. 'Positive.'

'Great, then.' She straightens up, smiling again. 'I was also wanting to ask if you've given any more thought to what we talked about last time? About having someone to talk to?'

And I haven't, of course, because after a session I shake off everything she said like a wet dog. But I lie, hoping it will make her stop asking.

'I suppose I've made a new friend,' I say. 'A pen-pal, of sorts.'

She perks up at this, her shoulders shooting up. Her eyes

shine with surprise and excitement. Maybe it's monotonous, what we talk about every session. My life playing out the same way day after day, no characters in it except me and Tom.

'Tell me about that,' she says, overjoyed, but clasping her hands on her knee to conceal it.

'His name is Kevin. He lives in Australia, we met on the Internet.'

I'm tense, trying to come up with a plausible answer if she asks about more specifics of how we got to know each other. On Tinder. Yes, I'm on Tinder, despite Tom. I use it all the time. That's probably something we should talk about.

But she doesn't. 'Uh-huh, and what kind of things do you talk about with Kevin?'

I shrug. 'I don't know. Regular stuff, our lives.'

'Do you open up to him about your feelings at all?' She puts her hands out. 'Not all of them, of course. But do you feel you can share them with him?'

Which is funny, because Kevin barely knows who I am, and every time he asks, I'm having a great day and I'm doing fine.

'Yeah,' I say. 'Sometimes.'

'That's great, Nicki.' She smiles like a proud parent. 'Have you told him about your past?'

'We're not at that stage yet.'

'Will you?'

I open my mouth and close it again. Of course I won't, but I can't tell her that.

'I suppose,' I lie.

I've lied to every therapist after Wallace. He was the only one I told the truth to. He's the one that made me realize that there's nothing in me that can be fixed. These people wouldn't help me if they knew the truth. They'd take one look at me and think, *Well, of course, what did you expect? You've brought this on yourself again.* The idea terrifies me, not because it would be news to me, but because it would prove my dad right.

The worst part was always when he turned to Mum.

'This is your fault,' he'd say. 'Look at what kind of girl you've raised.'

Rubbing her hands, her watery eyes turning towards me, she wouldn't say it with so many words, but it would be written clear on her face. I did my best with you, and look how you've turned out. The disappointment emanated from her shivering body and her trembling lips. *Do you know what he's going to do to me because of you?*

'Nicki.'

I snap back and assess the room. Leela is sitting in front of me, leaning over, concerned eyes.

'Yeah?' I say.

'You okay over there?' A crooked smile plays on her face.

I look down at my hands. I'm steady. My feet are planted on the floor.

'I'm fine,' I say.

'I was saying, I'm very happy for you. You haven't really had a proper friend since Kate, have you?'

I nod.

'It does get harder to meet new people as you get older,' she smiles. 'Would you like to practise some ways of expressing yourself to a new person?'

I'd like to put my head on the steering wheel and fall asleep to the echoing, all-consuming *beeeeeeeeeeeep*. I feel old. Joints aching, head tired, mind muddled, vision ever so slightly blurred. It's Leela's fault. She always drains me.

I'm not ready to drive home, so I text him. A few minutes later he replies.

How are you?

I catch myself in the rear-view mirror. There are bags under my eyes and I'm not okay, am I?

I'm great :) what are you up to?

Working, bored, he writes. *You?*

Getting ready to go out for lunch with some friends

What are you having?

I look around the car, to the passenger-seat foot area where I put all the rubbish. There's a flier for a new pasta place called Nonna's.

Pasta! There's a new place open just down the road that we've been dying to try

He takes a couple minutes.

I'm jealous, what's a bloke got to do to get in on the action?

I laugh, blubbering snot and tears on the steering wheel. Oh, I'm crying. I'm jealous too. I'm jealous of the life I've created. I miss something I never had. It's beyond ridiculous, and so I laugh at myself at the same time. It's pasta, I say to myself. It's lunch with some friends, why are you crying?

I miss Kate. Slurping up pasta sauce, making the face she always made when I was supposed to laugh at what she'd just said. Her jokes were never very good, they had to be sign-posted. Sometimes I miss it so much it hurts.

Nicki: *Get on a plane to Brighton, for starters*

Kevin: *You underestimate how far I'll go for food*

Nicki: *You don't get Italian food over there?*

Kevin: *No, we stick to kangaroo meat and dried spiders*

Nicki: *Disgusting*

Kevin: *It's quite appetizing*

Nicki: *I don't believe you*

Kevin: *If you come to Australia, I'll keep you hostage until you try it*

I smile at my phone, my thumb above the keypad. Of course, in his world, that's a possibility. I don't have Tom holding me here. I have a decently well-paid job as a secretary. In this alternate reality, I can go to Australia.

And in this alternative reality, I have no reason not to.

You'd make a great travel agent, I type.

Yeah? Don't I just make you really want to visit Perth?

Absolutely

Ditch the lunch

Already cancelled

I'll cook pasta for dinner

I snort.

I won't be there in time for dinner

Dinner tomorrow, silly. Time zones, you know

I take a deep breath. I should get going. Tom will be home by now, and he'll start worrying if I take too long after my appointment. I don't want the tirade of texts that accompanies his concern. The car park is empty and quiet.

Maybe one day, I lie.

I switch off my Tinder notifications, put the phone aside and get ready to leave. Tonight, I'm going to order some pasta.

17

Amber

I join the others after a mandatory meeting with the guidance counsellor. They're hanging at the usual spot outside,
seated on our benches. Melissa's sucking milkshake out of a
straw and I'd like to tell her how utterly, utterly lost I am.
The guidance counsellor kept trying to help me figure out
what I want to do. All I know is I'm going to Falmouth
because that's where Melissa is going. It will be me and her,
and Marnie will be in London and Kim somewhere else, and
things will be like they used to. I have no idea what I'll be
studying.

Melissa wouldn't get it. She's always known what she
wanted. I think she told me the first time we spoke to each
other that she's going to be a journalist. She already writes for
the school paper.

'Hey,' I say.

'How'd it go?' Melissa asks.

'All right.'

'Did you make a decision yet?' Kim says, peering at me
from under her fringe.

She's not asking a question. She's putting me on the spot
because she knows the answer.

'No,' I say.

'Marnie, tell her what happened.' Melissa is smiling, putting her elbow in Marnie's side.

Marnie rolls her eyes, and I think Kim reciprocates it. It's
too vague to see, she's subtle. They don't want to let me in on

their gossip. Marnie doesn't want to have to repeat herself to me. But Melissa is all smiles, all insistence.

'Okay, so apparently my mum's best friend's daughter was engaged to Mr Miller,' Marnie says, uninterestedly. 'Then she, like, found his Tinder profile and dumped him. I heard it from my mum.' A shrug. 'It was just pretty funny.'

Mr Miller got dumped because of us. Well, because of me, I guess. I could get expelled if anyone ever found out. I should delete his profile. My phone feels heavy in my pocket. I shouldn't keep the app. It's all evidence, but what about Nicki?

'Oh,' I say. 'Wow.'

'It's so sad.' But Melissa smiles as she says it. The unkindness of it surprises me. It's not like her not to care.

'Yeah, and it's not good for us.'

'For us?' Marnie raises her brows at me. 'You're the one who did it.'

It's sort of like being punched in the gut. It's so exhausting, keeping up with what they care about.

'It was your idea.' My voice is pathetically weak.

She shrugs. 'I've got lots of great ideas.'

'I was just thinking it might be bad if they figure out it was us who made the profile,' I say.

I could never survive an expulsion in my final year, ever. Mr Miller will survive this break-up. Nicki would survive being ghosted by Kevin, even though she might be confused in the beginning. I have to delete the app. I have to pretend this never happened.

'Yeah, but we're not still using it, are we?' Kim says. 'If it's not active any more, there's no way for them to find out.'

I close my mouth. I'm silent for too long, not knowing what to say, and it's weird now, Marnie looking at me from the corner of her eye.

'Weren't you messaging that woman on there?' Melissa says.

Marnie smirks. Kim's head perks up as she remembers this detail.

'Well, obviously not any more,' I say quickly.

In my eagerness to get it out, I might be too loud.

'Thank god,' Marnie says, her gaze lingering on me. 'It would've been so sad otherwise.'

Melissa laughs, putting an elbow in her side.

'Seriously, Amber,' she says. 'I was, like, worried about you still talking to her for some reason.'

I force myself to laugh. I'm cold. I feel solid like a rock and I'm careful that I make all the right facial expressions and every little gesture.

'Of course I'm not,' I say. 'Why would I be doing that? Jesus, Mel, I'm not a loser.'

I'm not, I think. I'm not I'm not I'm not.

But maybe I am, because I get my phone out and when I see the little icon for the Tinder app, I can't make myself delete it.

18

Nicki

After a long night shift, Edith is my last stop. It's around eight in the morning now. Tom will be gone by the time I'm back. I haven't slept in over twenty hours and I chug the last of the coffee in my thermos before I knock on her door.

She's usually awake at this time, pottering around with her flowers, a morning person. There's no answer. I use our spare key from under her doormat and let myself in.

'Good morning, Edith!' I call loudly, so I don't frighten or surprise her. I've walked in on my fair share of undressed seniors.

Still nothing. The lights are turned off, the curtains drawn just like they must have been left by the person here last night. The silence unnerves me. I've got my phone out already, prepared to call for assistance. I'm pulsating with adrenaline.

'Edith?' I say, and open the door to her bedroom.

She's lying in bed on her back, her face aimed at the window. For a terrible moment I think she's passed, and my workdays are going to be unbearable now without her to light them up. Then her head slowly turns towards me. I ease the grip on my phone, realizing how hard I've been holding it.

'Who is it?' she asks.

It's rare for her not to use a greeting.

'It's Nicki,' I say. 'How are you, Edith? Are you all right?'

I bend over the bed to check on her. Her face is fine, symmetrical, no stroke. There's no vomit around the mouth. Her eyes look normal. I know what to look for, I've seen these things before.

'I'm fine,' she says.

'You sure? You mind if I check you over?'

'Oh, if you must.'

I help her shimmy into an upright position against the bed-frame. She hasn't wet the bed. I lift her arms and touch her legs. She doesn't say a word, doesn't flinch, doesn't seem to be in pain. I finally allow myself to feel true relief.

'Why are you still in bed?' I ask. 'You're always up by this time.'

'I'm just tired, dear. Just tired.'

It looks like an attempt at a smile, but it ends up more like a brief twitch of her lips. She's getting older, I suppose. It happens to all of them. I take my time before I let go of her arm, forcing myself to accept this reality. Edith's been as healthy as someone my age the entire time I've known her. It was never going to last for ever, and I should have known that. I force myself to perk up.

'Well, would you like to get up now, then?'

'Maybe in a bit.'

'Breakfast?'

She nods.

'I'll make you some tea and a toast, yeah? Come out when you're ready.'

'Thanks, doll.'

I go out to the kitchen and put the kettle on. Take out some bread and marmalade, get the toaster going, realize I haven't asked her what kind of tea she wants. I go back, she wants Earl Grey, but she's unenthusiastic about it in a way that old British ladies usually aren't about tea.

I clear up the kitchen a little, and I hear her dragging her slippers along the hallway to the living room when the food is ready. The telly turns on. The volume is lower than usual.

I take the food out to her, surprised that she's still in her pyjamas covered by a dressing gown. The mail bowl on the table is empty. There's a women's football match on.

'I didn't know you were a sports fan,' I say.

'Oh,' she says softly. 'I didn't know what was on.'

'Should I switch it?'

She shakes her head. Edith's usually a hungry one, especially in the mornings, but today she doesn't reach for her food.

'Feeling tired today, are we?' I ask.

'Yes,' she says. 'Quite.'

The conversation doesn't flow like it usually does, it hits a dam. The commentator on the telly is loud and passionate.

'There's no mail today,' I say.

'That's all right.'

I think it's the first time she hasn't asked for it.

'Anything you'd like me to do? Should I hoover?'

There are crumbs on the living-room carpet and outside dirt by the door.

'If you don't mind,' she says.

I linger in the doorway, looking at her. The food remains on the table. Her face isn't aimed at the telly. This isn't the Edith I know, but she hasn't been the past few times either, has she? She's never asked me to check her voicemail before. She's never been as quiet and down before as she was last time. I didn't see it then, but now I do. I hear the mail slide down the letter box and hit the floor.

'That's the mail,' I say, trying to sound chipper. 'Maybe there's something there.'

She gives a slight nod. Most mornings, she'd jump at the sound. She'd order me to go get her mail right away. Now she says nothing. She sits on the couch, dejected, staring at the telly.

All she's got is a reminder that she needs to renew her TV licence. I take it back to her without even receiving a question about what it is. She already knew.

'It's your TV licence,' I say. 'We'll need to renew it in a few weeks.'

I feel like the bearer of bad news. Expected news, but bad nonetheless. I should go and hoover now; there are crumbs all over these floors, pieces of dirt and leaves that we've dragged into her home. But I'm tired, and it feels like such a wasted effort. What the fuck's a floor to someone like Edith? She won't notice, she won't care.

I sit down next to her. The Lake District leaflet is still in the bowl on her coffee table.

'Are you going to the Lake District?' I ask.

She looks at me, confused.

'You've got a Lake District leaflet here,' I say.

'Do I?' she says. 'I thought I threw that away. I was meant to go to the Lake District with my son.'

'That's fun!' I say.

But she doesn't look happy, and that's when I realize. He's the one she's been waiting for. When she asks for the mail, she's hoping for something from him. But there never is. I've never seen the man. Never heard his voice. For years I've taken care of her, and never has there been a visit. Maybe one day, a long time ago, she mentioned chatting to him on the phone. She would have been happy that day, and I wouldn't have realized why.

'Is he in the picture on your fridge?' I ask.

Edith nods. I remember now that she told me a few months ago that she's getting another grandchild, that her daughter-in-law is pregnant again, but have I heard anything else about the son since? No, I don't think I have.

I could say I'm sure he'll call one day. I could tell her of course he's taking her to the Lake District. But lying to her feels wrong. We both know the truth.

'What's his name, again?' I ask. 'Your son.'

A sort of twitch at the side of her face, like a blow. 'Roland.'

'What does he do for a living?'

It used to cheer her up, telling me about her son. I'm desperate to get that smile back. Not today.

'Bank,' she says.

'That's fancy.' I try a smile. 'You must be proud of him.'

'Yes.' Her eyes directed at her knees. 'Yes, I am.'

'It must be difficult for him to visit, being so busy.'

A small hum is the only response I get.

'Does he live far?' I ask.

'Surrey.'

'Yeah, that's a distance. And with a child on the way.'

Shut up, I tell myself. Bankers have weekends like everyone else. Surrey's an hour away, isn't it? She knows these things, and there's nothing you can do to change them. I'm angry at this son. All she wants is a trip to the Lake District. She has no other children, no siblings I've ever heard of, no husband in the picture, parents long since dead. The least he could do is give her a trip to the Lake District.

Edith says nothing.

I say, 'Should I hoover, then?'

When I go back to the office to finish up my shift, I look at her file. His name is listed as her next of kin: Roland Compton, son. There's no one else around; I check the kitchen and look out of the window. I dial his number and it makes me feel nervous. I'm intruding on something I have no right to get involved with. I'm imposing on a man I've never met.

'Hello?' he says.

I clear my throat quickly, caught off guard by how quickly he picked up. 'Hi. Is this Roland?'

'Speaking.' His sharp, short tone is so different from his mother's. It's like he has limited time.

'My name is Nicki,' I say. 'I'm one of the people caring for your mother, and—'

'Is she all right?'

'She's absolutely fine.'

'There's not been an accident? Because if I need to drive down there, I need to know that in the next five minutes so I can cancel my meeting.'

I look out of the window. I know this is my turn to speak, but it feels very pointless all of a sudden. This man is too busy for me. The thought of disturbing his existence, of changing his mood for the worse, it scares me. He seems like a person who can get angry.

'No,' I say. 'There's no need to drive down. Though we do encourage visits—'

'Look, Nicki, I'm actually at work right now, so you're kind of putting me in a difficult spot.' I can hear a loud coffee machine in the background, the barely restrained annoyance in his voice. 'Is there a particular reason you're calling?'

The Lake District. Edith's blank, despondent face.

'We check the phone numbers of our emergency contacts regularly,' I say. 'That was all I had to do. I'm sorry to have disturbed you.'

'Next time, send a text, won't you? It's a lot easier for me to get to.'

'No worries. Thank you for your time.'

'Thanks for caring for her.' And with that, he's hung up.

19

Amber

'Amber, dear.' My mum pokes her head out the kitchen doorway. Her hair's in a blonde bun at the top of her head.

Her lips are swollen after the most recent injection. That's why she's at home instead of with Stuart, a rare occurrence these days. She doesn't leave the house when her lips are healing. She sends me to get the groceries and calls in sick at work.

'Come in here a second,' she says, her malformed, bruised lips moving with the words.

'Okay,' I say.

She retreats and I take my shoes off slowly, biding my time. I've got a bad feeling about this, and I'm usually right.

I enter the kitchen apprehensively. Mum's standing next to the bathroom scales. It's been placed in the middle of the room.

I don't think my heart is beating any more.

She looks at me. 'Well, come on then.' Smiles. 'You know the drill. It's just scales.'

'Maybe—' My voice breaks, weak and hoarse, my throat dry. I try again. 'Maybe tomorrow—'

'Oh, honey, let's just get it over with.' She cocks her head to the side. 'It's been far too long since the last time and I don't want to forget again.'

When I was younger, I'd always pray that she would forget. And every time she went a month without taking me to the scales, I would be convinced it had worked. I don't know who

I was praying to, but sometimes they seemed to have my back. And sometimes they abandoned me.

I put my schoolbag on the kitchen island. I feel a bit dizzy, grasping the edge of the worktop for some stability. Mum watches me, impatience written all over her face. She nods to the scales.

I step on it. I'm not breathing as I wait for the number to appear. There are tears at the back of my eyes, and I keep them back only with the thin hope that maybe it won't be that bad. Who am I kidding? I look the same every day when I check the mirror.

The number shows and the scales beep. There's a convulsion in my chest. Mum cranes her neck to look, pursing her oversized lips.

'Wait.' I snivel, dry my nose with my sleeve. 'Just a second.'

I step off the scales as if it's burned me and I take off my jacket. It's not heavy, but maybe, just maybe, it's heavy enough. If Mum weren't here, I'd take off every piece of clothing I'm wearing. I throw the jacket on the worktop and get back on the scales.

Please. Please. Please.

The number has barely changed. My face feels wet so I guess the tears have escaped.

Mum checks the number. She looks at it for a long time. It feels like minutes go by. Then she turns her face back to me, her brows turned down in disappointment.

'Amber,' she says. 'Isn't this the same weight as last time?'

'I don't remember,' I whisper.

It's a bold-faced lie. Every number the scales give me stays in my mind until it's replaced by a new one. It's a constant at the outskirts of all my other thoughts.

'Well, why has nothing changed?' Mum demands. 'Are you lying about going to the gym?'

I shake my head. 'I'm not! I go every day!'

'Then how much are you eating?' She burrows her eyes into me, her hands planted on her hips.

I say nothing. I get off the scales.

Mum rolls her eyes. 'Oh, Jesus Christ! We've talked about this so many times, Amber. How much do you eat?'

I look down at the floor and ball my hands into fists. *Come on, speak*, I tell myself. *Say something*. I open my mouth and push the words as hard as I can.

'Too much.'

Mum sighs exasperatedly. 'Yes, I know. Do you want to be fat, Amber?'

I shake my head.

'No, you don't. You know what happens to fat women. They don't get love, they don't get boyfriends. Their husbands leave them for thinner girls. Do you want that to happen to you?'

Another shake. No, I want to be normal. I want someone to care. I don't want Dan to leave me after we have sex for the first time.

'That's why your dad cheated,' she says. I know this, I've heard it before. 'Someone slimmer and more beautiful came along and I became expendable. I was a fat, lonely, ugly hag, a single mother. You're not going to be like that, Amber.'

She's right. Mum was bigger back then, and I don't think she'd got fillers before. She'd never been on a diet before the divorce. But now look at her; she's slim, she's happy, she has a boyfriend.

She walks past me. My hair reaches after her with the breeze. I want to reach for her too. I want her reassurance that even though I'm disgustingly fat, I'm worthy. Everything is okay. But everything is not okay because the scales never lie.

I hear the fridge open and turn around.

'And I was going to make us a Cobb salad for dinner,' Mum says. 'Well, that's not happening now.'

She lifts out the box of chicken breast and puts her foot on the bin's pedal. She looks straight at me as she lets go of the chicken and it lands in the bin. I twitch when I hear the thud.

'Oh, don't cry,' she says. Her eyes look me up and down with disapproval, an edge to the side of her mouth. 'The only reason you have to cry is your weight. Is that why you're crying?'

I nod my head, snivelling, and dry some snot off with my sleeves. Yes, I'm crying because I am fat and ugly. I'm crying because I weigh too much to deserve food. I'm crying because I didn't have lunch today, and only a banana for breakfast, and I'm already hungry but there won't be anything else. I'm crying because no matter how hard I try, I always, always, always fail. If I could cut the fat off my body I would do it.

'Good,' Mum says. 'Every time you eat, I want you to remember just how bad you feel right now, and then you can decide if it's worth it.'

She gets out the vegetables and throws those in the bin as well. The eggs go. The milk is poured down the sink. I'm crying silently, watching her through blurred eyes.

'All the money I've spent on these groceries,' she mutters, binning the cereal, the apples from the fruit bowl, the cheeses, the granola bars.

The fridge is empty now. The cupboards contain nothing but coffee, sugar, flour, and a single bar of dark chocolate. Mum takes it. I try to divert my eyes and I wonder if she hears the growl in my stomach. I could start drooling at the sight of it. The tears rush faster, I'm so hungry.

She unwraps it and takes a bite. I close my eyes and listen to the crunching as she chews. I'm pathetic.

Mum looks around the kitchen and puts a hand on her hip as she eats. 'I suppose I won't be having any dinner either,' she says. 'God knows I won't be ordering takeout, what with all the saturated fat.'

And even though she was technically the one who threw all our food in the bin, I'm responsible for this. It's my fault she'll go hungry, even though she's as beautifully skinny as someone who's never given birth.

I strain myself and try hard not to let out the stronger sobs, the louder ones, the blubbering of snot and tears and the hyperventilating.

Mum fixes me with her eyes. She smiles lightly and puts a fond hand to my cheek. 'There, don't cry,' she says. 'I know it might be hard to see it right now, but I'm doing all this for you.'

And I wince with the tears I'm trying to hold back, and I say, 'Thank you.'

I stare at the box in the Kallax while I'm drying my tears and catching my breath. My stash. I'm so hungry. I don't deserve to eat.

But fuck it. I don't deserve to lose weight either. After all the times I've failed, shouldn't I realize that? I'm a disgusting pig and I deserve to be fat.

I pull out the box. There are five packs of Oreos in there and a couple of Kinder eggs. My dad used to buy me Kinder eggs after the divorce, every time I went to see him. I never told Mum about it. The divorce, that's when she stopped letting me have stuff like that. So I ate them in secret at Dad's, but then I stopped going there every week, and then I stopped going every month, and now I don't remember the last time I saw him in person.

I rip open the Oreo bag like the animal I am. *Pathetic, pathetic*, I tell myself. If I were any better, I would be able to fucking behave myself. I shove Oreo after Oreo into my mouth. They taste salty from my tears. I don't feel much else when it comes to the flavour. I throw them down my throat so fast I'm almost swallowing them whole. Some get stuck and make me cough, scaring me that I'll choke. What a fitting way to die.

I demolish that bag in five minutes. My mouth is so full of soggy Oreo pieces I can barely chew them; they stick to every part of my mouth and teeth. I catch a glimpse of myself in the mirror and I can't look away. I'm disgusting, and I force myself to face that reality.

My face is red and sweaty, the make-up ruined by my tears. My chin and my tits are covered in black crumbs and the corners of my mouth are white with Oreo filling and saliva. The fat falls in folds over my belly and legs, my shirt too tight to conceal them. What on earth was I thinking putting on this cute shirt today?

I rip open the second bag.

Because it doesn't matter what I do. Because I'm always going to get too hungry and be too fat. Because I'm simultaneously starving and so full I could be sick.

I keep eating and I keep crying. Why am I crying? Why am I upset? She did this for me. She's trying so hard to help me, and I wish she'd just see that I'm not worth the effort. Then I wouldn't have to disappoint her all the time.

My stash is empty now. My bedroom floor is littered with the bags.

I lie down in bed, tired. It feels like the food is filling me up belly to throat, pressing on every organ and muscle. I could put my knees on the bathroom floor and stick a finger down my throat, but I'm so heavy I don't want to move.

I wipe my face. My hands leave crumbs and sticky sugar on my cheeks and around my eyes. I'm too worn out to cry any more, but my throat still wobbles, my chest still burns. I curl up on my side and reach for my phone.

Melissa's profile picture smiles at me from the screen. I hate her. I hate her because she's skinny and I'm not. I hate her because she chose Marnie and Kim over me. And I love her because she'll always be the Melissa I grew up with and the shoulder I cried on so many times.

I need a shoulder right now, and hers isn't here. My finger hovers over Dan's name, and then I pull it back. This isn't something for him to see. This isn't the kind of girlfriend I want to be.

I open Tinder. I haven't spoken to Nicki in a week, I think. Not since I heard about Mr Miller. I wasn't planning to ever do it again. It didn't feel right, with the threat of expulsion hanging over me. Something about the whole thing feels illegal. She'll probably be angry at Kevin, and I can't blame her. But just for a little while, I want someone to give just a tiny, tiny bit of a shit. Is that too much to ask?

20

Nicki

Tom is with friends. They're at the pub, I assume, but I haven't pried, because I don't want to annoy him. I kiss him goodbye at the door and tell him to have fun. I don't ask him where he's going; I don't tell him I'll miss him.

But I think about him every second. I know he's drinking. When he's with them, he always does. And so I sit stiffly on the couch and force myself to drink a cup of tea, try to focus my eyes on the telly even as my mind drifts away. I pace a bit, anxiously moving from the kitchen to the lounge as if I keep forgetting something in the other room. He won't be home for hours yet, but my pulse is quick and loud.

There was a time when I thought he was enough. I'd made it that far with only one person to rely on, so why was this any different? Kate told me to leave him but I couldn't. She told me he wasn't right for me and I knew she was wrong. She didn't care that I'd have to spend the rest of my life alone if I wasn't with him, so I had to make a choice. I chose him and let her drift away. One unanswered call turned into many; 'Let's hang next week' was said over and over, but next week never came. There was a period of time I used to see her around the city and we'd chat like strangers for a minute, but it's been a long time since I saw her in a crowd. I don't even know if she still lives in Brighton.

I can't wait to have him back. The hours are long and lonely without him, my options of entertainment limited, everything unsatisfying in some way. And I'm scared to have him back, because I don't know what his mood will be.

In the end, I can't help myself. I've been good for a while now. I blocked Adam. Until he disappeared, I only went on Tinder to message Kevin. But tonight my fingers itch and twitch and breathing is difficult. Tonight I'm alone with only the telly for company.

I won't have time to meet with someone, I tell myself. It won't go further than messaging. I can allow myself that. I haven't slid all the way back yet. So I open the app, trying to tell myself that it isn't a failure.

I have a new message. It's surprising. With no new matches, there should be no new messages. But I check.

Kevin texted me an hour ago.

I'm so sorry, you must be pissed at me and I can't blame you

I didn't ghost you Nicki, I broke my phone and I've only just got a temporary replacement

I understand if you don't believe me

I'd like to hug the poor thing. Of course I'm not angry at him. He had every right and reason to leave. I'm just stunned that he's back. I was fully prepared for him never to return. This throws a curveball into my plans for the night, but Kevin is an enjoyable pastime. I can't remember the last time I was so happy to talk to someone who wasn't Tom.

I don't bother to wait before I reply; it's already been an hour. Kevin has repented for leaving me, whatever kind of sin that might be.

That's fine, I say. *I've not been heartbroken that you disappeared.*

Why would I be? It's nothing serious. I stare at the screen as I wait. He's not online, so I shouldn't expect the reply to be fast. I can't help that there doesn't seem to be anything more interesting to do right now. The icon beside his profile turns green. I reach for the remote and turn off the telly. I didn't realize I was watching *Criminal Minds*.

HI, Kevin types. Then, *Sorry*.

I smile, surprised at this excitement. But I'm glad. It makes me feel strangely warm.

He might not even be telling the truth about the phone. He might just have been bored of me for a week, and now he's found himself without something better to do. It doesn't matter. I have nothing better to do either. I check the time. Tom won't be home for hours.

I'm really sorry, he writes. *You're allowed to be angry at me, but I'm glad you're not giving me the silent treatment*

No, I say, *who would do something like that?*

Point taken

You can just tell me next time you grow tired of me

How could someone get tired of you?

I'm a tiring person

No you're not, you're invigorating

I put a hand over my mouth.

You'll make me blush

That makes us even

He's flirting again, despite the agreement that we'd just be friends. I lap it up like a hungry cat.

Nicki: *Isn't it really late over there?*

Kevin: *Technically it's now really early*

I'm a night owl, what can I say

Anyway, how have you been?

Nicki: *I've been well, not much new going on*

How about you? Must be difficult having to live without a phone

Kevin: *Like in the middle ages*

Nicki: *Did you catch the plague yet?*

Kevin: *No, just a shit ton of measles*

I laugh. I'm about to type, but I hold back when I see the three dots showing that he's already typing again. They go away, then come back. This happens a couple times. I know what it means. He's trying to write something that's difficult.

My chest feels tight. This is when he'll tell me that he's actually married with two kids and he can't speak to me any more. Or that he's falling in love with me and wants more than we agreed to. The possibilities are endless.

I'm not in a great place, he says.

I'm a little taken aback. We're not close enough for this, I want to say. I don't know how you expect me to help you when I can't even help myself. No one's asked for my support since Kate. That muscle has atrophied long ago.

How come? I type, because it's the polite thing to do.

My mum and I have a bad relationship

She has a way of making me feel terrible about myself

And I know that sounds ridiculous coming from a grown man, but it's the truth, and I feel quite upset

I gulp, my hand going to my throat. I'm thinking about my dad, of course. Sometimes my neck still feels sore from his hand wrapping around it and squeezing.

It doesn't sound ridiculous

It sounds like your mother isn't a great person

And I'm sorry about that. It's rough

That's not what I mean, he says. *She's only trying to be helpful, but she does it in a way that makes me feel useless.*

It's a tale as old as time. Every abused child will say their parent only hurts them out of love. I used to think so too.

You're not useless, I say.

No offence, but how would you know?

By comparing you to me, I think.

I know enough to tell that you've made something of your life, and what else can be expected of you?

More

There's always more

Kevin feels like a brittle baby bird in my hands. I'm not sure I like it. This virtual stranger is asking me for something I can never give him, this man I met on Tinder has given me more of himself than I know what to do with. I could close down the app. I could block him. My hand moves to do it. Running is the easiest option.

But I don't want to. I want to comfort him. I want to be of use.

I bite my lip.

When I was little, I write, *I saw my dad rape my mum on the kitchen table*

He held her arms behind her back and she looked at me the entire time, completely silent, her eyes full of tears

I felt like I had to do something, but I just couldn't

My dad was extremely abusive, to both of us. I can't remember how many times he hit me

The messages are delivered and seen. Radio silence. I feel queasy, my insides moving uncomfortably. I don't tell people this. Kate, and Tom, of course, and Wallace, but everyone else has found out through my files. I don't expect Kevin to know how to cope with this. The only reason I know how to do it is because I still have to live through it.

I'm so sorry, Kevin says. *You didn't deserve that.*

You don't deserve what your mother says to you

Who cares about her? Holy shit, Nicki, that's so awful and I'm sorry

Don't feel sorry for me, I'm fine now

It's a blatant lie, but it's exhilarating. Not a victim, a survivor. When I'm with Kevin, I choose who I am. I guess that's why I told him this. I'm not to be pitied, I'm to be admired.

I have a great job, I say, *and great friends, I'm healthy and happy, I've dealt with it.*

How does one do that? Kevin asks. *Man, you're impressive, I don't see how a human survives something like that.*

You don't. It kills you, just a little bit, and not enough to set you free. I still have nightmares about that moment. When I heard the sounds and walked across the hallway, in slow motion, because I had no idea what to expect. And I looked in through the doorway and was never the same.

But that's me, not the Nicki Kevin knows. That Nicki is the poster child of surviving childhood abuse. She went to therapy for a year and then the nightmares stopped and there were no more flashbacks, and now she loves herself and she loves all the people she's filled her life with.

By sheer force of will, I write.

What happened to your mum? he asks.

I twitch. I take a moment to inhale, deeply, then blow the air out between my lips.

Nicki: *She divorced him, she ended up getting a job, and now she's married again*
We still talk, she lives here in Brighton
Kevin: *And your dad?*
Nicki: *Died last year*
A heart attack in the little one-bed where he lived alone
Kevin: *Would be sad if it was anyone else*
Nicki: *Yeah*
Kevin: *Do you have any siblings?*
Nicki: *No, you?*
Kevin: *Brother*

Not close

Nicki: *What about your dad?*

Kevin: *Technically yes, but in reality not really*

Nicki: *Tell me about it*

Kevin's typing and then he's not.

Okay, but it's long

I've got time

It's like I've pressed a button no one has discovered before me, and Kevin's only been waiting.

He cheated on my mum when I was eight

He made an effort for a while, I'd see him every weekend, but I don't know

I think he just wanted to move on

Now we only talk on my birthday and Christmas

I'm not good at providing comfort. I don't know what to say and I sit there, knowing Kevin's waiting for a reply, knowing he deserves one after what he's revealed to me. The pure effort behind exposing yourself to someone like that.

He texts me again before I know what to type.

I'm sorry, I shouldn't have overshared

I started it, I say. *It's okay, I don't mind.*

I've never told anyone that I heard them the night she found out

I was sitting at the top of the stairs, listening to everything

I feel special. I don't know what I've done to deserve this.

Thank you for sharing that with me

Thank you? It's like a cat dropping a dead mouse at your feet

I start laughing. It's a small thing at first, a chuckle, but difficult to contain. And it bubbles over into something I haven't experienced in a long time: an uncontrollable laugh, loud and complete with stomach ache and gasping for air.

It's freeing. It's comfortable in its painfulness. I'm laughing for the sake of it now.

I manage to type, wheezing and shaking.

Again, I started it

We've both got some fucked-up families, don't we? Solidarity

It takes a couple of minutes until I've collected myself again. The smile remains plastered on my face as the laughter dies down. My abs hurt from the strain. My throat is dry. It feels good.

Thank you, I say again.

What for?

Giving me the best laugh I've had in ages

Any time, you know where to find me

I sit there smiling.

I lied, of course. My mum never got a divorce. If she'd ever mustered up the courage to leave him, she would have found me, and she would have let me know. But she never did; I haven't seen her since I moved out. The same goes for my sisters.

I was the oldest. Nadia was the youngest, Yasmin was a few years older than her. There are days when I feel terrible for leaving them behind. And there are times when I still hate them for the fact that my dad would never touch them. They were loved. I never knew what they did that I couldn't figure out. I guess that's why I was never close to them. They shared a room and I slept on my own. Dad gave them new earrings and gave me bruises the same day. I've never even tried to find them, and I have no idea what happened to them after I moved out. None at all.

Kevin doesn't need to know this.

21

Amber

I check what the time is. My laptop is staring at me from the desk. Yeah, I know I have to. There's only a few weeks left for me to apply for uni, and I haven't even decided on a subject. But I don't get up, because there's a message in the group chat and it's from Melissa, so I have to check first.

Amber, what are we doing for your birthday? she's asking.

Something feels weird in my chest, like I'm about to have a heart attack. That's right, it's almost my birthday. I'm going to be an adult; I've never heard of something more repulsive.

What do you usually do when you turn 18? Marnie responds, flamenco dancer emoji.

I'm going to need to have a party. My mum won't tell me no. If I don't, I'll look like a lonely loser. I'm not. There are plenty of people who will care enough about me to come to my party. Well, they'll care enough about the booze.

Of course we're having a party, I say.

I'll text everyone, Kim says, *is that cool?*

My heart is in my throat.

Yeah, it's a big house

Party time! Melissa texts, followed by some confetti emojis.

Sweet, Marnie says.

They're going to love me for this. I'm giving them a chance to drink and flirt and fuck, unsupervised by their parents. They can't say I'm boring if I do this. I'll look popular, I'll be wearing something cute and everyone will wish me a happy birthday. Everyone's going to come to my house. Why do I feel terrified?

The fact that it's almost my birthday just reminds me again of how close the UCAS deadline is. I get up, I go online and onto the Falmouth Uni website. The search bar is a black hole that scares me. How do you search for something when you don't know what you're looking for? I gulp. I've been through this before. I press the *View All Courses A-Z.*

I think Melissa wanted to be a journalist before I even knew what the word meant. That kind of determination baffles me. I wanted to be a ballerina at that age, and after that I wanted to be a doctor, a model, a photographer, and every other profession that Barbie has had. She's stuck to her thing for over ten years. She's worked part-time since fifteen, saving up for her living expenses, because her mum sat her down and crushed her dreams by describing the cost of university with tears streaming down her face.

That should be me. Melissa knows what she wants and she deserves to get her degree. It wouldn't make a difference to me if I couldn't afford it.

I take a deep breath and shake my head. Focus. I scroll down the list of courses. Architecture? Never. Computer games? It makes me shiver; that's disgusting. Fashion design? My mum would kill me for spending her money on something that'll only get me in debt.

I hear my phone buzz with a notification. It's probably Nicki. I glance over to my bed but I can't see what's on the screen. Never mind. I force myself to focus. Nicki can wait. Kevin isn't desperate.

English?

I pause for a moment, moving my mouse around the word. It doesn't cause a gut reaction. I could buy myself another three years of not having to make up my mind. I think about Mr Miller's classes and consider how I'd feel about spending the next few years of my life reading Shakespeare and learning grammar. It makes me feel cold inside. There's the gut reaction.

I lean back against the chair and throw my head backwards. *It's fine*, I tell myself. *I have time. I have almost two months.* My phone is calling to me like a siren. Maybe it wasn't even Nicki. Maybe it was Melissa, and she wants to hang out. She might be needing me now, needing me for the first time in ages, because Brandon's been an arse again. I really want it to be Melissa.

I look at my laptop again, biting my lip. Fuck it; I've done enough for today. I don't need to be on the website to consider my options. I close the browser and clear my screen of Falmouth Uni, of the future, of all the courses I don't want to take. Instead I jump onto my bed and grab the phone.

It wasn't Melissa. It stings for a little bit, but it's okay.

It's Nicki.

It feels weird talking to you on Tinder .

I check what the time is in Perth right now to make sure Kevin isn't texting her back in the middle of the night. It's late, but not too late.

How come?

Well, we don't talk about what you usually talk about on this app, she writes. *Also, we're not hooking up, which is strange.*

I don't mind it, I say.

I kind of know what's coming, and it makes me nervous.

Don't you have a phone number?

Of course Kevin doesn't have a phone number; he isn't real. *Fuck,* I think to myself. Will I have to get a Giffgaff sim or something? And then I come up with the best excuse.

I don't have a UK phone number if that's what you're asking
So Tinder is the cheapest option in this case

She's gone for a minute. Is it believable, though? No one uses phone numbers these days. Maybe Nicki's generation. Kevin would probably have other forms of social media, though. There's WhatsApp. Maybe she doesn't know what WhatsApp is, but if she asks if Kevin has it, what will I say?

She's back.

Oh, I didn't think about that

What about Messenger? I ask before she has the chance to. *Are you on Facebook?*

That's believable. Old people use Facebook. I can do Facebook. I can find enough pictures of Mr Miller to create a profile.

Yes! Nicki Jamali

It's such a pretty name.

I don't, I type. *But I'll make an account just for you.*

What a gentleman

I get on to Facebook, find Mr Miller's profile. I pull a picture we didn't use on Tinder, an old one of him in a suit with some friends. It looks like it's from his university days. It's strange to see him at that age.

I make a profile for Kevin. I give him the surname Price. Weird that she's never asked for one before, strange to know what hers is. It's like a missing piece that completes her as a person. I give him the birthdate first of March and I use my own email address because no one will ever find out. There are so many aspects of Kevin's life I haven't thought about before, things I didn't consider back when I was making that list about him. It's fun figuring it out. I choose his birthplace as Brighton and his alma mater as University of Bristol. His current home is Perth, of course. Single, obviously. I upload the profile picture. I spend some time googling to find an Australian beach picture to put as his cover.

And it's done. I feel a bit shaky, slightly nauseous, my fingers trembling. Kevin has never felt more real, and I can hear my heart pounding as I type her name into the search bar. She's not difficult to find. Her profile picture is the same as on Tinder.

She's a real person. There's so much context to her now. She doesn't have many friends, only in the low fifties. There's limited information on her profile: no workplace, no relationship status visible. She doesn't post much, but there are some pictures she's been tagged in by someone named Norah. Family pictures, mostly, where she's somewhere in the background, sometimes not even smiling or looking at the camera. They're all white. Nicki doesn't really look like she belongs. But then there's an image of her and someone named Tom, his chin resting on top of her head and her arms wrapped around his chest. Both of them smiling, hers a little awkward, her eyes directed at the camera. I guess it's an ex, then. Someone whose family she belonged to for a little while and then left.

There's not much else to look at. I have no more excuses not to send her a friend request now. She's waiting for it. This was my fucking idea, so why does it suddenly feel terrible? Kevin has become much more complicated to uphold. I'll need to maintain this Facebook account now, I'll need to create a list of friends and a life to display. There's not a lot of other options, unless I want to buy an Australian SIM card. Unless I want to ghost Nicki.

But I don't.

I lie down in bed and put my hands over my face. I'm laughing. I also feel like crying. Everything is so bizarre all of a sudden. A few days ago, Nicki provided me with real comfort.

I told her things I've never told anyone else. She feels like a friend. Hell, she feels more like a friend than Marnie and Kim. It's stupid. Of course she's not a friend. She doesn't know who I am. I just like talking to her.

That's all. It's just a friend request.

I press send.

22

Nicki

I wake up with a scream on my lips. My heart is racing and a cold sweat is dripping down my back, the sheets sticking to my skin. I don't know where I am. The room is unfamiliar to me, I have no memory of when I went to bed and where. I know my dad is angry again. I have memories of him, of his hands, of his loud, loud voice.

A soft breath beside me. I fling my head to the side. There's Tom. His eyes shut, his scent one I know well, asleep. Oh. I've had a nightmare.

My heart is still hammering, adrenaline coursing through my body. I put my hands over my face. It's been a little while since I had one of these, at least a few weeks. They were always going to come back.

I listen to Tom's breathing and check the time on my phone. It's half four in the morning. I should go back to sleep. It feels like I've just chugged two cups of coffee, so that's easier said than done. Everything inside me is awake and itching to run. I try to tell myself there's nothing to run from, but my body's made up its mind. I need to flee. I can't sleep.

I put my feet to the floor very slowly and quietly, transferring the weight from my toes to my soles to my heels. It's pitch black behind the curtains over the window. I get up and sneak out of the room, careful not to touch any of the floorboards that creak.

I go into the kitchen and pour myself a glass of water. It's heaven for my dry and aching throat. It does nothing to make me feel sleepier. There are goosebumps on my bare arms and legs. I wrap myself in a blanket from the couch and sit down in the kitchen.

The laptop is on the table, from when Tom was on it earlier. I open it up. I want to check if he was doing what I think he was. Yeah. Zoopla is still open, a house for well over £200,000, detached with three bedrooms. Clean and pristine and white. We can't afford this kind of house, we both know it. I wonder what kind of family would live like this. You'd have to put a cloth on the table before every mealtime, and small children would get food over those beautiful wooden floors.

Roland seems like the kind of person who would like this house. He wouldn't put any of the children's drawings on the fridge because it would ruin the look of it. There's probably a home office they're not even allowed to enter.

Thinking about him gives me an idea. I'd realize how silly it is if I'd stop to think about it, but I don't. There's nothing stopping me from taking Edith to go visit him. I imagine how happy it would make her, how her smile would be back again. Afterwards, he'll probably go back to not calling her. There won't be a trip to the Lake District. But she'd get to see him, just once. She'd get to see her grandson again.

I go to Google Maps. I try hard and bring up a memory of where Roland lives: Ash. I saw his address in the file. The drive would be almost an hour and a half. Petrol is expensive. I bite my lip and look at the screen. It's not a long trip, though. And the money, what else would I use it for? I think maybe I should do this.

I go to the bank website and log into our savings account. There's plenty in there to go around. It won't make a difference if I put in a hundred pounds less this month; we can't get a house for that.

I log out and I'm back on Google Maps. I check the route and try to make up my mind.

'What are you doing?'

I'm startled, and I slam the laptop shut. I turn my head. Tom is in the doorway in his boxers, arms crossed and his eyes tight little slits, his hair standing on end.

'You scared me,' I say.

'What are you doing?' he asks again.

'I had a bad dream. Couldn't sleep.'

He raises his head, glancing at the laptop. I can still hear it whirring, the soft hum of an older computer. He would be mad if he knew. I can't blame him, I know what this looks like. Why would I be going to Surrey? It would sound like a lie if I tried to explain the real reason.

'What are you doing on the laptop?' It's the kind of voice that demands an answer rather than requests one.

I open my mouth like a fish, trying to think of an excuse. YouTube videos, checking my emails, Zoopla, no – he's crossing the room and he's opening the laptop.

He stares at the map on the screen. His brows furrow, his jaw is set. I feel twitchy, my weight at the front of my feet so I can get up quickly, my heart beating fast and hard.

'What is this?' he asks.

'I was just looking,' I say. 'I'm not going anywhere.'

He looks from the screen to me. His face is a strange blank, neutral; I can't tell if he believes me or not. I can tell he's upset, by every little wrinkle on his forehead and the pursing of his lips.

It takes so, so long until he speaks.

'Okay,' he says. 'Well, you don't have any reasons to go to Ash.'

135

'Yes,' I say; I sound embarrassingly eager, like a child, pleading for his trust. 'I don't.'

The cursor moves across the screen, towards the right corner. I hold my breath. He clicks on History. He sees that I've been on the bank website as well. It's a different bank than my own, so he knows I checked our savings account. And now things look even worse, because why would I be looking for a route to Ash and figuring out how much money I have in savings?

There is no point trying to explain all this when he wouldn't believe it. The words would be wasted. I can feel myself bracing for the anger, turning my face away, looking down, closing my eyes. Breathe. Breathe. It'll be okay before long.

'Let's go back to bed,' he says.

He speaks like there's something in his mouth he's holding back. But this isn't the voice. Surprised, I look up at him. His eyes are serious, but his jaw is unclenched. This isn't anger. I don't know what this is. He closes the browser and turns the laptop off. He puts a hand on my shoulder. I flinch. The grip isn't hard. It's gentle, affectionate.

'Come on.' He smiles softly. 'You've got work tomorrow. Get some more sleep.'

I stare at him, blinking. 'You're right,' I say.

I stand up. He kisses me on the forehead, and we go back to bed. He's asleep again within five minutes, and I lie awake looking at his face. It feels like something has changed. Yesterday, he would have been angry at me for this. Today he kissed me on the forehead. I nuzzle up closer to him. I breathe in his scent.

I allow myself to think that from now on things might be different.

23

Amber

The doorbell rings and I go cold. I know who it is, I shouldn't be scared, and yet I am. My throat feels tight and my hands sweaty. This is a big day. I regret it already.

I go down the stairs and the doorbell rings again. I'm being slow, dragging it out, and it's ridiculous because I'm the one who set this in motion. Mum's out. I asked this morning, while she was having breakfast and I was watching. She's spending the night at Stuart's; that's why I decided today is the day.

I open the door. Dan is wearing joggers and a hoodie with the hood over his head. His skateboard's resting against the doorframe.

'Can I take this inside?' he asks.

'Uh, yeah.' I look around at the white floors. 'Just like, make sure you clean up any dirt.'

He comes inside and I wrap my arms around him. I want to say I love him. Instead I press a kiss to his cheek.

'Let me put this down first,' he says, zig-zagging out of my grip.

'Yeah, of course, sorry.'

He leans the skateboard against Mum's white wallpaper.

'You want to go upstairs?' I ask.

He shrugs.

I go up in front of him. I'm wearing a skirt. It's intentional, of course, but I'm intensely aware of it with every step. It's short and sways, giving him a front-row view of my ass and my panties. I'm wearing good panties, though. Black thongs, not printed childish ones. It digs into my crack but at least it must look good, right? Maybe if I wasn't so full of bumps and cellulite.

I look back, a cool glance across my shoulder. He immediately diverts his eyes from my ass to my face. His face seems redder than usual. It has to be my imagination.

'What do you want to do?' I ask.

We're on the first floor now, and I lean back against the railing. He looks down at my cleavage and then away; I peek at his crotch, checking if there's a bulge. There is, round against his jeans.

'I don't know,' he says. 'What do you want to do?'

I can hear my own heartbeat. I've decided to go through with this, though. It's too late to back down, and I don't even want to, not really. I just want it to be over with. Everything will be so much easier once I've done it. I brace myself and smile.

'You,' I say, and lean forward to kiss him.

My hands still tightly gripping the railing, my nails digging into the wood.

He responds immediately, sucking at my tongue like it's a lollipop. It's too wet. His hands are all fucking over me, clumsily grabbing at every piece of skin he can find.

'Wait.' He pulls back and looks down the hallway. 'Is your mum home?'

'No.' I grab his face. 'She's out.'

I kiss him again, his saliva slobbering on my chin. He presses his groin against mine and I can feel how hard he is. Something about it makes me shake. I hope he doesn't notice.

It doesn't matter. I've decided, today is the day I lose my virginity. I'm turning eighteen in a week and then I'll be more than embarrassing, I'll be sad. I'm not going to let that happen.

So I take his hand and pull him with me towards the bedroom.

'Oh my god,' he whispers. Maybe he's not aware he just said it out loud. It's kind of sweet.

We get inside my room and everything feels so much more real. He's kneading my breasts and panting.

'Are we actually doing this?' he asks, his eyes wide. 'Are we finally doing this?'

I don't trust my voice. I swallow hard and nod. 'Uh-huh.'

He grips my hair and pulls me close, his breath right next to my ear. 'Do you want to know just how badly I want this?'

Something about his voice is different, raw, unsettling. He feels wrong. Before I've had a chance to respond, he's placed my hand on his dick. I feel it through the denim. It's wider than I'd expected it to be, disproportionate to the length.

I'm going to be sick. No, I'm not. I'm just nervous. I'm going through with this.

My head is swimming.

I take my top off. This is the nicest bra I own; a push-up, black with sparkles, uncomfortably tight around my shoulder blades. It makes my tits look rounder and perkier than they are.

Dan reaches around for the clasp. I immediately swat his hand away. I can't take this off. They'll sag and hang, he'll see that one is bigger than the other.

'Wait,' I say. My voice trembles.

I get down on my knees. I'm glad to be on my fuzzy carpet. I look up at Dan. He's breathing hard, biting his lip.

I go for his belt. My fingers are too big, too shaky. I fumble and fail. Something wells up in my throat and I tell myself to shut up shut up shut up. Just do it. Just go through with it and it'll be done and the next time won't be as bad.

He unbuckles the belt himself, hastily, then unbuttoning his jeans and pulling down the zipper. His boxers are green. I don't know how to do this. I've seen it in videos, but I have no idea how to do those things with my mouth.

I look up again, hoping I'm sexy as I delay the inevitable. Dan suddenly doesn't look as excited. He furrows his brow.

'Amber, are you okay?'

I nod.

'You're fucking crying.'

This is news to me. I touch my cheek and find it wet.

'Do you not want to do this?' he asks.

I'm staring at my hand and the damp fingertips. I want to say that yes, I do. But I open my mouth and I can't make a sound. No, I don't want to do this. I want to go be sick.

'Are we doing this or not?'

I shake my head. I wipe the tears from my cheeks and stand up. There's a disappointed, angry scowl on his face.

'I'm sorry,' I whisper.

He doesn't respond. He zips up his jeans and puts the belt back in place.

'I'm not ready,' I say. 'Another day. Really soon.'

'It's fine,' he bites.

I feel like the worst person in the world.

'Do you want to, like . . .' I gesture to the bed. 'Sit down?'

'Sure.' His tone is vicious.

I realize I'm still not wearing a top. I take the jumper off the floor and put it back on. It makes me feel at ease to be covered up again. We sit down and he awkwardly adjusts his dick in his pants.

'I'm sorry,' I say.

He says nothing. I look down at my hands in my lap, still trembling, pick at the uneven edges of my nails.

He's on his phone. Texting someone rapidly, his sound on so I hear every key he presses. I try to sneak a peek of his screen and see the name of who he's messaging. It looks like a group chat. I bet he's telling them about what just happened. My stomach churns. I'm a fucking embarrassment.

'I should probably go home,' he says.

'You don't have to,' I say, but I don't want him to stay. 'I thought we were hanging out.'

'Yeah, I forgot this thing I have to do.'

He stands up. He's still hard. I wonder if it hurts. It's difficult to look away. It's like it's threatening me.

'Oh,' I say. 'That's fine.'

He looks around the room. I wonder if it looks childish to him, the furry rug and the pink walls, the teddies on my bed. I feel stupid.

'You're coming to my birthday party, right?' I ask.

It's so silly, begging your own boyfriend to celebrate your birthday with you. I wish I hadn't said anything.

'Yeah,' he says. 'I guess.'

It's awkwardly quiet again.

'Well, I'm heading out then,' he says.

I swallow hard and nod.

'See you,' he says.

He doesn't look at me before he goes. He's in and out like he was never here, and I listen to him bouncing down the stairs like he can't get away fast enough.

I fall back onto the bed and stare at the ceiling. I try to breathe calmly. This might reach Melissa. It will definitely get to Brandon. I hit myself on my temples with balled fists. I'm a fucking idiot.

Today was going to be the day. I'm not going to lose my virginity before eighteen. This is what it must have been like to be unmarried by twenty-five back in the day. I'm an old spinster. My vagina's full of cobwebs.

My hand fumbles for my phone, but I stop it. I find myself thinking that I wish I could tell Nicki about this. It would feel so comforting to have her tell me that it's okay, even though it's not, and that it'll be fine, even though it won't. But I don't know how to present this problem to her in a way that would fit Kevin. Kevin's not a virgin.

I think about the bulge in Dan's jeans. I imagine what's behind the green boxers. It makes it hard to breathe. I know what a dick looks like, of course. But the idea of having one in front of me is scary. I know what to do with it in theory, but my throat closed up when I was near it in real life.

Okay, calm down, Amber. Stop being such a baby. It's just sex.

I pull my skirt up and slip my hand inside my panties. I close my eyes, averting them away from my body.

I force him to the front of my mind. His hands on my body just now, touching my bare skin. The way his voice sounded. I have to wet my fingers with some saliva.

Unzipping his jeans. Green boxers. The fibres from the rug digging into my knees. Massaging his dick, imagining what sounds he'd make, moaning like he does sometimes when we make out.

I have to wet my fingers again. It's starting to feel good, though. Maybe I'm just fooling myself.

Him touching my ass, me holding his hard dick, reminding myself that it's hard for *me*. The way I look, when am I ever going to find myself in this situation again? Now, this is something I like. I move my hand faster. He's whispering my name. He's looking at me like he's never seen something more beautiful.

This boy wants me. It's in his voice, dripping from every word he says. 'Oh my god, I can't wait to be inside you.'

I imagine asking him, 'What do you want?'

His breath next to my ear, strained and interrupted, and his voice low and hoarse with excitement. 'I want you to fuck me,' he whispers, 'as deep and as hard as you want.'

I'm pulled out of the moment, my eyes flying open. He wouldn't say that. That was Nicki. She used that very same line on me our first conversation. I stare down at my heaving chest and the hand between my legs, confused. This is strange. This is Nicki. A woman, and so old. And yet.

I run my fingers over my most sensitive places and let my eyelids close. It's not hard to get back into it.

Especially because now, it isn't Dan touching me. I'm thinking about her. Her beautiful collarbones, her shiny skin, the tongue swirling around her lips, her eyes, half-covered by dreamy lids. Her hands everywhere, fingers slim instead of bulky, nails even and medium-long.

My breath quickens, my legs tremble. I don't let myself stop to consider what the hell I'm imagining. I keep going and going until I erupt.

My left hand hurts from how tightly I was clenching the sheets. I try to catch my breath. My fingers are wet and weak. I look down at my hitched-up skirt and the pulled down panties. This is when I allow myself to think.

What the fuck just happened?

24

Nicki: *What's your biggest fear?*

Kevin: *Unexpected questions*

Nicki: *Believable*

Kevin: *You caught me off guard, I don't know what to say*
I don't like heights, I guess

Nicki: *No one likes heights, but is that what you have*
nightmares about?

Kevin: *Not really*
If you're the expert on fear, then what's yours?

. . .

Kevin: *Hello?*
You started this, can't escape it

Nicki: *I'm thinking, give me a minute*

Kevin: *See, not that easy, is it?*

Nicki: *Oh shut it*

Kevin: *I got mine*

Nicki: *Spill*

Kevin: *I'm terrified that people don't have the opinion of me that*
I think they do
Like, they'll be so nice to me and I'll think we're friends, but
as soon as I leave the room they'll start talking about how much
they despise me and I'll just never know
I know it's silly

Nicki: *It's not silly*

Kevin: *Thank you for saying that*

Nicki: *I'm scared of people finding out who I really am*

Kevin: *Why?*

Nicki: *Because then they'd leave and I'd be alone*

Kevin: *No, they wouldn't*
You're wonderful

Nicki: *You're only saying that because you don't know the truth*

Kevin: *Which is what? What are you really like?*

Nicki: *I can't tell you that*
You'd despise me

Kevin: *You never know until you try*
What's the worst thing you've ever done?

Nicki: *Why are you asking that?*

Kevin: *Because I don't believe you*
And I want to prove you wrong

Nicki: *I'm not, but I appreciate the effort*

Kevin: *So, what is it?*

Nicki: *I'm never telling you*

Kevin: *I'll find out some day*

Nicki: *You can try*

Kevin: *Don't you doubt me*

Nicki: *You should take it as a compliment*
It means I want you to stick around

25

Nicki

Saturday is my day off, but I'm at Edith's house. I knock on the door because I don't feel entitled to go in by myself; I'm a guest now. Standing at this door without my work uniform feels strange.

I hear the dragging of feet against the floor inside, a fumbling unlatching and unlocking, and then the door opens.

'Hello, Edith,' I say.

She's in a nightie and a dressing gown as if no one's bothered to help her get dressed today. It makes me angry. She blinks in confusion.

'Nicki?'

'That's me!'

'You weren't meant to be in today,' she stutters, taken aback. 'And I wasn't expecting anyone until . . .'

Until six, when she's supposed to have dinner. It's only ten, which means we have plenty of time before someone comes over and realizes she's not home.

'Well, I'm not here for work,' I say. 'I have a surprise for you. Would you like to go see Roland?'

She looks at me with her mouth open; her dentures aren't in, and she looks very small and frail. Tinier than usual, her frame weak and her collarbones pronounced. It surprises me to notice this. Maybe I just haven't paid attention all those days when I'm in and out within an hour or two, scrubbing her kitchen or folding her clothes.

'Roland?' she repeats. 'I don't understand.'

'If he's too busy to come over,' I say, 'then I think we should go visit him. Would you want that?'

Her eyes are wide like she can't trust that this is happening.

'Yes,' she says. 'Yes, I would like that very much.'

I smile and put a hand on her shoulder. 'Great! Then let's go and get you dressed.'

We step on the mail and it rustles. Someone neglected to check it again, but that's not my job today, and Edith has lost her interest in it. Doesn't matter, because we're not waiting for anything any more. We're doing this ourselves.

I ask Edith what she wants to wear and get it out of her closet. When she steps out of the bedroom, she's more dressed up than usual. She's wearing a thick, woollen skirt over a pair of tights, and a sweater I haven't seen on her before. A pearl necklace around her neck and a little purse clutched in her hands. The colours don't quite match, but I'm not cruel enough to tell her that. It makes me feel a little warm on the inside. She still looks slightly dazed, disoriented as if she expects to wake up from a dream soon, but she's smiling. It's worth the money.

I help her put her seatbelt on in the car and back out of the driveway. I don't know when the last time is she's gone any-where in a car.

'How long will it take?' she asks.

'About an hour and a half, if traffic's good.'

The drive is smooth and the landscape outside is lovely. I realize that I haven't left Brighton in a long time. The world is so big and new on the other side of the window. My chest feels light and fluttery with excitement, with the sense that even though I'm sitting still, I'm stretching out my legs. I feel like I could keep driving to the end of the world. I feel like I never have to stop. Edith remains happy, smiling and humming a little to herself.

We're mostly silent. The truth is I don't think we have a lot in common. We don't usually spend a lot of time chit-chatting, not when I'm rushing about her house getting my job done. It's easier with the telly on or housework to ask about. She doesn't seem bothered by the silence, though. I don't think I'm on her mind very much at all. She's set on the future, on where we'll be an hour from now.

'When was the last time you went?' I ask.

'To Roland's?' Edith turns over to me, her eyes fixing in my general vicinity but not finding mine. 'Oh, I've never visited.'

This surprises me, but I suppose it shouldn't.

'I've never been to Surrey either,' I say, trying to push away the tragic realization just made. 'It should be lovely, from what I've heard.'

She doesn't linger too much on the fact that she's never been allowed to see her son's home. The gloom of my past few visits is gone, and she's happy and bright. She doesn't look old any more. She's back to looking like herself.

'So he says,' she says.

'How about Roland's father?' I ask. 'Has he passed away?'

Edith gives a little chuckle. 'Oh, I wouldn't know. He moved to Venezuela ages ago. Roland says he had another child.' She smiles with a lot of teeth, her eyes wrinkled up like she's trying hard not to laugh.

'Oh,' I say.

I don't know how else to respond to this. I don't find it funny, but maybe I should laugh, because it seems she does.

'I haven't had a husband in thirty years,' she says. 'Roland is the only family I have left, but he's more than enough.'

'Never thought of having more children?'

148

'We tried for years.' Her smile softens and her hand moves to her belly. 'Never kept any of them.'

'I'm so sorry,' I say, which seems futile.

She goes silent again. I feel like an idiot for the questions I've asked and the things I've messed up. I remind myself that this is only temporary. Soon she'll be with Roland, and that will be my doing. I'll make right what I did wrong.

She hums on another little song.

When we enter Ash, I pull over to a car park and put his address into the maps app on my phone. Edith knows it by heart, of course. I let the directions from my phone guide me the rest of the way.

I park on the street outside his home and help Edith out of the car. The house is very central, with a small front garden separating the front door from the street. It's an old house, bricked and huge, two floors. It even has a garage. I can't even imagine how much something this size must cost so close to London. I'm happy Edith's vision isn't good enough that she can see how grand this place looks compared to her small home. The curtains downstairs are closed and the doorbell echoes inside when I ring it.

I step back, allowing Edith to be the one at the front door. She moves some strands of hair out of her face, as if she wants to look her best. Her face aimed at the door, smiling already. We wait, but the door doesn't open. I check what the time is; almost noon. It's a weekend, so they wouldn't be working. It isn't early enough that they'll still be in bed, is it? Maybe they've gone out somewhere. God, don't let that be true.

I ring again. Edith's smile is looking a little more pained.

'It's a large house,' I say. 'Maybe they haven't heard it.'

But I can hear the sound bouncing off the walls in there,

going back and forth loud enough to breach the bricked outer wall. I suddenly think I might have made a huge mistake. This seemed such a good idea before I considered all the things that might go wrong. Yes, it's a Saturday, but don't they have a life? Don't they go to get groceries or go on little outings as a family when the son isn't in school? I force my breathing to slow. They might be back soon, if they've only gone out for a quick shop. But people don't go out for a quick shop with the entire family in tow, do they?

'Are they not at home?' Edith asks. Her eyes look slightly panicked.

'I don't know,' I say.

My voice is so weak and shaky, I might start crying. I can't admit to her that I made a massive cock-up of this. She doesn't see me that way. I tried to do a nice thing, and it's all gone to shit.

A door opens in the house next door. It's a woman with a little beanie on her head and a plastic bag over her arm. She peers at us; what a strange pair we must make. The brown woman with teary eyes and the old white lady with a pearl necklace.

'Are you selling something?' she asks.

'We're visiting my son,' Edith says. There's something sharp and proud in her tone, something like showing off the fact that she has a family member, that she has a son, and she's a wanted guest here.

'He's not in,' the neighbour says, her expression softening. 'They've gone to Spain on holiday, left yesterday.'

Edith stares, her shoulders sinking.

'Are you sure?' I ask.

'Yes I am,' the neighbour says, locking her own front door. 'They've asked me to mind the flowers.'

Edith is quiet.

'I suppose we should have called before we popped by,' I say, the lightness in my tone all fake. Let's pretend this is a regular occurrence, her visiting. Let's pretend she lives nearby and we haven't just travelled all the way from Brighton.

Edith looks defeated, and very, very small. Like all the air has suddenly gone out of her, the light disappears from her eyes. Her arms sink, letting her purse hang down by her side.

The neighbour smiles at me. 'Give it another go in two weeks, then.' She heads down the road.

And Edith is silent.

All the way home in the car, we sit in that silence. We sit in at a roadside KFC, where she picks at her food and doesn't take a single bite. It has enveloped us like something alive. She doesn't look out of the window. She doesn't hum any songs. Her face is blank, staring at nothing. She's put the pearl necklace into her purse and her hands now lie idle in her lap, clasping nothing, as if they're tired and worn out.

I wish there was something I could say. There's a lot I should be saying. I should take full responsibility for making this stupid decision without planning ahead, I should say it was all my fault we went all the way over there for nothing. I should remain cheerful and positive and make fun of the whole situation. I should talk about doing this all over again in two weeks, when they'll be back home. It's not like he's dropped off the face of the Earth. We'll try again. And when we're sitting in his lounge sipping tea, we'll tell him all about this trip and we'll laugh at it together.

But I say none of these things, because I don't think there will be a next time. I think if I show up at her doorstep again, she'll say no. She'll say there's no use. There's no energy left in her for another attempt. All the hope I gave her earlier today, it's gone now. The defeated, bleak resignation is back. I don't think I can remove it again.

So we sit in silence.

After I've driven her home, I come home to find that the electricity bill hasn't been paid. IMPORTANT, the envelope says. There are bold red letters inside informing me of how much we owe. The amount makes me woozy. I sit down at the kitchen table.

It's almost two hundred pounds. It must be two months since we last paid it. I can't remember who was supposed to do it. Probably me. Tom wouldn't forget. I want to bang my head against the table because of how stupid I feel.

I check the date on my phone. Oh no. I say 'Fuck' under my breath. Payday's a week away. The bill can't wait that long. I can't risk them cutting off the electricity. If they do, there's no way I can keep Tom from figuring out why.

I take a deep breath and tell myself it's fine. I open the bank app on my phone and hold my breath as I put the passcode in, as I wait for the page to load. The balance appears and I exhale with frustration. There's enough to pay this debt, just barely. But that doesn't leave anything for groceries for dinner, or for petrol for the car tomorrow.

I rub my forehead. I'm sure this wouldn't be a problem if I hadn't spent that money on lunch at KFC or used all that petrol to drive to Surrey and back. A headache is blooming inside my temples, shooting its branches into my skull. My heart is beating faster. I'm on the verge of panicking.

There's nothing to be done, I suppose. I'll need to use money from the savings account and put it back there when I get paid. I'll need to pray Tom won't check it until I do. That money is sacred, he's made that much clear.

I start making the payment. It's such a large number it makes me wince. I hesitate before I finalize it. That money will be gone if I do. There will be a hole in Tom's dream of owning a house, because of me. The rational part of me thinks I should just tell him and ask him to cover this bill if I get the groceries. I can't. I don't want him to know I messed up.

I press the button. The payment is processing.

The payment is rejected. I frown.

INSUFFICIENT BALANCE

That's impossible. Just a few days ago there were thousands in there. My chest is tight. Something is terribly, terribly wrong.

I go to the savings account. The balance is 0.00 pounds. There is nothing left of what we've been saving for six long years.

My first thought is that someone has robbed us. They've hacked our bank account and got our money. I'm about to leave the app and call Tom; I'll be crying by the time he picks up, I can tell by the wobble in my throat. First, I need a moment to come up with a story about why I was checking the savings account. I had no business in there. Should I tell him about the bill now? Won't it pale in comparison?

As I'm thinking, I scroll down, and I see the list of latest transactions. It catches my attention. There must be a trace here of whoever stole our money and how. Suddenly, I no longer feel close to tears. Everything stills. I stare at the screen. I can't be upset because I don't understand.

The last transaction, of every single pound we had, was made into the account of Tom Bayer.

26

Amber

I wake up eighteen years old. I can drink alcohol now. Legally, I mean. I'm allowed to vote. I stare at the ceiling and I don't feel eighteen. I'm supposed to have things figured out by now. Adults know what they're doing. Adults have self-control, adults aren't scared. But nothing changed overnight. I'm still starving, my stomach a black hole. I think about taking my clothes off in front of Dan and I still want to hyperventilate.

Groaning, I sit up on the edge of the bed. I'm so tired, my head heavy. I don't want to get up, I'm exhausted. I check my phone. It's late already; I slept for ten hours and somehow it wasn't enough. I'd like to go back to sleep. I've got a text from my dad.

Hi Amber! Happy birthday! I've transferred £100 to your account as a present

As good as can be expected. I can use it to buy clothes for the party tonight, something I can wear that doesn't make me look like a whale wrapped in fabric. Yes, that's what I'll do with it. I don't reply yet. He won't be waiting for an answer anyway. This is the extent of our communication on birthdays. I want to ask him if he even knows how old I'm turning, but if he gets offended I might not get anything for Christmas.

A message from Melissa as well: *Happy birthday babe! Love you lots!*

Omg thank u, I reply. *My dad transferred me some money, do you want to go to the lanes later? His treat.*

Kim and Marnie didn't text me privately, but I suppose I didn't expect them to. They've both written in the group chat.

Happy birthday Amber! from Kim.

And *Lol you're an adult now* from Marnie. I guess there's an implied congratulation in there.

I send them back an *Aww you guys are so sweet thank you!* and way too many hearts. That's how they'll know that I know, that they're not fooling anyone. No one unironically uses five heart emojis in a single text.

My birthday is almost the only day of the year that I log into my Facebook account. I have so many unseen notifications it won't even give me a number. I take a breath. It's time to find out how many people care about me.

I have five messages on my wall from today. There's one from Stuart, and I'm pretty sure I never accepted his friend request because I never check them, one from Georgia, who I used to be friends with in year three and who still goes to our school, and some from other classmates. Five is a pathetic number.

It's only ten, though, I remind myself. Most people won't be awake yet at ten on a Saturday. Five is a good start. A few months ago, Marnie got seventy-two birthday wishes on Facebook. The thought makes me nauseous. I'll never reach those numbers, but I should get more than twenty. Twenty's plenty. It doesn't mean I'm anything special, but it also means I'm not a complete waste of space. And people are coming to my party tonight, that counts. That matters even more.

Melissa's not online and hasn't read my text. I force myself out of bed.

After I've dressed and brushed my teeth, I head downstairs. Mum's laughter is flowing from the kitchen along with

Stuart's voice. I can't make out the words. I'm glad Stuart is here today. It will take the edge off her. I deserve that much on my birthday.

They start singing Happy Birthday as soon as I step in the kitchen. Mum's wearing a silk robe and her voice is shrill and high. Stuart's got no sense of rhythm. They're sitting at the table and I stand in the doorway, forcing myself to smile, waiting for it to be over.

Then I spot it. Instead of breakfast, there's a cake on the table. It's a Waitrose cake still in the box, but I'm not picky with these things. I stare at it. My stomach lurches like a wild horse. I can't remember the last time I had a birthday cake. Maybe it was when I turned twelve, one of the last birthdays I spent with my dad, and he got me a cake after dinner and made me promise not to tell Mum. As if he had to tell me that.

'Happy birthday, dear Amber, happy birthday to youuuuuu!'

Stuart does a drum solo with his fingers against the table.

'Thank you,' I say.

Mum gets up and hugs me. She smells like she's fresh out of the shower.

'Oh my god, I can't believe you're an adult now!' she shrieks in my ear. 'Goodness, where does the time go?'

I can barely think as I glance over her shoulder at the cake.

'They grow up so fast,' Stuart says. 'Happy birthday, Amber!'

'Thanks,' I mutter.

Mum holds me at arm's length and her eyes are watery. She smiles and dabs at her cheeks.

She gives my shoulder a squeeze and lowers her voice into a whisper. 'You've got a zit on your chin, love.'

I put my finger there and I can feel it, bumpy and sore. She goes back to the table and takes the cake out of the box. Stuart readies himself with the knife. I pull out a chair and sit down. I might start drooling. I have to control myself.

'What kind of cake is this?' I ask.

'Lemon and lime,' says Stuart, straightening his back with pride.

Of course he was the one to bring it. I don't disapprove of him any more.

'It's sadly all the present I had the time to get you,' he continues. 'Your mother failed to mention that it was your birthday until yesterday, and so I had to pop by Waitrose on my way over.'

'That's all right,' I say. 'Thank you.'

It stings to show him gratitude, but my relief is so much greater, the hunger so strong and so painful. I don't think I've had a proper meal in days, just small servings of grapes and nuts and other little things I can get my hands on.

He starts cutting the cake. Mum cocks her head to the side and smiles at me widely, her hands on top of each other on the table. I put my head on her shoulder because I'm so grateful and happy. The knife slices through the cake in one smooth motion, like it's soft as butter. Stuart slides a thin slice onto a plate, and it falls onto its side. Mum must have told him to not give me too much. I don't care; anything is enough.

Mum reaches her hands for the plate. 'Thank you.'

So she steals my slice. I sit up straight. I thought the birthday person always got the first one, but there she shovels it onto her spoon and brings it to her mouth, opening it wide to protect her lipstick. That's my mum for you; even though she's still in a robe, she's already got her make-up on.

Stuart cuts the next slice. I try to calm myself down, but

I feel like a hungry wolf who has to fight for the right to eat. I'm ramrod straight with my hands ready.

And then I realize there's only one other plate on the table.

Stuart must be lactose intolerant. Or maybe he just doesn't like cake.

Mum moans with her mouth full and her eyes closed. She swallows and smiles. Her teeth are full of crumbs and lightly stained with the lipstick. I'm not going to tell her.

Stuart puts a big slice on the other plate. I reach for it, and he picks up a spoon and digs in. I look around the table, searching for my own plate. Stuart nods, chewing with his mouth open.

'This is good,' he says.

'Oh, it's delicious!'

I'm starting to panic. My eyes dart back and forth, my head turning from side to side, but there's no plate for me, and Stuart's put the knife down.

He shakes his head a little. 'Amber, you're really missing out. I'm sorry, I just didn't know you were gluten intolerant.'

Wait, I think.

'Mum,' I say.

'Oh, right!' She chuckles, using her finger to remove a piece of frosting from the corner of her mouth. 'I've made you some fruit salad, Amber. It's in the fridge so I could keep it cold for you.'

'What?'

She looks at me, eyes wide, waiting for me to clarify the question. It hits me.

Oh.

I'm not getting cake. Mum told Stuart I'm gluten intolerant, and she's not going to let me have any.

My mouth opens. I close it. I wonder if they can hear my

stomach yelling, howling, my organs twisting and turning. I've been an idiot again. How could I think I'd be having cake on my birthday? Cake's not for fat people.

'What's the matter?' Mum asks. Her tone is sharp.

'I'll have some later.'

'Not hungry?'

I look at the cake and hold back a sob. 'Not really.'

Her eye twinkles. 'Oh, I know what you want!' She pushes her chair back and gets up, smiling like a mischievous child. 'You want your birthday present!'

I almost say no, and then I keep quiet.

'Come on, then!' She stands up and gestures for me to follow her. 'It's a girly gift,' she tells Stuart.

I push the chair back and stand. I don't really know what to expect, but I can't muster any excitement. All I want is cake, all I want is food. If she's not going to present me with a pizza, I'm not going to feel grateful.

We walk into the hall and she opens up her handbag, taking out a pink envelope.

'Here you go! Happy birthday.'

I take it and pretend to be excited. It's probably a gift card, and any other day, I'd be ecstatic about it. I don't want a gift card. I want cake.

She strokes my cheek. 'I hope you like it,' she says warmly. 'I thought it'd be perfect for you.'

Mum watches me carefully as I open the envelope, excited with her hands covering her mouth. I pull up the card inside. I'm seeing this wrong. There's so much on the page and I'm trying to make out some words that are coherent to me, but all I can see is the word *WeightWatchers* and the world is spinning and the words come at me too quickly from every direction and everything is happening so fast.

'Thank you,' I say.

'What do you think?' Mum asks, her eyelashes fluttering.

'What is it?'

'It's a six-month WeightWatchers membership! There's a coach, and meal plans with recipes, and workouts, and everything else that you need!' She grabs my arms. 'Isn't it perfect? It'll make you a whole new person by the time you start university! You're going to make so many friends and have so many boys flirting with you. Imagine wearing those skin-tight mini dresses to all the university parties!' She smiles. 'I never had that, you know. I was never small enough to be confident and popular, but you deserve to be. You deserve this.'

I nod. 'Thank you.' My mouth is dry, my throat is tight. 'It's perfect.'

I can't go back in the kitchen now, not to Stuart's smiling face. He'll ask what I got, and it's humiliating to admit that I needed this. That I'm so fat that my mum has to pay for me to get skinny. I don't want to see the cake any more. I don't want to pretend to be happy about this.

'I'm going up to get ready,' I say.

Melissa has texted me back.

Sorry hun! I don't have time today but send me pics ok?

Okay, I write, *no worries! What you wearing tonight?*

Idk, something cute

As she would, as she always does.

Of course you are you fucking style icon, ugh I'm so jealous

Omg shut up, you're too sweet, she texts. *Anyway I have to go, see you tonight love have the best birthday! I'm so excited!*

Her status changes to Inactive. I let my phone slide onto

the carpet. I'm sitting on the floor. I put my head against the wall and close my eyes. There's a wobble in my throat and my lips. My cheeks are soaked, the corners of my mouth tasting like salt. I pull my legs closer towards my chest and wrap my arms around them.

27

Nicki

I spend the whole day waiting. I sleep an hour or two at most and wake up exhausted, unable to return to a state of unconsciousness. The room doesn't get quite dark enough in the day, and my mind won't let me rest.

My head is swarming with the implications of what he's done. Half that money's mine, earned through the wiping and dressing and cleaning of old people who don't think I can speak English. Six long years of it, for what? It's all gone now.

I never thought he'd do something like this to me. Tom loves me. Even after this, I know he does. All the nights he's spent with his arms around me as I sob hysterically, as I don't even recognize who he is, as I scream that I want to die. All the times he wrestled knives and pills from my hands, firmly but gently, in the first few years of the relationship.

I'd shout there was no reason for me to be alive. He'd say that of course there was, what did I think he would do without me? He's my reason, he's my reason.

I remember my mum packing me and my sisters into a cab when I was little. Dad was at work. She told us to pack our clothes and she stuffed all her jewellery and our passports into the handbags we were filling. She told us we were going to Pakistan, we were going to where she'd grown up, and we were finally going to meet our grandmother.

I was scared. Her behaviour was so hurried, her movements quick and abrupt and her voice strained. 'Nicki, no, leave those shoes behind. You only need one pair.' She'd never raised her voice at me before. I knew my maternal grandmother only as a voice over the phone that laughed a lot and made jokes I didn't understand. I'd heard stories, of course, about Mum's upbringing, the heat of the sun and the large gatherings of family members, seen pictures of the elaborate clothing and abundance of jewellery, followed her down the grocery aisles as she looked for ingredients close enough to her childhood favourites. Mum loved Pakistan, cried at night for missing it, whispered into her phone to my grandmother when Dad was in the other room, tears on her face. 'Ammi, I want to go home.'

Nadia was crying in the cab, Mum hushing her. She paid the driver with cash, shoving it into his hand and saying, 'Thank you, thank you, thank you.' The train station. We'd never taken a train. He had not been mentioned, but somehow I knew Dad wouldn't be joining us. And my fear was mixed with excitement as it dawned on me that he would never yell at me again, he would never hurt me, he would never hurt Mum.

Dad wouldn't follow us to Pakistan. He'd been born and raised in England, and my whole life he'd been telling us how much better it was here than Pakistan. Mum would beg him to let her go for a week, and he'd refuse.

It took me until adulthood to realize that Dad didn't hate Pakistan, he hated the fact that her family was there. She'd have someone to protect her.

We were sitting on one of the benches as Mum tried to buy us tickets. I was rocking little Nadia, Yasmin was dangling her feet off the edge, and Mum returned with none of the urgency of before. Only sloped shoulders, tired steps, a defeated face; she sat herself down on the pavement.

She didn't tell me this then, but we'd run out of money. The debit card that Dad had given her was in his name, and he kept it at a balance that would never let us get anywhere far. Not enough for the train to the airport. Not enough for the plane to Islamabad. Not enough for a cab ride back home, or even the bus fare.

So Mum called him to come pick us up, knowing full well that she couldn't explain away all our suitcases and our passports and our presence at the train station. Knowing, too, what the consequences of this transgression would be.

And that's what I think about as I wait for Tom. Every time I check the account and see that empty bank balance, I think about my mum at the train station with her three children and our bags, sitting on the ground and dialling my dad's number.

I get notifications from Kevin. *Hi beautiful, it's my birthday today!*

I don't reply, and a few hours later he writes, *Are you ignoring me because you haven't got me a present?*

I disable the Tinder notifications. This doesn't matter right now, I want to tell him. Why should I care about your birthday? Why should I care about you? Look where caring's got me.

And Tom is late back, an hour after I know he's finished, no text to tell me he's delayed. He comes in smelling of sweat and fresh paint. I know he'll want to shower. He's whistling as he kicks off his boots and hangs his coat.

'I need to talk to you,' I say.

He hasn't seen me in the bedroom doorway and he looks up, surprised, then annoyed.

'Yeah, hello to you too, my day was good, thanks.'

'Tom,' I say.

The words stick to my throat, glue my lips shut. I open and try again, struggling, pushing. He doesn't look annoyed any more. He's straightened his back, his face shifting into a confused frown. This is unusual. It's unusual for both of us. Have I ever initiated a confrontation? Have I ever told him I need to talk to him? I don't think so. That's what he does, the difficult stuff. Facing things head-on, communicating.

I close my eyes. I remind myself of Mum at the train station.

'Do you know what happened to our savings?' I ask.

And I'm begging him, I'm pleading with him inwardly to tell me: Wait, something's happened to them? That must be an accident. They must have closed down the account and transferred the amount to me.

He looks back at me. 'What do you mean?'

'It's gone, Tom. There's no money left in the account.'

'Why were you checking the account?'

I cross my arms over my chest and shake my head. 'It doesn't matter why I was checking it, I—'

'Of course it matters.' His voice rises, it drips with anger; it's so familiar. 'You have no reason to go in the savings account.'

The tone sets me on edge, my heart racing, my pits full of sweat. It's reflex. My body knows what happens when he uses this tone. Stop, it tells me. Leave it. It doesn't matter. You'll get yourself hurt. You're playing with fire.

But for once, I don't care. Let it burn me. Rather that than ending up like my mother. I won't let that happen.

'Did you have a reason to take all of it for yourself?' I ask.

It sounds pathetic, even to me, like a child arguing back, my voice too high and not enough anger showing through. But it's been said. It doesn't matter how.

Tom rolls his eyes, hard. 'Yeah, I think I do. I know you'd put it all on some weekend trip if I gave you the chance.'

'So what if I did?' I say. 'I would have every right to! Half of that money is mine. I can do whatever I want with it.'

He steps closer, shaking his head. 'We agreed that money was going to our house. You can't just change your mind about that.'

'Yes I can! I worked for that money. I don't have to spend it on your house.'

'My house?' He snorts. 'That's just like you, isn't it, thinking about yourself and what you want, while I'm thinking about us and working to protect our future. It's not my house, it's ours.'

'That money is ours. You can't decide by yourself what to do with it.'

Any moment now. I expect the pain. Every muscle in my body is tensed and prepared, every inch of me is screaming to get out of his way. He's standing within range, every heave of his chest making me twitch. I stare right back. I don't let him silence me. I need that money back. I can't be my mum.

'I can,' he says. He sounds calmer now, as if he's realized the anger isn't working. His voice is at a normal speaking volume, his tone factual but firm. 'I understand that you're upset, but I can't trust you with access to this money right now.'

'What do you mean?' I interrupt. 'You can't fucking trust me, like I'm a child who'll spend it all on toys?'

'You're not mentally stable. You don't want to admit it, but you know it too. You're irrational. I can't trust you to make good choices about money.'

Is this how he sees me? I'm the crazy girlfriend. I'm losing my mind. I'm tempted to tell him. If only he knew just how insane I really am.

'That's bullshit,' I say. 'At least I'm in therapy.'

'What do you mean?' He cocks his head to the side, rapidly, like an invitation to a fight. 'You're saying I need therapy?'

'We've talked about this so many times! You know you do.'

'Oh, I've got anger issues? Is that what this is about again?' He laughs in my face, and it hurts worse than any blow. 'There's nothing wrong with me, Nicki. I was perfectly fine until you came along, and I've still never raised a hand at anyone except you. What do you think that says about you?'

The air's gone out of me. I can't find any words. He's right, of course. He's not a violent man. The boys at school, Wallace, I bet they've never touched anyone like they touched me. There's only one thing all these events have in common. Me.

'It's not me that's the problem,' Tom says. 'Anyone would lose their shit with you, believe me.'

It's not the first time he's told me this. He knows I'm defective, of course he does, and he loves me in spite of that. But it's the first time I don't hear his voice when he says it. It's the first time I hear Dad instead.

'You've nothing to say now, then?' Tom stares at me expectantly, raising his brows. 'Will you calm down now?'

And I want to say, yes, honey, I'm sorry, you're right. I was wrong to make a fuss. Let's pretend this never happened. But. He might be right, but that doesn't give him the right to take my money. But I have worked and earned it. But I can't end up like my mother did.

'It doesn't mean you can steal from me,' I say. It's a little too quiet, too soft.

'Excuse me?'

'You stole my money.' I speak loudly now. 'I'm not going to accept that, Tom. I need you to give me that money back.'

He snorts air through his nose, shakes his head. 'Stop it. It's not going to happen.'

'Yes it is!'

He makes to move past me into the bedroom; he's bound to want to take his clothes off and head into the shower. I position myself right in his way, my clothes grazing his, my eyes staring right at his neck. He stops.

'Yes it is,' I repeat. 'I won't stop until you do it.'

His hand is clenched into a tight fist. I don't dare look into his eyes. I know the expression in them, I know it all too well, and I don't need to see it.

'Nicki, get out of my way before I get properly mad.'

It's the voice. I feel like I could vomit onto his feet this very second. Everything inside me is telling me to run but I can't, I won't, I won't run to the train station and no further. Mum's hands shaking as she picked her phone up, the passports in our backpacks.

I force myself to look up. My neck straightens slowly, reluctantly. I meet his eyes.

It's the strangest thing. This isn't Tom. There's nothing in this face of the man I love, nothing in his hands of those that have stroked me so gently, nothing in his pursed, drawn lips of the smile that makes my heart jump. I'm puzzled as much as I'm scared. Who are you? Where did you go?

'Don't you hurt me,' I whisper.

'Don't make me.' It's a snarl. It's not a pleading request, it's a command.

'Say you'll give that money back or I'll walk out.'

'Jesus Christ, do you not understand? That's for the house!'

'I don't care what you do with your half, but I want mine back.'

We stare at each other. I don't know if he can tell that I'm trembling. His breathing is strained now, like he's just been out for a run, and I know he's about to blow. I'm due for an explosion.

'Tom—'

He pushes past me so hard I'm thrown to the wall. I slam into it, cheekbone first, losing my breath. I stay pressed against the wall on reflex, like a bunny frozen in fear, closing my eyes. If I don't move, maybe he won't continue. I assume this means no. He stomps past me into the room.

I don't turn around to look at him. I go out the doorway. Everything is happening very, very slowly now. Every step is like one underwater. I'm heavy. I put on my jacket. I reach for the keys on the hanger.

'What are you doing?'

I turn my head. He's back in the doorway, he's taken his shirt off.

'I said I'd be going,' I say. It's not difficult to get the words out. I don't feel much at all. It's a simple statement.

'Where are you going?' He comes towards me.

'I don't know.'

I step into my shoes. I'm looking down at the floor when he grabs my arm.

'Hey, stop that. You're not going anywhere right now.'

I've got one foot in a shoe and the other leg feels shorter now, I'm asymmetrical. Tom is frowning. He doesn't seem angry any more. I can only see confusion. God, how good it feels to be confusing, to be a surprise.

'Yes I am,' I say. 'You can't stop me.'

'Nicki, please.'

His grip isn't tight, it's slowly loosening, his fingers losing their strength. His eyes are big and pleading, his brows downturned.

'Stay and we'll talk about this.'

'We already talked about it.'

'I know, but, honey, please.' He shakes his head desperately, his mouth twisted into an unhappy smile. 'You know I have issues. I lost my temper, that's all.'

'That's not all.'

I turn my cheek to him. I don't know if he left a mark, but it's sore, and it aches.

'Come on now.' He chuckles. 'If I hurt you, I didn't mean to. That was accidental. You were in my way, Nicki.'

I stare at him. That's a lie. That's a bold-faced lie. It feels like for the first time ever, I distrust him. I don't know what's true of what comes out of his mouth. The situation is absurd. Like a wake-up call, the shove into the wall replays in my head.

'You're just like my dad,' I say.

The colour drains from his face. Does he realize it alongside me, or did he already know? He just lied to me. These are all excuses, these are all lies. And if they're not true, there's nothing separating his actions from my dad's.

'You know I'm not like that.' His tone is frantic. 'You can't say that.'

But I could, and I did. I pull my arm from his hand. I shove my other foot into a shoe.

'No, please.' He grabs me again. 'Please, I swear it won't happen again, just stay and we'll talk.'

'Tom, I said no.'

I'm surprised by the harshness of my voice. It's so strong, it's so stern. It works. When I pull my arm back again, he doesn't try to go for it.

'Don't walk out that door.' His voice is a quiver now, like he's close to tears. 'Please, don't leave me right now. I can't live with myself—' He snivels. The crying that never comes. 'I can't live with myself if you think I'm like that.'

I don't mean to say it. I don't know why I do. He's turned into my dad, all of a sudden, and I want to tell him all the things I never had the courage or the opportunity to do.

'Then don't,' I say.

And it's the last thing I say before I go out of the door.

28

Amber

Get yourself together, Amber, the party's in an hour. I stare at the mirror and tell myself this. No matter what I do, I can't make myself look pretty. The foundation doesn't sit right on my skin. The concealer can't conceal my acne. My cheeks remain chubby no matter how much I contour. *Get yourself together, this is your chance.*

This is my big moment. People are going to have fun, people are going to like me, I'm going to look so popular. This is going to be a great party.

Mum and Stuart have left. She went away with cheek kisses and reminders of how many calories there are in alcohol, and he was winking at me behind her back.

Now the party's in an hour, and I have nothing to wear.

I haven't eaten anything today, but all my dresses make me look pregnant, my stomach protruding like a bowling ball. I try putting some high-waisted jean shorts underneath to tighten things up, but I can't button any of them. They've been at the back of the wardrobe for a few summers now.

I try Mum's spandex. I'm smooth and thinner than I've ever been naturally, but I can't breathe. Every organ is in pain. The spandex go back in Mum's closet, and all my pretty dresses go back into mine. I bundle them into a ball that I force into the very back, where I can forget about their existence.

I take a deep breath, reminding myself I have an hour to get dressed. It's not enough time.

I look at the trousers I have. A pair of simple black jeans, as stretchy as they go, that should be fine. At least they're high-waisted.

I fill my bed with all the tops I own. The nice ones, with glitter or straps or nice cleavage, are all short-sleeved. I look at myself in the mirror with my thick, meaty arms hanging by my sides. I look like I think I can pull this off. The only thing worse than being fat is lacking self-awareness.

For a few minutes, I sit down on the floor and struggle to breathe. My chest is empty and my throat tight. I'm shaking. I exhale and exhale and exhale until I finally feel like I can breathe again. This night is too important. Everyone is going to be here. Why can't I just look nice for once?

Goddammit. I pick up a boring cream blouse and put it on. It covers most of my arms, it's baggy enough to hide my stomach. I guess I can't ask for more than that.

But Melissa is beautiful. She's wearing a jean jacket over a tight mini skirt and a transparent top, showing off a strappy bralette. Her top is sparking, purple, beautiful. I'd ask her where she got it if I could wear something like that.

'Happy birthday!' she shrieks.

She wraps her arms around me, squeezing and shaking me, pressing her body against mine. She smells good; the scent is fruity and artificial, like gum or sweets. It's hard to hear what she's saying over the music and the laughter.

'I'm sorry we're late.' She lets go of me, stepping aside to let the others in. 'Kim fucked up her eyeliner.'

Kim gives her the finger without looking up from her phone. Until now, I hadn't really seen that they were there too.

I shrug, like it's nothing. 'Don't worry about it.'

I did worry about it. It was stupid of me to be scared they wouldn't show up, but I was terrified. I should've known Marnie would never pass up a party, and of course Melissa goes where Brandon is.

Melissa puts a strand of hair behind her ear. Her eyeshadow is glittery. When she moves, I can hear the bottles in her bag clinking against each other.

'Is Brandon here yet?'

'Not yet,' I say.

'What kind of crap are you playing?' Marnie asks.

'I don't know this song,' I say defensively. 'I don't know who's connected to the Bluetooth speaker.'

Which is true, because I knew she'd say this, and I didn't want to be the one with the wrong music taste. I left that in the hands of whoever felt like facing her judgement.

She shoves her way inside like a bulldozer. 'That's fine, I'll take care of it from now on. I've got the perfect playlist.'

She disappears into the lounge with a shout for a greeting.

'What's this address again?' Kim asks. 'Charlie's asking.'

'Who's Charlie?' I say.

'I don't think you know him, but he knows Adel.'

'Oh, okay,' I say, even though I don't know Adel. I realize I don't really know who they've invited.

I give her the address. She gives me an unenthusiastic peace sign.

Melissa goes into the kitchen and I follow her. Philippa from English is sitting at the table, talking to someone on the phone. She raises a hand to Melissa. I don't think she's even wished me a happy birthday today. I don't think we've ever exchanged words.

Melissa mixes us some vodka and orange juice at the work-top, whistling as she does.

'You finish your applications yet?' she asks.

Stone in my chest. 'No, not yet.'

'I sent them out yesterday. I'm terrified, man.'

'Them? I thought you were going for Falmouth.'

'Well yeah, but I need some options. I'm relying on a scholarship.' She hands me the drink in a plastic cup. 'Drink up!'

We take big sips at the same time. I close my mouth and scrunch up my nose and Melissa coughs. It's my first drink of the night.

'Damn, that's strong.' She laughs.

'Thanks,' I say. 'I won't be needing a refill at this rate.'

'How's the party been so far?'

I shrug, reaching for words. 'It's been pretty tame.'

I don't want to tell her that Dan gave me a bracelet from Claire's and then started trying to connect his Wii to the telly because he wants to play *Mario Kart*. I don't want to tell her that there's people out there whose names I don't know, that until she arrived I was stuck listening to Georgia going on about her horse even though I don't give a shit about horses and I haven't been friends with Georgia since year three.

'Aw, that's sad.' Melissa furrows her brows. 'You deserve the best birthday party.'

'It's fine,' I say. 'Like, it's just too early for things to be happening.'

'Okay. I'll get everyone drunk if you ask me to.'

The music changes. Arctic Monkeys is playing now and I know it's Marnie's doing.

'Are you angry because I'm late?' Melissa asks, peering at me over the edge of her cup.

'No. It's not your fault. Kim's shit at eyeliner.'

But she didn't have to get ready with the others at Kim's

place, did she? She could have arrived early and done her make-up in my mirror. Kim and Marnie could have come too. They didn't ask me if that was what I wanted. They didn't ask me if I wanted help setting things up. If you got ready here, I want to say, then Kim's eyeliner skills wouldn't matter.

'Well, I'll make it up to you anyway.' Melissa pulls a smaller bag out of the one she carries the alcohol in. It's from New Look. She pushes it into my hands. 'Happy birthday!'

I open the bag and pull up what looks like a piece of fabric. Small enough to be a thong. I turn it as I try to identify what it is. Oh. It's a crop top. It's cute, it's pink, the short sleeves ruffled.

'Oh wow,' I say.

And I think *Goddammit, Melissa, do you think I can fit into this?* It would look pretty on her, it would look gorgeous on her, but it would barely cover my fucking nipples.

She smiles excitedly. 'Do you like it?'

I think I'm angry at her. She's never seen me wear a crop top. She knows I can't put one on; can't she see the folds of fat through my baggy clothes?

'I spent so long in the shop looking for it,' she says.

'I love it,' I say.

'Try it on!'

Philippa is mumbling quietly into her phone on the other side of the room. The music is booming louder. Marnie, again.

'No, I'll try it on later,' I say. 'I don't want to spill anything on it.'

I hope the receipt is still in the bag.

'Come on, it'll wash off!' She tugs at my arm. 'We can go up to your room so you can change!'

'No, I don't want to,' I say. 'I just—'

'Pleeeeease!' She gives me big puppy eyes and a sad pout. 'It'll look beautiful on you. What else were you planning to wear anyway?'

I pull my arm from her grip.

'What do you mean?' I ask.

She looks confused. 'Sorry,' she says. 'I thought you were changing. Like, there's nothing wrong with your outfit. I just thought you'd be changing.'

I'm not stupid, Melissa, I want to scream. I'm not completely oblivious to fashion. If I could wear the kinds of clothes you do, don't you think I would? If I could wear anything except this, don't you think I would?

Her face doesn't change to embarrassment. She doesn't scramble to save the situation. She just gives me a look like, 'Oh, really?' and then she shrugs.

'Well, it doesn't matter,' she says. 'I won't force you. It's your birthday. That shirt is really pretty.'

She's just saying that, it's not true. 'I'll try it on later,' I say. That's also not true.

She slips away, heading towards the living room. I want her to stay, I want to grab her by the arm and tell her I have something to say so that she won't leave. I have nothing to tell her.

When I follow, the doorbell rings. I switch course to the front door and open it. It's Brandon, football hero. He's the tallest guy in our year.

'Hello,' he says. 'Happy birthday.'

'Thank you.'

We're both smiling at each other awkwardly, he clears his throat a little. This is our first conversation ever. I don't like Brandon. Maybe it's the fact that he shares Marnie's genes,

177

and by association I assume he's the male version of a bitch. Maybe it's because—

'Babe!'

Melissa flies past me, jumping into his arms. He almost falls as he catches her, widening his stance to maintain balance, her legs wrapping around him.

'Holy shit!' he pants, laughing. 'Give a guy some warning.'

He stumbles past me towards the living room, following the sounds of the party. She's clinging to him like a koala, looking at me over his shoulder with a huge smile. She mouths something. I don't catch it.

I go after them. As soon as he enters, Marnie flips him off with both hands. The room smells like weed. I can't see anyone smoking. I need to air the house out before Mum comes back tomorrow.

My home is full of people whose faces I recognize but don't know the names of. Some seem not to be from our school at all: unfamiliar, older, legs wide and voices loud like they own the place. Very few people are dancing, most of them are just standing around and laughing too loudly. I search for a friendly face. Kim is dancing with some other girls. Dan is playing the Wii, he's sitting on the couch with James from chemistry, hollering, laughing. I have a few shots. I can feel them going to my head, fogging things up, making the floor slippery.

Someone bumps into me as I head over towards Dan. 'Sorry,' he says. I don't know him. He doesn't look at me twice, like he doesn't realize that I'm the birthday girl and this is my party.

I sit down next to Dan. He doesn't say anything, his eyes are fixed on the screen. I put my hand on his thigh, and I'm not sure why. I guess I want to claim him. Everyone in this room needs to know I'm not by myself. I have a boyfriend. I can't look lonely and sad at my own birthday party as everyone else is talking and having fun.

Dan is cursing, James is hysterical with laughter. Melissa is grinding herself against Brandon with her low-cut top. Philippa comes into the room, her phone off her ear. She spots me and waves enthusiastically, walking over with her high heels like she's on stilts.

'Oh my god,' she says. 'Happy birthday!'

'Thank you!'

'This party is so much fun!'

I nod. Yes, it's fun. People are enjoying themselves. That's all that matters. My birthday party will be remembered as fun.

'It is, isn't it,' I say.

Here's where things start to go wrong:

James from chemistry suggests that we play truth or dare.

I don't want to, but I don't say anything. It's my party, but everyone else is so excited. Marnie's immediately willing to turn the music down. Dan and Brandon move the coffee table out of the way to make room.

'Careful,' I say.

'I'll watch,' Georgia from year three says.

She's sitting in the window, smoking. I don't know if it's weed or a regular cigarette. I can hear that there's a few people outside, and two guys are staying on the couch.

The rest of us are sitting in a circle on the floor, like a dozen people. There's screamo playing at a low volume. I'm drunk by now – that stage of drunk you don't notice until you stand up and everything goes woozy. I've been drinking from Dan's cup, something sweet and strong. I sit next to him and put my arm inside his and my head on his shoulder. Melissa's sitting on Brandon's lap. I'd like to do the same, but not to Brandon, obviously. I'd crush Dan if I tried.

'Who wants to start?' Marnie says. She's sitting cross-legged with surprising flexibility, her knees almost down to the ground.

'Me,' Brandon says. 'Hit me.'

Marnie smirks, raising her brows. 'Truth or dare?'

'Truth.'

A quiet oooooh goes through the circle. Marnie smacks her lips.

'Do you use my fucking shampoo?'

'Oh, come on!' James groans. 'We don't want to hear this!'

'Easy,' Brandon says. 'Yeah, I do. The girls love it.'

Melissa giggles. She's pathetic, playing with her hair like she's eleven. I wish I could tell her she's embarrassing herself, but I won't. There's a sudden blankness in her face, a fakeness to her laugh, because he said 'the girls' like there are lots of them.

Marnie rolls her eyes. 'I knew it, you dick.'

People are having a great time at my party. No one's passed out yet, no one's been sick, there are no stains on the carpet, and every single person is drunk. Kim's top has slipped down below her bra and no one's told her. Georgia laughs at everything anyone says and Marnie is shouting. Melissa's rubbing herself against Brandon like a cat in heat. Dan touches me, discreetly, as the questions and the dares move around the circle, stroking my back and my stomach, down to my thighs. His breath reeks of alcohol when his mouth bursts open with laughter right next to my face.

The game continues. Kim has slept with three people, we learn. The last time James pissed his bed was when he was twelve, which he's not ashamed of now, but will be tomorrow.

Brandon is dared to chug a mix of vodka, whiskey sours, and tequila, and he does it, his face green and his cheeks big. I enjoy watching it. Georgia isn't watching any more; I don't know how voluntary her involvement is. She has to let Matthew, who I think is a theatre kid, send a text from her phone, and he asks her mum to pick up a pregnancy test. We are roaring.

When Georgia spins the bottle, it points to Melissa and Brandon. Melissa volunteers to take this one, because Brandon did the last. Melissa chooses dare.

Georgia chuckles innocently. 'Um,' she says. 'Um, okay, give me a second.'

She laughs, a snort escaping in the middle like she's a pig. *Oh, boy*, I think. I might feel bad for Georgia, struggling to think of something, as tame as she is. I hear she still wears printed panties. Melissa looks at her with her head leaned back and her arms wrapped around Brandon's neck, then grins at him because Georgia can do her worst and it will be no match for her.

'Oi, come on,' James says. 'We haven't got all night.'

'Okay!' Georgia says. 'Okay, just, like, French someone.'

Melissa cocks her brows.

'Well, that's fun.' Marnie slaps her hands onto her knees. 'As if she wouldn't be doing that anyway.'

'Hey, who said it had to be Brandon?' Melissa says.

James from chemistry clears his throat and straightens his shirt collar.

'Who said it could be anyone but me?' Brandon says. 'You think I'll let you make out with some other dude right in front of me?'

'What if it's not a dude?' Melissa licks her bottom lip.

He acts shocked. 'Well, then I'd be all for it.' Giving a cheeky wink.

The boys laugh. Dan is so loud I stick a finger in my ear. *Oh*, I think. Melissa's about to kiss Marnie. It's the obvious choice. It's one of her best friends, it's the only bi girl in here, and it's not like they haven't flirted at parties before.

Marnie looks smug, like she's thinking the same thing.

But then Melissa turns to me. She puts her hand to my cheek and pulls my face closer, and as she's still sitting on Brandon's lap and I'm clinging to my boyfriend, she presses her lips to mine and slips a tongue in.

She's a good kisser. Her mouth matches mine so well, the amount of tongue is perfect. She tastes like sweets and I want to eat her. I think, *So this is why people like kissing.* This feeling, that starts low in my abdomen, and the voice in my brain crying for more, more, more.

She moves away. My mouth stays open, hungry, pleading for her to return. Her face stays close, smirking, a drop of saliva hanging off her bottom lip and I want to lick it off. *Please*, I think, *just one more time.* Just one more.

If she gave me enough time, I might have gone for it again. But she turns back to Brandon and shrieks, flinging herself onto his neck. I stare. I can feel her saliva on my wet lips.

The room is oohing and awing and Melissa is laughing. Dan doesn't say anything, but I feel him stiffening, moving his legs, and I think he has a boner. I don't care. I keep looking at Melissa even as Brandon looks like he's eating her face, holding her hair in his hand with a tight grip.

And I think, *I wish that was me.*

29

Nicki

I'm in my car in a car park near the beach. I think I've been driving for a while, but I have little sense of time. It's dark outside. I wanted to get near the water. I watch it through the windscreen, watch the moonlight on the waves.

It's not until the car is still and the engine is off that I'm fully able to think about what I've done. Oh my god. Did I leave the only man who'll ever love me? *Did* he love me? I snivel. My nose is running, my eyes sting. I take a tissue from the glove box and then a deep, deep breath. It's best not to think about this. I close my eyes and press the back of my head against the headrest.

I want to go home. And a voice in my head asks me, again, *Do you want to be like your mother?* And I think, *Aren't I already?* I have thirty pounds and a car at my disposal. I get out and go to the edge of the car park, walk onto the beach. Pebbles under my feet. The wind hits my face and the waves hit the shore.

It's cold and I wrap my arms around myself. Everything smells of seaweed. My phone still dings with occasional notifications from Kevin. I wish he'd just leave it. I made the mistake, six years ago, of convincing myself I could trust someone, that the emotional toll of loving another human being was worth it. Look where that's got me.

No, best not to think about this. I pull myself away from these thoughts. There are more pressing issues.

I'm getting hungry, and I made no plans for where I would sleep tonight. That's what I need to sort out first. Once, a very long time ago, I showed up in the middle of the night at Kate's place. It was the second time Tom had hurt me. There was a bruise forming on my face and I think she could tell, from my weepy, incoherent babbling and the lack of an overnight bag, what had happened.

She kept asking: *What happened? Did he do something? What happened, Nicki, tell me what happened.* I could never rely on her help again. She'd force me to give him up, she'd make up her mind even if I kept my mouth shut and never told her. I cried on her couch that night with my lips pressed tightly together and her holding my hand, and I knew we'd never be the same again. I knew I'd have to leave.

Kate's couch is no more. I could bundle myself up in the car and hope I don't freeze to death. I could look at Airbnb and see if they've got anything I can afford for a night. But then what will I eat?

Tinder is cheaper than a hotel. I pick my phone up and open the app. It's been a while. It feels quite like walking back into the house you left before you went on a week-long holiday. Everything feels strange and your furniture has a thick layer of dust.

My inbox is full of messages. They're all older than three days. These men won't be interested any more; they've got their fix by now. I run my hands through my hair and start swiping. Right. Right. Right. It doesn't matter what he looks like, I don't deserve to be picky.

There's no one on this app that I'm too good for. I got cocky today. For some reason, I forgot what I'm worth. Silly me, expecting honesty and loyalty. I need someone to put me back in my place. I need someone to spit on my face and choke me with his cock and remind me of my place in the world. Maybe then I'll be able to go back. I won't seethe with rage. I'll know that Tom is the best I'll ever get and I don't deserve more than that. He's right. No one would put up with me as long as he has.

I have a headache. I don't see who I'm swiping on any more; the pictures blur together, the names don't register. Okay, that's enough now. I'll start getting matches and messages in a bit.

The sea is dark and inviting. I go all the way to the shoreline, crouch down and put my fingers in the icy water. This water could stop a heart. You'd freeze to death before you drowned. My stomach roars with hunger.

By the time I walk back to the car, my teeth are chattering. I drive to the nearest Tesco. I go to the café there and eat a bland, dry sandwich, followed by a bag of crisps and a can of Coke. The fluorescent lights in the ceiling are incredibly bright. The voices around me, the scraping of the trolley wheels against the ground, the beeping from the registers, it's all incessantly loud. I'm the only one in the café area. The teenager that served me, blue-haired with a nose ring, is sweeping the floors around me, eyeing me occasionally. Hoping I'll take the hint. I checked the opening times; they're closing in five minutes. When I'm done eating, I get up, and she smiles at me as I leave. The moment is gone so fast, I don't have time to smile back.

My phone vibrates in my pocket. I check it. I have a match. Then the phone starts ringing. Tom's face appears on my screen, a picture I took of him during our first year together. He's wearing a beanie and his nose is red with the cold. He's awkward in pictures, usually, his smile forced or non-existent, his eyes angry. In this one he's laughing with his head to the side, and he looks so beautiful.

I press decline.

I check my Tinder match instead. His name is Richard. He's ten years older than me, his hair starting to grey. He looks like he votes Tory.

He messages me first.

Hi

Hi, I send back.

What are you doing on a night like this?

Just at Tesco, getting some groceries. Got any plans for tonight yourself?

Ah, not yet

Night is still young, though

Instead of going back to the cold car, I decide to walk around Tesco. I stroll up and down the aisles without a basket on my arm or any money in my account. The evening is calm apart from a couple of families with smaller children, who almost run into me as they come rushing round corners.

Whereabouts do you live? I ask Richard.

I'm up by Falmer. Any particular reason you're asking?

I don't have any plans for tonight either

Well, maybe we could do something about that

Nicki come back

It takes me a moment to understand the new notification I've just received. It's Tom. I don't have it in me to swipe it away. I stare at it on the top of my screen until it disappears; disappointed, rejected.

What do you have in mind? I write to Richard.

I look at his picture. He's decent. He's getting wrinkly and he has a lot of birthmarks. There are no full-body pictures, so I assume he doesn't frequent the gym. It doesn't matter. I should be lucky that he wants me, that anyone does. God knows he wouldn't once he got to know me. Only one person has ever done that.

Nicki

I'm in the snacks aisle, browsing the crisps and popcorn flavours.

Well, you could come over and find out

There's a group of teens in front of me loading their trolley with family-sized bags of crisps on top of bottles of vodka and Fanta. They're so loud, their voices shrill, their laughter piercing. I want to slam their trolley straight into them. I turn down into the drinks aisle.

Oh really? When?

I think about what I have in my handbag. No clean underwear or socks for tomorrow. No toothbrush. No condoms, most likely, and not enough money for the morning-after pill. Well, maybe one of the cheap brands.

Tom is calling me again. Ignore.

It'll just have to work out. What does it matter?

'Miss.'

I look around. It feels like I've just been shaken. There's an employee, a young guy, standing next to me, filling up the Pepsi shelf.

'Are you all right?' he asks.

I nod. My mouth is too tight and my jaws too hard.

'You were sort of zig-zagging,' he says.

'I'm fine.'

I sound like a troll under a bridge. I walk away from him, quickly, paying attention to where I step. I'm fine. It's fine. I can walk in a straight line.

Whenever you want, sweetheart

And I feel like I could burst into tears at being called something so affectionate, so loving, so full of care. Like he could brush a strand of hair out of my face and I would fall in love instantaneously. Like he could kiss me with more tenderness than passion and I would melt. It's pathetic, I know. I just need to feel wanted.

But this isn't what he wants me for, I remind myself. I know that. I know what he wants from me. At least it's something I can give him. At least it's something I'm good enough at.

I open the phone to start typing a reply. I think I could be in Falmer in twenty minutes tops.

Then I look up, and I see Kevin.

30

Amber

Melissa kissed me.

It repeats in my head, hitting me over and over again like the first time.

Melissa kissed me.

The music is muffled from the other room. I can hear people screaming and laughing. I'm sitting at the kitchen table, looking down at my hands. Chipped nail polish and a rubber band around my wrist, I'm trembling. I'm drunker than I realized I was. Everything feels so smooth, so blurry.

A bottle slams down on the table. I look up. Melissa's standing there, her head cocked to the side with a quizzical look on her face. Her collarbones shine in the light from the kitchen lamp.

'You okay?' she asks.

'Uh-huh,' I say.

She puts the back of her hand against my forehead. 'You don't have a fever.'

Her hand moves away and my head moves with it. I stop myself.

'I'm fine,' I say.

'Drink some water.' She prances over towards the sink.

She's taken off her shoes and is wearing ankle socks that expose the star tattoo on her ankle. The front door is opening and closing and people are laughing. Melissa produces a glass of water and returns to me. I drink.

'You've had a bit too much,' she says, hand on her hip, leaning against the table.

'It's my birthday,' I say.

'Watch out so you don't spend the rest of it vomiting into a plant pot.'

It's unsaid. It's there. I think I could reach out and touch it. I'd take it in my hand and show it to her. Like a question. Like a request.

'You really don't look good.'

Everyone else is too close. There is no door to the living room and no door to the kitchen. They're so loud and so present. I want her away from here.

'I want to go outside.'

She looks a little worried. 'It's raining?'

I look out of the window. She's right. It's drizzling, pattering against the glass and running down in streams.

'The porch's got a roof,' I say.

We go out of the kitchen door. It's cold outside, and windy. The little yard is dark, the grass overgrown because Mum's never touched a lawnmower. Melissa's covered in goosebumps and has her arms wrapped around herself.

'There better be a good reason I'm out here,' she says.

'I wanted to be outside,' I say.

'Is that your birthday wish?'

She's so close. Her fake lashes flutter against her eyelids. There are still remnants of her lip gloss. It tasted good. It tasted like raspberry. I want to taste it again.

'Amber.' She's moving away. Her face is scrunched up, annoyed. 'What are you doing?'

I step back. I don't know what I'm doing. Was I doing something? I'm not doing anything. I'm dizzy. Oh god. I think I moved in. I think I leaned in towards her face.

'How drunk are you?' she asks.

There's laughter in her voice. I'm being mocked. She thinks I'm ridiculous. She's laughing at me on the inside but she's holding it back because it's my birthday. I've made a fool of myself.

'That's what you did,' I mumble.

She cackles. She holds my shoulder like I can't stand by myself.

'Oh my god,' she says, sounding shocked now. 'That was just for fun.'

I stumble, I feel weak. I should've known. Now I look like an idiot. I should've known she doesn't want to kiss me. Not me, when she's so beautiful, and I'm an ogre. What was I thinking?

I was thinking she must've liked it as much as I did. I was wrong.

'Yeah, I know.' I might be sick. 'I was joking.'

She gives me a strange smile, all uptight and fake, like the smile on a mannequin. 'I know,' she says. 'Like, being straight and all.'

Yes, we are, of course we are. Melissa is straight. I've always known this. I know she's in love with Brandon. But am I straight?

I remember that time I was touching myself and started thinking about Nicki. I usually pretend that never happened. But this feels just like that. Something I didn't expect to enjoy, something that I shouldn't like. Something that's very different from any time I've made out with Dan. But it doesn't matter what I am. Melissa is straight.

Her brows are furrowed with concern, her eyes watching me intently. I refuse eye contact; I don't want to cry in front of her. I hope I'm not tearing up.

'Are you okay?' she asks.

'Yeah.' I make my voice higher, chirpier, put all my effort into sounding okay.

'I got surprised,' she says. 'I'm not upset or anything, I was just—'

'I want to go back inside,' I say.

'Okay.' She tries to lead me and I shrug her off.

'I'm fine.'

'Are you sure?'

I nod. 'I need to go upstairs.'

'Do you want me to come with you?'

I stare at her. She can't be this stupid. That cluelessness is fake, that concerned smile is going to break into laughter as soon as I'm out of earshot. She knows. Why would she kiss me if she didn't know I'd kiss her back?

'No,' I say. 'I might be sick.'

'Ew.' She sticks her tongue out. 'Gross.'

For a split second, I think she's referring to me.

I lie down on my rug. I rub my face against the fibres. And I cry. I let the mascara run and the foundation dissolve. It doesn't matter. There's no point in trying.

I think about Melissa. Her beautiful smile and big teeth. Her head against my shoulder. The way it felt to kiss her. Her lips so soft, her breath tasting of alcohol and fruit, her lip gloss sticking to my face.

It's not like I want a relationship or anything, I just wanted to kiss her. I just wanted to kiss her, I just enjoyed it, that's all. She just makes me feel warm on the inside, that's all. She just tastes so good, that's all. And maybe I want to do more than kiss her.

But she doesn't want me, and she kissed me anyway. She

kissed me, and I don't think I've ever been that embarrassed. I don't think I'll ever look at her and be able to not think about that moment outside. 'Being straight and all,' she said, like she doesn't know. She's good at pretending. When I go downstairs she'll hug me and it'll break my heart, and I know she'll be thinking about it too.

Everything has changed. I get up off the floor. I look around my room. There are so many memories of her in here. Us playing with dolls, her braiding my hair, sleepovers we spent giggling under my duvet, all the times she cried to me that Brandon is refusing to commit. All of that is gone.

It's not going to be okay when we go to Falmouth together. The realization hits me right in the stomach. Ever since Kim and Marnie appeared, I've been waiting for us to go to Falmouth. Leave them behind. Be like we used to. It's not going to happen. It's never going to be like it was.

All because I tried to kiss her. I didn't try to kiss her, did I? But I wanted to. I leaned in. I think I did. And she knows I did.

But it's her fault. My chest is heaving. *She* kissed me. She made me think I could do it.

I keep a Polaroid of us on my desk. It's from when we were ten. She had freckles then, and dark hair. I wasn't fat yet; I had big, pretty eyes and a tan. Back then, I was good enough for her.

I rip up our picture. I tear it to pieces. We'll never be the same. We'll never both be pretty and happy and smiley, arms around each other. *Fuck you*, I think, raining pieces of Polaroid onto the floor. *Do you think any of them love you as much as I do?*

I'm fat, but I wouldn't treat you like Brandon does. I'm not as cool as Kim and Marnie, but I'd never leave you. I wish she'd see that. I just wish she'd see it.

The sobs subside with time. There's cheering downstairs. I should get the music turned down before a neighbour complains. My hands are still trembling. I'm not sad any more. I'm angry.

I take a deep breath and leave my room. I go back downstairs and the music booms inside my head, I hold onto the railing as I walk.

Back in the lounge, it seems like the crowd has grown. There are so many faces I don't recognize and the room is dark and full of bodies. In a corner, Melissa is dancing with Brandon and Dan. I take a drink, spill some on my feet.

I join them, throw my head back and start to dance. Melissa smiles at me, pulls me along into the dance. She's so pretty. She's so unbelievably pretty. But then she grabs Brandon by the waist and kisses him on the neck.

I think, again, that I wish she could know just how little this asshole cares about her. I wish there was a way to show her.

Maybe there is.

Something's taken root inside me, an idea that isn't blooming yet.

Brandon's right next to me, a hint of sweat mixed with his cologne. Melissa is no longer attached to him. We make eye contact and he smiles. The speaker is playing 'I Gotta Feeling' by The Black Eyed Peas.

I don't plan to do it. It happens by itself. *She deserves this*, I think. And then I'm kissing him.

He tastes of booze and weed. He has a bit of stubble that rubs against my chin.

It doesn't last long. He never even kisses me back. He pulls away as fast as I've pulled him in.

'Whoa,' he says. 'Amber—'

I've just made a mistake. I put my fingers to my lips. What I've done doesn't feel real. I thought it might linger on my face. There's nothing.

I've made a mistake.

Dan stares at me, and then I realize that everyone else is doing it too. There's no more shouting. Everyone's silent, and every single head is turned in my direction. I take a step back, turn towards Melissa.

Her expression isn't right. It's not angry, it's nothing.

'Melissa,' I say.

She just stands there. I'm trying to figure out the words to say, and I whisper, 'I'm sorry.' She's close.

'You bitch,' she says, but her tone is not full of rage. Just surprise.

She turns around and walks out, the crowd parting for her. Brandon runs after her.

James from chemistry does a wolf whistle.

31

Nicki

It can't be right. Kevin is in Australia. But he's standing right there in the meat aisle, his side towards me, a long black coat hanging down his legs. I stare at him.

And I almost get killed by a trolley.

'Oh my goodness, I'm so sorry!'

There's a woman in a puffy winter coat staring at me with a horrified expression. Her phone's fallen to the floor. There's a baby in the little seat of the trolley, twisting and turning like it's trying to escape. I've lost my balance and cling to the trolley as I pull my legs back up from underneath it, keep myself from falling.

'That's all right,' I say. 'It barely touched me.'

'Are you sure? Are you sure you're okay?'

I glance over her at the meat aisle; I watch as Kevin moves away from us. I lied. My hip radiates a sharp, shooting pain.

'Yeah,' I say. 'Yeah, I'm fine.'

'Oh, Jesus, I can't believe this.'

The baby starts crying. The mother bends down and takes hold of his face.

'Hey, now, honey, please don't do this right now,' she says.

I crouch to the floor and pick up her phone. The screen is cracked.

'You dropped this.'

'Oh,' she says, and slaps a hand over her mouth as if she was about to swear. Like the baby would have the comprehension skills to understand. 'Thank you. I'm so sorry.'

'No worries.'

She takes the phone and I go round the trolley, quickening my steps. I can't see Kevin any more, he's disappeared around the corner. My shoes slap against the tiles. My hip hurts when I put weight on my left side.

I pass through the meat aisle and look to the side. He's not there. The other side is crowded, another group of loud teens blocking my vision. Girls in fur coats with heels they stumble in. I push past them. He's not here either. I look down the aisle to my right. Empty.

I go back the other way, looking down the aisles as I do. He's nowhere to be seen.

And then I catch myself being ridiculous. I stop in my tracks. I could laugh at myself in the middle of this supermarket. It wasn't him. It can't have been. Kevin lives on the other side of the world. I shake my head. I get rid of the idea that I saw him. It was just someone very similar. But I only know Kevin from pictures, and this man was far away, and I only saw one side of his face.

Either way he's taller than I imagined Kevin to be. He looked more unkempt than the pictures, too. Hair too long, stubble.

I rub my sore hip and pick my phone back up.

You still there? Richard asked a minute ago.

I exhale. *Yeah, sorry*, I type, my finger above the send button.

And then I get another text from Tom.

32

Amber

I wake up. I'm in bed, I'm fully dressed; my face feels hard and dry with cracked and peeling make-up that I never removed. I check my phone because I haven't cleaned up yet. It's early. Mum's return is hours away; she doesn't get up before noon. And I have a text.

I'm sorry, Kevin, but I can't talk to you again. My boyfriend just tried to kill himself.

Boyfriend. Nicki has a boyfriend. I sit up in bed and stare at the screen. I remember last night.

I remember eating what was left of the cake, all of it, in my room, with the music and the laughing booming through the floor.

I remember being sick into Mum's en suite toilet until I could taste nothing but the vomit and the toilet bowl was full of half-digested cake.

I remember seeing Kim's drunken snaps from McDonald's, with Melissa, Dan, Brandon, and Marnie after they'd left. The picture where Melissa's sitting next to Brandon, his arms around her shoulder, with a soft sort of smile on her face and a huge guffaw on his.

I remember the frantic texts to Nicki. My fingers darting across the screen, hyperventilating more as each went unanswered, screaming into the air but never loud enough to break through the shouting downstairs.

And yes, I remember the terrible look on Melissa's face, the complete blankness and the straightness of her mouth, her arms hanging by her sides. I remember how she was there the first time I ever got drunk. She was plastered until I started wandering off to find a place to be sick, and suddenly she was acting completely sober and showing me to the bathroom and holding my hair.

It's like watching a train crash as it unfolds in my head. I look over to my desk. The little pieces of our picture are still on the floor, too small to glue back together. Why the hell would I do that? The picture's gone forever now; it's not a digital camera, it's a fucking Polaroid.

My head hurts. There's an awful taste in my mouth, and I don't know if it's vomit or alcohol or Brandon.

I close my eyes. Breathing is difficult. My chest heaves quickly and I try to slow it, exhaling loudly. I don't want to think about this, I don't want to remember. It can't be real. But images of Melissa are playing on my eyelids. Melissa with her mouth nearing mine, shiny lip gloss, before I'd even registered what had happened. Melissa, arms wrapped around her chest, her breath visible in the air, outside in the yard. Melissa looking at me when I'd just kissed Brandon.

I want to bang my head hard against the wall. This is fine, I tell myself. Everyone saw my humiliation, but only one of them matters. I made a huge mistake but she will forgive me. She's known me for thirteen years, she has to. She has to. I didn't do this out of malice. Did I? Why would I do something like that?

But she hasn't texted me. If things were fine, she would've texted me.

I go to our chat and start typing.

Melissa, I'm so sorry

I'll tell her everything if I have to. It doesn't matter any more. Yes, I did want to kiss you. You didn't want to kiss me back and that's fine. I'll never try again. I don't need that. I just need you. Won't it make sense to her? Won't she understand? How could she not? It's Melissa, after all. This is the kindest person I know. We've been a pair since we were little. If there's anyone who could forgive this, it's her.

She's online. She says nothing. Suddenly, it says Inactive next to her name. She's gone.

Please let me explain

And I write out, *I love you*, but I don't have time to press send. She's back.

Leave me alone, she says.

And that's it. I send the text but it doesn't go through.

I love you – Not delivered

This time, she's actually gone. No pouring our hearts out, no angry rant, no tearful confession. Not even that.

This can't be happening. Melissa is never talking to me again. Last night, it felt like things would never be okay. But last night I was drunk and upset and confused. I could've fucking dealt with it. This? There's no coming back from this. There's no solution to having kissed the boy your best friend loves.

I inhale. I exhale. There's something in my head like a thunderstorm, a throbbing and gnashing and something beating on the walls of my skull. I have no friends. It's a painful realization. Kim and Marnie, if they ever counted, are gone now too. I definitely can't call Dan. Who do I text when everything hurts this much? Who do I go to when I have no idea what to do next?

Nicki. I have Nicki. It's ridiculous and I know it, but by any definition of the word, she's a friend. She has a boyfriend but that's okay. She hasn't left me yet.

I don't really know what I wrote to her last night. I go to our conversation and read through the texts. I don't remember these, but I remember the feeling of them; the desperation, the panic, the urgency.

Nicki, I need to talk to you
Please I'm not okay
I did something bad
Please text me back
Everyone hates me now
I'm drunk and I'm not okay
Nicki
Please
Help me
I need help

And her response, curt, factual, straight to the point. Earth-shattering. *I can't talk to you again.*

It shouldn't be a surprise that she's been lying to me. I should know that you can't believe what you see on Tinder. And yet I never saw this coming. Nicki, looking for nothing serious, because the boyfriend can never know. Because she's already got someone and she doesn't need you.

My head is pounding and my throat is dry. I don't know how I feel. I feel betrayed, like I've just come home to find her in bed with someone else. And I feel elated. Nicki is just like me. As heartless, as cruel, as completely clueless, bumbling through life like a wrecking ball into those close to her. She can't be angry at me now, that I'm not Kevin, not after how she lied to me. And if she knows that I'm not him, she won't have to hide me from the boyfriend. I'm not a secret lover. I'm not a threat. She can talk to me again. I'll be able to tell her what I did last night. And as awful as it was, she's the only one who can understand me.

Nicki, I don't care that you have a boyfriend

But the message isn't delivered.
No.
I type it out again and press send once more.
No.
She's blocked me.

33

Nicki

I met Tom when we were both working at a restaurant. I had highlights in my hair back then; I was new in Brighton, and he was the new employee. I was told to teach him the register. We were looking at each other sort of awkwardly; I wasn't sure where to start, and I laughed, and he made a sweeping motion towards the register.

'Well, it's pretty easy.' I logged myself in and taught him how to choose a dish and how to remove things.

'Now, this is important,' I said. 'If they want to add chips, or cheese, or anything, you don't choose that here. You go a step back, like this, and then it says "extras". That's where you add it, and look, it's added onto the price.'

'You have to pay extra for the cheese?'

'It's very important. Alex gets really angry if you don't add it this way.'

'No, of course. We can't be giving out one-pound cheese slices for free.'

I laughed. He looked a bit proud of himself, and I thought about how good-looking he was.

'This is the button where you open the register.' I pressed it and the cash drawer flew out.

Tom's eyes opened wide. 'Whoa. They should not be leaving me in charge of this much money.'

And I laughed again, well aware he was joking. 'Well, if you steal it I'd have to tell.'

He turned to me. His smile was enchanting. 'Not if we steal it together,' he said.

'Hello again.'

I look up from the hospital floor. It's the doctor who took him away earlier, sealing him into a little plastic-curtain box from which I was banished, who ushered me back to the waiting room and pointed me in the direction of the vending machines.

'Oh, hi.' I rush to my feet, but she holds up a hand.

'Don't worry, you can sit.'

I've risen halfway up, too far to go back. I straighten myself out the rest of the way.

'It's okay,' I say. 'I need to get up anyway.'

I'm suddenly aware that my butt hurts from the hard, plastic chair, my legs throbbing from the lack of activity and the uncomfortable position. The doctor smiles at me.

'God, tell me about it,' she says. 'These chairs are rough.'

I think that I should attempt a laugh, but I can't be bothered to. My chest is so full of worries, my head blurry with anxieties. I could put my hands around her neck any second if she doesn't tell me soon what's happening. All my limbs feel like they're full of something carbonated.

'Well, you won't be here much longer.' Another smile. 'We'll be discharging him in a couple of minutes, just filling out the last of the paperwork.'

'So he's okay?'

It feels too soon to let myself be relieved, to allow myself to release all the tightness in my body. Hopes that are too high fall so much harder.

She nods. 'Tom's all right. He's a little banged up from the fall, but he's not injured. There's no damage to his windpipe or his neck. Just a bit of bruising.'

Something like a snivel escapes me. I almost lost this man. I almost found him dead on our floor. But he's still here, and it's hard to take in, it's difficult to reject the worst-case scenario. The doctor looks at me with such pity, like she might pet me on the shoulder and go, 'There, there'.

'Okay.' I pull myself together, force my voice not to wobble, dry the tears from the corners of my eyes. 'So what happens next?'

'That's entirely up to you. Tom has been given the number of the community mental health team, and he's also free to discuss things with his GP.'

'But.' I frown. 'You can't just let him walk out of here.'

She cocks her head to the side like she's talking to a child. This doesn't match my idea of what should happen. If this were a film, he'd be restrained and put in the psychiatric unit. They'd be telling me they have to keep him for at least forty-eight hours.

'We can't keep him.'

But neither can I. My mouth is open, but I don't know how to express to her that I can't take him home. I can't be put in charge of him, responsible for him. I don't know what to do, I don't know how to help him. He almost died last night, because of me. I can't let that happen again. He feels so fragile. I'll break him.

'But he just tried to kill himself,' I say, incredulous, wondering if maybe she's got things wrong, somehow thinks this was just an accident.

Her smile is unwavering. 'In healthcare, we like to distinguish between suicide attempts and suicidal gestures. Tom's was the latter. I don't believe he's in any danger as long as he gets some help.'

This doesn't make sense. Either you attempt suicide, or

you don't. Why won't they help him? I can't do this by myself. I'm not good for him. I'm the reason he's in here. Whatever she wants to call it, I know what I saw. I know what he told me in that text.

But I also know what these professionals are like. They always know better than you. I'm too tired to fight her. I nod, slowly, feeling disoriented. Something heavy has been put upon my shoulders, and I can't shake it off.

'What's important is that he has people around him he can trust to take care of him and be there when he needs them,' the doctor says, then smiles. 'And he clearly does.'

When I blink, I'm back in Tesco the night before, messaging that man on Tinder.

'Come on.' The doctor nods to the side. 'Let's go and see him.'

We take a cab back home. We're silent. The driver is playing some kind of house music on a very low volume. I'm grateful for his presence. There are so many things to say, and I'm not ready.

Tom's hand rests on the side of his neck, right above the ugly, purple bruise. It looks so out of place. It unsettles me. Tom never gets injured. I'd like to reach a hand out for his, the one that lies on the seat between us, palm up, fingers curled.

We get home, we go up the stairs. We take our shoes off and hang our coats. He hasn't said a word since they released him. He hasn't spoken to me since I found him last night.

'I'm so sorry, Nicki. I'm so sorry.'

I squeeze my eyes shut to get rid of the image. It's around eight in the morning. I don't know how many hours I spent waiting in A&E.

Tom stops, facing the wall, his eyes downturned. He opens

his mouth and my heart jumps in anticipation. Then he closes his mouth again, the words remaining unsaid, the thoughts inside his head still a mystery. I can see his throat move as he swallows.

'Hey,' I say.

There's a twitch at the corner of his lip to acknowledge that he's heard me. What do I say? I can't ask him why he did it. We both know why. I can't tell him what I did last night, and hurt him even further. Do I tell him that I'm staying? It seems like it's understood, like I've silently agreed to it. He couldn't think I'd still be going, after this.

'How do you feel?' I ask, and it feels like the most obvious question in the world.

There's so much he can give me, now. We can end this conversation wrapped in each other's arms on the floor, crying. After each of my attempts, or maybe they were gestures, by the doctor's definition, there's been an outpour of emotion. I've revealed every part of my thought process to him until I feel raw and exhausted. He's known me inside out. That's what he can give me now. He can tell me how my words made him feel. He can tell me how much it hurt to see me go out of the door. Why he took the money. Why he gets so angry. Why he did it.

He gives me none of that.

'I'm tired,' he says, his voice low and croaky, like the doctor was wrong about any damage to his throat. 'I think I'll go to bed.'

I nod. There's nothing else to do. Instead of grabbing him and demanding answers, instead of telling him the truth, I watch him go. The door closed behind him. The shuffling of his feet and the rustling of his clothes.

I'm tired too. The energy is seeping out of me every second, spilling onto the floor and spreading across the room. But I have more obligations before I can sleep.

I go into the living room. For a second, I see him on the floor again. I feel the fear and the panic and the desperation of last night wash over me again. I hold on to the doorframe and take a deep breath. He's okay now. He's okay.

The living room is messier than I remember it. I had more pressing things on my mind last night. There are beer cans on the couch and the coffee table, sticky stains on the wooden floors. In the middle of the room is a heap of rope and pieces of ceiling, glass from the lightbulb, the lampshade lying on its side. Tom's phone is still on the couch, out of battery.

I pick up the blue polypropylene rope. I hold it tight in my fist. I used scissors to cut it open last night; I was sobbing, I'm pretty sure, terrified of scratching his skin. What did I do with the scissors? Oh yes, I put them in the kitchen sink, too worried to leave them in the room with him in case he decided to try again. As if he would try to slit his wrists with our blunt kitchen scissors right in front of me.

I bin the rope. I sweep up the pieces of lightbulb and ceiling, wondering what I'll tell the landlord when I ask to have it repaired. I clear away the beer cans and wipe away the alcohol-smelling stains. The lampshade goes in the back of the storage closet, where we won't have to look at it. I'll get something new from Ikea. I take out the bin bag, though it's only half full, just to get it out of our home. It's gone now, it's over.

When I come back inside, out of breath from the stairs, the place looks fine again. All that's left is the strange spot on the ceiling in the middle of the living room, the spot with missing paint and the electric cord hanging out of a hole. I'll get that sorted too. How could I leave when there's so much left to fix?

I pick up my phone. There's a message that I'm struggling to send. I stare down at the screen in my hands.

There's a part of me no one ever gets to see, because I know exactly how ugly it is. It's unloveable. It's despicable. I hate having to reveal that it exists. And I wonder if maybe I should just block him without sending the text first. No explanation, I'll just go away. His life won't be any emptier than it was a few months ago.

I close my eyes and focus on my breathing. That's what Leela would tell me to do. *Don't make any rash decisions, Nicki. Think and breathe. Consider your options and breathe. Take your time, and breathe.*

I'm sorry, Kevin, but I can't talk to you again. My boyfriend just tried to kill himself.

He deserves that much, not to be left wondering. But the word boyfriend, it makes my stomach turn. I might as well tell him I'm a terrible person and a serial cheater, such an awful partner that I drove the person I love to a suicide attempt.

A suicide attempt, while I was chatting to some random man online. Telling him how badly I'd like to fuck him, letting him talk about me like I was a sex toy. If Tom had waited another hour or two, he might have died while some other man was inside me. While I was drenched in his sweat, naked in his bed. I can't think about that. I'd never be able to live with myself if that had happened. And for what? All that, for what? Some money I have no use for. I don't know what I would have done with those savings. They're not as important as Tom is.

Kevin won't miss me. I'll give him an easy out. I press send, fast, before I can change my mind.

The doctor said Tom needs someone to be there for him. I can never let myself do this again, ever. No more Tinder. No more men. Tom needs me. He loves me. I can't hurt him like this again, I can't risk messing up this badly again. So Kevin needs to go. It's for the best. I block him. I open the Tinder app and block him there too. *This is the last time I'm opening this app*, I promise myself. I have to make things right.

34

Amber

We're not home alone this time. The extractor fan is running loudly in the kitchen, where his mum is cooking their dinner, his little brother Tim is running up and down the hallway bouncing a ball against the floor and walls. Sometimes their mum yells at him to quit it, then doesn't follow up.

Dan is on the bed and I'm on the floor on the other side of the room. Sitting on the bed is too close. He doesn't look at me a lot. He's fiddling with his fingers. The game he was playing before I interrupted him is still on the TV screen. I guess this is a flying visit and we both know it.

He grunts, and I suppose, again, that I don't deserve more than that. I put my knees closer to my face.

'I looked for you at school today,' he mumbles.

'Yeah, I didn't go.'

This guy wanted to break up with me at school. I get why he wouldn't want me to come over, and I appreciate the fact that he hasn't done it over text, but god. The public humiliation would kill me. As if the party wasn't bad enough.

That's why I didn't go to school. I told Mum I felt ill and she didn't question it. I'll have to go back at some point, but right now . . . The idea of seeing Melissa in person. Of the way people will be looking at me, everyone knowing, everyone talking behind my back. Of the few who will smile at me with pity and offer me a seat at their table, not because they want to sit next to me, but because they feel bad for me.

It really does make me feel ill.

'It's the last week anyway,' Dan says.

'I'm sorry.'

He nods, slowly, like an acknowledgement. I just want him to tell me it's okay. I want this apology to be enough.

'I guess that's kind of nice,' he says. 'Like, it doesn't make a difference, though.'

'No.'

So we're breaking up, then. Not surprising. But my heart sort of sinks, not because I'll miss him, but because I don't want to be as utterly alone as he'll leave me. I don't want to be a tragic, single virgin. No boyfriend, no friends, no one.

'Is this a break-up?' I ask.

He looks up. 'What did you expect?'

I avert my eyes. I'm ashamed. It was a ridiculous question.

'You tried to hook up with my best friend,' he continues. 'You can't just say sorry and make me forget about it.'

'I know.'

'Like, I don't know if there's anything worse you could do to someone you're dating.'

He's probably right. I'm the worst person ever.

'Is this why you didn't want to have sex with me?'

I close my eyes. The question makes my head hurt. I don't want to think about that, I don't want to be reminded. The shaking, the crying. No, this isn't why. But I don't know how to tell him what the real reason was.

A nod. That's all I can do.

'So you were into someone else our entire relationship.'

I peek up at him through my hair. He looks thoughtful, like he's trying to figure out how he's meant to feel right now, his brow furrowed, his mouth a little open.

'Yeah,' I say. But I don't think we're talking about the same person.

He shrugs. It hurts. I look at him and I don't think I'll lie awake at night thinking about him, I don't think he'll leave a hole in my life that nothing else can fill. But the nonchalance of that shrug, it hurts. I want him to cry. A single tear would be enough.

'Well, I guess that's all I need to know,' he says. His voice still steady, his eyes still dry.

'Okay.'

I stand up. Should I hug him? Should I try to kiss him? How strange that I had no idea, when he gave me that shitty Claire's bracelet, that it was the last time we'd ever kiss. And this is the last time I'll ever be at this house, in this room. All these lasts, they make me feel nauseous. The last hug from Melissa. The last text from Nicki. The last party I'll probably ever go to. The last year of school.

He doesn't get up from the bed. Looks like there won't be a hug. He looks at me.

'Do you have that bracelet I gave you?'

I blink. That bracelet must have cost him five pounds.

'No,' I say. 'Sorry. I didn't realize you'd want it back.'

Because if I had known, I wouldn't have minded. I'll never wear that bracelet. I don't even know where it is. I stuffed it somewhere in my room and there it will stay. Did he think I'd be wearing it every day like a reminder of him? Did he think that even though he doesn't give a shit about me, I'm so madly in love with him I couldn't possibly part from the only present he's ever given me?

'It's cool,' he says. 'It doesn't matter.'

'No,' I say. 'I guess it doesn't.'

I don't have dinner. I haven't eaten anything today and all I want to do is lie down. But I look at myself in the mirror and

I'm not as bloated as I usually am at this time of day, and it's worth the hunger. It's chilly today, indoors as much as outdoors.

I look for the bracelet from Dan and I can't find it. But in the pile of presents and bags from last night, I find something else. It's a card in the New Look bag from Melissa. It looks like it was meant for a five-year-old, because Barbie is on the front. I struggle to breathe when I see that. My fingers fumble to open the card.

Melissa's written: *Happy birthday to my best friend in the world! I love you Amber*

I know why there's a Barbie on the card. Because on my sixth birthday party, just a few months after I first met her, she gave me a Barbie doll. The first birthday present I got from her. And when I think about it more, I think I remember what that doll's outfit was. She had a pink crop top that looked just like the one in this bag.

Mum's having dinner when I go downstairs to grab a glass of water. It looks like a chicken breast with some vegetables. She didn't cook one for me; she didn't ask if I was hungry. I want to thank her, because I don't think I'd have the strength to say no. I avert my eyes from her plate, I remind myself of what my body looks like.

'Hi, honey.'

'Hi.'

I take a glass from the cupboard and turn on the tap. Mum's watching me from the table, chewing. It feels like she's waiting. She's waiting for me to ask about dinner. She's waiting for me to stare at her food and start drooling like a dog.

I don't. I get my glass of water and I'm ready to leave.

'You okay, Amber?'

I wonder what she'd do if I told her everything. There's this woman I was talking to online, she thinks my name is Kevin and I'm a man, but we became friends and now she's gone. I kissed Melissa's almost-boyfriend at the party and now she hates me and I have no friends any more. My boyfriend just broke up with me.

'Yeah,' I say. 'I'm fine.'

She smiles. She looks so proud of me.

'Good,' she says. 'I love you.'

'I love you too,' I say, and leave.

35

Nicki

Norah shoves Tom into me in the doorway.

'Oh, look at that!' she exclaims gleefully. 'You're right under the mistletoe!'

This is Tom's mother. Her cheeks are rosy. She's wearing one of those ugly Christmas sweaters, except I don't think she knows it's intentionally revolting. There's a huge wreath on her chest.

Tom rolls his eyes and puts his hands on my waist. I look up at him. He's trying hard not to smile. He kisses me, all lip and no tongue, and I can hear the flash on his dad's phone as he takes a picture of us. In my hands, the stockings Tom filled for his family. As he pulls away from me, Norah rushes over to her husband.

'That's beautiful!' she says. 'Post that on Facebook!'

'You're not going to ask us about that first?' Tom says, the sternness feigned, his hand still on my side.

Norah drinks from her glass of eggnog and twinkles her eyes at us. She's tipsy, laughing often and loudly.

'Oh, don't you start,' Phil, his dad, says, holding his phone far out in front of his face, using it with one determinate finger at a time, in the way of older people. 'I won't give you a tag if you don't want to.'

Sally, next to him on the couch, rolls her eyes. 'Grandpa, you tag people, you don't give them a tag.'

She would know; her phone is in her face every moment, including this one. I think she's fifteen now, which is strange.

Seeing her once every year gives me the impression that I'm always meeting someone new; an older, snarkier niece who has replaced the one from last Christmas. When Phil playfully nudges her arm and calls her a little know-it-all, she flinches to the side like an unfriendly cat.

'Dad,' Tom says with exasperation.

He laughs, looking at me, and then lets go, heading over towards his parents. He seems light and carefree. It soothes me to see him so smiley.

We haven't talked about the attempt since it happened. I haven't asked about his reasons, and he hasn't offered any. He hasn't said a word about the spot in the ceiling, leaving it to me to try the landlord every few days in case he eventually picks up. The bruises have faded, as if nothing ever happened. I'm still overcome with worry every time he seems more down or quieter than usual. It takes me a few extra minutes to go out of the door when he's home, convincing myself that he'll still be there when I come back.

I haven't asked for the money back. He was right that I don't need it. His cause is a greater one. That money's gone and I don't mind. *I'm not my mum*, I tell myself. *This isn't the same*.

We tiptoe around the subject of therapy like it would send him over the edge if I suggested it. I know it might upset him. I know it might anger him.

I cross the room, taking the stockings to the fireplace. I hang them next to the ones Norah and Phil have purchased. They look fancier than ours, more expensive, the material thicker and softer. There's one with my name on it. It always makes me feel tremendously strange to be part of such a family. And then I remind myself that really, I'm not, and it's out of politeness. It's a game we're all playing. We pretend I belong here when I don't. They're good people, Tom's parents, and so they'd never let me know that I'm an intruder.

I never celebrated Christmas until I met Tom, but I remember Eid when I was growing up. It never felt cheerful. Dad would act happy, and Yasmin and Nadia would receive money and gifts, but Mum and I would be on edge. If anything was wrong with the feast, it was Mum's fault. I don't think there was ever a holiday that he didn't start yelling at her after the guests had left or we were returning home.

Jessie comes bumbling out of the kitchen. Niece number two. Norah calls her name and opens her arms wide, smiling big. Jessie's almost two now, I think. She doesn't have a lot of hair, but what she does have has been gathered into a little red bow at the top of her head. Tom's brother follows her out, picks her up off the floor.

'Where you going?' he asks. 'You've got a dirty little nappy that needs changing.'

I can smell it from where I'm standing. He looks up and our eyes meet. I smile. Johnny smiles back, exasperated, his daughter squirming to get out of his grip.

'I'll take her.' His girlfriend, Laura, dries her hands off on her apron and takes the toddler from his arms. 'I've just finished with the dishes.'

She's too young for him. I think she'd barely graduated university when he knocked her up. It wouldn't be like her to complain, though. Laura's always smiling, always chatty, always laughing.

'Here we go,' she says. 'Let's get you cleaned up.'

'Sally, get off the phone,' Johnny says. 'It's Christmas.'

She makes a typical teenage 'ugh' sound, a sound I never would have made to my own dad.

'Oh, leave the girl alone,' Norah says. 'She can't be having much fun with all these old people around.'

'Hey, who says I'm old?' Tom says.

'You're not young,' I tell him.

He puts his hand to his chest in a dramatic display of offence, as if I've greatly wounded him. I stick my tongue out at him. I smile. *Christmas*, I tell myself. *I'm having a lovely time, I have a family, they're all kind to me. Remember to enjoy yourself.* I feel like I should leave the room, the house, stop forcing myself on these people. I wonder how Kevin is spending the day. He might be on the beach, tanning, while it's rainy and cold here. No, I shouldn't be thinking about him. I make myself stop.

'Could someone check on the oven?' Laura calls from upstairs.

'I'll do it!' I say. I assume she's put the Yorkshire puddings in, then. That means it's almost time to eat; the turkey will soon be ready. I rush in there to save the day.

The worktops in the kitchen are overflowing with containers of Brussels sprouts and gravy. Cleaned dishes are drying by the sink. All four advent candles are burning in the window. The turkey is still in the oven and the Yorkshire puddings are beneath it, turning golden and beautiful, but still a little too pale to take out.

'How are they doing?' Johnny asks from the doorway.

'Not quite ready,' I say.

'I'll mash the potatoes,' he says.

I still find it funny. My dad would never volunteer for something like that. My dad wouldn't do a thing around the house that he trusted my mum to do correctly, because why would he? All he needed to do by himself was stuff the washing machine, because she'd once managed to turn one of his shirts grey and he refused to give her another chance.

'Earth to Nicki,' Tom says.

His arms creep into mine from behind, wrapping around my waist. I jump at the suddenness of it. He laughs and plants a kiss on my cheek.

'Is the food nearly ready?' Phil calls. 'We'll miss the King's speech if we don't eat soon.'

'Before you start complaining, do you want to come in here and take care of the food yourself?' Johnny shouts back, his sleeves pulled up and his hands working hard on the mashing.

What a way to talk to your father. If I did such a thing, I would be on the floor by now with my cheek on the tiles. Suddenly, I don't know why I'm here. These people all love each other. They belong together, by blood or, in Laura's case, by choice. She fits right in, though. She knows the in-jokes, she makes the Yorkshire puddings. She has hobbies in common with Norah that they talk about, people they can gossip about. Unlike me.

'Give me a second,' I say.

I get out of Tom's grip and smile to assure him that everything's fine. It is, isn't it? There's nothing wrong in this house. They never raise their voices at each other, even less their hands. Phil is going through the channels on the telly. Sally's still on her phone. Norah is moving the stockings around. I must have put them up wrong. She smiles at me, not mentioning my mistake, acting as if nothing's the matter, unapologetic about correcting me. I'd like to tell her I'm sorry. If I could leave, I would.

I go up the stairs. Laura is still in one of the bedrooms, cooing at baby Jessie lying on the bed. I feel faint. I go into the bathroom and close the door. I wonder what these lovely, normal people would think about me if they knew what I truly am. All the men I've been with since I met their son. The things I do to him, the things I make him do to me. The person I turn their sweet, loving Tom into. Because this is who he truly is: hugging his brother, laughing with his parents, speaking gibberish to Jessie.

Part of me hates them. It's not their fault, but I'm jealous. I'm angry that this is their everyday, and I never had this. It isn't fair that these things all belong to them for no reason other than luck. I don't remember the first time my dad hit me. What could I have done by that age to deserve that?

My hands are trembling. I touch my face and realize I'm crying. I'll need to stay in here for a while. I'll let them enjoy themselves before I force myself on them again. It's for the best.

I can't ruin Tom's Christmas. He'd be so sad if I told him how I felt. Everyone would be so upset, so offended, if I left. I wish I could tell someone. I wish I could tell Kevin. No. I shake the thought out of my head and I deal with it alone.

In the car on the way back, Tom says, 'Nicki, we should talk.'

I turn my head, resting against the cold window glass. He broke a silence that was easy and comfortable. He planted a seed of worry in my heart, because what could it be except bad news?

'Things have been strained lately,' he says, his eyes on the road, not because he's a careful, attentive driver, but because he's nervous, and it's easier not to look at me as he says this. 'I haven't been as good to you as I should have.'

Oh. It's an apology. I used to crave them, long for them, cling to them with bleeding hands and white knuckles.

Suddenly, I feel tired. It's like a song I used to love but I have listened to too many times. It's got old.

But the apology doesn't come.

'I want that to change,' he says. 'All this fighting, the arguments we get into, I want it to stop. I don't ever want to raise my voice at you again.'

And I think, *I'd like that too.* But I don't feel the hope in my heart that I've come to expect at times like these. I feel empty. Yes, I know this is what he wants. It sounds nice. But it's also a fantasy, just like the dream of owning a home. We pretend. It isn't real.

'Okay,' I say.

His mouth twitches into a brief smile, his eyes pass over to me before he looks back at the road. 'From now on, things will be different.'

I've heard it so many times by now, I can't stir up an emotion. It won't be different. He hasn't touched me since the night of his attempt, but we've done this dance before. Months without a fight, and then a spark catches hold of the fuse and everything explodes. I haven't been on Tinder since that night either, but I've abstained in the past too. I'll always relapse in the end. It's foolish to hope otherwise.

But I'll let him be a fool.

I smile. 'Okay.'

He takes one hand off the wheel and grabs mine with it. I squeeze right back. He brings my hand to his lips and plants a kiss on it, smiling all the while, letting his lips linger on my skin. I love him so much in this moment, I could almost let myself believe he won't hurt me again.

36

Amber

I don't feel well. Christmas morning I sit on the floor of the shower because I'm too exhausted to stand up, my legs shaking and my head swimming. I press my forehead against the wall and let the water run over me; it's hot, because every part of me that isn't being drenched in warm water is freezing cold. I don't know why I'm tired. Since I stopped going to school, I've napped almost every day. I don't get up until noon. Mum thinks I've got the flu. She says at least I'll lose weight this way, being sick and not having an appetite. Well, she's wrong about that, because I haven't been sick since my birthday party. And I do have an appetite. I am starving, but she's not cooking. The fridge is so bare. I can't remember the last time I had a full meal.

I daydream about Christmas turkey on the shower floor, and then I get up and get dressed. I put on extra layers and the thickest jumper I have. It makes me look ridiculously round.

'Oh, look!' Stuart says when I enter the lounge. 'It's an escaped snowman!'

I guess they're serious, spending Christmas together. They're drinking mulled wine. I'm not offered any, and I shouldn't mind, because of how utterly disgusting it is, but I'm so hungry.

The Christmas tree is as beautiful as ever. Mum doesn't let me touch it. She spends hours hanging the golden baubles and draping it in tinsel, until it shines as much as the jewellery she's wearing. She looks so glamorous today, with a wide-skirted dress and big diamonds in her ears.

'Were those earrings a Christmas present?' I ask.

She looks at Stuart, beaming with pride and squirming with joy. 'Yes, they were!'

She kisses him, leaving his lips red from her lipstick.

'Amber, would you like any Christmas food brought back?' Stuart asks.

They're going to a restaurant tonight. Stuart's parents are dead, I think, and well, Mum won't let my existence stop her from celebrating in her own way. I have no memories of my mum stuffing a turkey and making gravy on Christmas. They're going to have cocktails and unlimited access to a buffet. The thought makes my mouth water. I'm suddenly furious with her, leaving me at home with an empty kitchen while she gorges on holiday food. I bite my tongue so I don't say something bad.

'Oh, she's got the flu, remember?' Mum smiles at me. 'I don't think she'll be hungry yet.'

'Well, no harm in bringing something just in case, don't you think?'

She has her hand on his chest, tapping her nails against his shirt. She's probably thinking of another excuse. *Just tell him I'm too fat*, I want to say. It's not like he can't see it.

'I'm fine,' I say.

'Would you like to open some presents?' Mum asks, her face perking up.

'Let's!' Stuart says.

We converge around the tree like a cult of Santaworshippers. Mum's excited like a child. There are fewer presents these days than back when I was little, when the pile wouldn't fit under the tree. This year Mum and I've got two, and Stuart has one, because I didn't get him anything.

Mum starts, sitting on her knees, ripping the paper off the

224

gift that's from me. It makes me nervous to watch her tear it up with her long nails, clamouring to get inside. It feels like nothing can satisfy such excitement. And I'm right.

She holds the box in both hands, the paper dropping to the floor, turning it around and around. I should have known it would be a disappointment. It was difficult to find her something. She can be so picky. I settled on a collection of travel-sized perfume bottles, hoping at least one would be to her liking.

'Amber, is this from you?' she asks.

I nod.

She smiles. It looks so forced. 'Goodness, they're really small, aren't they?' She laughs. 'How adorable.'

'I guess,' I say.

If I hadn't tried, it wouldn't have mattered this much. But I actually did try, and I thought I might have got it right, and I failed anyway.

She puts it on the floor and shimmies over to me, wrapping me inside her arms. 'Thank you, honey.'

I don't say anything, because I don't know what to say.

I wanted to buy a Christmas present for Nicki. While I was browsing all those shops looking for something for Mum, I wondered what jewellery she would like, what kind of clothes she would wear. I wondered if she reads books and if she'd like one. I wish I could ask her. I might have got her address and sent her something, made it look like it was from Australia. Maybe a stuffed koala she could keep in her bed, and I could pretend I was the one in her arms.

We open the rest of the presents. Mum got Stuart a pair of slippers, and he bought her a back massager. She squeals, putting it around her neck, jumps as it turns on and laughs at the vibrations.

My presents are both full of clothing: a red dress, a pair of ripped jeans, a nice tank top with a low cleavage. They're all a size eight. I don't need to try anything on to know they won't go over my hips. We all know I'm not a size eight.

'Aren't they pretty?' Mum says, the massager still on. I know what she's leaving unsaid: this is motivation, this is something to look forward to.

I'll shove them deep into my closet, where they don't need to remind me of how big I am. I don't feel motivated. I feel disappointed in myself. The worst part is, I would wear these jeans if they were my size. They're pretty. But I couldn't button this pair, and my fat would fall out of the rips like I was trying to burst out of my clothes.

Stuart is smiling like an idiot. I wonder if he paid for these.

'Thank you,' I say.

After they've left for the night, I still haven't eaten. My stomach hurts, and I'm proud of myself for ignoring it. I lie on my side on the couch. *Home Alone* is playing on the telly but I haven't watched in a while.

I scroll through Instagram to see how everyone else is celebrating. Georgia has posted pictures of herself out riding with a Santa hat over her helmet. Marnie has a video of herself singing 'All I Want for Christmas'. Kim has pictures on her story of her family and overflowing tree.

I check their accounts every day. It's pathetic, I know. They've unfollowed me, and I suppose I should unfollow them too, but I doubt they notice that I haven't. Kim has started featuring a guy in her stories, someone I don't recognize. Marnie still posts daily outfits and videos of herself singing. Sometimes they're all hanging out, and I catch the only glimpses of Melissa I can get these days. I don't know why I keep looking for her. It sends my heart up into my throat and I feel like crying every time I see her.

She blocked me on everything. There was a weak moment when I considered opening a new account just to see what she's up to, but there's a limit to how ridiculous I can allow myself to be. I just miss her.

So I look at her face in the background of Kim's stories, laughing or dancing. And sometimes I do cry. Ugly, loud tears that feel like they're going to rip my chest out. I scream. I bang my head against the wall because this is all my fault, and I'll never talk to Melissa again.

When I feel like that, I'll reach for my phone. I'll reach for Nicki. It's reflex and it's wishful thinking. There's no one on the other end. I would just like to wish her a merry Christmas, or I tell myself that's all I want. I'd like to know she's enjoying the holidays.

Dad is calling me. I mute the telly and sigh.

'Hi,' I say.

'Hello!' He speaks too loudly on the phone. There are voices and laughter in the background and I wonder where he is. 'Merry Christmas, my love!'

'Thanks.'

'How's the day going?'

I'm hungry, alone on the couch in front of a stupid kids' movie. I'm angry at him for even asking.

'It's fine,' I say.

'Did you get any nice presents?'

I can barely hear what he's saying over the chatter. He's next to a woman who has an annoying and loud laugh.

'Yeah,' I say.

It's always awkward speaking to him. I never really know what to say, because I know he's not really interested. If he

227

was, he'd actually come by some day. He says he will, but he doesn't. I can't remember the last time I saw him in person, or the last time I heard his voice outside of my birthday and Christmas. I can't blame him. I'm not interested in him either.

'I'll be sending over some money later. It's so hard to know what to buy teenage girls.' He laughs awkwardly.

'Where are you?' I ask.

'I'm at a Christmas party with some friends. Is it too loud? Hold up, I'll go outside.'

I wait. I can hear his breathing, the voices around him changing, a sliding door opening and closing. Everything goes silent apart from his breath.

'Is that better?' he asks.

'It's okay.'

'Jesus, it's freezing.'

Another awkward silence. It feels like when you have to sit next to a stranger on the bus and you should say something but you have no idea what.

He clears his throat. 'How's your mother?'

She's probably having a great time. She might be drunk by now, her arms wrapped around Stuart, laughing and dancing and eating.

'She's good,' I say. It might not be what he wants to hear, but who cares?

'Great,' he says. 'Did you apply to university yet?'

Wow, he knows what year I'm in. Has he been keeping track, or did he calculate it based on the year I was born? Does he remember what year I was born? The surprise gives way to the same old dread. It's less than two weeks until applications close. My stomach feels weird.

'No,' I say. 'I'm still, like, deciding.'

'Ah, well, that's good. You should take your time with decisions like these.'

I look at how long the conversation's gone on; it's been three minutes. They have felt like forever. We're both quiet now. Dad coughs.

'Look, honey, it's getting real cold out here,' he says.

'Uh-huh.'

'I should get back inside before I catch pneumonia, but it was nice talking to you.'

I want to pat him on the head and tell him that he doesn't have to lie to me. He doesn't have to make these calls at all. He's wasted three minutes of both of our lives, and I'm obviously very busy over here.

'Yeah,' I say. 'Merry Christmas.'

'Merry Christmas, Amber.'

Mum and Stuart get home late. I'm already prepared to go to sleep; it's only midnight, but I'm so tired. I'm still on the couch, from which I haven't moved a lot. *Elf* is playing now, which is stupid, but I don't pay enough attention to the telly to bother changing the channel.

I can hear Stuart rummaging in the kitchen and Mum comes in the lounge with her big coat still on, her cheeks all red from the cold. She bends down and kisses me, the corners of her mouth all wrinkled with smiles.

'How's the day been?' she asks. 'Didn't you have a great Christmas?'

'Yeah,' I say. 'It was cool.'

'I had a delightful time!'

'Good for you.'

She leaves the room, unsteady and giggling, stumbling into Stuart's arms. He rolls his eyes at me over her shoulders, like we're in on a joke together. They disappear. I can hear steps up the stairs, and then Stuart's head pokes into the lounge.

'Hey,' he says. 'I'll go up and take care of your mother, but there's a box in the fridge of turkey and mash, some Yorkshire puddings. In case you get an appetite.'

He leaves. I'm furious. Mum explicitly told him not to bring me any food. I shouldn't be eating. He has to know this; can't he see the way I look? I shouldn't eat, but there's food in the fridge now, and I'm just so hungry. I hate him for doing this to me. Does he want me to be fat? Does he not know I have the self-control of a toddler in front of a marshmallow? I bury my head in the cushions. I scream into them, muffled and desperate. There's food in the fridge.

It's not his fault that I can't help myself, I know that. But how can he not realize how difficult any person would find this when they haven't eaten for a week? Deep breaths. I think about going out there and binning the food before I can think about it further. I don't do it. I don't trust myself to take that box out of the fridge and not devour it all. The thought of food makes my intestines turn and my stomach make strange sounds. It feels like a deep, hollow pit. I need to drink some water to soothe it. But my water glass on the coffee table is empty, and I can't allow myself to go into the kitchen to refill it.

So here I lie. Nauseous and sleepy, the screen of the telly blurred in my eyes. The best course of action is going to bed and sleeping. When I'm asleep, I won't feel hungry. When I'm asleep, I can't eat. But I would get way too close to the kitchen if I went for the stairs.

I don't know what I'm watching any more because I can't think of anything except food. A large, juicy turkey, drowning in gravy, soft, soft mash. *Fuck off, it wouldn't be that good*, I tell myself. *It's microwaved leftovers we're talking about. You don't need* that *this badly*. And yet I can't keep myself from glancing at the doorway, from licking my lips, from seeing food on my eyelids every time I blink. My stomach hurts.

Two a.m., I get off the couch. I can't hold myself back any more. I lose my grip over my body and I rush over to the kitchen. I'm a little shaky. I open up the fridge and I feel like crying at the little white plastic box. This won't sate me. I'm so hungry.

I don't have time to microwave the food. I don't have time to sit at the table. It feels like the hole in my stomach is expanding, sucking the rest of me inside, pulling everything I am into a black nothingness. All I have time for is grabbing a fork and sitting down on the floor.

It doesn't taste very good. This food isn't meant to be eaten cold, and the gravy is thick, the potatoes lumpy, and the turkey slices hard. It doesn't matter, though. I'm too hungry to care. I scoop the stuff into my mouth as fast as I can swallow it. I can't stop myself; my arm moves reflexively, urgently, grabbing more and more food. My body is screaming for it. It will feel so good not to be hungry. I can't wait to be free.

I hear the steps on the stairs, but there isn't enough time to act. It's too late to put the food in the bin and try to wipe my shirt clean. Either way, I can't seem to stop. The food is more important than anything. I don't need to protect myself, I need to eat. I need to eat, eat, eat.

And Mum's standing in the doorway in her dressing gown, her face bare and her toenails painted. I look up at her from the floor like some sort of troll. I can see myself in her eyes, and I want to die. I'm gross, I'm disappointing, I'm hopeless, I'm fat. I'm fat, fat, fat, fat.

'Amber,' she says. Not angry, just tired. Disappointed, like

231

I'm five and she's found me with my hand in the cookie jar before dinner.

'I'm sorry,' I say. 'I was so hungry.'

My voice wobbles, breaks. It feels so futile to try to explain. I can only give excuses. Excuses that just reaffirm what she's looking at.

'Oh my god.' She takes a step forward, her face scrunched up in disgust. 'What are you doing?'

I bring the box to my chest, shielding it from her, protecting it like a child. I'm still hungry. I need this food.

'Oh, Jesus. I'm not going to take the food away from you, you pig.' Mum shakes her head. 'What's the point in trying? I've been trying for so many years with you, and I'm sick of it.'

I look down.

'Maybe you should try bulimia,' Mum barks, sounding angrier now. 'It might be your last hope at this point.'

Yes, I think, *an eating disorder, that's what I need*. The problem is I can't stop eating.

'Look at you,' Mum says. 'You're fat. I used to hope it was baby fat, but you're not a baby any more, are you? You're just fat.'

She kneels down in front of me, her robe grazing the floor.

'Look at me when I'm talking to you.'

I take a deep breath and force my eyes up. I look at her and it hurts. There's so much anger in her eyes, so much disappointment, so much regret.

'I try so hard to help you,' she sneers. 'I have told you what this road leads to. You know I wasn't always this skinny, and I've told you how awful it was. I hated my body, I hated my life. The only man I managed to get was your useless father and then he left me for someone prettier. You know all of this, but do you even try? Do you even try to help yourself?'

Of course I do. But I don't tell her this, because I'm at fault here. I shouldn't be eating Christmas food on the kitchen floor right now, I shouldn't be eating at all, and yet here I am. Unable to control myself once again. That's not her fault. That's mine. No one can do anything about that except me.

'I'm sorry,' I say again, and she snorts.

'I don't want you to be sorry,' she says. 'I want you to be skinny.' She sticks her finger in the mashed potatoes, she swirls it around and brings it back up covered in mash. 'Merry Christmas to me.'

She looks at the finger like she's considering something, and then she sticks it into my mouth. She forces her finger between my lips, pushing the mash onto my chin and my tongue, shaking her finger inside my mouth and splattering it everywhere. I can taste her hand cream, the one that smells like mango and tastes like chemicals.

'Eat it,' she says. 'If this is what you want, eat it all.'

She stands back up. She wipes her finger off on the robe. I can feel a clump of mash on my chin, dribbling down my lips mixed with saliva. *Mum*, I want to say. *Mum please help me.* I don't speak. She leaves before I have the chance. Her steps up the stairs are aggressive, threatening.

Nicki would be able to help me stop. If I could just text her, I'd be able to take my hands out of this plastic container.

I shouldn't want this food any more, but despite the taste in my mouth and the hard, aching pain in my stomach, I look down at the box and I reach for more. I don't want it. I need it. My hand scoops more onto the fork. I cry and I keep eating.

37

Nicki

I'm back to work a few days later. I go into the office in the morning, when the snow is still on the ground for the few hours that it will stay.

Alice is sitting at one of the desks, her beanie on and a cup of Starbucks in front of her. We nod at each other. I check my schedule, and it looks weird. I have someone new in my rotation, a lady called Susan Gardener. Most notably, there's no Edith in my timetable. None at all. I always see Edith, I go at least once every day.

'Alice,' I say. 'Do you know why I haven't got anything with Edith this week?'

'They didn't tell you yet?' she says. 'Edith died.'

That's impossible. She was tired the last time I saw her, yes, but she was fine. Edith was always healthy. She was barely eighty, she had many years left. I turn around. Alice doesn't look like she's joking.

'What?' I say.

'I'm sorry. I thought they would've told you, you being her favourite and all.'

Somehow, this makes me feel worse. Edith was my favourite, but I never imagined that I was hers. I should have known this earlier. I don't know what difference it would have made, but I should have known.

'What happened?'

Alice shrugs. 'She had a stroke on Christmas Eve. Jamie

found her in the kitchen, she was already unconscious. She passed on Boxing Day, never woke back up.'

I feel nauseous. I think about Edith, who was always smiling and always so polite, lying alone on the kitchen floor on Christmas Eve. It should have been me. It's a silly thought, but it should have been me. Jamie's always behind. I would've been on time. I might not have saved her, but I would've held her hand before she lost consciousness. I was her favourite.

'Wasn't she with family?' I ask.

'Ah, I think the son was in Mallorca when we called. Sad, isn't it?'

She says it so flippantly, with barely any emotion, eyes on her nails. Yes, of course he is. He was supposed to be there for two weeks. He's celebrating Christmas there.

'You all right?' Alice asks.

I snap out of it. I shake myself back into reality. She looks at me curiously, like there's something about my reaction that's wrong. She makes me feel bad for feeling upset. Sad, she said, but she doesn't look sad; she doesn't care.

'Yeah,' I say. 'I'm fine. I'll head out to Mr Peterson, then.'

During the day, I pass by her house. I don't need to take that route to get to my next old person, but I do it anyway. I drive by slowly, watching the circling seagulls, looking at the closed blinds and the empty garden. Anyone going past would have no idea that this house is now unoccupied. I drive away.

I get home and Tom's done early. I'm overcome with so many emotions when I see him on the couch. I'm relieved that he's here, because I can't be alone. I'm sorry for all I've done to him, because despite it all he's still here. He's here for me to wrap my arms around and burrow my head into. His shoulder is here for me to cry on. His hand strokes the back of my hair, and he doesn't ask what's wrong, even as I sense the tension and the surprise when I burst out sobbing.

I'm angry because Edith was all alone when her son had promised to take her to the Lake District, because he was supposed to have spent Christmas with his mother, because she had to die by herself. I'm sad because every day from now on will be without her.

'It's okay,' Tom says, pressing his cheek to my forehead.

It's good not to be alone. It's good to have him to cling to.

38

Amber

I might pass out.

Everything is spinning, my legs are wobbly. I stumble off the treadmill and sit down on the floor. I try to breathe, and it's hard. There's white in front of my eyes. Is that concerning? It's probably a good sign. I pushed myself hard enough. That's how you get results.

I put my elbows on my knees and close my eyes. I let my head fall forward and onto my arm; I'm too tired to hold it up. Even my neck is aching and burning. My stomach doesn't feel right. I'm a little scared I'll be sick. I won't be able to make it to the bathroom in time. If I try to stand, I'll collapse. I'll be sick all over myself in the middle of the gym, in front of all these strangers. I can't let that happen.

My vision was too blurry to check the calories and distance on the screen before I sat down, but they must be good. I almost feel like laughing. I could take a picture, I could show it to my mum. It's been a long time since I managed to make her happy.

'You all right?' a voice says.

There's no risk I'll run into Melissa at this new gym; she's still attending the old one as far as I know, and she wouldn't switch to one so far away. There's no reason Melissa would talk to me anyway. But for a second, it sounds like her.

My head shoots up. Stars in my vision, blood pumping hard and painfully in my temples. It's not Melissa. It's one of those pretty gym-girls, the fit ones with their perky butts and flat stomachs. The ones who store all their fat in their tits. The ones who go to the gym in only a sports bra and leggings, because they've got nothing to hide with tank tops or hoodies. There isn't a drop of sweat on her slender figure and smooth skin. The make-up is flawless, her lips pursed in concern and her mascara-covered lashes fluttering.

'Yeah,' I say.

Which I'm not, because she's here, and I'd like to crawl into a hole and hide. I can't even begin to imagine what I must look like to her.

'Okay,' she says, hesitant, standing back straight. 'Take it easy, yeah?'

I nod and look down, hiding my make-up-free face with the acne and redness and the sweat and the chubby, chubby cheeks. She leaves and I'm glad. I bet she wouldn't be this exhausted after a simple run. She could keep going much longer than I just did and she'd look just the same; she'd find it refreshing even.

I take my phone out. I still check my chat with Nicki regularly. It's not that I expect her to unblock me. I just hope she might. So I send off another little *Hi*, and it comes back undelivered, like it always does, just one more in a long line of other texts that she hasn't received and never will. I exhale. It's okay, it's okay.

I didn't run for nearly as long as I thought I did. There's no reason to take a picture of it. I clear the screen and wipe down the treadmill.

There's always a moment of excitement when I step outside the building. I look around, look down both sides of the street. She's never here. It would be too convenient if she was, I know that. I don't have that kind of luck. But there's still a stillness, an anticipation, as I look. Then my heart sinks and I think to myself: *How silly.*

It was stupid to change my gym to one that takes me twenty minutes to get to by bus. I tried telling myself that it was only because I couldn't go to my old one any more, not if Melissa was still going. I tried telling myself it was better to move further away, in case she also switched while trying to avoid me. But there's only one reason I ended up in Kemptown. It's because I once asked Nicki where she lives, and it's here.

I probably won't see her around. I know that. But I go to the gym every day, so it's not impossible, right? I kind of wander around afterwards. Not much else to do before school starts again. It feels more productive than lying in bed. It's more likely to lead to something than the countless undelivered texts. I start walking down the street.

It's cold out. I put my gloves on and I'm still freezing. There aren't a lot of people around, just dog owners and people rushing from one place to the next. A lady with a child in a stroller walks past me, the baby wailing loudly. My teeth are clattering. I've done this every day for over a week now. If I told anyone, they would think I'm insane. I can't blame them. This is pointless. I won't be out long today, not in this cold. I decide that I'll just go down to the bus stop and get back home.

Nicki isn't suddenly going to show up just because she lives in the general vicinity. Hundreds of other people do. What are the odds she's going to be walking this exact street at the same time as me? This is probably the last time I'm going to try this. Tomorrow, I'll just take the bus home as soon as I'm done. I won't hope for a glimpse of her. I breathe into my hands to warm them up.

Nicki isn't going to show up, I tell myself. But then she does.

It takes me a while to realize that it's her. She's just a random woman walking in my direction with a Tesco bag. Maybe it's the beanie she's wearing covering her forehead. She looks different in real life; she's not the all-consuming presence I imagined, the confident, sexy seductress she was in our first text conversation. She's so small. She's short, shorter than me. She doesn't strut. She walks like she doesn't want to be seen, with her eyes on her phone and her shoulders hunched inwards. I thought she'd look glamorous, with a lot of make-up on and her hair always recently blow-dried. Her skin isn't foundation-smooth or free from dark circles. Her hair is long, but it looks frizzy and long overdue for a trim. She's wearing plain jeans and a black coat. She looks anonymous, she blends in. If I didn't recognize her, I wouldn't have looked at her twice.

I realize I've stopped. I'm staring at her and I don't know what to do next. My planning never got this far. She wasn't ever going to appear, it was futile all along, wasn't it, so why should I think out what to do if she actually did? She's getting closer. There are so many things I could say right now. I could say 'Excuse me' to get her attention and ask her where the bus stop or the bank or the library is; I could get to hear her voice for the first time. I wonder if it would be as disorienting as her physical appearance, so different from the one in my head. I could grab her by the arm and I could tell her that I'm Kevin. That would get her to listen.

But why would she want that? I've lied to her. She wanted Kevin, not me. Never me.

Everything happens too fast. Suddenly she's right next to me, about to walk past, and I still don't know what to say. She looks up from her phone and our eyes meet. It doesn't feel very real. At the same time, it feels way too real. She actually exists. She's a human being outside of my phone. It doesn't feel possible that she won't recognize me, not when she knows me as well as she does, not with all the things I've told her that I've never said to anyone else.

But of course, she doesn't recognize me. Her eyes meet mine for a second and then they drift back; she doesn't pause, she doesn't flinch, she doesn't slow her steps. I can hear the rustling of the plastic bag in her hand. I can feel the faint breeze of her passing, that's how close she is. My hand moves like I'm about to reach for her. It would be so easy to touch her, to make her tangible. Is that what I want? Is that what this is about? I don't know. I don't know if hearing her voice would be enough. I don't know if what I need is for her to come back to me.

She's past. I resist the urge to turn around and follow her with my gaze. It would look too obvious, it would be too strange. I have to remain calm. I pick up my phone and pretend to realize I've been going in the wrong direction, then I put it back in my pocket and turn around. I'm not stalking her. I just need a little more time to consider my options and decide what to do. So yeah, I follow her. I can't let her get out of my sight. I can't let this moment go to waste.

Suddenly I've forgotten what a normal distance to have to a stranger is. The fact that she's moving away from me makes me want to run. I want to keep her close so she can't disappear around a corner. I force my legs to keep a normal pace. She's maybe six feet away; that should be fine. That seems about right. That shouldn't rouse any suspicion if she turns around and sees me.

I can't believe she's here. If I called out, she would hear me. I can tell her deep, personal things about herself and she would look at me with confusion. She wouldn't even be able to say what my name is. I look like a stranger to her, but really, I'm not. I've lied to her about a lot of things, but she knows me better than anyone else.

She glances back at me, quickly, like she's trying to do it

subtly. She must have sensed that I'm here. I keep walking, acting like I have no reason to stop, and I hold my breath. She might break out into a run now. She's being followed by someone she's never seen before. But she doesn't quicken her pace, and she doesn't look back again, and she doesn't put her phone back in her pocket to pay more attention to me. I suppose I am a teenage girl; I don't look very intimidating. She knows who's behind her and she has assessed that I'm not a threat, so we keep walking.

I check my phone every once in a while, and I look at our surroundings so I don't act suspicious. I follow her for ten minutes, way in the opposite direction of where I'm going, in a neighbourhood I don't know at all. It's not a surprise when she walks up to one of the apartment buildings and gets her key out. It's a tall building, it looks pretty modern. I jump behind a tree, though it's not wide enough to cover me, and I watch her. I'm going to lose her now. This is my last chance to speak. If I don't, I'll just be a creep who followed her home. And then I think that maybe I already am. I didn't mean to stalk her, I just wanted to think about what to say, but it went on for too long. Anything I say now is going to be creepy; she'll either realize I followed her from somewhere, or she'll think I found her address somewhere else. She's never going to text me again. I lost my chance.

I watch her as she unlocks the door and walks inside. She doesn't look back once. I think I could run up to the door and catch it just before it falls completely close, and maybe she'll already have started up the stairs or rounded a corner or entered her flat, and she won't notice me. But what would I do then? I don't know. I just know I want to go after her.

I don't. The door closes, and I let it. I close my eyes and

press my forehead against the bark of the tree. This was always a stupid idea. This was never going to lead anywhere. But something feels strange in my chest. It's like a fluttering excitement, a pressure inside me that's building with no release in sight.

I know where she lives now.

39

Nicki

Edith is buried on the first day of the new year. A beginning and an ending. I could write about that if I were any sort of poet.

I put my hands on the sink and let myself rest. I look at myself in the mirror. Breathe. There's not enough oxygen in here. A strand of hair is hanging in front of my face and I pull it behind my ear. I look sickly. I hope it's just the bathroom lighting. I straighten out my black dress.

A knock on the door, soft. 'Are you okay in there?'

I swallow and clear my throat, make my voice sound nice and normal. 'Yeah, just a second.'

I might not be okay, but he worries. There's no reason to tell him the truth. There's no reason to consider how I'm actually feeling. My emotions are far away, and I don't much mind it. I don't reach out to try to grab and examine them, I let them be. They're not needed right now. I could tell Kevin all about them, but that's not an option. It's best not to feel them.

I leave the bathroom. Tom has a concerned frown on his face. I smile to ease his worries, and I take his hand, running my fingers over his knuckles.

'Are you ready to leave?' he asks.

Am I? Will I ever be?

He drives us. The world outside is grey, but it's not raining today, not yet. The clouds are dark and menacing. I watch it all through the window, my hand against the glass. There is a part of me that doesn't want to get out of the car. We have reached the church too fast, Tom has found a parking spot too quickly and slid into it with too much ease. I'd like a bit more time.

'They'll be starting in two minutes,' he says. 'Come on.'

He's right. I don't want to interrupt this funeral, barge into it in the middle of the eulogy when no one in there will even recognize me, when I'm not part of the family.

The inside of the church is not like I imagined it. I hoped there would be more flowers on her coffin. I thought there would be more people to mourn her. How could you live a life this long without gathering a string of people along the way? But there's only one bouquet on the dark, featureless coffin; it's a boring one, simple red and white roses that would work just as well on Valentine's Day or Christmas or a birthday. There's no character in them. I'm suddenly devastated that I didn't bring any. I imagined that I would take up too much space, steal too much attention, if I put myself in the spotlight by walking up to the front of the church and placing a bouquet on the coffin. Her family would be wondering who I think I am, why I have that right, why I act as though I have more claim to her than they do.

But there is barely any family here. There are three shapes seated on the front row, two big and one little. One turns its head to us and gives a confused, surprised smile. It's the son whose face I've seen so many times on her fridge. He looks very much the same, if perhaps a little older and more worn, and of course he has a tan.

'Sorry,' Tom says. 'Are we early?'

'No, no,' Roland says. 'You're right on time.'

The woman next to him looks back at us too. It's the heavily pregnant wife, her face round and her hand on the giant bump in front of her. Their little boy is sitting between them.

He's much older than in the picture; he must be around seven, and he almost reaches up to his mother's shoulders. I realize I can hear the tapping of his impatient feet against the stone floor.

Part of me wants to leave. There is no way now to avoid detection. I was hoping the party would be large enough that I would go unnoticed, that I wouldn't need to explain my presence to her family members. Funerals bring people out of the woodwork, don't they? Everyone who never called you suddenly pretending to care. But there's no one here, and I know I can't leave. I was one of her favourites. She deserves more than three people at her funeral. I smile hesitantly at Roland.

'Please, have a seat,' the priest says. He is lighting some candles at the front. 'We should get started soon.'

I reach for Tom's hand. I'll need to apologize, afterwards, for how clammy and hot mine is. He moves towards the front, but I lead us into a middle aisle instead. Front row is for family, and this feels more appropriate.

The daughter-in-law bends over the little boy and tells him something. I can only hear the sound, none of the words. Roland is on his phone now. His face is bright with the light from the screen.

'Well, now,' the priest says, putting his hands together. 'It doesn't look like anyone else will be joining us, so let's begin.'

It's over quickly. In the end I find myself alone in our row as Tom goes off to find the toilet, and Roland stands up and looks back at me. He smiles and I know he'll be coming over. I stand up to greet him.

'Hi,' he says. 'Sorry, I don't think we've met.'

'No,' I say, 'we haven't. My name is Nicki.'

'I'm Roland. How did you know my mother?'

He doesn't remember the phone call, then. Of course he doesn't, I wasn't worth remembering.

'I was one of her carers.'

'Oh, really?' He looks even more surprised now. 'I didn't expect anyone else to show, to be honest. That's why I was a little shocked to see you.'

No one else from the company attended. I don't blame them, I haven't been to any of the other funerals either.

'She was a special woman,' I say.

'Well, I truly appreciate you being here,' he says.

His son is playing with a fidget spinner now. The mother looks on, leaning against the pews, and doesn't tell him to stop. I suppose there is no reason to.

'What happens now, then?' I ask.

'She'll be cremated. I'm not sure what to do with the ashes yet, but we'll figure it out.'

'Well, I meant today.'

'Ah.' He laughs awkwardly. 'To be honest, I haven't planned anything. I didn't expect anyone to show, like I said. We were just planning to head back home.'

I feel bad for being relieved. I was fully prepared to attend a gathering afterwards, the awkwardness of tea with strangers all pretending to be sad, unruly children who haven't got the sense to. It's such a relief that I won't have to. And it's awful that I feel this way, because it's the least I could have done for her.

'Oh, okay,' I say.

'I'm sure the priest wouldn't mind you hanging about for a bit,' Roland says. 'You know, if you'd like to have a little prayer, light a candle. Maybe we should do the same, actually.'

He looks back at his family. The wife shakes her head. He's

trying to convince me that he's not a bad son. I don't know if he is, and I don't care. It doesn't matter why Edith was alone, and is alone still, only that it's true. And I don't really know what one is supposed to do inside a church. Mum used to pray. Every time things got bad, she'd be on her knees on the prayer mat she kept secret from Dad. Her prayers never worked. That's all I know about religion, because Dad was never a fan. And Dad made the rules.

'That's okay.' I force myself to smile.

'She wouldn't want a fuss,' he says.

I nod. He smiles awkwardly, too widely, and the silence is uncomfortable, disconcerting. I wish Tom was back, he would know what to say.

'I'm sorry for your loss,' I say.

It feels like something I should have done a while ago. But then it didn't feel like it was necessary, because he doesn't look like a man who's lost anything. His face is dry, his manner carefree.

'Thank you,' he says. 'And thank you for being here. I'm sure she would have appreciated it.'

And when, I think, *have you ever cared about what she wanted?* The anger comes over me suddenly. She would have appreciated if you'd taken her to the Lake District. She would have appreciated if you'd gone to see her at Christmas. I'm angry at his smile, at the boy with the fidget spinner, the wife scrolling through her phone, the tans they all have. Edith deserves more than this. She deserves a church full of people who cared enough to be sad that she's gone. She deserved to die in a hospital bed surrounded by family, not alone on her kitchen floor to be found the next day.

Roland clears his throat. The anger is gone as suddenly as it appeared. It's not his fault. Sometimes these things just happen. This isn't an evil man; he has a child, he thanked me for coming, he bought a bouquet. It's not a crime he'd rather go to Spain than the Lake District. It's not a crime to have a job and a family and not enough time for your ageing mother.

A movement at the corner of my eye catches my attention. It's Tom, standing next to the door of the church. I'd like him to intervene, but he's taking the polite approach. He smiles at Roland and raises a hand, but he doesn't approach.

'I should go,' I say.

'Of course,' Roland says. 'I wouldn't want to keep you. Thank you, again, for coming.'

In the car ride home, I fiddle with my phone. I miss Kevin. Whenever I had something I wanted to keep my mind off, I'd replace it with him. This is a moment when I would be messaging him, if things were different.

'Are you okay?' Tom asks. He looks over for a moment before he brings his eyes back to the road.

'Yeah,' I say, before I've even thought about it. 'Yeah, I'm fine.'

'You're quiet.'

I put my phone on my lap, screen down. I close my eyes.

'It's just sad, isn't it?'

'She was old. She lived a good life.'

'No, I mean . . .' A deep breath. 'The funeral was so small. She died alone, and barely anyone showed up to her funeral. Like no one ever cared.'

He gives me a smile of compassion. 'You cared.'

But I didn't care enough, did I? I didn't call her during the holidays to check up on how she was doing. As soon as something happened in my life, I let her slip my mind. I barely thought about her after Tom tried to kill himself. Maybe I only cared when it was convenient for me. And what did I do? I drove her to Surrey. I could've done so much more. I could have called Roland for her, I could have invited her to spend the holidays with me, I could have stopped by any day after work.

But I never did. And on some level, I know that I cared about her. Why else would I be feeling like this right now? The question is, did she know? What is the point if she never knew? She must have felt so alone and so unloved when she died.

'I know,' I say. 'It's silly.'

I'll end up like her. I could count on one hand the people that would show up to my funeral, and they're all Tom's family. I have no friends. I have no colleagues I stop to chat with unless I absolutely have to. Kate would never get the news that I'd died, and Kevin's on the other side of the Earth. He'd never realize I was gone. If I didn't have Tom, I could end up like that lady in London who was dead in her flat for years before being found. Maybe they'd never bury me.

A single bouquet on the coffin, that's me. A crowd so small it's awkwardly silent, that's me. No one who is there out of anything except obligation.

Yeah, it's definitely a moment when I would be messaging Kevin.

40

Amber

After the gym, I sit outside her building. I know it's weird, but I don't have much else to do these days. I eat an apple because I felt very sick while I was working out, and there aren't that many calories in an apple. My bum's cold and wet from the bench. There's a seagull eyeing my apple from a distance.

It's become routine to do this. Every day I tell myself I'll go straight home, and then I walk in the wrong direction. I can't seem to stop myself. I'd just like to catch another glimpse of her, that's all. I tell myself I'll stop once I've seen her again. I don't know if I believe that. Before I saw her the first time, I told myself that was all I needed. And I'm still here. But it would be nice to see her in a calmer, more prepared state. I want to make sure she's okay. I want to study the expression on her face for any signs of sadness, any dark circles from lack of sleep, any wrinkles from anxiety. I want to consider her body language and whether she's depressed or not; I want to see if she's thin enough to see bone, or if she's eating well and taking care of herself.

If she just unblocked me, I could send her a single text and make sure she's okay, and she'd never have to hear from me again. All she'd have to do is answer.

I toss the apple core far away and watch the seagull attack. I'm still hungry, but that's a good sign. I haven't eaten too much. Just a granola bar for breakfast, and an apple.

I look up at her building. It's fun to wonder about which

floor she's on, which window belongs to her. I have seen people in there, so it's not impossible I'll spot her some day. At the kitchen sink washing dishes. In the bedroom changing. I'd look away, then. I'm not a creep. I did think about her that one time, and it makes me feel a little sick to remember it, but of course I'd look away. I might be tempted not to, but it would feel too strange.

Or maybe I'll see her curled up on a couch next to this boyfriend she never told me about. Maybe I'll see them dancing in the lounge. Maybe I'll see her being fucked by him on the bed. These scenarios are less appealing. They make me feel strange, make my stomach hurt.

I'm starting to get cold, and I think I'll be heading home soon. It's creepier the more time I spend here.

But that's when the front door of her building opens, and my heart is high in my throat. This has happened before, and it's never been her. I always stop breathing and raise my neck to see better and then I see some old man stumble out with a walking frame, or some woman with a stroller and an energetic lurcher. Still, I can't help it. The moment the door opens I fix my eyes on it.

And this time it is her. I recognize her as soon as she appears in the doorway, pulling on a pair of gloves. She looks up at the sky like she's trying to determine if it's raining. She's wearing the same beanie she had on last time and her hair hangs long over her chest.

She goes down the steps and I'm standing up. What the fuck am I doing? She's coming in my direction, paying me no attention. What the fuck am I doing? I'm walking straight towards her. I'm not subtle. I look at her as I do it and we make eye contact, and I don't look away. It's too late. I raise my hand and I feel like an awkward toddler, like an alien trying to emulate a human greeting. There's a half-hearted attempt at a smile on her face, nothing but a small gesture that she sees me and she recognizes that it's the polite thing to do, but she's not going to put feeling into it.

'Hello,' I say, my voice sharp and loud, carrying across our distance with too much eagerness.

I tone it down. My throat is shaky, voice uneven, chest tight. I'm probably shaking, but she probably can't tell.

'Sorry, do you know where Montague Street is?'

This is an address I found a few days ago. It's only a street down, which makes it plausible I would've got lost here. I could make up a random street name, but I don't know how long she's lived in this area. If she knows it too well, I'd look weird as fuck.

She pauses. She's so close. It's hard to focus on very much, just staring at her face. Yes, there are dark circles under her eyes. Her skin is pretty clear, though it looks dry. She doesn't wear make-up, but I already expected that from last time. She doesn't look like her cheeks are hollow from starvation. Her eyes don't look like they're raw from crying. I knew this would be the case, and still it stings.

But it doesn't hurt as much when I'm staring at her face. She's real, she's real, she's real. I could touch her. If I stepped a little bit closer, I would know what she smelled like.

I think about that time again, when I touched myself, and how I imagined her to look and feel. I can't believe she doesn't recognize me but I've imagined what she looks like without her clothes. It makes me feel a bit faint. Maybe I am a creep after all.

'Think it's down that way.' She points to our right, a movement without much passion. 'Couldn't get more specific, sorry.'

Her voice is a shock to my system. I've imagined it a lot; there's a voice in my head that I hear her messages in, but it's not this. It's lower, with a rasp to it like she's a smoker. I don't know if she is, she's never said so. I almost ask right now, but that would be ridiculous. I'm not supposed to be Kevin right now. I'm a stranger to her.

Her accent is a little bit different to mine. It's slightly northern, and I realize I've never asked her where she was born. I assumed she'd been in Brighton all her life. Now I think she might be from somewhere around Manchester, maybe closer to Scotland, a little bit Geordie, maybe. It could be anything north of London, as far as I know, because it isn't pronounced. It's a small scar she carries with her from a long time ago, a reminder of a different place that left a mark on her.

It takes me a few seconds to gather myself together. I must look like a proper idiot as I stand there with my mouth open, her voice playing over and over again in my head, a hundred thoughts crashing over me at once.

'Thank you,' I say.

A strand of her hair is attached to one of her lashes. It's so thin it's barely visible, only by the light that hits it and the line of a shadow it casts on her cheek. Her gloves are purple and fuzzy, the fingers thick and broad.

'Sure,' she says. Her lips moving, almost a smile, a bit of teeth showing.

She's pretty. She's prettier in real life than in the pictures. The relaxed lack of effort is good for her smile, and the sun hits her brown eyes just so, turning them golden and warm. Her hair is so dark. Despite the circles under her eyes, despite the little wrinkles, and despite the blemishes on her nose, she's prettier than I will ever be.

And now she'll be gone, because all I had was this request for directions. I want to keep her here. Fuck, I even consider coming clean just to make her stay. If I shout out her name, she'll be so surprised and confused she'll have to. If I tell her who I am, she would need to hear the whole story.

But I can't do that. The saliva is sticking in my mouth like glue, I know I'll ruin every chance of ever speaking to her again if I let on who I really am.

And she leaves, her boots squelching in the watery mud on the ground. I watch her until she's out of my sight.

41

Nicki

Leela seems more serious than usual. Her smile is contained and careful, her hands neatly clasped on her lap. It concerns me.

'How are you doing?' she asks.

Just tell me what's going on, I want to say. *Whatever it is you need to say, let's get it over with.*

'Good,' I say. 'I'm doing good.'

Just so I say something, because what does it matter what else I tell her? She can't do anything about the fact that Tom tried to kill himself or that Edith is dead.

'Nicki.' She closes her eyes briefly, a twitch at the side of her face. Exasperation mixed with desperation. 'I need you to be honest with me this time, okay? Tell me how you're really doing. Please.'

It opens the floodgates of my armpits. It makes it hard to breathe. She can't be demanding this of me. I can't do it. I can't tell her the truth, because—

Because what? It's hard to think clearly. All I know is that I need to stay far away from her.

'Nicki, breathe. You're safe here. Can I touch you?'

She's reaching her hand out for me. But it doesn't look like hers. The nails are too short, the fingers too stubby, the hand too hairy. I manage to shake my head. I press myself against the chair. Leela's hand retracts.

'Remind yourself of where you are. You're here with me. I'm Leela. I'm your therapist.'

Yes. Yes. I shake my head, squeeze my eyes shut hard.

I breathe deeply and dig my nails into the armrests. Leela smiles.

'You here?' she asks.

'Yeah,' I say. 'I'm here.'

'Ground yourself however you need. Would you like me to continue speaking to you? Does that help?'

'I'm fine.'

'I'll give you a minute.'

I shake my head. I don't want a minute. Drawing it out is such torture.

'What's going on?' I ask. 'Why are you not taking notes?'

Leela sighs, embarrassment crossing her face.

'I was hoping you'd tell me how you are,' she says. 'But I won't force anything.'

So I don't speak. She waits, and I let her, and then she gives up.

'We need to discuss your treatment,' she says.

I nod, apprehensive. It feels like bad news.

'As you know, we've had twenty sessions together now. It's been almost a year. We've made no discernible progress during that time.' Her eyes are apologetic, as if this is her fault, as if it's not just a defect within me. 'I know why this is difficult for you, Nicki. I know what happened with your first therapist, and I'm deeply sorry for it. But this doesn't work unless you're willing to make an effort, and you've never opened up to me.'

I suppress a sudden, intense urge to laugh. I used to be willing. I tried this before. Look where that got me.

'It's important for us to give this time to people that it will really help,' Leela continues. 'Therapy just isn't for everyone, and that's okay. And we think that maybe, it isn't for you.'

'You're ending my treatment.'

It doesn't give me the sense of relief I would have thought it should. After all, why do I come here? When has it ever made me feel any better? But at the same time, it feels like I'm being left to drift on my own. There was one thing that could have saved me, and it didn't. I truly am a lost cause.

'This is a short-term service,' she says.

'It's not a short-term condition.'

She smiles at me apologetically. *No*, I want to scream, *I'm not upset I won't be speaking to you any more. I'm upset that the only lifeline available to me failed to do what it was supposed to.* I'll always be like this. It dawns on me, suddenly, that in a way I still held out a little hope. *Things will be different one day*, I told myself. They won't be. I've tried all possible solutions and I'm still me.

'I've got this list for you.' Leela reaches over to her desk and grabs a document. 'These are some self-help resources and some phone numbers to crisis hotlines.'

I look at the paper in her outstretched hand. It's laughable. I've called a hotline like that. All the medications and all the therapy have done shit to help me, so how would a teenage volunteer on a phone be able to fix me?

'I don't need this,' I say.

'Nicki, I can feel you're being a bit hostile right now. I recognize that this is difficult, but I want you to understand that we don't want to leave you without support. It's just support of a different kind.'

I take it, reluctantly, because I don't have the energy to argue; I'll put it in the bin later. Leela looks so relieved, so happy, for a moment. I try to stop being angry at her. It's not her fault she couldn't help me. It's not the NHS's fault they couldn't help me. No one can.

'How do you feel about this?' she asks. 'I know it's scary, you can be honest with me.'

I feel. So. Much.

'It's fine,' I say. 'Like you said, not that it was doing anything anyway. Doesn't make sense to keep coming here if it doesn't work.'

'Now, you know that's not what I said.'

I don't say anything. I clasp the document she gave me hard in my hand, crumpling it.

'Okay, so.' She puts her hands together, she puts on a brave face. 'Our next session will be the last one. What would you like to work on during these final two sessions?'

'What?'

'I was thinking maybe we could try some strategies for coping with difficult emotions, practise grounding yourself when you have flashbacks . . .'

I frown. We have around one and a half more hours with each other, and she thinks she can cram into it all the skills I need to be released into the world without therapy. What does she think she can do of any value during one and a half hours?

Over twenty sessions and I've got nowhere. This isn't worth it. I always knew this. I told Tom this. I made the effort yet again and it didn't work. I won't waste any more time.

'No,' I say. 'I think I'd rather just go.'

Leela laughs, insecurely. 'Well, you're already here, now. I can cancel the next session, but—'

But I'm standing up.

'It doesn't matter. Thank you for trying. I appreciate the attempt.'

'Nicki.' She rises too, reaching for my arm, stopping herself before she touches me. 'It's okay to be upset about this, but I don't think this is an impulse you should act on.'

I can feel my face contorting, my throat hurting. I've never cried in front of this woman. I can't allow it. I can't be weak in front of her. Deep breaths. Why are you upset? You knew this all along. God, I've been so stupid to get my hopes up.

'It's fine,' I say. 'Really. But being here is pointless, as you said yourself. So just drop it.'

I leave. I leave the last session of therapy I'll ever attend. The door banging shut behind me, tossing the 'resources' into the bin.

I get in the car and lock it. It's really difficult to breathe. I can feel my eyes rolling back and I grip the steering wheel hard, watch my knuckles whiten. Not right now. I can't do this right now.

But I can hear his voice. Wallace. His breath smelling like the mints he always chewed.

'Nicki, with the kind of trauma that you've endured, I've found that there's a foolproof method of reaching recovery.'

His hands unbuttoning my blouse one by one. Did it feel right? Of course it didn't. Young and dumb as I was, part of me knew all along that this wasn't therapy. I guess I was desperate. I guess I looked at him with eyes that said, *Please, I'll do anything. I'll try anything. Just fix me.*

I thought it was possible. I thought I could be cured.

'I call it exposure.'

And I knew there was no point resisting when it would be no use. I'd resisted in the past. I'd shouted in the past, said no, tried hitting back. The boys at school didn't care about that. They were stronger than me, they found it funny, and they laughed and held my arms. They told me I was bad at blow-jobs, but they still kept going.

Just like Wallace would. Why try to stop it when it would

just keep happening? Why try to resist when this would always be my reality? Better to just get used to it. Best accept my lot in life.

I shake my head, bang it into the headrest. I stare at my knuckles; I focus on reality. I feel like a helium balloon floating across the sky, rising higher and higher, out of bounds of everything I could attach myself to. There is nothing to grasp to keep me on Earth.

I need someone to grab me. I fumble for my phone, struggling to see the screen properly, putting my password in wrong a couple times. Breathe. Breathe. I get in.

I open up a conversation with Tom, but I stop before I start typing. If he asks why this is happening, I'll have to tell him what Leela just said. If he asks why I don't go back inside to ask for her to help ground me, I'll have to reveal that it wouldn't work. Therapy won't help me. The efforts would begin all over again, the constant worrying, the hiding of sharp objects and the phone calls to the NHS telling them to take me in, the enquiries about hospitalization. He just wants the best for me. He would worry so much. I can't do that to him.

Instead, I unblock Kevin.

42

Nicki: *Hi*
Kevin: *Hi*
Nicki: *Sorry about blocking you*
  Are you angry
Kevin: *No*
  I'm happy you're back
Nicki: *I feel wrong asking but I need help*
Kevin: *Talk to me*
Nicki: *Why do you still want to help me*
  You should hate me after what you found out
Kevin: *Don't tell me what I should do*
  I want you to be happy, and I want to know that you're okay
  I care about you
Nicki: *I should have cared about you*
  You were upset when I blocked you and I should have been there
Kevin: *It hurt*
  Which is why I won't do the same to you
Nicki: *I'm sorry*
Kevin: *I'm sorry too*
  What's wrong?
Nicki: *Everythings falling apart*

43

Amber

I'm sick on the first day of spring term. Not intentionally; I don't stick my fingers down my throat or anything. Mum said I should try bulimia but I don't like the taste of vomit. I'm sick anyway. On the bathroom floor retching into the toilet, nothing coming out of me but transparent bile. There's not much else for my body to eject. I've been good again since Christmas, I've done well. I haven't eaten anything except some fruit every day.

It doesn't make me feel much better. I sit back against the wall. Being sick is tiring. I'd like to text Nicki, but I can't tell her the real reason I'm nervous. First day back in school. My penultimate term. And I don't have any friends.

I considered telling her, yesterday. When she told me that she's in a relationship but she's always been a cheater and she doesn't actually work as a receptionist. When she told me she was raped, repeatedly, by the first therapist she saw, and now she's been abandoned by the system again. I was too relieved to be angry at her, too surprised to feel betrayed, too busy trying to comfort her. She lied to me too. She pretended to be someone else too. If I told her, she would have to understand, it would be hypocritical of her to be angry at me. I don't feel like a bad person any more. She did this too, and I forgive her. I don't feel particularly hurt. All that was wrong was her occupation, her relationship status; so what? I know *her*. Those things don't matter.

But the thing is, even if she doesn't get mad, she would

definitely get weirded out. She thinks I'm a thirty-six-year-old man. She wants Kevin, not me. She'll take one look at me, eighteen and fat and a virgin and unfunny, and she'll say no thanks. It was nice but I'm not interested any more. What does someone like me have to offer her? Why would she want to talk to me? It's a risk I can't take.

I check Instagram. Yeah, still blocked by Melissa. Figures.

'Amber!' Mum shouts from downstairs. 'Won't you miss the bus?'

Yes, I will, but I wouldn't mind. I check the time. I can still make it, and I guess there's no point delaying it. I get up and wash my face.

First period is English. I sit far, far in the back. I'm too big to be invisible, but I do my best. Mr Miller is at his desk, sorting through some papers while looking increasingly concerned, pulling a hand through his hair with a frown on his face.

Kim and Marnie are some of the last to enter. I almost thought they wouldn't show up; I was hoping they'd switched classes, or maybe they were skipping. They look the same as they did in December, which is strange. So much has changed that they should have, too.

Marnie stretches her neck out and holds her head high like a meerkat, scanning the classroom like she's looking for something. Her face has something disapproving in it, superior. It's me she's looking for. And she spots me. Her expression turns into one of amusement instead, her lips jerking up to a smile. She pokes Kim in the side and she sees me too, and they both look like they find it so very funny. Maybe it's the fact that I dared show my face in this school again. Maybe I've gained weight. Maybe it's because it's the first time they see me without make-up and they never realized how ugly I truly am.

Maybe Dan has been telling them about how we never had sex because I'm too immature and ridiculous.

I look down. I don't want to see them laughing. I don't want to be tempted to read their lips and try to figure out what they're saying about me.

Lunch is hard. I won't eat, of course, but I still feel like I should make my way to the cafeteria. I have a single orange in my bag, and I wouldn't mind some water. My head hurts and I feel tired.

And then I enter and everyone's sitting at the tables with their friends. There is no empty corner for me to squeeze myself into.

I see Melissa with Kim and Marnie and some other girls. She's dyed her hair again, and cut it shorter. It's a vibrant red now. It suits her. But then she'd suit any hair colour. It would be great to be able to talk to her now, to explain what happened, to apologize the way I was never allowed to over text. She's laughing, she looks up, and she sees me. Of course she would. I stand out. We look at each other for a few seconds. I feel an inexplicable urge to smile; not like we're old friends, not like I'm happy to see her after the holidays, but in an apologetic, regretful way. Maybe I should raise a hand instead, just to see if she'll do the same.

She doesn't look sad. I shouldn't want her to, but it hurts. A part of me wants her to be suffering like I am. How could she not be heartbroken when we were best friends for thirteen years? How is she going to move on like it was nothing? I'm stupid for thinking these things, because of course it was nothing. I was wrong to think it was anything else. I was wrong to think I ever mattered to her like she did to me.

Like she's trying to emphasize that, she doesn't acknowledge my existence. She whips her head to the side, her red hair obscuring her face.

There's the boys' table. Brandon is on his phone. Dan is listening to one of the others talking, smiling. I guess it was silly of me to think he might be a little upset after our break-up. Just like Melissa, he's moved on. He looks happy. He's not cowering alone in a corner, on his phone to avoid talking to people. He's fine.

I thought it would make a difference to these people that I'm out of their lives. It didn't, and they're rubbing it in my face. If anything changed, it was for the better. They're all having so much fun now, they're all enjoying themselves so much more. Life without me is great.

'Amber!'

It's Georgia's voice. She's sitting to my side with two friends I don't know. She smiles in a way that's almost hysterical.

'Do you want to sit with us?' she asks.

I consider it for a moment. It would be nice to sit with someone. It would make me look less like a loser. The idea of being fat and alone in everyone's view is scary.

But I can't. Georgia is too nice, and she doesn't actually want me there. It will be awkward. They will force conversation with me and pretend to enjoy it. They won't be good enough that I won't be able to tell, every single second, just how badly they want me to leave. Yeah, that's appealing. That sounds fun. And when I'm gone they'll talk shit about me, rolling their eyes and groaning, and Georgia will have to apologize and say she didn't realize just how bad it would be and it just seemed like the right thing to do because I'm so alone and sad and fat and she felt bad for me. We're not friends any more, we have nothing in common.

'No thanks,' I say.

I eat my orange alone in the library.

44

Nicki

I lie in bed listening to Tom in the kitchen. The clattering of dishes and the boiling of the kettle. I need to pee, but it seems such an impossible task to get up. Instead I turn over and bury my head in the pillow, trying to ignore my bladder.

I didn't sleep much last night. Too many nightmares, too many thoughts. I don't want to get up. I don't want to go to work. I don't want to eat. All I want is to lie here. It's the only thing I have energy for.

The door opens behind me. I can smell him as he gets close, treading softly on the carpet.

'Hey.' He puts a hand on my shoulder. His voice is right next to my ear. 'Don't you work early today?'

'I called in sick.'

'Are you?'

No, I'm not ill. I'm just tired. If I told him this, he'd be concerned again. He would ask me when my next appointment with Leela is, and I would have to lie or tell him the truth. The things he would insist on.

'Yeah,' I say. 'A bad headache. My throat's sore.'

'I'm sorry, babe.' He presses a kiss to my cheek, his lips lingering.

I don't tell him to get away because I might be contagious. I want to convince him to stay, take his clothes off and crawl back into bed with me. We could lie under this duvet all day, skin to skin, staring at each other's faces, his hand on my cheek and my neck.

'Do you want me to pick up anything from the pharmacy?' he asks.

'Thank you.' I squeeze his hand. 'But I think I'll already feel better when you get back anyway.'

'Okay. Take care of yourself. Get some rest.'

After the front door closes, I turn onto my back and stare up at the ceiling. I guess I need some water; my throat is dry. All the sinks are so far away. I stay in bed. Ideally I'd be going back to sleep. I could let so much time pass without being conscious of it, but I'm not sleepy.

I can hear my phone buzzing with a notification every once in a while. It's on the nightstand, which isn't very far away, but my arm is too heavy. I could reach it if I tried. All I need to do is lift my arm. I don't. I look at the phone and I look at my arm. It's probably Kevin, so there's no reason I shouldn't respond. Maybe it's Tom checking up on me. The idea of speaking to anyone just seems so draining, so effortful. I need to try so hard. I don't want to do that right now.

When Tom comes back, I've managed to move over to the couch. I've made the effort to seem like I'm doing okay. I'm still in my pyjamas. Getting dressed, at this point, doesn't feel like it would require more effort than it did to finally empty my bladder. The difficult part would be selecting what clothes to wear. It's just fabric, and I'm too tired to feel anything about fabric.

His face is icy cold from the outside and he keeps his hands by his sides instead of touching my face with his frozen fingers. He hasn't even taken his jacket off when he kisses me, as if he was in a hurry to get back to me.

'How are you feeling?' he asks.

'Better,' I say. Which I suppose isn't a lie, because I managed to leave bed.

He takes off his jacket and sits down next to me. He motions for me to move closer, and I do, putting my head on his shoulder. It makes me feel at home. It makes me feel secure.

'You poor thing,' he says. 'Better how? Do you still have a headache?'

I nod, tired.

He places his hand on my forehead, cold from outdoors. 'No fever.'

I feel so taken care of and I smile up at him, running my hand down his cheek.

'Do we have any food that's expiring today?'

I give him a curious look, trying to see if I can understand why he would be asking about that. He looks like he's up to something, like a mischievous child who's proud of misbehaviour.

'I don't know,' I say. 'Why?'

'Well, I was thinking, unless there's something we need to get rid of, maybe we should order some pizza.' He smiles, sitting down on the couch next to me, an arm around my shoulder. 'I think you could do with some pizza today.'

There's an instant wetness in my eyes, my chest aching to cry. What a man I have. There's so much love in his eyes, such affection in the words he's just said. I put my hand on his face and press my forehead against his. He's been thinking about how I'm not doing well, he's been worried about me, he's been wondering what he could do to make things better. This is what it's like to be loved.

I'm grinning as if this pizza is life-changing.

'I'll assume that's a yes?' He laughs.

I nod. 'Let me just check the fridge first.'

'We can let it rot, Nicki.'

'It's okay.'

It's not the pizza I care about, after all. The concern was enough. Even if we end up putting a chicken in the oven, I'll go this entire evening feeling all warm and fuzzy. I put my phone down and stand up. Suddenly, it's not difficult any more. My legs obey me just like that, and walking over to the kitchen is as simple as it should be.

I check the fridge and determine that nothing here is going to suffer from not being eaten immediately. Tonight I'll be having pizza in front of the telly with the man I love; I'll be dressed in my pyjamas, I'll put my legs over him and my head on his shoulder. I'll let him choose what to watch, because I'll only be looking at him.

He looks up at me from the couch. He looks serious. I see that he's holding my phone in his hand, and I stop smiling.

I didn't close the screen before I left, did I? I left it open on the coffee table.

'Nicki,' he says, 'why do you have Tinder?'

45

Amber

No lunch and no friends means there isn't much to do during my free periods except find somewhere to sit and scroll through my phone. It took me a couple of days to find a good spot. It's too cold outside, too cramped in the cafeteria. There's lots of hangout spaces, but there's always people. People chatting with their friends, watching silly YouTube videos together, making out with their boyfriends and girlfriends in full view of everyone else. People looking at me like I'm a fucking alien because I'm all by myself in a corner, too big to make myself unnoticeable.

In the end, I started going to the girls' toilets. I sit down on a toilet lid in a locked cubicle, where no one can see anything except my legs, and at worst they think I'm constipated because of how long I'm in there. Doesn't matter; they can't tell who I am by my feet.

That's where I go now. I hang my purse on the hook on the door, put the lid down, and sit. I can hear someone peeing in another cubicle. There's a bit of toilet paper on the floor and I'm careful not to get it stuck on my shoes. I listen as the other person flushes and washes her hands and I get my phone out.

I have a text from Marnie. That's a surprise. I didn't even get those back when we were friends. She's sent me nothing but an image. It's confusing, but for a moment, I think that maybe it's a screenshot of a text from Melissa, talking about me. Does she miss me? Does she wish she could talk to me again? Does she feel bad for me?

I was wrong. The picture is of me walking down the hall-way; it looks like it's from a couple of minutes ago when I was heading in here. My butt looks huge and way too wide. She's drawn a pink, curled little tail on my ass, like a pig's, and a couple of pig ears to match, sticking out from the sides of my head.

She's typing. *Pig*, is all she says.

I wonder if she's with Melissa right now. She can't be. If Melissa was aware of this, she wouldn't be allowing it. She wouldn't let Marnie turn me into a pig and then send it to me.

I don't reply to Marnie, and she's noticed.

Too scared to face some consequences, piggy?

I can't believe you thought he'd cheat on Melissa with YOU

I take a deep breath. There's a quiver in my throat like I'm about to cry. I don't let myself; someone might come in and hear me at any point. Marnie's not a bad friend, not really. She's protecting someone she cares about. I was just never worthy of that, I guess.

I don't want to seem weak. It would be pathetic to roll over and take this, it would give her more ammunition, and I don't want her to think even more badly of me than she does. So I pretend I don't have a huge lump in my throat and I'm hiding in a toilet cubicle.

I get it, you're mad, I write. *But you literally have nothing to do with this, it's me and Melissa's business and you don't even know the full story.*

The full story doesn't make me look much better, so I have no plans on telling it to her. But maybe she'll believe there's more to it than she'd thought, and maybe she'll believe that Melissa had something to do with it too. She kissed me that night, didn't she? No one was pissed about that, no one called her a slut. They're not even technically dating.

You don't think I know the full story? Marnie replies. *That's weird because Melissa says that I do.*

Do you want me to ask her again?

Because she's right here

I feel ice cold. She is there. Maybe she suggested making me into a pig. Maybe she was laughing the whole time. Maybe she's the one who got annoyed when I didn't reply. Maybe she suggested the whole thing.

Melissa's in on it. That's how much she hates me now. I start snivelling, covering my mouth with my hand. I don't wear make-up any more, so there's no need to worry about any mascara.

Lying slut, Marnie writes.

Or maybe it's Melissa.

46

Nicki

'Nicki.' His voice is firmer, harder, angry that he has to repeat himself. 'Why do you have Tinder?'

He gets up from the couch and we stand facing each other.

I feel like a deer in headlights. I feel like I'm about to die. My body, useless, is shutting down. I'd like to say something, but my brain has no words and my mouth will not move. I'd like to stand firm, but I can't feel the ground beneath my feet and my legs are soft, weak, incapable of carrying me.

The ridiculousness of the fact that I'm still in my pyjamas, my bottoms frayed at the seams and the t-shirt oversized, my feet bare.

'Jesus Christ.' Tom looks away and drags a hand over his face. 'You're not going to say anything, then?'

What is there to say? Excuses, empty words. Things will be different from now on, I could say. But what's the point of lying?

He looks at my phone screen. I can see his jaw tightening, I can see his other hand clenching by his side. He could break bones like this. He's looking at my profile, of course. He's reading my chats to determine the extent of my betrayal. He is going to see every. Single. Part. Of. Me.

The man from the night of his suicide attempt. Kevin. Marcus. Adam. All the others. He is going to see who I truly am. He is going to be so disgusted at having slept next to me for all these years that he's going to shower for a week.

But I'm overwhelmed by a sense of relief.

It's over now. There is no need to hide, because I have been found. All the hard work I've put into pretending to be the person he wants, all my efforts at seeming normal, it's over. I am so tired of it all. I am so drained. It feels so good to free myself of this mask, to get this burden off my shoulders. I am known.

'Fuck.' He puts my phone on the table; it is too much, I know. I am difficult to know fully. He looks at me again, his mouth slightly agape. 'How long have you been doing this?'

'Always,' I say. 'I've always been like this.'

Before Tinder, there were the boys at school. There was Wallace. Men at clubs. Employers. Anyone who would have me, I took it. I couldn't stop it.

Tom doesn't look angry. He looks sad. 'All the time we've been together?'

There's a tug towards the lies, the comfort of the made-up world we've lived in. *Of course not, they don't mean anything, I love you, Tom.* But I can't do it any more. I don't have the energy. I can't pick the act back up.

'Yes,' I say. 'Not for the first few months, but then . . . Then I went back.'

That was the first time he hit me. I'd been out until the early hours of the morning, and I came home to our first fight. Where have you been, what were you doing, who were you with? I didn't tell him, of course. But a part of him must have sensed it, and he struck me. My first thought was *I deserve it*. After what I just did, he has every right.

'Six years.' He stands up, his expression that of someone who is lost. 'How many of these men have you slept with?'

'I don't know,' I say. I haven't kept count. I don't think I could.

'Fuck,' he says again. He's looking around, his breathing quickening. 'Fuck!'

It's a shout now. It makes me flinch. Here's the rage, the justified, well-deserved anger I knew was coming. I brace myself, feel my heartbeat picking up a pace. But I don't move. I've made this bed, and now I'll lie in it. Giving him the satisfaction of retaliation, that's the least I could do after all I've done to him. The pain I've put him through, the lies I've told.

'Too many to count,' I say.

His eyes find me, his chest heaving. His eyes have the darkness I know so well.

'Most of them blur together,' I say, and I know it's cruel, I know it's harsh, but I can't stop myself. I feel so much lighter with every sentence I say. 'A lot of them I can't properly remember. Not even their names.'

'You fucking whore,' he says, voice low. Familiar.

And I know what I deserve, and I just want him to stop dragging it out.

And he does.

47

Amber

Today is the day.

They reminded us in school, of course. Every single class, the teachers felt they had to mention it.

'All right everyone, I hope you've got your UCAS applications done. Who's sent them in already?'

Hands flying up, most of them. Mine too, because I couldn't let everyone else know I don't have it under control. I felt fine until I saw all those hands going up. I thought a lot of us probably haven't got it fully figured out yet; everyone else will have picked a uni, I guess, but maybe not the course they want. Or the other way around. And then I realized that I'm the only one who has no idea what I'm doing and my stomach tightened and my hand went up. Months, it's been months, and I keep putting it off, and I can't do it much longer. I can't keep pretending I have it under control.

'Who here has decided to do English?' said Mr Miller, smiling with futile hope, awkward hands held together, no one saying anything. A cough somewhere in the classroom, and Mr Miller cleared his throat and moved on.

No, I'm not doing English. But it's the last day I have to fill in this application. And I still have no idea what to apply for.

Now I'm at home, and the UCAS homepage is staring at me from the laptop screen. I haven't even logged in yet.

These are the next three years of my life. That should really matter to me, shouldn't it? Mum's right; it's my time to reinvent myself. I can be skinnier by the time I get there, not slim, but closer to it. There will be new people who won't know me, who will have no idea about the mess I've made. No more looks in the classroom, no more free periods spent hiding in a toilet cubicle so I won't be seen alone. Everyone will be alone. Everyone will be needing friends, and they'll be desperate enough that even I might be good enough.

But I'm kidding myself, because there's only so many things you can change about who you are. I won't be any skinnier. I won't be any more likable as a person. I'll still be fat, I'll still be single and never have got laid, I'll be making up stories about my friends at home because everyone else has some.

There won't be any friends. When's the last time I managed to make a friend by myself? In reception, when I met Melissa, and even then I'm pretty sure she did most of the work. Just like she did for the next thirteen years. I don't have that kind of charisma. I would've never known Marnie or Kim or Dan if it wasn't for her. Why would things be any different now?

I was supposed to have her around still. We were meant to do this together. That's gone to shit. I knew one thing about this application and that's where I wanted to go, but what's the point in Falmouth if she'll spend the entire time avoiding me? I know nothing about Falmouth Uni or the city, I've no reason at all to go. It would be so nice to bang my head against this laptop right now.

Instead, I go scrolling through the subjects. Accountancy is up first, which makes me feel like vomiting. Animal behaviour and welfare, what the fuck am I supposed to do with that? It's not even a veterinary course. I scroll down and reject course after course because nothing interests me. Nursing, like I would ever be wiping people's butts for them. History,

278

not even one of my A levels. I don't know the order of the ways Henry VIII got rid of his wives.

Life feels so big, it stretches out in front of me beyond where I can see it. I've never thought to look very far until now, never planned further than a week ahead, at most. That's all over now. I need to decide what I want to do full-time for the next three years, costing my mum tens and tens of thousands. Three years is such a long time. I know what I want to eat today. I know what clothes I want to put on tomorrow. In a few hours I'll probably have an idea of what I want to watch on Netflix tonight. I have absolutely no clue what I want to do with the rest of my life.

Down the list I go, barely looking at the words any more. I force myself to unblur my eyes and keep focus. There are so many subjects I can't even take the time to contemplate them individually. I go with my gut reaction, which is always *Ugh*, and then I move on. There are five pages initially, but when I've gone through all of them, even more appear. It never ends. Physics, entering nerd territory. Philosophy, I don't even know what that means. Easy ticket to a degree, I guess.

I rub my eyes. My finger's a little sore, so I stop scrolling to give it a break. That's when I notice that I have psychology on the screen. Psychology. It gives me pause. I consider the word. It makes me think about doctors sitting around and listening to other people's problems. I've never cared much about other people's problems, but I do like the idea of sitting around. And it makes me think about Nicki.

I bite my nail and stare at the word. I've never considered psychology before. I've never known someone with a mental illness before. It always felt foreign, like something I knew existed but somewhere far, far away from me. It's not like that any more. It's right next to me, pressing and urgent and painful in a way I never imagined. Wouldn't that be a great problem to solve?

I open up a new tab and google the best universities for psychology. I look through them, check out what the modules are, the career options they list for the degree. I don't know what all these words are, so I search for them. There are countless psychology books available. I read the blurbs and I can't remember the last time I read a book, but I save these titles. They interest me. I'll look at which ones are available in the school library.

Wow. It doesn't make my stomach turn. It makes me excited. I could be a therapist one day, or a community health nurse, a psychologist, anything. A job I never knew existed: eating disorder counsellor. I might like that. I'll stop anyone from ever feeling as fat and as hungry as I do. Not that I have an eating disorder, but . . .

I'll stop anyone from feeling as lonely and afraid as Nicki again. I'll save any scared child who went through what she did.

I write a personal statement. *I have a friend named Nicki*, is how it starts. And I channel everything into it.

She's told me about the nightmares, the flashbacks, the emotions she goes through. She's told me about therapy, the uselessness of it. The way that one man used that position to abuse her further. I just want someone to help me, that's what she said. I just want someone to help me but no one knows how. She told me I wouldn't understand, and I tried to. Maybe I can try harder. Maybe I can understand. It's silly, but I think that maybe I might end up figuring out how to help. At least one person I could help. I could provide some therapy that isn't useless.

The statement comes easily, the words flowing out of me and onto the page.

The future has never been very clear before, just blurry. Now there's suddenly something there, something beyond school that doesn't involve Melissa, something that exists even after university.

I'm ready to send in my application. I look at my list of choices. Psychology at a bunch of different universities in places I've never been to, a subject I'm not even doing for my A levels. Fuck it, I'll get into at least one of them.

I submit it.

48

Nicki

Everything hurts. I dragged myself into bed last night without fully realizing how bad it was. I was tired, I was confused. Then I woke up and the duvet was causing me pain. It wasn't soft and comforting, it was heavy and hard on my sore body.

My vision is blurry and unclear. The sheets are red, my head sticking to the pillow, skin and hair covered with dried blood. I move the duvet to the side. My pyjamas are stained too; I'm glad I never got dressed yesterday. I think about all the laundry I have to do. There's a terrible headache throbbing inside my temples, my body is so weak, everything hurts, and I can't bear the thought of lugging all this to the kitchen.

Rolling over makes me lose my breath. It feels like I've just been stabbed. My head pulsates, my ribs are on fire. I hear myself squeal weakly, softly. I manage to gather myself together and look at the clock. It's past ten. I was supposed to be at work two hours ago, I think. I can't remember right now. Everything is so fuzzy. They've probably been calling, but I can't remember where my phone ended up yesterday.

Yesterday. It sparks memories. My body tenses, I fold myself inwards on reflex.

Is Tom home? I listen carefully for sounds. The flat is silent. I can hear the cars down on the street, the steps of my upstairs neighbour. The telly isn't on, the shower isn't running, there's nothing being cooked in the kitchen. Tom must be at work.

He left last night. I watched him go from the floor. I remember staring at his shoes as he rummaged around for his phone and his keys, muttering to himself.

He won't be calling home to apologize this time. I know it. There won't be a heartfelt reunion, there won't be any more promises. He won't look at this face and recoil in shame at what he's done. This time is different. This time, it was properly my fault. It wasn't an overreaction. Six years of his life, that's what I took.

These things can't be thought of right now. I brush them aside.

I need to get up. I need to find my phone and call work. Maybe they assume I'm still ill, like I told them yesterday. But maybe they don't, and I have bills to pay. Slowly, I turn over onto my other side. I clasp a hand to the edge of the bed, bloody and bruised, nails broken. I need to get up.

I bite down and do it. My body screams as I sit up. Every muscle is on fire. Breathing hurts. The clothes stick to my body with the blood, and trying to pull them off is too painful. My stomach is full of sharp needles. I breathe deeply, tears in my eyes. *Okay. Okay. Get up.*

My legs aren't that bad. They carry me just fine, though my stomach hurts all the more when I stand upright. It makes my head swim, my vision darkening and blurring. I hobble out of the bedroom with an arm around my stomach, squeezing one eye shut, because it hurts a little less that way.

There are drops of blood on the floor all the way to the living room. A dent in the wall where my head went. It might have been better if I'd died last night, and didn't have to answer to the landlord about this damage.

My phone is still on the coffee table, almost out of charge.

Tom hasn't been in touch. I didn't expect him to really. So many missed calls from work. Texts in all caps from Janet, my manager. *WHERE ARE YOU? CALL ME BACK RIGHT NOW.*

I press on her name and listen to the dial tone. Please, let her not fire me.

'Nicki!' Her voice cuts like glass, making me wheeze, holding the phone further away from my ear. 'Where on earth have you been?'

'I'm so sorry,' I say. My voice doesn't sound right, all sorts of hoarse and weak, throat burning. 'I'm still ill. I got a bit worse.'

'Well, Jesus,' Janet says. 'You need to phone in next time. We have lots of folks on your schedule today, and we had to figure out how else to take care of them. You can't come in at all?'

I close my eyes. How could I walk into the office looking like this? Would I say I got hit by a bus? I can't do it. I can't help Mr Anderson out of bed when I'm just as much in need of it. I couldn't carry a tray of food the way my wrists feel. There isn't even Edith to brighten up my day.

'No,' I say. 'No, I'm really not well.'

Janet sighs. 'It would've been useful to get some notice.'

'I'm sorry. I just didn't wake up in time.'

'Well, you've put me in a bad spot,' she says.

I expect her to continue, but there's nothing else. She just wanted to remind me that I'm a burden.

'Sorry.'

'This won't be happening again, yeah?'

'Of course.'

'Will you be well enough tomorrow?'

My stomach turns at the idea. 'No. I'll need a few more days.'

'How many? I need to write it in, you know, so we can plan.'

I start to feel dizzy. It seems like a simple question, but I don't know the answer. I can't think.

'Nicki?'

'A week,' I say. 'Sorry. A week.'

It won't be enough time for the bruises to disappear, but it will give me an opportunity to come up with a story about them. I wonder if I will get sick pay for this. A week of wages is a lot. It doesn't seem like the right time to ask, after all the trouble I've caused.

After hanging up, I go to the bathroom. I empty my over-full bladder with the lights off and the door open; the lamp in here would be too bright for me in this state. My back aches as I bend over, as I stand back up, as I move.

I wash the blood off my hands. It makes the bruising more pronounced. The skin is broken in some places. I look in the mirror to see what I have to deal with in terms of my face.

The dim lighting does little to protect me. I don't recognize myself. This person, with her tousled hair and bruised face, her broken, swollen lip and cut cheek, skin varying in colour from green to black, one eye so swollen it's barely open, she looks like my mum. I stare at her. It's been over fifteen years since I last saw her. I don't know if she's still alive. I don't know if she still regularly looks like this. So many times over the years, I swore that I would never be like her.

Everything feels horrendously real. I sit back down on the toilet lid, and I start crying.

I manage a shower. I manage to change from my bloody pyjamas into a big t-shirt. I don't manage to take the sheets off the bed or try to clean up the blood.

It's been half a day since I woke up, and that's all I've done. I don't feel hungry, though I feel like I should be. There's nothing in the fridge that I can eat raw. I miss Tom. I want him to hold me and tell me everything is okay. I want the apologies again, the reassurance that everything will be fine. Kisses on my forehead, plasters on my wounds. Someone to wipe away my tears. But he won't do that. He won't do that after what I did, and so the idea of seeing him is simultaneously terrifying. All the anger that I saw yesterday, it won't be gone.

I don't know what to do. Nothing can go back to the way it was before he found out. I've probably lost him for ever, I'll probably never be forgiven, and I shouldn't be. I don't deserve forgiveness. I don't deserve a return to normality. But then, what else is there? There's nowhere I can go, there's nothing I can do. I have no home except here with him. I have no one besides him.

He'll come back, and he won't want me to stay. Who could blame him? No one wants to sleep next to someone like me at night. It can't even be fathomed what kind of existence we could create together after last night. Will he look at men on the street and ask me if I've been with them? Will I come home at night and tell him about who I just got fucked by?

I don't know what to do, and there's no one here to tell me. I text Kevin.

Hi

I mean to send a second text explaining how I feel, what the context is, what I need help with. That I'm not okay. But I can't. I stare at the screen and my fingers won't move, I try to think and I don't know what to say.

Everything's a lie, Kevin. Everything's a lie and my life is a

286

*mess. Do you still care about me now? Do you still want to hear from
me when you know the truth?*

Minutes go by. I wish messages could be unsent. I could
delete it, but then he'd be able to see that I have. Suddenly,
the text under his name says Active Now. I can feel my heart
pounding instantly. The message is marked as read.

You okay? he asks.

Yes, I type, and don't send. Erase. Type it out again. Erase.
Type *No* instead, erase.

I put my phone down. I take a deep, quivering breath. I've
never told anyone before. Ever. Not even Kate, even as I cried
in her arms, as she begged me to tell her what was wrong. I
know how stupid it makes me look. How weak. I remember
how I looked at my own mother. Never, ever was I going to
let someone think I was like that. They would never understand how different it was with me and Tom. No one would
ever believe that—

That what? I make him hit me? It's all my fault?

Do I believe that?

I pick my phone back up.

Not really

We had a fight

The message is read. I wait. I watch the dots appearing,
wait for him to finish writing.

Want to talk about it?

No, I don't. But at some point, I suppose I'll have to.

One step at a time. I take a selfie and send it.

It takes him a long time to reply. For a while there, I don't
expect him to. I can't blame him. Things just got complicated. I just got real, and the reality of me isn't pretty. The
reality of me isn't something any decent person could possibly want.

Did he do that to you?

Yes, but it wasn't his fault. Yes, but I provoked him. Yes, but I deserved it, I think. I've never told anyone. As much as Kate pleaded with me, I knew what she'd do if she found out. I'd rather let her go than tell her. I'm tempted to do the same with Kevin, block him and leave his life for ever, go on as if he never existed. Jesus, what will he think of me? I didn't need Kate to judge me, I don't need Kevin to judge me now. I'm not as weak as I look, but then I guess I am. Fuck. I struggle to breathe. I've never told anyone and it's so hard.

He found my Tinder app

And? That doesn't make it right

I hurt him

It doesn't give him the right to hurt you back

I'm crying, just a little. I'm looking silly, aren't I? It must seem so strange to him that I would be defending this man. Don't I have a backbone? Am I just like my mother? I can't explain to him just how much I love Tom, despite everything.

Kevin: *Nicki, listen to me*

You have to leave him

Nicki: *I can't*

Kevin: *Why not?*

Nicki: *I have nowhere else to go*

Kevin: *I will help you in any way I can, but you have to get out of there*

I can't let him do this to you

Nicki: *I love him*

I know it doesn't make sense, but I love him

Kevin: *It doesn't matter that you love him*

He doesn't love you back
Nicki: *Yes, he does*
Why else would he care enough to do this?
Kevin: *Has he talked to you today? Has he checked how you're doing?*

I squeeze my eyes shut. He's bound to still be angry, so of course he wouldn't be worrying about how I'm doing. Of course he wouldn't. I don't deserve his concern after what I've done. And still. The absence of contact stings.

I open my eyes again.

He doesn't care. If he did, he wouldn't be doing this to you

But that's not true, is it? Because I care about him more than anything in this world, and look at all I've done to hurt him.

All I can see is his face last night. The soreness in the side of my chest is constant, the ache in my head persistent. My own face in the mirror.

If he doesn't care about me, I write, *then no one does.*

Another thing I've never told a soul. I'm unloveable. *Do you still want to stick around?* I force myself to press send, I wipe my tears as it's marked Seen. I've been seen. I've been seen in a way I never have before, by a man I've never met. I've let him see me and it can't be undone, and maybe I don't want it to be. Because I feel just like I felt last night: relieved, light, relaxed. And tired, so tired.

Kevin: *That's not true*
I care about you
Nicki: *Only because you don't know me*
Kevin: *Tell me what I need to do to prove it*
Nicki: *You can't*
Kevin: *Tell me*

I'm sobbing, my nose running, and it hurts to wipe it. Makes me sob harder, from two different kinds of pain. Kevin's sent me a link to some kind of organization offering shelter for victims of domestic violence. It makes my stomach turn to be reduced to that phrase.

I find myself gasping for air. My chest is so tight. The world is getting unclear, blurring at the edges, fading. I know what this is – I'm going back. Dad. I try to shake it off me, steady the reality around me. My phone screen lights up so suddenly I flinch. But it's a little light in the darkness, a little piece of what's real.

Nicki, talk to me

Typing is difficult, my vision distorted and my fingers stiff and clumsy.

I can't do it

Yes you can

Tom is the only thing I look forward to during the day. If it weren't for him, I'd have nothing to wake up to. I'd have no one to cling to when things get bad. I'd have nothing to keep me grounded, nothing to make me smile, no one to hold me. And I need, so desperately, for someone to put their arms around me hard enough that I can feel it. Does it matter if he loves me? Does it matter if I love him? I need him.

Nicki: *You don't understand*

Kevin: *Then explain it to me, and I'll try*

Nicki: *He might not be perfect, but neither am I*

Look at what I've done to him, and so much other shit that you don't even know about

We deserve each other

And no one but him could ever love me

I think thoughts I haven't allowed myself to think in a long time. I think that without Tom, I'll have to kill myself.

There's nothing else to do; I don't know how to go on without him.

That's not true, Kevin writes. *I love you.*

I look at the room around me. There's our picture from the trip to Naples. And on my phone there's the link that Kevin just sent me.

49

Amber

I move fast from the classroom to the toilets, it's the only way I won't be seen. The key is to hunch your shoulders and look at the ground so no one sees your face. It would be so embarrassing if anyone noticed how I spend every free period, like a lonely loser with chronic constipation. It would be embarrassing if anyone remembered I even exist. I prefer to be invisible for the last few months I have left here.

I've seen Dan, distantly, a few times. I don't know if he's ever seen me. He probably doesn't want to remember that he ever sank low enough to call me his girlfriend. There's a new girl he hangs out with a lot now, someone whose name I don't know. Someone skinny with shiny hair and a perfect fake tan. She's got braces, though, so there's always that.

Brandon and I walked past each other in the hallway once. I didn't see him coming in the opposite direction until it was too late and he was right in front of me. I wish I'd had the time to duck into another room or turn around. We made eye contact. He didn't smile at me. I looked away. And that was that. I cringed as I remembered what I'd done to him. He probably remembers the way I tasted that night, all alcohol and orange juice, how I must have smelled of sweat and booze as I pressed up against him.

Kim and Marnie ignore me in English. They share gum and laugh, angling their phone screens at each other and taking selfies doing the peace sign. Mr Miller doesn't try to stop them, as usual. Sometimes he looks just a little distraught, and I almost feel bad for him. I never noticed that expression on him before. The little drop of his shoulders as he gives up and sits back down, pretending we'll all be doing our work.

I don't see Melissa really. Sometimes there's a speck of bright red hair in an ocean of people, and I strain to catch a glimpse before I remember that as long as I can't see her, she probably can't spot me either. All the better if she doesn't. I don't want to see that look on her face again.

So I walk fast to the toilets, and I sit myself down. I put my face in my hands. I'm tired these days, weak like I've worked out, even though I haven't been yet. My muscles are sore today, my thighs aching from the gym last night. I was there for two hours. The pain's a sign it's working; Mum once told me that. Until I have to go down any stairs, I like it. I picture the fat inside my body dissolving, melting away like ice cream.

I message Nicki. *How are you settling in?*

I've been thinking about her a lot today. She was on my mind all throughout class. I don't know why I didn't text her earlier. I guess because I was waiting for her to do it first. She was so busy yesterday, and she'll still have much bigger things on her mind. I don't want to intrude. And at the same time, I worry. Maybe Tom called her and she went back home. Maybe he showed up at the shelter and he knows where she is. Maybe the shelter is absolutely terrible.

She logs in. I log out, so I don't seem like I've been waiting for her.

I'm okay, just lying in bed right now

I exhale. She's okay. I give it another five seconds before I open the app back up and reply.

Kevin: *How is the place?*

Nicki: *Decent, can't complain*

Pretty crowded, but that's to be expected

Kevin: *Clean?*
Nicki: *Yes, it's good actually*
Mattress is pretty hard but I got some sleep
Kevin: *And how are you? Are you okay?*

She takes her time with that one, like it's something she has to think over.

I'm in less pain today, the bruising around my eye has gone down, and they don't think I need to see a doctor if I don't want to
And you don't?
No

How superficial things feel today. This is small talk, like we've just run into each other at a bus stop and haven't spoken in years. I don't like it. It's so different to how things usually feel with her: effortless, enjoyable. This feels like Dan, or hanging out with Kim and Marnie without Melissa.

She hasn't mentioned what I said yesterday, and I don't think she will. I guess that's what we're doing with it. That's fair; she's going through a break-up. She just got beaten up by her boyfriend. I shouldn't have sprung something like that on her. I could at least have had the decency to add that it's platonic, that I love her as a friend, or some dumb shit like that. But I didn't mean to do it. I was overwhelmed. I was just as surprised as her.

But it's true, isn't it? I realized that as soon as I saw it in writing. *I love her*, I thought, shocked. This is love, and it ambushed me. I'm thinking it now, too; I love her. This is what that feels like. Much better than any time I said it to Dan. It's like with Melissa.

Has he called you? I ask.
No, and I haven't called him either, didn't say a word
I'm proud of you
It's a bit callous, isn't it? After six years

Look at yourself in a mirror, and then come back to me about who's callous here

Like a child, I hope this makes her laugh a little bit. I think about the way her laugh sounds, I'm sad I'll never hear it, and it keeps hitting me again and again. I love her. It hurts me to see her in this much pain. I look at the picture she sent me last night, I've looked at it so many times, and it makes me wince. I want to protect her from all harm. She doesn't deserve it. Maybe I do fantasize about finding this Tom, and giving him a piece of his own medicine.

I'm essentially useless. Like I'm trying to pick up something that's falling but I'm too far away and my arms just aren't long enough, and if I stretch out far, I could almost graze it as it goes past. Crashing onto the floor.

I wish I could help you, I say.

You do, she writes, and it gives me a little flutter. *I appreciate your concern.*

Concern is fine, but in the end it's all words. There's nothing I can actually do. Yesterday, she told me I wouldn't care about her if I knew who she truly was. That isn't true. But words are never going to be enough to convince her, and I know this. I know this because I do know her, and that's not the kind of person she is. She needs action.

I mean actually help you, I write. *If you were closer to me, I could let you crash on my couch instead of a shelter*

Yeah, not a problem, I can definitely go over to Australia, who needs work anyway?

Fuck that, I could give you a job at my company if you needed one

My screen is without activity for a while. She's still logged in.

Do you really mean that? she asks.

And I realize that it might actually be working. I straighten my back. Tell me what I can do to prove it, and it's done. In this moment, I'll say anything she needs to hear.

Of course, I say.

You're too kind to me

Barely kind enough

Now maybe she knows. I feel strange: weak and dizzy. She's not arguing any more. I think it worked. I did something that actually helped. She knows I care. She knows she has someone that cares. Mustn't that be the best feeling in the world?

I did mean it, I write. *I would be happy to help you if I could*

I'm really tired, she says.

That's okay, I say.

And then she sends me a smiling emoji, cheeks blushing and eyes squeezed. It makes my heart do little cartwheels in my chest. Again I think, *Fuck, I love her*.

And the worst part is, I think she might love me too. But she doesn't know I exist.

50

Nicki

This is temporary. That's what I tell myself when I wake up, alone, on a mattress that's too thin. The wall in front of me bare, the room smelling like nothing familiar. It looks like a prison cell. There is nothing in here except the little night-stand and my suitcase open on the floor. I sit on the edge of the bed and I tell myself this is temporary.

Elsa, my case worker, said this is an emergency room for women who arrive at short notice. In a few weeks, I could get one like the others have, with my own kitchenette and an en suite. I don't want to be here in a few weeks. I told her as much, and she said she'd help me find a place of my own. It almost offended me, the suggestion that I would need help. I'm older than her, I have a full-time job, I know how to do this. I've lived by myself before. But it's been a long time.

I'm not like the other women here, I wanted to say. I'm not an eighteen-year-old with a baby on my hip, I don't have a drug addiction. But that's before I saw the others, when she showed me the communal kitchen and the common area with the couches and the telly. One of the women is fifteen years older than me and dresses in skirts and cardigans; she was reading *Jane Eyre* that day with a pair of glasses on her nose. I met another woman named Susan, who has a five-year-old and a teenager and who looks just like any one of my co-workers. Once I bumped into someone in the kitchen who couldn't have been older than twenty, she had a nose ring and she told me she was studying for an exam, books

297

spread out before her on the kitchen table and the kettle boiling for her tea.

I'm exactly like these women, I thought. The only thing we have in common is we've made some terrible, terrible choices when it comes to men.

I get up, get dressed and take my toothbrush and toothpaste out to the bathroom. It isn't occupied today. Sometimes it is, and I have to stand outside the door, toothbrush in hand, like I'm queuing in the supermarket. I wash my face and brush my teeth. The mirror is splattered with toothpaste stains and fingerprint marks. I can hear people out in the kitchen; by the sounds of it, it's Susan and the boys. A kitchen timer going off and her loud voice yapping at them.

The common room is empty right now. It's easy to sneak back to my room undetected. There's a pile of my dirty laundry on the floor in the corner, and I know I should take it down to the laundry room soon. I'm almost out of underwear. I couldn't bring very much; I didn't have time or the suitcase space. But the laundry room makes me nervous. It's right on the other side of the wall, and I've heard women congregate in there while they're waiting for a wash. I don't want to be ambushed by someone else while I'm in there, forced to make small talk. Assessed up and down with curious eyes, unsaid questions in the air about who I am and why I'm here. I look dreadful still, with my face bruised and swollen.

Out of all people, these women would understand. They wouldn't judge me. But what they've been through, the men they've had, is all so very different from my situation. Tom isn't a bad man. I've provoked and betrayed him for over six years, and I got what was coming for me. He never raped me. He didn't hit me every day, every week, or even every month. It's never been quite this bad before.

He wouldn't kill me if I went back. These women, that's what they've been through. That's what's at stake for them. I don't feel deserving of this room I have. Everything that's happened to me has been my own fault, and there are so many worse situations out there. The lady I saw the first day I was here, her wrists were full of scars. Vertical, not horizontal, a sign that she was serious. I wonder if someone's out on the streets because of the bed I'm occupying.

But I don't need Elsa's help. I'm well acquainted with Zoopla, and I've been scrolling through all the flats within my price range in Brighton. One agency has got back to me so far. I have my first viewing today, a place there weren't a lot of pictures of. It's central, though, and it's cheap. Most importantly, it's far away from Kemptown. I don't want to ever risk running into Tom again.

I take my meds and a painkiller, drinking from a water bottle I keep in the window. The viewing is in an hour, and I'll pick up some food on the way. I haven't cooked anything in this kitchen, and I'm not planning to. It's an even more social place than the laundry room.

I haven't been back to work yet. I took out another week of sick leave. I'll have to go back at some point, and I know that, but not right now. Getting out of bed feels insurmountable every morning. Leaving my room is something I dread, rushing back and forth fast, peeking round every corner and dodging other residents. Returning to work would require me to return to a normal existence. Getting up at a decent time, having a few meals a day, going to work and back, going to the supermarket to stock up on food and snacks and tampons. I'm not ready for that kind of reality yet. My days are slow and easy underneath the duvet. I don't know how to do the job without a car either. I take the bus everywhere these days. I had to leave the car behind; it's in his name.

I brush my hair. I prepare to run out to the front door before anyone can say hi to me.

'Hello, hello, come on in!'

The man from the agency is wearing a grey suit and smiles like someone from a dental commercial. There's a familiar surge of danger in my chest; I suppose I'd hoped a woman would be showing the property because a woman picked up the phone when I called.

He looks harmless, he probably is, and he needs to get this flat rented out, so of course he wouldn't do anything to me. It's just the standard risk assessment.

'Thank you,' I say, stepping in.

This is barely a hallway. It's a tiny passage, just big enough for the door on the other side to open. The man from the agency points at it and says, 'That's the kitchen.'

'Okay,' I say.

'You live alone?' he asks.

I don't really want to admit it. I'm in my mid-thirties now, and I shouldn't be at this stage of my life. It's been five years since Tom and I went to view our flat. Well, it's his now, I suppose. He didn't like the way the windows faced west instead of east.

'This is temporary,' he said. 'Until we can buy our own place.'

'Yes,' I say. 'Just me.'

The agent's phone rings. He takes it out of his pocket. 'Hold on, let me get this. I'll be right out here if you have any questions, have a look around and I'll be with you soon.'

He squeezes past me out of the front door. He leaves it open and I can hear him speaking, his voice echoing in the stairwell.

I open the kitchen door and look inside. It's about the size of a decent bathroom. There's a hob and an oven and a mini fridge, and just enough counter space for a chopping board or two. I'd never imagined I would be viewing properties without a freezer, and I wonder how I'd buy ice cream if I wanted some. There are no windows in the kitchen. The bin blocks one of the drawers.

I go back in the narrow hallway and open the door on the right. It's the bedroom, or the lounge, or maybe it's both. It's quite big, with bay windows facing the street. I look down at the road. I can hear the cars, and the beeping of the pedestrian crossing. The bed is a double, which isn't too bad. There's a wobbly wardrobe and a couch that looks worn down. The space is too big, and it could do with something more. Maybe an armchair, a desk, a dresser. The carpet is stained. When I touch the windowsill, my finger comes up full of dust.

I cross the hallway for a final time and find the bathroom. It's of the long, narrow kind, a stained-glass window just above the toilet. Some of the tiles are cracked. The shower is dirty, yellowing in the corners. The floor is wet, and I don't know if it's from a leak or the tenant just took a shower before they left. I don't go in. I don't want to see the state of the toilet.

There are questions that Tom always asked when we went to a viewing. Things about the property, the electricity, the plumbing, the works. I try to remember them. I try to remember what he asked when we viewed our flat all those years ago, the ones that made him decide it was a good option. What am I supposed to ask? I don't know what to look for.

The man from the agency is still on the phone outside, smiling a huge, fake smile as if the person on the other end can see it. I don't want to live in this place. I'd like a freezer and a dishwasher, a washing machine, a clean bathroom, a lounge. He sees me and says that he has to go, saying an overly friendly goodbye and stuffing his phone back in his pocket.

Elsa doesn't need to help me with this. I can do it myself. I don't want to stay long enough to get my own room. *This is only temporary*, I tell myself. Once I have a place to sleep, I can take as long as I need to find something I like more.

'That was fast,' the man from the agency says. 'How do you like the place?'

'What's the council tax band?' I ask.

Later, back at the shelter, I've filled out an application form. I've had to name my employer and my salary and I've promised the agency I don't have any children and I don't have any pets. I take a picture of the document and send it to the email address I was given. I wonder if Tom's taken my name off our lease yet.

I've only heard from him once. It took him almost a week to do it, but last night I got a text.

Are you just going to stay away then? is all it said.

Fuck, I'd been waiting for it. I'd been bracing myself so I could resist the temptation to go back, I'd dug my feet into the ground so I could hold on to this independence no matter how much he begged and pleaded and insisted. None of that. Not even asking where I am, if I'm safe, how I'm doing. I left the sheets bloody and the evidence from the carnage everywhere, and it didn't occur to him to ask if I'm okay. *I'm not. I'm not okay, Tom.* So I guess I am staying away.

If he'd asked, I don't know if I could have resisted. I don't want Elsa's pity or Susan's questions, or the flat viewings and the sneaking to and from the bathroom. I want to go home. I want to sleep in my own bed, with my arms wrapped around him, his face there for me to kiss every morning when I wake up. His chest to put my head on when I come back in the evening. Cooking food in the kitchen instead of living off Greggs sandwiches and Tesco ready meals that I frantically heat up in the dead of night. Home, and normality, and him. I'd let him punish me as much as I deserve, just to get back home.

But he won't ask me to come back. Of course he won't.

I open the text back up again, stare at it. Does he miss me? Probably not. He's probably doing great. I never replied. I consider it again now, my fingers over the keypad. No, I won't. There's no point when I know things can never go back to the way they used to be.

I close the chat down. I imagine myself living in the flat I viewed earlier. It's almost impossible. Where would I get the money to buy a telly, or a microwave, or a washing machine? And where would I put it all? I don't know how to fix leaky pipes. I don't think I'd be able to sleep with the road so loud outside. If my application gets approved, I don't see myself getting excited about it. It wouldn't feel like good news.

But this is only temporary. I go back on Zoopla, scrolling through the same flats I've already seen, hoping to find some new ones.

51

Nicki: *You know I'm using you*

Kevin: *For what?*

Nicki: *You make me feel better. I unload on you, I come to you when my mood is bad. I tell you things I wish were true and I tell you things depending on what I need to believe that day I'm using you and it isn't fair*

Kevin: *Isn't that what everyone does?*
   You look at a person and you wonder what they can give you
   That's just what human beings do
   We use each other because we need to

Nicki: *That's not what I mean*
   Of course you get something from a friendship with someone, but not like this, it's more like I'm a patient and you're a therapist, except I don't pay you

Kevin: *You don't have to, I'm on the NHS*

Nicki: *I mean I don't give you anything in return*

Kevin: *Why am I still here, then?*

Nicki: *Why don't you tell me? Because I don't have a fucking clue*

Kevin: *Of course I get something out of this*
   You make me feel likeable

Nicki: *You are*

Kevin: *See?*

52

Amber

I hope you know how fucking disgusting you are

It was a number I didn't recognize. Now, when I'm walking down the school hallway, I imagine that any one of these many people could have sent it. So many faces I don't even recognize properly, some I think might have been at my party, names I don't know. Never spoken to them, but their looks feel so hostile sometimes. Or maybe it's not one of the glares or the hidden laughter, and it's someone who doesn't even bat an eyelid when they see me.

It was probably Marnie, and I know that. It might equally well have been Kim. But the whole school must know by now, it must have spread like wildfire throughout sixth form, and so many people were there at the party. So many know Melissa, or Brandon, or Dan. Popular people who others actually give a shit about. And of course they'd remember something that humiliating. Any one of the people I pass might be looking at me with a blank, neutral face that doesn't reveal anything, and at the same time they could be thinking, *You slut*. There's so much laughter from every corner of the building, all the time, and any of it might be directed at me.

Look at her. She tried to cheat on her boyfriend when she should have been grateful to have one. Right in front of the whole year. She thought Brandon would get with her when he had someone like Melissa.

It's all about the speed. I always get to the toilets fast, swing closed the cubicle door behind me. *Breathe, breathe, it's fine.* No one can see me here.

I hope you know how fucking disgusting you are

As if there's some way I could have missed it.

But today, I don't get that far. I push into the room and I'm stopped in my tracks. Melissa is staring back at me. She's standing at the sink, her hands by the tap. The water is running. Her mouth is shut tight, like she has nothing to say, her eyes unreadable. Her red hair is so very bright from this close.

And that's the last thing I'm aware of.

'How are you feeling?'

The school nurse has her face way too close to mine, her tongue between her teeth as she concentrates on placing a little plaster on my forehead. It stings and I wince.

'I'm fine,' I say. I'm not fine. I feel so cold, so tired, like everything's been drained from my body. My limbs weak and shaky. There's a throbbing in my head from where it hit the floor when I passed out.

'Did it just happen suddenly?' she asks, sitting back down on her swivel chair. 'Were you feeling okay earlier today?'

She looks concerned, a wrinkle on her forehead. She even put away her chewing gum when we came in, spat it out into the bin.

'Yeah,' I say. 'I was a little tired, I guess, but I'm fine.'

She sucks in her lips and nods. 'What did you have for breakfast today?'

'Nothing.' And to alleviate the wrinkle on her forehead and get rid of the worried, anxious tone in her voice, I add, 'I didn't have time.'

'Have you had lunch yet?'

I'm technically meant to be having lunch right now, but I haven't eaten anything today. Is that why I fainted?

'Not yet,' I say. I try a smile to reassure her.

She looks at me, her head tilted to one side. Like she's thinking, like she's considering me.

'Are you going to grab some lunch right now, then?'

'Yeah,' I lie.

But maybe it's not a lie, because she makes it seem like the lack of food is the reason I fainted, and I don't want this to happen again. I didn't know it could. Has it got out of hand? It hasn't, has it? If it had, I wouldn't look like this.

'I feel okay,' I repeat.

Ignore the nausea, ignore the trembling hands, I'm hiding them by gripping on to the bed.

'Have you been getting your period okay?' she asks.

I frown. Does she think I'm pregnant?

'What does my period have to do with it?' I ask.

I don't want to have to tell her that there's absolutely no chance I could be pregnant.

'Is it regular?' the nurse says.

'No,' I say. 'But that's not new. It never has been.'

'Hmm, okay.' She smiles. 'I'll give you an out for today, okay? You're free to leave. I'll call a parent to pick you up.'

'You don't have to,' I say.

But she stands up. 'It's not a question, Amber. How else would you get home? The bus? I can't have you fainting out in public by yourself.'

I can't say it's not a good point. I shut my mouth and watch her leave the room.

Melissa's sitting at the other end of the nurse's office. Her hands are clasped on her lap, and some of her fringe is over one eye. I told her she didn't have to bring me here, but she insisted. She walked me all the way in awkward, angry silence, and plopped herself down on the chair. She should have left by now, but she hasn't.

There's a lot I could say to her. All the hundreds of texts I've crafted over the past month, that I was never able to send. It just won't come out. I wasn't prepared for the day to go like this. I didn't think I'd end up in the nurse's office, and I definitely didn't think Melissa would be in here with me. Her legs are crossed, appraisingly. This isn't how it was meant to happen. I'm supposed to be prepared, in a familiar environment, with no risk of being walked in on, with unlimited time and not forty more minutes of lunch.

Do you hate me? is what I want to ask. But it would be stupid, because I know what the answer is. And I don't want to hear her say it.

'Thank you for staying,' I say quietly. 'You didn't have to.'

She shrugs. Two months ago, she would have called me silly for saying something like that.

'I'm . . .' I say, and lose my footing, or my strength, or my voice, and can't get it out, and have to try again. 'I'm sorry.'

I have formulated this apology many, many times. I should know how it goes by now. But my head is such a whirlwind of reasons and excuses and explanations and feelings and expressions of regret and guilt and love. There is too much to pick any one of them to speak of. There are too many things to say and not enough time.

'Okay,' she says, almost like a question. Like, is that it? Why do you need to tell me that? Why do you think it makes a difference?

'I'm not into him,' I say. 'Like, I wasn't.'

Her brows lift. 'You could have fooled me.'

You, I want to say. *It was you.*

'I was mad at you,' I say. 'I was mad at you for making new friends you cared about more than me, for obsessing over that guy when I was right there for you.'

'I don't care about them more than you!' She looks offended, her face twisted, her mouth big. 'You were my best friend.'

'But you spent all that time with them, without me. I saw pictures of you guys when I wasn't invited. You didn't say anything when Marnie was mean to me.'

Melissa crosses her arms, her eyes rolling like she can't believe what she's hearing. 'And did you say anything when Marnie was mean to me?' She spits the last word out, shaking her head in disbelief. 'They make fun of me all the time, they have all these in-jokes that I'm not part of. They're not my fucking friends. You were.'

I'm so confused I don't know what to do except sit there, rethinking every interaction between Melissa and the others that I ever saw.

'But you started hanging out with them instead of me,' I whisper.

'Only because you never wanted to spend time with me any more,' she says sharply. 'You just wanted to go to the gym and I don't like working out. You'd never listen to anything I was saying. You'd always say no if I wanted to go to McDonald's or watch *Bake Off*. So what else was I supposed to do? I didn't want to be friends with Kim and Marnie! I just have to be nice to Marnie because she's Brandon's sister and if she liked me then maybe he would like me too.'

I'm just sitting there and I don't know what to say.

I fucked up. She's right. I never had time because I was always at the gym. I always said no to McDonald's or cafés because then I'd start eating. We couldn't watch *Bake Off* because then I'd want food. Melissa didn't leave me. I left her.

'I know it doesn't make sense,' I say. 'But I guess I wanted to show you that no one else really cared about you as much as I did.'

She laughs, a short, hard laugh. 'Well, you were right. And the only thing you proved is that you didn't care about me either.'

I shake my head. 'I wasn't right. Brandon does care about you, you saw that. And Kim and Marnie care about you too, even though they don't show it.'

Her eyes are wet. It's been a long time since I saw her cry. It makes my throat wobble too.

'Brandon and I aren't together,' she says, slowly. 'He never wanted that. We've stopped hooking up now. Well, mostly.' Another little shake of her head, a snivel.

I'm sorry is on my tongue. *I'm sorry* is dying to get out. *I'm sorry* is the only thing that I can think of to say. *I'm sorry* is too difficult, too heavy, too pointless.

'I'm not going to Falmouth.'

'Same,' she says. 'I can get a loan to cover the tuition, but not the living costs. So I guess I'm staying here.'

'I didn't know that,' I whisper.

'Yeah, you did. I told you all the time, you just didn't care enough to listen.'

I lower my eyes. I think I was too busy calculating the calories of lunch. I think I was too distracted staring at her food. I think I was just so hungry I couldn't take in what she was saying. But of course she told me. She told me everything, and I've told her nothing.

She doesn't know why I don't eat. She doesn't know I

kept talking to Nicki. She doesn't even know I never had sex with Dan.

She dries her nose with her sleeve. 'I should go.'

And as she stands to leave, pulling her bag up over her shoulder, it comes out again. 'I'm sorry.'

She looks me straight in the eyes. 'I know. But that doesn't change anything.'

And she's right.

'I miss you,' I say.

'I miss you too,' she says. So matter-of-fact, so cold. Like she wasn't almost just crying in front of me.

I'm not allowed to hug her this time, I know that. I'm not allowed to dry her cheeks and tell her it'll be okay. It's not okay.

'You don't need him,' I say. 'You don't need someone else to make you happy, you don't need to be in a relationship.'

She says nothing to that. Her face is unreadable, but there's a soft smile there. Awkward, misplaced. Not genuine.

The door opens and the nurse comes back in, smiling, completely incapable of reading the room. Melissa flashes her a quick smile and heads out. The nurse looks at me. I wonder if she can see any redness in my eyes, anything wet on my cheeks.

Her voice is as chirpy as ever. 'Your mum will be here in a jiff,' she says.

At a red light, Mum checks her make-up in the rear-view mirror. Twisting and turning it and pouting her lips.

Being in the car is making me feel nauseous. I'd open the window but I know she'd get mad at me because it's too cold outside. Instead I just rest my head against the side and close my eyes.

'Well, I hope it was worth me taking time off work to come and get you,' she says. 'You don't look too ill to me.'

'Sorry,' I say.

I wanted to get the bus home, I want to tell her. *I tried telling the nurse not to call you.*

'You won't be sick, will you?'

I open my eyes and she is glancing over at me with her brows raised, probably assessing my face for greenness or puffy cheeks.

'No,' I say, and I hope it's true.

'Hmm.'

The light turns green. Her eyes dart back to the road and we move forward again. I wish we were home already.

'I don't understand why you'd be fainting,' she says under her breath. 'I haven't been feeding you crap, and you're still going to the gym, aren't you?'

'Yeah, I am.'

'See, you're healthy.' A disappointed sigh. 'As healthy as you can be.'

I wrap my jacket tighter around myself to hide my size, and the folds of my stomach when I sit. I swallow hard as I try gathering the courage to tell her.

'She made it seem like it was because I haven't eaten.' It sounds pathetic even as I say it.

Mum laughs. 'Oh, she said that, did she? You're not anorexic, Amber. Look at yourself.'

'Maybe it was, though.' My throat is so dry and tight. 'I haven't eaten a real meal in a really long time, and I don't feel very good.' I watch her jaw clench and her grip around the steering wheel tighten. 'Maybe I should have a salad tonight.'

'Maybe you should stop stuffing yourself full of sugar,' she snaps. 'Maybe that would save you some calories for salad.

Do you think you're starving? Because I think you have a pretty long way to go.'

I think about children in poor countries with visible ribs and swollen bellies, collarbones and elbows sticking out, all skin and bone. I look at my own face in the side mirror and it's pudgy and round, not sunken in, not slim.

'Stop trying to come up with excuses,' Mum says, harsh. 'That's all this is, an excuse to eat.'

'You're right,' I say. 'I'm sorry.'

But this time, I don't know if I mean it.

53

Nicki

Elsa comes for a visit. It's the middle of the day, so most of the women are out. I feel obligated to make her a cup of tea, and so we're in the kitchen. She's sitting by the table, chair facing me, while I lean against the worktop and wait for the kettle to boil.

'Have you been back to work yet?' she asks. It's so casual, like it's not a big deal.

I shake my head. 'Haven't felt up to it yet.'

I don't ache any more. The bruising on my face is gone. I can lift things again, and I can sleep on my side without crying from pain. But I don't want to go to work. I want to lie in bed, drag myself out to the bathroom, and then go back. They called me a couple of times last week, and I don't really feel entitled to any more sick leave. I took a week's holiday. It's not like I'll need it anyway, it's not like I'll be going anywhere.

'That's all right,' Elsa says. 'These things take time. If you want to, I can call your workplace and discuss the situation with them. Legally, they're not allowed to fire you because of this.'

A sudden burst of nausea, the room spinning. God, no. I can't imagine what everyone would be thinking if they knew. I don't want them to smile at me with all that fake sympathy and their voices dripping with concern, offering their help, the condescending faces of people who know you can't take care of yourself and who've deigned to help you. Oh, you poor thing.

Why didn't I leave? Why would I let someone do that to me? I always seemed so capable. They always thought I was stronger than that.

'No,' I say, too sharply. 'That won't be needed.'

Elsa smiles. I can hear the water boiling fiercely in the kettle. I turn around towards it, taking a deep breath when she can't see my face. I get the tea bags and pour our cups.

'Thank you,' Elsa says, wrapping her hands around the cup I've just handed her. Her hands are red and dry from the cold outside.

'Do you want milk or sugar?' I ask.

'Oh, no, I'm fine.'

I plop a cube of sugar into my tea and sit down. She's stirring in her cup, blowing gently on the surface. Her lips are so violently pink it must be lipstick. She's pretty, tall and blonde and blue-eyed, as if she's just stepped out of a Nazi poster of the ideal woman.

'How was the viewing yesterday?' she asks.

It was awful. The flat was unfurnished, but I'm desperate enough I reckoned I could get an air mattress and tough it out. This is only temporary. But it was so cramped, like someone had built an entire flat out of an average-size bedroom. In the kitchen there were visible pipes on the wall. The carpet was stained.

And I went for it anyway. It was almost humiliating to send in the application. Here I am, an adult woman with a full-time job, fully independent and capable, and I'm begging you to let me stay in this tiny, dirty, cold basement flat the size of a hotel room. The worst part? They rejected me. I wasn't even good enough for it.

'It was all right,' I say. 'I applied for it, but I just heard back a few hours ago that someone else got it.'

Elsa looks at me like she feels bad for me. I don't know if they told me the truth about why I was rejected. Maybe it was because my salary isn't high enough, or because I'm not a student that can be easily kicked around, or because my surname is too foreign. It isn't the first time. This is the third viewing I've had and the third rejection I've received. I've exhausted most of the properties on Zoopla within my price range, and soon I'll have to go higher. Or I'll have to rent a room in a shared flat with strangers, like I'm twenty again.

'It's such a mess, isn't it?' Elsa says. 'Gosh, I know it took me ages to find my current place. You don't need to worry about it.' A kind smile. 'As long as you need it, there's a place for you here. We have someone moving out next week, and then you can get a proper room.'

I strain my cheeks and mouth.

'If you'd like,' she continues, taking a careful sip of her hot tea, 'we can start looking into some council housing options. I'm more than happy to pull a few strings. They're usually very accommodating in these circumstances.'

'I'm all right in my room,' I say. 'It's only temporary.'

'Okay.' Her smile so wide it's pushing her cheeks into her eyes. 'Let me know if you change your mind. That's always allowed.'

Maybe I do need her help. I don't want to live in one of these places I've been viewing. Without Tom's salary, I can't afford anything else. So maybe I am incapable of doing this by myself. Because the thing about temporary is that at some point, it's going to end.

Tom's texted me again.

I think we should at least talk about this

I didn't know there was anything else to talk about. The little icon for an unread text is staring at me from my phone.

Of course I want to go back. I could forgive him for this. But I don't think he can forgive me. I've tried so many times to imagine what it might be like between us after all this. After what he found out about me, after what I've seen in him. It doesn't work.

I don't like thinking about the future. It's such an abstract, untouchable thing. But tomorrow it's going to be here. And the day after, and the day after that. Elsa doesn't know this, but there is no plan. I don't know when I'll be going back to work. I don't know how long I'll be stuck in whatever shit-hole will accept my tenancy application. All I know is that I want none of it.

I don't want to go back to work, spend every day pulling old people in and out of bed and the shower, for the next thirty years. Spending the weekend lying in bed, in a place that doesn't feel like home, because I've always told myself it would be temporary, but I can't afford better. Nothing to look forward to, because every week will be the same. No friends, no Tom. The one thing that brought me happiness, gone. The one thing that made me feel special, the one thing that wasn't routine. None of that.

On and on and on, just like that, until I'm eighty years old, and I'm Edith. No one will come to visit me. I'll plead for the carers to talk to me and spend time with me, but their time is limited and their interest is paid for. No one will be at my funeral. No one will care.

I was a fool to give up on the money Tom took from me. Things would be different if I had half those savings. Now it's too late and I can't do anything.

I don't want this. It isn't temporary, it's going to be my life.

How do I stop it? How do I stop it?

Something needs to change. Something bigger than getting a place of my own, something bigger than never seeing Tom again. Should I quit my job? Should I move to a different city? And even though I feel despondent, I'm excited. I haven't made a decision by myself for so long. I haven't had a change in years. The days have all been the same for a long time.

Not any more.

I get my laptop, and I find myself looking at pictures of Australia. The Sydney Opera House and white-sanded, blue-watered beaches. The red deserts and eucalyptus trees. Kangaroos and koalas. I look at Perth, with high-rise buildings and parks with green grass and palm trees, beaches in the sunset.

And I text Kevin.

When you said you'd let me crash on your couch, did you really mean it?

54

Amber

It felt good to tell Melissa. Isn't that strange? She didn't forgive me, and she'll probably never talk to me again. It looks like nothing has changed. But it feels like something has.

After all this time being blocked, every message I've sent that didn't go through, every night I was crying and wished I could apologize. I guess the outcome wasn't that important, as long as I got to say it. I was wrong about what happened between us, and it feels strange to know that. But it feels good. Like it didn't fully make sense before, but now it does.

That night, I slept well for the first time in a very long time. And I woke up wanting more of this feeling. I don't know fully what it is, but it feels good, it feels final and cathartic, and I know it came from apologizing to Melissa. Now I want to apologize for everything bad I've ever done.

I've been thinking about telling Nicki the truth. Didn't everything feel new and big and exciting when she revealed what she'd been lying about? Didn't it bring us closer? She trusts me in a new way now. It makes me feel worse about lying to her. It would be so wonderful for her to know the truth.

I fantasize about meeting her for real. In a situation where she'll recognize me and won't treat me as a stranger. Something that isn't fleeting but means something. Just a cup of coffee or something. I'll let myself have a Starbucks so she doesn't ask me why I'm not eating. Things could be so different from the way they are now.

But there's someone else I should apologize to first.

'Okay, I suppose, yes.' Mr Miller smiles awkwardly as people begin to chuck their backpacks over their shoulders and stand up, chairs squeaking against the floor. 'Yes, that's the time now. Class dismissed.'

His voice is drowned out by the chatter and laughter as the rest of the class files towards the door, phones out and their attentions somewhere else entirely. Kim and Marnie don't look back at me. I see Marnie throwing her head back laughing and I wonder if it's about me again.

'See you all on Thursday!' Mr Miller pipes. A defeated wave at their backs.

I've never heard someone say goodbye to him. I'm standing at the back of the class in my usual spot, waiting for the others to disappear. Pretending to fumble with my pens and erasers on the desk, stuffing it all into my bag.

I haven't made up my mind. That's why I'm stalling. Because right now, I could just pick up the pace and walk straight out of the door, giving him an awkward, obligatory smile as I go. I might still do that.

But I don't. I approach the desk and we make eye contact, and now it's too late. He smiles, surprised.

'Hello, Amber,' he says.

'Hi,' I say. 'I need to tell you something.'

I'm trembling a little. I put my hands on my lap to hide them from him. I took a seat opposite him, and now he's sitting with his head in his hands, slightly tilted. A very serious face, but not really any expression on it.

I wish he'd just show any sign of what he feels about this. He could get mad at me, and I'd accept that. It would be better than this silent, uncomfortable, unreadable nothing.

'I know it was a bad idea,' I say. 'Like, it was stupid. I didn't realize what would happen. And I'm sorry.'

He nods, slowly, like he's still taking this all in. *Please say something*, I think.

'Will I get suspended?' I ask.

The thought would have been scary to me a few months ago. Now it's nothing. It would almost be a relief to get out of here.

'No,' he says, and suddenly he's smiling a little. 'No, Amber, I won't be telling the head teacher.'

I'm confused by the casual tone and the unbothered face.

'You're not angry at me?'

'Don't you think I knew it was some of my students who created that profile?' he says. He gives a short little laugh. 'The options were limited.'

His voice doesn't sound very ridiculous now. It's funny, but I'm barely thinking about it. It's a little high, but not that out of the ordinary. A completely normal voice. I wonder why we ever found it hilarious, and why it ever mattered so much to us.

'But you could still be upset,' I say.

'Well, I won't say it was an all right thing to do. But you know that. It was a nuisance, but nothing to do about it now.' He shakes his head. 'It was only a prank, wasn't it?'

I can't remember any more, what it was. It was funny at the time. It wasn't going to have a lasting impact. I guess we were bored. I guess one of us suggested it and everyone else felt they had to agree.

I didn't tell him about Nicki, of course. There's a limit to

321

how much catfishing I'll admit to, that I think he would be able to accept. Maybe that's why I don't seem as bad to him as I actually am. As far as he knows, it was only a few loose conversations and some ghosting. That's just part of online dating.

'You obviously know it wasn't a great thing to do,' Mr Miller says. 'I don't need to convince you of that. But we all do stupid things when we're young, don't we?' He smiles, full of teeth. 'It might be hard to believe, but I've been a teenager too.'

'But I got you dumped,' I say.

He looks a little sad, now, the smile not reaching his eyes. 'No, I didn't get dumped.' He looks down at the desk, almost embarrassed, like he's sharing too much with me. 'Adult relationships are complicated. I left her. I told her I hadn't made that profile, and she didn't believe me. She didn't trust me enough to believe me, and you made her reveal that.' He shrugs. 'That's it. What you did – it had no other consequences than that. And I was happy to know it, I was. I wouldn't want to spend the rest of my life with someone who didn't trust me. So it's fine.'

He looks back up at me. A wrinkle of concern appears on his forehead.

'Amber, are you okay?'

Fuck, I'm crying. I quickly wipe my eyes. I inhale deeply to hold back all the tears and the snot wanting to get out.

'Yeah,' I say. 'Yeah, I'm fine.'

There's a little quiver in my voice, and I know he's heard it. I expected to leave this room with my mum being phoned and a lawsuit being threatened. It must be some kind of crime, what I did. I should be happy that it hasn't gone that way, and instead I'm tearing up.

'No, you're not,' he says. 'I promise you, Amber, it's okay.

You're very brave for telling me. I think that's admirable. I'm not angry at you.'

That's not why I'm crying, though. I'm crying because this is the forgiveness I wanted from Melissa, and that she couldn't give me. This is something I didn't think I was worthy of, but here it is. I feel like I've shed all the pounds I've been trying to lose for so long. I'm so light.

'Thank you,' I say.

'You're okay,' Mr Miller says. 'It's all right.'

I leave school when my eyes don't feel red and sore any more, and I think I'm beyond the risk of crying in public. Everything looks very bright outside.

I need to do it. I need to tell her.

I never even realized that what I'd done to Mr Miller was hanging over me like this, but now it's gone, and I can breathe again. I've made things right. I couldn't do that with Melissa, but I could do it with Mr Miller. I'll delete the app after this, I'll stop pretending. It will feel so good to be a decent person again. And if he can forgive me like this, there's no reason Nicki can't.

The lies I've told her are so much bigger, which means the relief will be so much greater. She knows me. She cares about me. Of course she will forgive me.

I take my phone out and I smile when I see her name. I have a text from her already, like she knows.

And then I stop smiling. Oh my god. Oh my god.

I open the text to read the whole thing, desperate to find out that it's not as bad as I thought. But it is.

So, I just did something impulsive, don't be mad
I got a plane ticket to Perth
I'll be there in a week!

55

Nicki

Sometimes I wake up and I wonder, *What the fuck am I doing?*

I'm about to uproot my entire life and move to the other side of the world. I'm about to leave a stable, paid job that I've had for years. I've never even been outside Europe. I've never been on a flight longer than four hours. My tickets are cancellable and refundable. I can change my mind at any time. But I don't want to do that.

Elsa was surprised. 'In a week, though?' Trying to sound like she wasn't judging me too hard.

I didn't tell her that if I didn't go in a week, I might not go at all. If I hadn't bought those tickets as soon as I decided, I might have chickened out. I won't give myself the chance to change my mind.

'There's nothing holding me here, is there?' I said.

'No, I know, maybe, but still. I think these things are usually thought over for a while.' A small silence, as if she was expecting me to change my mind at this minor prompting. 'Would you like to have a conversation with our counsellor? I know you said you don't want therapy, but I think it might be useful for you to discuss this with someone. Examine what your motives are, and if this is really something you want. I only worry about you.'

But I'm tired of people worrying about me. I know very well what my motives are, and I know that I want this. Here, I'm stuck in something old and tired and something I haven't wanted in a long, long time. Everything good about my life is gone. In Australia, I have a chance at something new. It has been so many years since I last had a friend whose couch I could crash on. There's one person in this whole world who would attend my funeral if I died tomorrow, and he's on the other side of the world. I need to make sure he'd actually be able to show up.

Even he was shocked and sceptical when I told him.

What do you mean? he asked. *How long are you staying?*

As long as you'll have me, I suppose, I replied. *It's a one-way ticket*

Kevin: *Are you serious?*

I didn't realize you were actually considering this

Nicki: *I asked if you meant what you said, and you said you did*

Was that a lie?

Kevin: *Of course it wasn't*

I was just expecting to get a bit more notice

I'm not sure I'll have the guest bedroom done in time, haha

Nicki: *I'm fine on the couch*

I just thought you'd be more excited

Kevin: *Of course I'm excited!*

I typed out *My ticket is refundable*, but I didn't send it. I can't think of it that way, I can't think of it as a reversible decision.

I'm looking at visas on my laptop. I don't need one to enter the country, but I will need one for work. It might prove a bit tricky. I text him again just to check.

Hey, I know you said you could offer me a job, but I realize that's asking a lot and I don't expect it at all

If it's not possible, I'll figure something else out, I just wanted to make sure

The truth is I'm not sure what it would be. Without a work visa, I won't have any way of making money. Without an employer, I don't know how I'll get a work visa. If he can give me a job, I'll go. It feels insane to think about it. Nothing else is holding me back except for unemployment. If I get a job, I can go.

I google pictures of the Australian outback while I wait. My heart is beating hard against my ribs. I'm going to delete Tinder. I've made up my mind about that. I've made this decision so many times, but this time it's for real. This is a true fresh start. Nothing has to be the same in Australia, nothing will be. I won't let things slip through my fingers this time.

My phone's notification signal goes off. I reach for it.

Yeah, I could do with an admin assistant

If you need a job, that's no problem

It reminds me of the feeling of receiving a text from Tom the day after our first date. It reminds me of getting that phone call after a job interview. An excitement that's over my entire body, almost overwhelming, itching for me to let it out.

I appreciate it so much, I write. *I don't suppose getting a work visa would be a problem? Would that be something we can get done if you employ me?*

Oh yeah, it shouldn't be an issue, I can help you apply for it

I just want to make sure about something

My stomach turns a little. Something's going to be pulled away from me. *What?*

Is this really what you want? It's so very sudden and it's a very big change

You can take months to think about it if you want, I'll still be here, but please do think about it

326

I roll my eyes. Just like Elsa, just like Tom, he thinks I can't make my own decisions. I've been made into an eternal child because of the trauma I've been through, I'll never grow up, and I'll never be treated like one of the adults. It's tiring. It convinces me even more about what I have to do. I'll show him, I'll show them. I'm going to thrive in Australia.

It is frustrating that no one ever believes I know for myself what I want and need, I say. *I do.*

Why would I stay here? I don't have any friends here, I don't have a family, I don't like my job, and now I don't have my relationship any more

There is no reason for me to stay and I can see that myself, I don't need you to tell me to think it over. If you don't want me to come, then tell me that, but don't do it because you don't think I can decide this for myself

The messages are read, and I get radio silence for a while. It's uncomfortable to get upset with someone. I expect him to get angry in turn. With Tom, this would have started a fight. Kevin's never been angry at me before. I don't want him to look at me that way. I shouldn't have said anything.

That wasn't what I meant, Kevin writes back. *I'm sorry you took it like that.*

I just meant you've gone through a break-up and you're feeling fragile right now, and maybe you expect this to solve things that it can't

And I don't want to see you disappointed and with your life uprooted for that

It's fine, I say. *I need a change, that's all*

I won't stop you, he says.

I'm going to Australia. The last piece of the puzzle was just solved. I feel giddy with the excitement.

I dial Janet's phone number. This is not temporary, I remind myself. This is irreversible. It doesn't feel like a warning. It's not a deterrent. It's exactly what I want. No more Paki this or Paki that. No more helping people who've always voted Tory use the toilet.

'Hello?' says the voice in my phone.

I clear my throat. 'Hi, it's Nicki. There's something I need to tell you.'

56

Amber

I don't know which burger to get. Woozy, dizzy, I look up at the bright screens above the McDonald's counter. The letters merge together. It doesn't matter what I get, I'll have two. I'm so extremely, incredibly hungry.

'Hi,' I say. 'Could I have a Big Mac and a bacon mayo chicken?'

The man on the other side of the counter isn't one of the teenage employees, which is good. I would hate to worry that it was someone from my school. He must be approaching fifty and he nods as he puts my order in.

'Meals or just the burgers?'

'Meals,' I say. 'Both of them.'

I know one set of fries won't be enough.

'What drinks?'

'Two Cokes, please.'

A woman comes up to the counter to collect her order. I can smell the chicken nuggets from her tray.

'And some chicken nuggets,' I add.

'Anything else?' he asks.

I imagine that he's thinking *Is that all, you pig?* I shake the thought out of my head. I'm ordering for a group of friends, if he asks. I'm not going to eat all of this myself.

'That's all,' I say. 'Takeaway, please.'

I pay and go sit at a table in one of the corners. I pull my hoodie over my head. No one I know can see me here. It's the most pathetic thing I can imagine right now, to be seen by people at school. There's the fat, lonely girl from English. No wonder she looks like that. It should be illegal for these people to serve her, it's just cruel.

My food will be ready soon, it's okay. I put my head against the wall.

When Nicki asked me if I was serious about that offer, I thought she wanted reassurance. Of course I would give it to her. I wouldn't lie to her. She just wanted to know that I'm here for her, and I am. But not like that.

Fuck. I don't know how to tell her now. She spent most of the money she has left on this plane ticket, and I can't give her that back. She'll never talk to me again. Just a few days ago, all she'd invested in me was time and emotions. Now it's way more than that. What I'm doing is suddenly way worse than it's ever been before. It's passed the point of being forgivable.

But I have to tell her. She's about to quit her job and give up her spot at the shelter and end up in a country where she knows no one and has no place to stay. Of course I have to tell her.

Don't cry, don't cry. I'm struggling to breathe, but I can't cry in this McDonald's.

I'm not ready to say goodbye to her. I'm not ready for her to leave me. I don't have anyone else.

My food is ready. I go up to the counter with my shoulders hunched. My stomach rumbles so loudly I think everyone in the restaurant can hear it. I hope there's no one here that knows me.

'Thank you,' I whisper, grabbing my two bags.

I can't stay inside to eat, of course. Then my cover story is blown and everyone will see me eating this food completely by myself. Someone from school might walk in. But I can't go home either; I don't know if Mum is there. It's too risky to try to sneak these bags past her up into my room.

I go behind the restaurant, where the rubbish bins are. The car park is too public, too visible. I'm hidden back here, invisible to the world. I sit down between some bins. The ground is wet and cold, and I'll get my trousers dirty. I can't really be bothered to care.

Nicki's going to be gone soon. Not in Australia, obviously. She'll still be at the other end of town where she's always been, and maybe I can still sit outside her house. Maybe I can still see her after the gym, until I go away to uni. But I'll never speak to her again. I'll never hear her voice, her real voice, the one she'd use for Kevin instead of a stranger she's giving directions to. The voice she'd use for someone she actually cares about.

But I'm not someone she cares about. I'm not Kevin. She's the most important person in the world to me, and as far as she's concerned, I don't exist.

I cry onto the last few bites of my burger. This doesn't feel as good as I always imagine it will. I daydream about food, I stare at what other people eat, I cry from hunger, but it never tastes like I imagined. It doesn't feel nice and satisfying. It's frantic and nauseating and too filling and my stomach hurts, my throat is tight. This isn't normal. This isn't right. Has anyone else ever sat by the McDonald's bins stuffing their face full of food? I don't know how to stop. I should be able to stop. Something is wrong with me.

But of course I'll tell Nicki. It's not like I can keep talking to her after she goes to Australia anyway. She would either know that everything I've told her is bullshit, or she'd think I'd stood her up. One way or another, this whole thing is going to end. And I should do it as soon as possible to minimize the damage done. It's just a plane ticket. It's just a bit of money. When I get my student loans in autumn, I could even pay her back.

It's fine, I tell myself, it's fine. But what the fuck am I supposed to do when she's gone? This food doesn't make me feel better. I can't talk to this food about my problems and my feelings. I have no one, no one, no one.

But that's selfish. That's not a good reason. A good reason? The fact that I've never seen her this excited. She's never told me she looks forward to something. I don't think, until she told me, she'd ever used an exclamation mark while texting me. A week ago she was telling me she had nowhere to go and no one who cared about her. Now she sends me pictures of her online shopping for shorts and thin blouses, flip-flops and sunglasses.

I love to get excited with her about this. I love imagining her in these summery clothes, I love dreaming about her in the outback. Sometimes I let myself get carried away with these fantasies. I convince myself that it's true, and it feels so good. It's so good to see her have something to live for. It's so good to help her out of this slump. It's so good to have provided her with this thing to look forward to. And it's so much easier, so much nicer, to pretend that it's real. I know this isn't going to happen. But I want it to just as badly as she does. I'd feel like the cruellest person in the world taking this away from her. I would ruin everything she wants and everything she's happy about.

I will, I mean. Nothing else is an option, I remind myself. The dream has to end at some point, and better it does now than in a week. I have to ruin her life, I have no choice. It stings, it hurts. But I need to tell her before she does something irreversible.

57

Nicki

I go to Primark and pick up more clothes. Most of what I own is for British weather, and I'd boil in Australia. It feels strange to shop for shorts, t-shirts and sunhats in early February, when there's still snow up in Scotland and the ground is still slush. It's difficult to find anything except jumpers and sweaters.

I have a couple of items slung over my arm, and I'm browsing through the summer dresses. I haven't worn things this pretty in a long, long time. Clothes have been nothing but protection against the elements for years, because who cares what I'm wearing? Cute mini dresses, workout tops with strapped backs, there hasn't been a point in those. I look carefully at this dress. It's long and pink, the shoulder straps are thin, there are brown buttons all the way from the V-shaped cleavage to the bottom. It's not revealing, it's not figure-hugging. It won't accentuate my waist, and it's simple. But the idea of wearing it excites me in ways I don't even understand.

My dad would always ask me, 'Who are you wearing that for? Why dress up like that for school?' He told me I wanted people to look at me. He told me I liked to make boys have disgusting thoughts about me. In the end, most of the clothes I owned were purchased by Mum. She knew what he would accept: plain, full coverage. No flashy colours, no fancy little details. Nothing that stands out from the crowd.

I pick the dress off the rack. I've seen teens wear more

elaborate outfits for an afternoon run to the supermarket. This isn't anything special, but it's nothing like what I usually wear. A simple cardigan, a tee without print, a few different colours of jeans. I'll try this on in the changing rooms. I probably won't buy it. It will make me look like I'm trying too hard, but I'd like to see how it fits. I just want to know how the material feels against my skin.

Across the rack, there's a face I recognize. And the hands, and the shoulders. And the weak, awkward smile. I've slept with this man, he's been inside of me. But for several, gut-wrenchingly painful moments, I don't remember the name. I don't remember the context: where he lived, what we talked about, what we did, if it was good. And for these moments, I feel so much shame. There's been so many of them I can't even remember. There's been so many they're no longer people, they've turned into a parade of smiles and dicks and the sounds they make when climaxing.

And then I remember his name: Adam. This is Adam.

It's like getting an electric shock, being reminded of that night. I showed weakness in front of him. He saw parts of me that were not for him, that I want to keep to myself. I don't want him to know me like that. Weak, traumatized, victimized. I don't want him to know me at all.

I duck down below the rack, let only my eyes stay above it. He's running his fingers over a pair of jeans, he hasn't seen me.

He looks so different out here in the real world. He's wearing a leather jacket and his jeans are ripped. I never imagined he existed outside of his bedroom. That's a strange thought, isn't it? But I never wondered where he works, where he shops, if he has a family.

This part of my life, it doesn't touch anything else. I leave

334

it behind when I leave their houses. When I'm out in the real world, that part of me can't show. And now it does. Now it suddenly exists. I feel overwhelmed by shame, I'm drowning in it. Jesus, how disgusting I am. I barely had a full conversation with this man before I let him fuck me, and then I left.

His face turns in my direction. We don't make eye contact, I'm too quick for that, but I think he's seen me. *Fuck*, I think, *fuck*. I walk away fast. I don't hear him say my name. Maybe the glance was too brief, or maybe he doesn't want to speak to me.

I can't bump into him. I make my way over to the changing rooms quickly, forcing myself to breathe. This won't happen again, I tell myself. I won't be in this country much longer. I can feel myself slipping through time like it's a crack. I'm liquid, not firm. I don't want to do this in public.

I get into the changing rooms. I pull the curtain across my cubicle and slide down on the floor, my back against the wall. No one can see me now. I put my head in my hands and I can see Wallace. I can see the boys at school. I can see Dad. I can see Tom. They're not real. I bang my head against the wall and I remind myself they're not real. Reality is in the fabric in my lap, the hard floor against my butt. That's real, that's real.

It's not a bad one. One final quivery breath and I feel steady enough to stand. I am firm again. I am real. Looking in the dressing-room mirror reminds me and comforts me.

I get out of my clothes and I try on the dress. My arms are full of goosebumps when I wear it. I don't think I've felt this pretty in a long time. I move around and let it swirl around my legs. What happened today is never going to happen again. I'm out of here soon.

This is a fresh start. I'm never going to go on Tinder again, all of these men are out of my life. No more sex I don't enjoy with people whose names I'll forget. No more wishing I could say no and waiting for things to be over. I am breaking every bad habit that I have and I am never looking back.

I'm going to Australia.

58

Amber

I have two more days to stop this. After that, there's nothing I can do. And I have a headache.

Mum has guests over and I can hear them laughing downstairs. I don't know these people, and I won't go down to say hi. It would be an embarrassment to Mum; she's too pretty for a daughter like me.

I am so angry at Nicki right now. I'm so angry I punch my pillows and grunt, unable to shout or Mum would hear me. She didn't ask me before she did this. She should know this isn't a good idea. I want to hide behind the fact that I've just turned eighteen and I had no idea where this would lead. She's the adult, she should know better than this. She's never even heard Kevin's voice, but she's willing to go across the world to him. Spend all her money on him. Quit her job for him.

And I know it's all my fucking fault, of course I do. The anger doesn't last long. I sink into bed and push my hands into my temples. I thought I had so much time to make this thing go away, but now it's here. Two days from now, she'll be boarding the plane to Perth. I might be sick again.

There's a picture on my phone right now that she sent me a few days ago, of her in a changing room in a pink sundress with a Primark price tag on it.

Should I get it? she asked.

And she looks so beautiful, the pink bringing out all the

beautiful warm tones of her brown skin, her collarbones showing. And her hand is over her eyes, like she's trying to hide her face, but her mouth is visible below it, smiling. Fuck me if I were to take that beautiful smile off her face.

You look so gorgeous, I said, and I felt like I should have been ashamed to admit it. I should have been scared to use such a strong, powerful word, like a magic spell. But it slipped out of me, and it felt right. What do I have left to lose? What can I fuck up now that isn't gone soon anyway?

All I got back was a blushing, smiling emoji.

I've looked at this picture so many times now. It's almost over, and I wonder if this is the last piece of her I'll ever see. I wonder if she'll return the Primark dress when she realizes she won't be wearing it in Australia, or if she'll keep it until she can wear it in the Brighton summer sun.

The more I drag this out, the worse it is, the crueller I am. Two more days, I need to do this. I text her.

Hey, I need to tell you something

I'm typing slowly like an old person. It feels like there's something in my chest, something hard and heavy, something painful. I stare at the message. I force myself to send it, and there's no going back, there's no unsending it. She's online immediately. I find myself holding my breath.

What? she asks.

Oh my god, I think, *where do I start?* There is so much. It's like when you're in an awkward group of new people and an adult forces you to introduce yourselves to the others, tell them a bit about yourself. Like I could fit an entire person into a few sentences. Like I could explain to her over text why I've done what I have and who the fuck I think I am. I play with the idea of pressing the call button. I wonder if she'd pick up.

It feels impossible to put it all into words, but there is one essential piece of information that she needs.

I'm not in Australia, I type.

And I stare at the text. I can't make myself press send. I picture the confusion, the hurt, the denial I'll be met with. Getting this message will feel a little bit like having a rug pulled away from under your feet, only to discover there's no floor underneath, and suddenly you're falling aimlessly. But maybe I'm wrong about that, and all I'll get is anger. Righteous anger, but still.

I can't make myself press send. I delete the entire message. It was too much, it was too fast. She has no idea anything is wrong and I'm just making things worse that way.

I type something else instead. *You've made my life a lot brighter*, I write. *I want you to know how much you mean to me.*

I want you to know that I love you

And again, I think, what do I have to lose? What I said to Melissa, it's true for me too. I don't need her to love me back. I'm tired of it all, all these emotions, all these people I feel like I might die without. Melissa is gone and I survived. Dan is gone and I survived. I'm still a virgin and guess what? I'm still alive. These things don't matter right now. Nicki will be gone soon, and it won't kill me either.

She reads the message and she doesn't reply. I don't know what I expect from this. I think it would break my heart if she felt the same way.

Suddenly she's typing. My lungs stop functioning.

You mean so much to me, is what she says. *Sometimes I think you're the only person I've ever known who's never lied to me about who they are.*

You're the only person I know actually cares about me

And I'm so grateful for that

My head is swimming. I feel so overjoyed, so happy I could cry, because she doesn't doubt it any more. I got it through to her. She doesn't second-guess my intentions, she knows I care. And she deserves to know that, she needs to know that. She needs to know she's lovable and wonderful and I would walk through fire for her.

But then the full extent of what I've done dawns on me.

You're the only person I've ever known who's never lied to me about who they are

I haven't, have I? I was always myself with her. She knows me. But I'd be delusional if I thought that was all that matters. Every word I've ever told her has been a lie. I'm not thirty-six years old. I don't live in Perth. I don't own a company. My name is not Kevin.

I've ruined this woman. Telling her the truth would devastate her. It would rip her to pieces. She has been through so much. I can't put her through more.

Fuck. I can't do it.

My hands are shaking now. I think about how she told me no one else could ever love her after Tom. I think about how she felt she had nowhere to go. This is the first time in years that she has had hope. She finally has somewhere to go.

I can't take that away from her. I can't do it. This betrayal goes far beyond all the money she lost on the plane ticket, the job she no longer has, all the planning she's put into this trip. This betrayal isn't ever going to leave her, and I can't do that to her.

My name is not Kevin, I write.

But I don't send it. *Do it*, I tell myself. *It's done either way. This is the best way to let her find out. It's going to happen one way or another.*

But I imagine the pain I've caused. I imagine her tears, her pleas for me to be joking. What the fuck is this going to do to her? I can't stand to think about it. I have to shake it out of my head. I'm crying. There is no way I can deal with that pain. I can't be there for that.

I erase the message.

What's your address? she asks. *How do I get there when I land?*

I can't do it.

I'll pick you up at the airport

59

Nicki

There isn't much packing to do. I keep my little toiletry bag with the toothbrush and toothpaste on the windowsill, and I'll stuff it into the suitcase tomorrow morning after I've brushed my teeth. All the clothes I own are carefully folded inside the suitcase, except for the outfit I'll be wearing while travelling. I put it on the chair for when I get dressed in the morning. I put more thought into those clothes than I should have, and I felt like a teen on her way to a first date. It's just a pair of jeans and a V-neck sweater, but it was a big decision. Part of me wants to make an impression. I want to step out of that airport as pretty as he must have imagined me, until he can change his mind.

I have a t-shirt I'll be wearing underneath, so I can take the sweater off in Perth. It'll be too warm for it.

My hands are shaking and I try to steady them. I've never seen Kevin in person before. He might look nothing like his pictures. People do that, don't they? I wonder what his voice sounds like, what his scent is. I don't even know how tall he is. What if he's shorter than me? What if he's massive?

This is the first time I've gone abroad on my own. I've gone on holiday with Tom, with my family back when I was little, but never by myself. I try to remember everything I need. A plastic bag for the liquids, but I only have my tooth-paste, so I'll get that at the airport. My passport, make sure it's in the handbag and not the suitcase. The online check-in is done, the boarding passes have been saved in my phone. I've checked multiple times that they're actually there and won't disappear if I'm without wi-fi.

I see if I can close the suitcase. I press the lid down hard, squish the clothing down, and manage to pull the zipper. That's good. There's a little bit of space left for my pyjamas and the clothes I'm wearing right now. The Primark stuff added some extra volume to the few belongings I have. The pink dress is stowed away safely in a corner.

My phone buzzes in my pocket, so suddenly it makes me jump. I don't get a lot of phone calls. I pull it from my pocket and I see a familiar picture on the screen. I should probably remove it.

Tom.

For a second, I think he knows. Why else would he suddenly be calling me right now? He hasn't bothered to get in touch for over a week. Somehow he must have sensed that I'm leaving and he'll try to change my mind. I want him to. What a strange feeling, but I want him to try to make me stay. There's no one else in this country who has cared enough to express that they'd miss me. At work, I was dismissed with a huff and some grumbling about being short-staffed. Elsa accepted my leaving without any more coaxing; it frees up another room.

I'd love for there to be someone who wants me to stay.

I accept the call and put the phone to my ear.

'Hello?' he says, urgently.

I haven't heard his voice in so long. I didn't expect it to hurt as badly as it does. It hits me like a train, his voice, and all the memories that come with it. All the *I love yous*, all the nice words, all the whispered pillow talk when our love was young and new. I thought I'd spend the rest of my life with him. His breath against my neck and his lips in a smile. I'll never forget the shock of the first time he struck me.

'Hi,' I say.

It doesn't sound as strong or as stern as I wanted it to. It sounds pathetic, weak.

'Why haven't you been answering my texts?' he asks.

Anger, already. Voice low, words short.

I don't know what to reply to that. I left you, I could say. You hurt me, again, and it's unforgiveable.

I say nothing. I'm a little girl in front of my dad again, and he's asking me why my skirt is ripped, and I know that whatever I tell him, the outcome will be the same.

'You can't just leave like that,' Tom says. 'You can't leave without a word. That isn't fair.'

I swallow hard, drowning in my own saliva. 'It wasn't fair of you to hit me.'

'Don't play the victim here,' he says, voice drawling with disgust. 'You can't seriously tell me I'm the one who did everything wrong in this relationship. Not after all the shit you did to me.'

'Then why are you calling me?' I ask.

'Because we have stuff to work through! I have the right to process this. I want to talk.'

'I don't.'

A momentary pause, and I can hear him inhaling slowly and shakily, like he's trying to contain himself.

'You should be grateful I would ever speak to you again,' he says. 'You're lucky I'm willing to even consider forgiving you.'

His voice is so loud I put the phone at a distance from my ear. Adrenaline is rushing and my limbs are unsteady. He can't hurt me now, I remind myself. He can't touch me. But it feels like his hand will come out straight through the phone, or that somehow, some way, he will know where I am, and soon I'll hear banging on the door.

'I don't care,' I say. I almost whisper it, it's so hard to press the words out.

'What?'

'Tom, I don't care if you forgive me. It doesn't matter. I don't forgive you.'

Silence. Heavy breathing. I sit down on the edge of the bed, too weak and dizzy to stand up. I can't believe I've said it. I've forgiven him for so many things. It's enough now.

'I didn't ask for your forgiveness,' he says, surprised.

And yes, I'd noticed that too. No crying and no apologies this time.

'Okay,' I say.

Another long, strange pause. I look at my suitcase, open on the floor, and I think about Mum. I think about the time we ran to the train station, about the bags she packed for us. I think about the silent wait for Dad to come pick us up. I remember the stern, disappointed look on his face as he held open the car door for her, and I thought he was going to close it on her head. And I think that I will never, ever do what she did. It would be such a disgrace to her if I were to let this opportunity go, if I were to cancel this plane ticket. She never got to do this. I will do it instead.

'What the fuck is that supposed to mean?' Tom says, his voice going up. 'You think I'm to blame for that fight? That fight wasn't because of me, it was because of you!'

My mum was not weak. My mum did not deserve what Dad put her through, what he's maybe still putting her through. My mum was kind. Dad hit her anyway. Tom would have hit me no matter what I did.

'And what about every time before it?' I ask. 'You didn't know what the fuck I was doing. So how was it my fault all those times?'

I sound so calm. I hold my hand up in front of me, and it's steady. I stretch the fingers out, look carefully. Not a shiver, not a twinge. I smile.

'Don't bring up stuff from the past,' Tom says. 'We're talking about you now, not me.'

I have no idea what to feel about the fact that I'll never see this man again. I've spent every day with him for six long, gruelling years. When I wake up in the morning, I still expect to see his face. When I go to bed at night, I feel cold and alone without his body to press against. But no one gets mad at me any more. There's no yelling. My body is healing so wonderfully it's barely sore any more. I don't know how I feel. But I don't feel bad. I don't feel sad.

'No,' I say, 'we're not.'

I pretend he's my dad, and I pretend I'm Mum. And I do what I would have wanted for her, what I always wished she would do; I end the call. I'm amazed at the fact that I've done it and I'm frozen in front of the screen, trying to take in what I just did. I'm never going back. And there isn't a single part of me that wants to.

A second later he's calling me again. I decline the call. I go into my contacts list and I decline another incoming call. There is no third attempt, because I press the block button.

He is gone. It feels so final. I'll never fully scrub out his smell from my body, and I'll never entirely erase his smile from my mind. But he is gone, and I am never going back.

60

Amber

'Amber?'

I look up from my phone. The screen is black, but I'm clutching it hard in my hands, bending the plastic cover with my fingers. The face that looks back at me seems kind. She's a redhead, freckled. She smiles and nods at the door.

'Come on in,' she says.

I rise on unsteady legs. *She won't believe me*, I think. Look at me, I don't look like I have a problem. But it feels different this time. It isn't my voice in my head now, telling me I'm fat; it's my mum's. I don't know if I should trust her. I follow the doctor into her office. She closes the door behind me and gestures towards a chair. I sit, my phone still tightly in hand. Like I'm holding on to the edge of a life raft.

The GP sits down opposite me, swirling her chair out from behind her desk.

'So,' she says chirpily, 'how can I help you today?'

Do you really want to do this? Mum's voice asks me. *Do you really want to be fat for ever?*

I clear my throat, struggle to speak. These feel like words that shouldn't be spoken, like words that belong to someone else, and not to me. The GP looks at me patiently, not letting the smile waver, and I wonder how long it takes me. It feels like hours. Maybe it's only a few seconds.

No, I think to myself, *I don't want to be like this forever*.

'I think I have an eating disorder,' I say.

61

Nicki

I've not had breakfast, and I've rolled my suitcase through some dog shit. It's all over the wheels and splattered onto the side. I stand in a corner by the check-in desks, frantically rubbing it off with tissues. It smells horrendous. The air outside is early-morning cold, with the sun just barely rising. Shivering hands, visible breath. The world is very quiet this early.

I can't believe I'm doing this. I let my alarm ring once before I immediately got up. Sneaked quietly to the bathroom so I wouldn't wake anyone up, dressing in half-darkness in a race against the cold. Ever since, I've been in a state of disconnect from the world. Nothing feels real. I'm not sure I'm not dreaming. It feels a little like floating, a little like I'm listening to the world around me through a thick wall of cotton. I can't believe I'm doing this.

I manage to clean most of the shit off the suitcase and go to check it in. The man asks for my passport and I scramble to get it out of the side pocket of my handbag. I'm apologetic and he's unimpressed.

Security goes by fast. I expect there to be a queue and there isn't, I barely have time to transfer my toothpaste into a plastic bag. I expect to be stopped and searched, because I feel like things should be going wrong, but I'm waved through the scanner like I'm taking up too much of their precious time.

I feel very lost and overwhelmed. My flight isn't until two hours from now. I was way too cautious, way too worried about missing it. I can't imagine missing it. This is the single most important day of my life.

I locate my gate, but it won't be opening for ages. Seeing the flight number and destination on the screen makes me want to throw up. This is the last chance I have to turn around.

Until my last pay cheque comes in, I have twelve pounds in my bank account. It's just enough to buy me an expensive airport coffee and a book in WHSmith. It's a long flight, I'll need something to do. I spend the last money I have and then I find a place to sit down. It doesn't feel like I should be allowed to be doing this on my own. I've never been inside an airport by myself. What the fuck am I doing? My heart beats very fast. Not in a bad way. Not in a bad way at all.

I take a sip of my coffee and open my phone. I text Kevin.

I'm at the airport!

62

Amber

I look at the message on my phone. It's six in the morning and there's no reason for me to be awake right now except for this. I've been waiting for it all night. I'm lying in the dark under my duvet, the light from my phone screen burning my face.

I imagine that she's just joking. This has all been just an elaborate prank. There never was a plane ticket, she never did quit her job. But it wouldn't be very funny, would it? I don't think it's a joke. She's actually at the airport.

I go on the Heathrow website and look at the flight schedule. Her flight is going to be on time. I check when she'll be landing. It feels like an eternity away. I imagine myself picking her up at the airport. I'd be standing by the arrivals exit and I'd spot her immediately, her head turning from side to side as she's trying to locate me. She would recognize me and she would smile at me, not like she did before, like she would at a stranger. She'd smile at me like I'd smile at her. I'm not Kevin in this fantasy, I'm me. I'm me but she recognizes me anyway and she walks faster to get to me and she hugs me. It would feel so wonderful to touch her like that.

I go to our messages. *I'm at the airport!*

Nothing feels very real when it's really early in the morning. Nothing feels real when you haven't slept. I'm so tired, so confused, I wonder if I'm dreaming. I have to be. I can't actually be about to let this happen.

I know this is the last chance I have to make things right. There won't be another opportunity to stop her.

Text me when you've landed, I say. I add a heart emoji.

I look at the picture a final time, of her in that pink dress. She'll be wearing that in Australia, under the sun. I love her, but that doesn't matter. One day I'll think back on this time and everything will be clear, the confusion will be gone. I'll make sense of everything. Right now, this doesn't need to make sense. I don't need to think about it any more.

I go to the Tinder app and delete Kevin's account. It asks me if I'm sure. *This information can never be retrieved again. This decision cannot be undone.* I say I'm sure. I delete his account and I delete the app off my phone. It's easy.

I go on to the Facebook app and do the same thing. *Are you sure? Your profile will be deleted for ever.* Kevin will be gone for ever. Yes, I'm sure. I delete his profile. It's nothing serious.

63

Nicki

This is the last time I'll be on British soil for a long time. The man in the aisle seat of my row gets up and I smile at him as he steps back and lets me walk past. I squeeze into my window seat; I'm lucky to sit where I can see England for a final time and where no one will be kicking my legs while moving in and out. I push my handbag underneath the seat in front of me.

My chest feels like it's full of little sparkles. Fireworks popping and burning, sizzling and shooting upwards. I run my hand through my hair and look out of the window. It's started to drizzle and the sky is grey. There is frost on the grass.

I take my phone out and look at the last message I have from Kevin. I'm going to see him in sixteen hours. The thought makes me dizzy. Sixteen more hours until my new life begins. But then, maybe it already has. This trip is certainly new. This flight isn't my old life. Maybe this isn't the end of the old, but the beginning of something new.

I put my phone in flight mode and I buckle my seatbelt.

Acknowledgements

This book is about loneliness. I have always been lonely; I still am, but writing a book isn't something you do by yourself. Writing acknowledgements like this always reminds you of just how many people you have in your life, and I have had some great ones.

I'd like to start by thanking all the online friends I've made over the years. To Maren, Christina, Georgia, James and Phoebe – I don't know where most of you are now, but you made my life bearable while you were in it. I wasn't catfishing any of you, by the way, and I hope you were also who you said you were. Out of all of you, two deserve special attention. James, thank you for being one of my first and most supportive readers. You once told me that you thought writing was what I was supposed to be doing, and that's always stuck with me. I think you might've been right. I hope you're doing well today. I hope you finally achieved some happiness and peace of mind. Phoebe, to date you're my longest-running friendship and the person who's read and critiqued my writing the longest. I don't think I'd be the writer I am today without your support. Please never show anyone those early works I let you read. Let's pretend they never existed.

I owe everything to the wonderful team at Penguin and Michael Joseph, and in particular everyone involved with WriteNow 2020. You saw potential in my work and you have offered me opportunities beyond what I could ever have imagined. I'm sure this book wouldn't exist without this programme.

Thank you as well to my fellow WriteNow participants of the 2020 cohort, it's been lovely to know you and go through this journey alongside you. But the person I need to thank more than anyone else is Madeleine Woodfield, my lovely editor from the very beginning. I can't believe how lucky I was to have you assigned as my mentor during WriteNow. You helped me make this novel the best it could be, but more than that, my entire career is thanks to you. You got me my agent. You got me my book deal. Thank you for all the work you've put into this book and for the many times you've had to read through it, and thank you for taking a chance on me and advocating for this novel.

Thank you to the incredible sensitivity readers who helped me portray experiences that aren't my own. Guntaas and Georgina, your feedback was invaluable and greatly appreciated. I couldn't have done this without you. Any mistakes I've made are entirely my own fault.

Thank you to Emily Glenister, my wonderful agent. Your support and incredible feedback have meant so much to me, and I can't wait to continue down this career path with you by my side. You're the best agent for anyone with words of affirmation as their love language.

Thank you to Kashish, for being the first friend I made in real life. There's more of you in this book than I'd like to admit. I hope you don't mind.

Thank you to my family for your ongoing support and patience with me. To my mum, who introduced me to the joys of books and reading. To my dad, who is never surprised when I tell him about new accomplishments or good news. To both of you for keeping me alive through my most depressed years. To my sisters, because even though I know you never read a single book, I hope mine might be the exception.

I need to thank the most important person in my life. Diego, you are my favourite person and the best life partner I could have chosen. Words can't describe how much better you make every day simply by existing. You've picked me off the floor so many times, and I don't know where I would be without you. Thank you for your feedback on this book and your support while it was being written, and thank you for loving me.

A final, special thank you to my pet mice. You understand nothing I say or write, but you keep me sane.

Resources

The things that Amber and Nicki struggle with are very real. If you have faced any of these problems, know that you are not alone and that there is help available. This is a non-exhaustive list of some support organizations that might be able to help you.

Sexual Assault and Domestic Violence

Centre for Women's Justice
Provides legal support for victims of male violence in
   the UK.
Website: centreforwomensjustice.org.uk
Phone number: 0207 092 1807

Scottish Women's Rights Centre
Provides legal advice and representation for victims of male
   violence in Scotland.
Website: scottishwomensrightscentre.org.uk
Phone number: 0141 331 4183

Muslim Women's Network Helpline
Supports Muslim women dealing with a range of problems,
   from domestic and sexual abuse to mental health problems.
Website: mwnhelpline.co.uk
Phone number: 0800 999 5786

Rape Crisis

Provides support to survivors of rape and other forms of sexual assault and violence in England and Wales.
Website: rapecrisis.org.uk
Phone number: 0808 802 9999

Rape Crisis Scotland

Provides support to survivors of rape and other forms of sexual assault and violence in Scotland.
Website: rapecrisisscotland.org.uk
Phone number: 0808 8010 302

Refuge

Provides support for men, women and children experiencing domestic violence.
Website: refuge.org.uk
Phone number: 0808 2000 247

Women's Aid

Provides support and services to women and children who have experienced domestic abuse all across the country.
Website: womensaid.org.uk

Scottish Women's Aid

Provides support and services to women and children who have experienced domestic abuse in Scotland.
Website: womensaid.scot
Phone number: 0800 027 1234

Welsh Women's Aid
Provides support and services to women and children who
    have experienced domestic abuse in Wales.
Website: welshwomensaid.org.uk
Phone number: 0808 8010 800

Eating Disorders and Mental Health

Beat Eating Disorders
Provides information and support on eating disorders.
Website: beateatingdisorders.org.uk
Phone number: 0808 801 0677 (England),
    0808 801 0432 (Scotland), 0808 801 0433 (Wales),
    0808 801 0434 (Northern Ireland)

NEDA
Supports people and families affected by eating disorders.
Website: nationaleatingdisorders.org
Phone number: 800 931 2237

SANE
Provides emotional support for people struggling with
    mental health issues.
Website: sane.org.uk
Phone number: 0300 304 700

Samaritans
A free helpline offering emotional support for people facing
    any struggles or difficulties all across the country.
Website: samaritans.org
Phone number: 116 123

Mind
Offers support and information about mental health.
Website: mind.org.uk
Phone number: 0300 123 3393

LGBTQ Support

Stonewall
LGBTQ charity offering support and information about
    LGBTQ issues in England.
Website: stonewall.org.uk
Phone number: 0800 050 2020

Stonewall Scotland
LGBTQ charity offering support and information about
    LGBTQ issues in Scotland.
Website: stonewallscotland.org.uk
Phone number: 0800 050 2020

Stonewall Cymru
LGBTQ charity offering support and information about
    LGBTQ issues in Wales.
Website: stonewallcymru.org.uk
Phone number: 0800 050 2020